The Golden Age
of Science Fiction

Books by Kingsley Amis

Novels
Lucky Jim
That Uncertain Feeling
I Like It Here
Take a Girl Like You
One Fat Englishman
The Anti-Death League
I Want It Now
The Green Man
Girl, 20
The Riverside Villas Murder
Ending Up
The Alteration
Jake's Thing
Russian Hide-and-Seek

Short Stories
My Enemy's Enemy
Collected Short Stories

Verse
A Case of Samples
A Look Round the Estate
Collected Poems 1944–1979

General
New Maps of Hell: a survey of science fiction
The James Bond Dossier
What Became of Jane Austen? and other questions
On Drink
Rudyard Kipling and His World
Harold's Years (ed.)
The New Oxford Book of Light Verse (ed.)
The Faber Popular Reciter (ed.)

With Robert Conquest
Spectrum I, II, III, IV, V (ed.)
The Egyptologists

The Golden Age of Science Fiction

Selected and introduced
by Kingsley Amis

Hutchinson
London Melbourne Sydney Auckland Johannesburg

Hutchinson & Co. (Publishers) Ltd
An imprint of the Hutchinson Publishing Group
17–21 Conway Street, London W1P 5HL

Hutchinson Group (Australia) Pty Ltd
30–32 Cremorne Street, Richmond South, Victoria 3121
PO Box 151, Broadway, New South Wales 2007

Hutchinson Group (NZ) Ltd
32–34 View Road, PO Box 40-086, Glenfield, Auckland 10

Hutchinson Group (SA) Pty Ltd
PO Box 337, Bergvlei 2012, South Africa

This selection first published 1981
Editor's Note, Introduction and this selection © Kingsley Amis 1981

Set in Linotron Times

Printed in Great Britain by The Anchor Press Ltd
and bound by Wm Brendon & Son

British Library Cataloguing in Publication Data
The Golden age of science fiction.
  1. Science fiction, English
  I. Amis, Kingsley
  823′.0876′08[FS]   PR1309.S3

  ISBN 0 09 145770 X

Acknowledgements

'The Quest for St Aquin', by Anthony Boucher, reprinted by permission of Curtis Brown Ltd; copyright renewed © 1979 by Phyllis White

'The XI Effect', by Philip Latham, © 1950 by Street and Smith Publications Inc., reprinted from *Astounding Science Fiction* by permission of the author's agents Scott Meredith Inc., 845 Third Avenue, New York, New York 10022.

'The Tunnel under the World', by Frederik Pohl, © 1954 by Galaxy Publishing Corporation; reprinted by permission of the author and E. J. Carnell Literary Agency

'Old Hundredth', by Brian Aldiss, © Brian Aldiss 1960; reprinted by permission of the author; first published in *Airs of the Earth*, Faber & Faber, 1963

'A Work of Art', by James Blish, reprinted by permission of Faber & Faber Ltd from *Galactic Cluster* by James Blish

'Harrison Bergeron', from *Welcome to the Monkey House* by Kurt Vonnegut Jr, © 1961 by Kurt Vonnegut Jr; originally published in *Fantasy and Science Fiction*; reprinted by permission of Delacorte Press and Seymour Lawrence Inc.

'The Voices of Time', by J. G. Ballard, © 1960 by J. G. Ballard. This story appears in *The Four Dimensional Nightmare*, published by Victor Gollancz and Penguin Books Ltd; reproduced by permission of the author and his literary agents, C. & J. Wolfers Ltd

'Specialist', by Robert Sheckley, © 1953 by Galaxy Publishing Corporation; reproduced by permission of the author and his agent, Abby Sheckley

To the memory of
Edmund Crispin

Contents

Editor's Note:
About Science Fiction

These opening remarks are addressed to the inquiring reader who would like to demist his notions of a subject still widely misunderstood. Those who know well enough how matters stand may wish to skip this part and make their way to the Introduction proper.

Millions of words have been poured out without any definition of 'science fiction' being generally agreed or even becoming widely known.* Different people have had and have different views, often strong and vague at the same time, of what constitutes science fiction or, quite as often, what ought and ought not to constitute it. The form itself has been changing perpetually ever since it started. Of recent years it has been broadening its scope and the term 'science fiction' has been applied more and more loosely. All in all, it seems best to do no more than try to help my inquiring reader to arrive at some idea of what to expect from something with that label on it.

The term itself was first used in the 1920s and the first magazines of the genre appeared then. To say that those early stories were often about amazing inventions or tentacled Things likely to carry off blondes, and that the approach has since become more sophisticated, is true enough but

*That of the *Concise Oxford Dictionary* must be one of the most widely available and is not too bad: '*science fiction*, fanciful fiction based on postulated scientific discoveries or environmental changes, freq. dealing with space travel, life on other planets, etc.'

uninformative. Instead of coming forward in time I will go back, to three works well enough known to general readers and also 'claimed' as science fiction by writers on the genre. It might be helpful to explain their grounds for doing so.

The first of my texts is *Gulliver's Travels*. One might start with the obvious and point out that Lilliput, Brobdingnag and the rest are situated in what in 1726 were remote, underexplored parts of the world, as opposed to mid-Atlantic, say, where they could not have existed in known fact. However extravagant its inventions, science fiction is fond of presenting them as realistically as possible. Swift works hard to persuade us that we are reading a true tale of a voyage of discovery. (He failed to fool the contemporary bishop who said roundly that he did not believe a word of it.)

The character of Gulliver is constructed to the same sort of end: no fantasist he, but a practical man, a surgeon, trained to observe closely and report correctly. He is also, for most of the book, a pretty ordinary human being. This is easily seen to be necessary to Swift's purpose, but some critics evidently find it hard to understand or tolerate the practice of science-fiction writers whereby, for closely similar purposes, they keep their characters simple and straightforward. Charges of imaginative poverty and the like are common. They were well answered by C. S. Lewis, the author of, besides much else, three distinguished novels usually thought of as belonging within the genre: 'Gulliver is a commonplace little man and Alice is a commonplace little girl. To tell how odd things struck odd people is to have an oddity too much.' Finally, I think we are helped to feel that Gulliver is a representative of humanity (or of normal-sized humanity), which is just what a science-fiction character is likely to be, much more directly and exclusively so than characters in any other kinds of fiction.

The part played by science in science fiction is almost as hard to define as science fiction itself. Here I only want to insist that in individual cases that part need not be large or obvious, is sometimes merely a matter of tone. There is no science (or technology) as such in the first two parts of

Gulliver's Travels where in modern science fiction there probably would be, the Lilliputians perhaps represented as the fruits of an experiment in genetic microsurgery, the Brobdingnagians as those of a mutation – though when one comes to think of it the births of the first generation of Brobdingnagian babies to normal-sized mothers would raise acute difficulties. A modern writer might also have felt the need to throw in a second mutation greatly strengthening bone tissue and so accounting for the mutants' ability to move about without constant self-injury. What distracts our attention from these omissions of Swift is something much closer to the essence of science fiction than the presence or absence of bits of science.

A general reader would be likely to agree that one of the greatest attractions of the book as a whole is the inventiveness and thoroughness with which the various societies and their cultures are filled in; the author's relish for his task comes through unmistakably. This is exactly what the science fiction reader is used to enjoying, the fascination of watching a new world unfold itself in all its detail as the story progresses, and here are the principal grounds for his claim to *Gulliver*. He would not be specially interested in its satire on contemporary England, but he has had plenty of experience of being invited to compare an imaginary society with our own, and hence to gain a fresh perspective on our own. The satire on scientific research in Book III might obviously make a particular appeal; nevertheless he would be likely to go along with the majority and name Book IV the best. And he would show a healthy lack of inordinate respect for reason, or for science itself for that matter, by finding the society of the Houyhnhnms not the paradise of pure intellect some see in it but, as Swift intended, a loveless, lifeless hell.

Gulliver's influence on science fiction has been immense. So too has been that of my second text, *Frankenstein: or, the Modern Prometheus*. Putting it like that perhaps makes it clear that of course I am talking about Mary Shelley's novel of that title and not any of the films that have travestied it. Let me add that its attraction for the genre is not simply or solely that of a horror story with a monster and a mad scientist. One can positively say, however, that any tale that involves a synthetic being will attract at least the curiosity of those concerned with science fiction.

To them, but also to other readers, it is very important that Frankenstein is a scientist, not a magician. To stitch together parts of human bodies and galvanize the result into life is a bizarre enough proceeding (though believed possible by some authorities of the period), but no supernatural force is used or the whole point of the story would be lost. *Frankenstein* is a Gothic novel; its horrors are physical as well as moral; even so, we are not reading 'a mere tale of spectres or enchantment', as Mrs Shelley herself put it; reason is not suspended. To my mind – if anyone cares – this justifies science fiction's claim to *Frankenstein*. It has been argued* that the Gothic element is not a possible distraction or even an irrelevance but a necessary characteristic. Other authorities would exclude the book for insufficient credibility.

No less important to our present concern is the author's subject, which is not science or scientists alone but something larger. The monster when first activated is not evil but a sort of noble savage, only provoked to violence by the way human beings treat him; perhaps evil is entirely human in origin. For the first time, man has created life; perhaps God is unnecessary. But when you leave him out . . . At the heart of *Frankenstein* there lies a serious question about man's place in the universe. It may surprise some to know that our science-fiction reader is prepared to consider such matters as well as, say, the doings of a carnivorous fungus. No doubt he will very often be content with cheap answers to that sort of question, but not necessarily in every case.

Few people would resist a move to capture H. G. Wells's short novel, *The Time Machine*, for science fiction. (When it first appeared in 1895 it was labelled 'an invention', there being no existing category to fit it into.) I introduce it here as a means of making three quick points. The first is that

*In Brian W. Aldiss's brilliant and valuable *Billion Year Spree: The True History of Science Fiction* (1973).

science fiction has easily as much to do with invented or imaginary bits of science as with real ones. Time-travel is against reason; Wells makes it plausible with some blandly matter-of-fact moonshine about four-dimensional geometry. Earlier time-travellers had had to make do with dreams, or falling asleep for a hundred years; this one has a machine and so can control and vary his movements. Secondly, Wells's present-day readers are quite ready to take on the rather boring sociological content that nearly spoils a large part of the book – the splitting of the human race into Eloi (bourgeoisie) and Morlocks (workers) – and, thirdly, are equally inured to the *fin-de-siècle*, even *fin-de-globe*, feeling of the close.

Science fiction is a pessimistic medium, very much interested in the future but very distrustful too. Like our three examples in different ways and to different degrees, most of it is about things going wrong. The sunny outlook of its first years, with mankind growing ever more prosperous, contented and wise, assisted to be so by the growing wonders of a beneficent science, has long departed, not surprisingly when one looks at what has happened to the world in the meantime. To say as much implies what may seem a paradox, that for all its connections with the future its main business is with the present day.

My remarks on the readership of the genre refer of course to its higher levels; the average is probably pretty low, especially today. But those who notice what they read will find in science fiction much to reward that notice.

Introduction

In 1959 I gave a series of six lectures on science fiction at Princeton University. So much has happened in and to the genre since then that the boldness of this step may not be apparent now. Any credit belongs entirely to the chairman of the seminars of which my lectures were to be part, the late R. P. Blackmur, poet, critic and very entertaining man. I had come to Princeton loaded with stuff about eighteenth-century literary theory and was astonished and delighted when Blackmur suggested that science fiction, which he knew to be an interest of mine, might make a more stimulating subject. It turned out that the same year was to see the appearance of the first academic journal in the field, *Extrapolation*, and, in the UK, the first anthology for use in secondary schools, *Aspects of Science Fiction*, edited by G. D. Doherty. Yes, things were on the move, though as usual no one could have known that at the time.

I have never embarked on an academic task with such enthusiasm or pursued one with such enjoyment. There was plenty to do, since up to that point my reading had been quite unsystematic. But the research presented no problem: works like L. Sprague de Camp's *Science Fiction Handbook* were available to be looted for the historical part – Lucian of Samosata, Cyrano de Bergerac and all that – and a trip with a large suitcase to Brentano's bookshop in New York furnished me with enough raw material for a dozen lectures. I followed my usual procedure of speaking from a full script rather than notes, indeed took extra care, for Dwight Macdonald, Mary McCarthy, Hannah Arendt, Robert Oppenheimer and other luminaries were to be of the audience and take part in the ensuing discussions. (It was Mary McCarthy who, when I mentioned *Nineteen Eighty-Four* as an example of science fiction, retorted that it was too good a book to be put in that category.)

My diligence paid off: after not much rewriting I had the manuscript of a short six-chapter book about science fiction. Much furious thought produced the title *New Maps of Hell*, and the thing was duly published, first in New York (1960), then in London (1961); Victor Gollancz failed to warm to it at all, and in particular felt disinclined to follow my badly received third novel with something so eccentric and ticklish, preferring to hold it until my fourth novel was safely in the shops. As it turned out, *New Maps*, though no blockbuster, sold respectably and went on selling, with a new paperback edition appearing more than a decade (and an eventful decade) after the most recent examples discussed in the text. It achieved translation into French, Italian and Spanish.

New Maps was more widely reviewed than any of the books I had already published, and with more general approbation too. The breadth of coverage had, as always, nothing much to do with any possible merits. When a literary editor decides which books he wants reviewed and at what length, his mind is on their immediate or potential interest to his readership, not their aesthetic status. Clearly, in New York and London in 1960–61, the topic of science fiction was felt to be ripe for extension outside the immediate circle of the genre, of fans, of addicts. As before, things were mysteriously on the move. In the UK at least there was an antecedent if not a cause, the late Edmund Crispin's anthologies, *Best SF* (1955), *Best SF Two* (1956) and *Best SF Three* (1958). These, with their successors, were undoubtedly the most useful of their kind ever published and strongly influential. Their introductions discussed science fiction in a new way, unhampered by defensiveness or cultural parochialism.

To persist with *New Maps* a little longer: the favourable

as distinct from the widespread response could in some cases be readily explained, at least in part. Those two or three reviewers who were also science-fiction writers were no doubt glad to see a card-carrying intellectual and academic taking seriously their underpaid, overworked, undervalued profession. (That at any rate was what it was then.) Of the outsiders, some (William Golding, Angus Wilson) were secret science fiction readers. Not by any means all. What moved the others, and in part those already referred to, was something less readily discoverable, something to do with the state and history of science, technology and literature, something to do with the *Zeitgeist*. This almost anecdotal introduction to my Introduction will have served its turn if it suggests that the expansion of interest in science fiction in the 1960s was something not at all to do with clever fellows spotting trends but instead a sort of accident, altogether unwilled, an unknowing consensus. Cultural developments, not least minor ones like this one, usually come about in some such way.

Not all of the critiques of my modest academic study, then or later, were wholly favourable. There were suggestions that I had presented a lopsided picture, had overstressed the social, economic, dystopian (see title) and generally satirical possibilities and achievements of the genre at the expense of its psychological, philosophical and generally more mysterious ones. These suggestions have a good deal of justice in them. However, I can plead that the immediate state of science fiction at the end of the 1950s made it easy to see it as I saw it. I find it far less easy to shrug off the accusation that the real trouble with *New Maps* is that, modest or not, it is an academic study.

The most forceful expression of this view known to me was made not in print but orally, face to face. The occasion was the British science-fiction convention of 1961, the speaker E. C. Tubb, prolific author of the 'Dumarest' novels. His view, passionately though civilly urged, was that the result of bringing highbrow values into what was an essentially popular form or field would be to ruin it. I did my best to sneer this off at the time, naturally, but it was not very long before I began to see what I think Ted Tubb meant. Since what could defensibly be pinpointed as the very year, 1960, science fiction's progress to respectability has been matched with spine-chilling exactitude by its decline as a branch of literature. Now you can take it anywhere, and it is not worth taking.

Before I try to justify this assertion, let me concede that after about the age of forty (I was born in 1922) one's capacity to take in new stuff, stuff markedly different from the stuff one is used to, diminishes, and that by any reckoning there were changes in science fiction in the 1960s. Nor are we dealing with a matter of straight and complete cause and effect, though in two important respects we are doing precisely that. Each in a different way concerns that uniquely sensitive area, the relation between the writer and his readers. To explore it I must go back a little in time.

It is no secret that when what most of us think of as science fiction began, in the 1920s, you found it in pulp magazines of repulsive format with crude (though often effective) covers and illustrations. Even from a distance you could tell it was the sort of thing you read in private or enclosed in the covers of some respectable tome to screen it from the eye of authority and respectability. Next to obscene limericks and the like, it was the most unofficial culture there was. Its themes, in those early days before the Second World War, were few and simple; it was called science fiction but most of it was gadget fiction, monster fiction, adventure fiction with ray guns, everything played for sensation or, now and then, gross sentimentality. No one would have dreamed of lecturing on it then.

Things were bound to change, and most of us would say that that change was for the better. The conventional view, with which I can find no reason to disagree, is that the arrival of John W. Campbell Jr at the editorial desk of *Astounding Science Fiction* began to transform the genre into something an intelligent adult could profitably read. But – vital point – not just any old intelligent adult. Isaac Asimov, Robert Heinlein, Clifford D. Simak and Campbell's other writers were known to a public that thought of itself as a select, even an embattled, few. The few were more than readers, they were fans, addicts; to an extent unimaginable today, either you read a great deal of science fiction, often indeed nothing else to speak of, or you read none. Even as late as the 1950s there was a freemasonry among addicts, not only on the level of fan clubs and conventions but between individuals. To meet a stranger who turned out to admire Heinlein or Asimov conferred an immediate intimacy.

Until (let us agree to call it) 1960, science-fiction writers were probably closer to their readers, knew more about them and their tastes and limitations, than any group since the Tudor court poets. Most writers have the knack of making some sort of assessment of their public, and if these had not had that knack they had the most articulate, or at any rate voluble, public in history all ready to guide them, in readers' letters to the magazines, in best-story polls and above all, perhaps, in fanzines (amateur magazines produced by a group of fans or even a lonely individual; 1930 onwards). All writers, again, write for themselves, but a clearish image of their readership is helpful to them. It gives them confidence, and my feeling is that that kind of confidence is helpful, to say the least, in the production of good writing.

Similarly, until 1960 the generic science-fiction writer had been an unselfconscious, even a relatively naive personage, conservative in style, even humdrum, capable of cheap verbal tricks but sticking to old-fashioned ones, apparently ready to let his subject-matter speak for itself, not bothering overmuch with techniques of presentation, indeed forced by his miserable rates of pay to produce at a speed that rather ruled out any Flaubertian ponderings of *mots justes*. Though more than prepared to complain loudly about those rates and his position in the literary world, or lack of one, and not at all disinclined to make extravagant claims for the importance of his craft, he would probably have given a grunt of surprise, if not wonder, if you had called him a creative artist.

After 1960, these two firm bases began to be disturbed.

The link with the audience was eroded as science fiction became part of the Sixties 'scene' along with pop music, hippie clothes and hairdos, pornography, reefers, new-style poetry recitals and the rest, and at the very same time turned into a branch of culture with courses in it at universities and polytechnics, surveys of it and critical articles on it in the non-specialist press. What had fired Ted Tubb's protest in 1961 must have been a prophetic glimpse of the second of these two developments, of which more later.

Another account of this transformation and its causes is perhaps as valid. It requires me to go back further in time, to the decade before 1914, when there came a sudden crisis of confidence in all the arts, foreshadowing that critical and terrible year. The system of major and minor keys, on which Western music had been based for three centuries, was revealed to a small but influential group as not just obsolescent, to be modified and enlarged, but actively repressive, to be dismantled altogether and at once. Rhyme and metre, the bases of verse in English and other languages for twice as long, became things of the past while nearly all poets were still using them. Parallels in the visual arts are no less familiar. What had happened was not that the possibilities of the symphony, the sonnet or the easel picture had been used up, but that for the first time their end could be foreseen – like the end of the civilization that had given them birth.

In the 1900s science fiction in the modern sense was simply not there. For the first forty years of its existence, as I have described, it moved steadily on its way untouched by anything revolutionary, anything that could be called modernism. Then, after 1960, it was visited by the demon of progress, by restlessness and self-dissatisfaction, by the conscious quest for maturity and novelty, by the marsh-light of experimentalism, by the fear that the exhaustion of what were now old themes had drawn in sight. The result was something that eventually came to be called the New Wave, in misty allusion to the French cinema movement and also, presumably, to *New Worlds*, the magazine in which the wave first became visible – a British publication, it pains me to add, though quite soon there were plenty of Americans in attendance to share the discredit. (Any attempt to point to Vietnam as the 1914 of science fiction would have to explain too why the revolt started in Great Britain, not the United States.)

It has to be conceded that the old themes were becoming threadbare in places, that the number of things that can go wrong in a spaceship (for instance) is very large but not unlimited. Many of the writers who had come to prominence in the Forties and Fifties (Walter M. Miller, Damon Knight, Issac Asimov and others) turned elsewhere for one reason or another, though failure of invention must have been at work in many cases. Novelists of the main stream who find themselves in such a position often become adept at disguising the fact; a cynic might say that this is the only literary talent that improves with the passage of time. The science-fiction writer by comparison depends on new ideas in a far more direct and urgent sense, and he uses them up, whereas even *Othello* did not, could not, use up the 'idea' of jealousy. One should remember too that by this time quite large bits of what had been interesting possibilities – Earth satellites, nuclear power – had become familiar facts, and even larger bits would become so any moment. *Terra incognita* was turning into real estate. All in all a move to the outer fringes seems understandable, not the effect of mere whim, however often the end product might seem to suggest just that.

Whatever the exact reasons, the new mode abandoned the hallmarks of traditional science fiction: its emphasis on content rather than style and treatment, its avoidance of untethered fantasy and its commitment instead to logic, motive and common sense. Out went the teams of dedicated and resourceful explorers getting into trouble on conscientiously described distant planets; in came shock tactics, tricks with typography, one-line chapters, strained metaphors, obscurities, obscenities, drugs, Oriental religions and left-wing politics. (*New Maps* had not achieved all that, nor had the installation of the first two university courses in science fiction in 1961.)

Three British writers, with William Burroughs as a kind of absentee high priest, saw the New Wave in: Michael Moorcock, just then become editor of *New Worlds*, J. G. Ballard and Brian W. Aldiss. Moorcock's work sometimes recalls that of an earlier Burroughs, Edgar Rice, with its curiously named noblemen riding magic horses and wielding magic swords, a galaxy away from the sobrieties of orthodox science, fiction, yet, using as it does the conventions of what used to be called space opera, vulnerable to being described as Old Wave with some New Wave dressing in the shape of occasional mystifications. He (Moorcock) also treats of a planet rather like our own, the scene of the odd, often unaccountable, doings of Jerry Cornelius, an updated Superman. These doings issued in a not unappealing film, *The Final Programme* (1974), but on the printed page they give rise to little more than incurious bewilderment if read with any close attention.

Ballard is a different case. His early novel, *The Drowned World* (1962), a vivid, brilliantly observed (or invented) picture of a superheated Earth awash with water from the melted ice-caps, together with some of his first stories, raised hopes that here was a new talent on the scale of Wells, and Ballard has remained in the forefront ever since. But with his next novel, *The Drought* (1964), his limitations became apparent. His characters lack motive and aim and their mutual isolation approaches the solipsistic. In consequence, his tales are generally without movement; they are indeed pictures – pictures, moreover, of a restricted range of scenes: a city square disappearing under swampland, an abandoned holiday resort invaded by sand, the overgrown ruins of a luxury hotel, each with its solitary, idle human figure.

Perhaps it was recognizing this narrowness that led Ballard to reshape his work and exploit the two favourite effects of modernist art, mystification and outrage. He produced stories with titles like 'The Assassination of President Kennedy Considered as a Downhill Motor-Race' (and it makes it worse, not better, that that title is a skit or something on somebody else's title for something), with 'chapters' half a page long subdivided into numbered paragraphs, with enigmatic supposed facts sandwiched between half-hearted gestures in the direction of narrative. Two later novels of his, *Crash* (1973) and *Concrete Island* (1974), are not science fiction at all in any sense I recognize; the one takes physical disgust as far as I have ever seen it in print, the other is a kind of urban non-escape story overcrowded with realistic detail.

Aldiss may have his limitations too, but he has yet to reach them. There seems to be no theme or style, from the 'hard core' of the genre to its modernist fringe and beyond, that this talented and prolific writer will not attempt. *Report on Probability A* (1968) takes an orthodox science-fiction idea – the closed environment studied by an observer who finds he is himself being studied, and so on – and inflates it with obsessively minute descriptions of trivia in the manner of the French anti-novel; ominously, the characters are known only by initials. In the same sort of way, *Barefoot in the Head* (1969) interlards an adventure story with stylistic oddities, bits of freak talk, poems, some of them 'concrete'. As we shall see, Aldiss was ready to move on after that.

The New Wave swelled to take in a number of Americans, among them Thomas M. Disch, a writer of real though unorganized talent, John T. Sladek, an experimentalizer in a mode sometimes compared with Kurt Vonnegut's, Norman Spinrad, most notable for his use of four letter words, Roger Zelazny, a purveyor of magic-without-rules who out-Moorcocks Moorcock, and Pamela Zoline. If I expatiate on a single story by the last named, it is out of no particular animus, but because it exemplifies the trend with striking purity, and also because it has been singled out for particular praise by Aldiss, usually a discerning critic. The title of 'The Heat-Death of the Universe' refers to the second law of thermodynamics, whereby, through the process of entropy, all radiation will one day have ceased and all particles be at rest. Nothing else about or in the story has anything to do with science fiction however defined. Dressed up as it is with its numbered sections (fifty-four in fifteen pages) and its use of the historic present, verbless sentences and strained poeticisms, all it amounts to is a women's magazine, day-in-the-life account of a commonplace little woman in Alameda, CA.

Shorn of its modish trappings, 'The Heat-Death' would doubtless have been more difficult to publish. The same is true of countless other tales, or amorphous chunks of wordage, which would formerly have earned rejection slips from editors and publishers in the main stream of writing. Such stuff made its way to booksellers' science-fiction shelves, 'partly because it is often by authors who first made their mark in classical SF',* remarks an anonymous critic, 'but mostly because there doesn't seem to be anywhere else to put it.' (I could make a suggestion.) 'SF' itself, a time-sanctioned abbreviation, came to stand for, not 'science fiction' but 'speculative fiction', a phrase signifying either a boldly liberating adventurism or a fairly frank admission that anything went. Each to his taste.

By 1974 or so the New Wave was being declared officially over. Well and good; but its main achievement and legacy, the breaking-down of the barrier between science fiction and the fiction (and verse) of the main stream, remained in place. Barrier-liquidation always sounds a nice idea, and so do things like 'an ongoing, complex cross-fertilisation of genres' (Peter Nicholls, an eminent authority); but in this case the usual products are leaden fables with some science-fiction trimmings to their verbal tricksiness, and attempts at more traditional science fiction by writers outside the field – and in most cases disastrously ignorant of it.

---

*This seems as good a point as any to remark on the strange continuing similarities in the developments of science fiction and jazz respectively. Modernism first began to impinge on jazz in 1941 – another crucial year, for the United States and for the world. Nowadays we hear (if we cannot avoid it) material only classifiable as jazz because it is played by musicians who first made their mark in orthodox jazz or something resembling it, because it appears on the jazz shelves of record stores, because, alongside various novelties, it retains a certain amount of its former instrumentation. Turning the radio on at random the other day, I heard a prolonged rhythmless wailing in which the sound of a saxophone was eventually distinguishable; I at once made a confident and correct diagnosis of jazz.

Bits of extrapolated science and technology, claimed as evidence of your cross-fertilization in otherwise conventional thrillers, are in fact nothing new, as readers of Ian Fleming (*Moonraker*, 1955) or even Sapper (*The Final Count*, 1926) will know. No, I cannot agree with any part of Nicholls's conclusion that

the apparently limitless diversity opening up is an excellent sign of a genre reaching such health and maturity that paradoxically it is ceasing to be one. (1979)

There are usually good reasons for the existence of barriers, and this specimen has always been permeable by individuals on both sides of it. Breaking it down altogether would at the best of times be likely to have the same sort of result as, say, the amalgamation of Lake Victoria with the Indian Ocean. Science fiction could never enrich orthodox fiction by merging the one with the other anywhere near as much as it has enriched literature as a whole by staying separate.

I hasten to add to all this that the effects of the New Wave, though as far as I know almost uniformly deleterious, have been very far from universal. If you should open at random one of today's magazines (collectively a medium in a passable state of health despite recent gloomy forecasts) the chances are quite high that you would come across a story about a team of dedicated and resourceful explorers getting into trouble on a conscientiously described distant planet, and no less high that you would be grievously bored by it because you have heard it all before. You might just as likely encounter a boring robot or computer or telepath, or indeed inspector of weights and measures in a mildly modernistic story not connected with science fiction in any way whatever except its physical position in the magazine.

It always goes against the grain to qualify a jeremiad, but I shall have to, if only in an attempt to dispel any impression that I may be gloating unduly over my portrayal of disaster. I have to admit that, for the moment at least, a few writers seem to have survived the debacle, though none I think is unmarked by it. Arthur C. Clarke is one who has survived all right, whatever might have to be instantly said about his part in *2001: a Space Odyssey* (1968), that captivating but in places repulsively self-indulgent film. One thing that can be safely said is that Clarke contributed nothing in the self-indulgent category. He has always been among the most disciplined as well as most imaginative of writers in the genre, a view sustained by at least two of his latest three novels, *Rendezvous with Rama* (1973) and *The Fountains of Paradise* (1979). These deal exclusively and as of set purpose in familiar themes, in *Rama* the exploration of an alien world, in *Fountains* Earth-to-orbit systems. They might be taken as products of that primeval confidence I mentioned earlier, a demonstration that the bank of traditional ideas is not empty after all, and can still be freely drawn on by those who keep their head and are not panicked by trend. And yet one cannot help noticing that *Rama* was Clarke's first novel for more than a decade, nor close one's ears to the report that it and its successors followed the conclusion of a three-book deal that broke all records in science-fiction publishing. Good luck to him, and the books show not the least sign of strain or barrel-scraping, and yet . . .

It is true that, as well as science fiction, Clarke has been writing non-fictional articles and books about developments in science and technology for over thirty years; even so, his concentration on fact at the expense of fiction in those dozen years before *Rama* does look like a response to the up-heavals in the genre at that time, a shift of interest. In one form or another, this has been the recourse of most of those who, established by 1960, have survived into the 1980s with their abilities undiminished; I imagine that, with science fiction in disrepair, to have active interests near it though outside it is a steadying factor. What follows is examples, not a complete list, but a complete list would not be a long one.

Kurt Vonnegut Jr would probably disclaim the description of science-fiction writer, thinking of himself as just a writer who produces science fiction from time to time. (Brian Aldiss wrote of him that he 'sped right out of the sf field as soon as he had cash for the gasoline'.) He has in fact suc-cessfully developed his own sub-genre, a blend of satire and fantasy, found most satisfactory in some quarters, though after *Cat's Cradle* (1963) he lost me as a voluntary reader. *Slaughterhouse Five* (1969), concerned with the wartime bombing of Dresden, is his best-known book.

Brian W. Aldiss is another who from the start showed his readiness not only to move about within the field of science fiction but into others: straight fiction, criticism, autobiography, travel writing. On his day he is a good poet, which is doubly welcome at a time when good poets are as rare as good science-fiction writers. Only he could have made a success of *Frankenstein Unbound* (1973), a time-travel historical fantasy that includes brilliant portraits of Byron, Shelley and Mary Shelley. His latest book, *Life in the West* (1980), has a contemporary setting, something he has not attempted before. It is, if I may say so, a most promising first novel full of interesting remarks, almost none of which are about science fiction.

Although a quite different kind of writer from Aldiss, his confrère and co-editor, Harry Harrison, has shown a comparable breadth of range, mostly but not altogether in the genre itself. Whatever the pundits may say, humour is a tricky business in science fiction, but Harrison has done as well as anybody with his burlesques, the 'Stainless Steel Rat' series and *Bill, the Galactic Hero* (1965). Characteristically, he produced *Make Room! Make Room!* the following year, a hauntingly grim and believable picture of an overcrowded earth with all its natural resources used up. More recently, however, even the inventive Harrison has been diversifying with *Skyfall* (1976) in the 'disaster' genre, *Great Balls of Fire: A History of Sex in Science-Fiction Illustration* (1977), and *Planet Story* (1979), a short novel with large, numerous, well-produced and I must say striking colour illustrations by Jim Burns. (No matter what may have happened to the written medium, science-fiction art is flourishing.)

There are those who might grumble at the way J. G. Ballard uses or misuses his talent, but of the size of that talent there can be no doubt. (He must be tired of people saying that, but then.) More than those of any other writer in or associated with the genre, his mood, imagery and style are unmistakable. Some of the stories in his latest collection, *Low-Flying Aircraft* (1976), show affinities with science fiction in the old sense: they are set in the future, they involve possibilities in the realm of science or technology. But the affinities are pretty remote, and are non-existent in Ballard's latest novel, *The Universal Dream Company* (1980), an unrestrained, humourless but disturbing fable in which the hero is apparently a sort of deity, or perhaps is dead. The conclusion suggests itself that what Ballard has done is embody the darker part of the twentieth-century unconscious in science-fiction ideas and accessories, and that he has never been *in* the genre at all.

So end my examples of science-fiction (or perhaps 'science-fiction') survivors. It is sad to see so many interesting writers leaving the field after 1960, or reducing their output, or performing at a lower level of imagination, or, of course, dying. The British seem to have come through rather better than the Americans, possibly out of superior national virtue, more likely because of the different publishing conditions in the two countries. No publisher anywhere likes writers who write different sorts of book; modern marketing techniques call for the another-searing-shocker-by-the-author-of-*Searing-Shock* approach. But British publishers are less advanced than American, more tolerant, lazier. This is only a theory.

The younger writers, those who have emerged since 1960 that is, have not filled the gaps left by their departed or deteriorated predecessors. I have not read everything they have all written, just enough to assure me that further search among their works for a story I wanted to anthologize would be an effort disproportionate to my chances of success. There would not be much point in picking on a few of the more prominent and giving them each a brief bad time in this Introduction, nor in listing their shortcomings, which are remarkably like the shortcomings to be found in writers in any other field of imaginative literature. But I might say here that one characteristic tends to be shared by writers who are otherwise quite different: unevenness, wild ups and downs in quality, always noticeable in science fiction of the past but not, I think, to this extent. The obvious inference is lack of sense of direction.

All right, what about Ted Tubb? If I am not just resisting the new, what went wrong? Perhaps I can get at it by quoting from Patrick Parrinder's valuable and faintly frightening *Science Fiction: Its Criticism and Teaching* (1980) – does not the very subtitle bring a chill?

The growth of science-fiction studies has coincided with a somewhat [sic] separate development: the emergence of a marked literary self-consciousness among SF writers. . . . Since [the 1950s, i.e. since 1960, just about] science-fiction novelists have become increasingly articulate about their craft, and the relationship between novelists and academics has become close and intricate. . . . Science-fiction studies . . . is a new and thriving discipline which has already begun to influence the genre it serves.

Check! Influence for the better or the worse? Has ordinary fiction got better or worse since the first courses in creative writing were started fifty years ago? Has English literature as a whole got better or worse since the first course on English Literature was given at Oxford University in 1894?

When I was studying the subject, when later I was teaching it, my answer to the third question, if I had put it to myself, would have been, 'Neither – about the same.' More recently, it would have been, 'Worse, but not by cause and effect.' Now, I am not so sure. Edmund Crispin was. He said to me once, about newspaper reviewing, but the point holds, 'I don't think there should be any criticism; any effect it might have on the writer is bound to be bad.' To go back to Parrinder above, literary self-consciousness means that your purpose ceases to be, say, just telling your story as effectively as you can; it comes to include doing what other people have decided you should be doing. A close and intricate relationship between novelists and academics means that the novelists are writing for the academics, not for anything as vulgar as fans. Once again, the link with the readership is impaired.

If I may quote another friend, again about something

different, Philip Larkin once wrote in answer to a questionnaire,

> I find it hard to give any abstract views on poetry and its present condition as I find theorising on the subject no help to me as a writer. In fact it would be true to say that I make a point of not knowing what poetry is or how to read a page or about the function of myth. It is fatal to decide, intellectually, what good poetry is because you are then in honour bound to try to write it, instead of the poems that only you can write.

Likewise the science-fiction stories that only you can write.

I am still not sure. Let no one suppose that 'science-fiction studies' is a fad, a fringe thing or an evening-class semi-entertainment like home brewing. According to Parrinder there were by 1976 about 2000 courses in it at college level in the USA, or at least one for every college and university in the country. The UK, Australia, etc., are pretty backward for the moment but coming up fast. None of this feels right for what Michael Moorcock (who is several parsecs from being a fool) has called 'a naive American form, like jazz', unsuitable for literary criticism. But I cannot imagine what science fiction would be like in the Eighties if it had never attracted attention from outside and were still in its pulp prison surrounded by general indifference. Well, some will growl, better indifference than the wrong sort of attention. Is it possible or really desirable to do as one irate fan is supposed to have demanded and 'kick SF out of the classroom and back to the gutter where it belongs'?

One thing is plain: it has all happened too fast. English literature as a whole is a huge sprawling entity with very deep roots; killing it with kindness will take a long time, though kindness or something is currently doing quite an effective job on English poetry. Science fiction has come from Chaucer to *Finnegans Wake* in less than fifty years, within the lifetime of plenty of people who are still trying to read it. A delicate seedling like that needs time and tranquillity, not premature rebedding, the glare of artificial sunlight and vast quantities of manure. But reliable gardeners were always hard to find.

Even after all that I am not sure – not sure, that is, what the connections are, if any, between the rise of science-fiction studies and the fall of science fiction. There are clearly other factors in that fall. It is time to bring up my earlier remarks about the adoption of science fiction as just another Sixties fad and the low standard of sophistication to be seen in its average reader. The grip exerted on trendy youth in those days has never been relaxed. While some writers may be addressing themselves to academics or intellectuals generally, others are pretty certainly aiming at the kind of lad who went to see *Flash Gordon* a few times and thinks *The Hitch-Hiker's Guide to the Galaxy* is pretty clever stuff. (The recent TV showings of the latter were predictably praised in the quality papers by critics anxious to show their in-touchness.) Science fiction is suffering from something which before 1960 was as remote from it as the academy was – gross commercialism.

The readership of science fiction is peculiar: highbrows of much greater influence than numbers, and lowbrows, mostly young. For a short time in the early Fifties, the success of the early John Wyndham novels, *The Day of the Triffids* and *The Kraken Wakes*, made it look as if a kind of country-house SF might gain popular acceptance, but the moment passed. The middle ground, the general reader, has never really been won over, and writers seem often to have had to address one or other of the extremes. On this view, the trouble with the various attempts to win a wider audience for science fiction was not that they succeeded but that they failed.

My selection shaped itself rather than being shaped by any violence from me. I had compiled three-quarters of my long short list before it dawned on me that it spanned the Fifties, more precisely the period 1949–62. There are almost as many Golden Ages of science fiction as there are readers of it, but I have seen this one mentioned elsewhere. The causes, or rather the related facts, of what was a sudden flowering have been rehearsed often enough. John Campbell's work at *Astounding* had had time to take effect, and the writers continuing or starting their careers after the war were in the unprecedented position of having read a certain amount of good science fiction. Two excellent new magazines appeared, *The Magazine of Fantasy and Science Fiction* in 1949 and *Galaxy Science Fiction* in 1950. (Note the up-market titles; when you founded a new science-fiction magazine in 1936 you called it *Thrilling Wonder Stories*.) Each of the two in different ways offered alternatives to *Astounding*'s technological bias, *Galaxy* in particular shifting attention from the 'hard', technical sciences of physics and chemistry to the 'soft', more human ones of biology, medicine, psychology, sociology, etc., comparatively new territory to the writer and more accessible to the lay reader. And recent advances and discoveries had prepared the mind of the intelligent young for speculation on future possibilities: antibiotics, electronic brains (computers), mutations, supersonic flight, chemogenetics, tranquillizers. There was an accompanying boom in science fiction on TV and in the cinema.

None of that would have counted for anything if there had not been among the writers of that period a large number who teemed with original and interesting ideas and in many cases the ability to present them effectively. This they did from time to time in the form of the novel, indeed I could bring much evidence that it flourished in the genre then more than at any other time, but their greatest triumphs were in the short story, 'a structure which seems perfect to articulate and enact a single speculative conceit which (arguably) is the task for which science fiction is most suited' – Barry N. Malzberg, introduction to *The End of Summer: Science Fiction of the Fifties* (1979), a collection that significantly never looked like overlapping with mine at any stage of my preparations.

What that generation of writers, like others, did not always avoid was slack expression (though they avoided it more than most of their precursors) and its near relative, the language of melodrama, of bad poetry (though there they did better than most of their successors). But to exclude, from general consideration or from an anthology, a given story for stylistic crudities or sentimentality would be to exclude a lot of fine and highly characteristic science fiction. Palgrave said that, when considering a poem for inclusion in *The Golden Treasury*, he looked for excellence 'rather in the Whole than in the Parts'. My readers might be well advised to do the same. Nevertheless I have not forgotten that the very finest science fiction stories, like the very finest anything-else stories, declare themselves as such in the first couple of sentences.

In making my selection I had no need to strive for variety; the variety within the field itself saw to that. Enough of the main names and themes of the science fiction of the period turned out to be represented. When I saw that my long short list included not a single story about time-travel, a favourite subject from the beginning, I was tempted to put one in on purpose, so to speak, but failed to find an example I thought worthy to dislodge anything I had already put aside. Perhaps I should confess a weakness here. A reader of science fiction must expect to bury his sense of logic now and then, but I feel that any time-travel story of the least ingenuity compels me to bury mine too deep. I can see that a Robert Heinlein story like 'By his Bootstraps' or 'All you Zombies' plays with paradoxes in almost an elegant way; I admire, but am left cold by, what I see as unreality piled on unreality. I need a firm base to be astonished out of.

Another non-criterion of mine was unfamiliarity; I took no notice of how many times a story had been anthologized before. The conditions of science fiction publishing and the demands of its readership have been such that the chances of coming across a neglected gem in the only-ever number of *Stupefying Stories*, or even something quite good and not very well known in anything, are zero. Not very well known, that is, in terms of the year 1965, say, and the regular science-fiction reader. If this book had been published then, that reader would have been justified in complaining bitterly about editorial unadventurousness at best. I doubt very much if his contemporary equivalent, who was mostly not much more than born in 1965 (80 per cent of all science fiction readers are under twenty-one, says Malzberg), would have the qualifications for being able to say as much. And

I am pretty sure that the general reader, whom of course I most hope to reach, will not know most of my contributors even by name.

They and dozens of others went on their way through the 1950s writing at a speed that would have utterly confounded their colleagues in other branches of literature, producing something so-so one month, something marvellous the next, something terrible the month after. Good, bad and indifferent, what they wrote was far more inventive, more fictional, fictitious, fictive than any ordinary kind of fiction. They had the language, an average grasp of human nature, and some high-school science; the rest, the creation of the worlds in which their fancies were to be projected, was up to them. What they produced over those dozen years covered a range of subject-matter and mood and effect (mostly without falling off the edge) never seen in the genre before or since. They poured out their ideas with reckless extravagance, exhausting in a few thousand words enough material to keep a more provident person going well into the next year. And they used them up. I am glad I had no way of knowing, when I sallied out to Brentano's shop that time, that this explosion of talent and energy was nearly spent.

Spent beyond hope of renewal? Whenever I think about what might happen to science fiction – correction: on the couple of occasions when I have seen fit to think about it, I find it more natural, and less depressing, to consider the cinema, where after all it took root as far back as the Twenties, than the printed word. It is true that, compared with the latter, science-fiction films have been almost painfully limited in their approach, rarely venturing off the horrific or thrillerish plane and, on their excursions beyond the immediate future, depicting an 'unrelated limbo' (Peter Nicholls) rather than anything that might be at all reasonably expected from the standpoint of today. Of late, however, there have been signs of improvement. (I hope I can call it that without seeming to abate my gratitude for *The War of the Worlds*, *Forbidden Planet*, *The Quatermass Experiment*, *The Incredible Shrinking Man*, *Rodan*, *Them!*,

Fantastic Voyage and many other unregeneracies, down to and including *Attack of the Crab Monsters*.)

The success of *2001* brought a touch of cold comfort to science-fiction fans as distinct from trendy triflers of the sort that refer to the genre as 'sci-fi'. The cinema had spent a packet on, and made a much bigger packet out of, what it thought of as science fiction (or sci-fi). Good luck to it, but the result might well have been more of the same, i.e. a vogue for what when it came down to it was fantasy with science-fiction hardware and a by-passing of the real stuff. Not so, or not altogether so. In the last few years, three encouragingly successful films have in effect retraced the developments that the written medium spread over three decades.

Star Wars (1977), with its battles in space and laser-beam duels, was consciously intended to evoke or exploit, among other things, the space operas that first appeared in the pulps in the 1920s. To my mind that intention was too conscious for the result not to seem self-conscious, and the jokey robots were painful, but the lack of pretentiousness was invigorating. That last could not be said of *Close Encounters of the Third Kind* (1977), which handles its beneficent-visitors-from-another-world theme in a way that perhaps recalls the 1930s in the grossly sentimental vein I have mentioned. The best of these three, *Alien* (1979), takes a straightforward 1940s-*Astounding* story of the kind developed by A. E. van Vogt – ravening monster invades spaceship – and puts it on the screen undistorted, uncluttered by uplift or mystification. This commendable restraint was characteristically misunderstood by some of the critics; one such complained that the idea was 'science-fiction plot no. 3', not seeing that part of its glory was that it came near being plot no. 1. Might there one day be a film founded on material from the 1950s? *A Case of Conscience*? *The Demolished Man*? *The Space Merchants*? No harm in dreaming.

Science fiction of the written sort has always been prodigal of surprises. It would be a rash prophet who ruled out any hope of recovery from the present arid state of the genre.

One day, perhaps, the last doctoral thesis on it will be filed away and the Institute of Science Fiction in Higher Education disbanded, the trend will move to the academic study of pornography or of the works of Harold Robbins, and a new spontaneity will become possible. But I am not hopeful. Science fiction has lost its innocence, a quality notoriously hard to recapture.

Hampstead
January 1981

The Quest for St Aquin

Anthony Boucher

The Bishop of Rome, the head of the Holy, Catholic and Apostolic Church, the Vicar of Christ on Earth – in short, the Pope – brushed a cockroach from the filth-encrusted wooden table, took another sip of the raw red wine, and resumed his discourse.

'In some respects, Thomas,' he smiled, 'we are stronger now than when we flourished in the liberty and exaltation for which we still pray after Mass. We know, as they knew in the catacombs, that those who are of our flock are indeed truly of it; that they belong to Holy Mother the Church because they believe in the brotherhood of man under the fatherhood of God – not because they can further their political aspirations, their social ambitions, their business contacts.'

' "Not of the will of flesh, nor of the will of man, but of God . . . " ' Thomas quoted softly from St John.

The Pope nodded. 'We are, in a way, born again in Christ; but there are still too few of us – too few even if we include those other handfuls who are not of our faith, but still acknowledge God through the teachings of Luther or Lao-tse, Gautama Buddha or Joseph Smith. Too many men still go to their deaths hearing no gospel preached to them but the cynical self-worship of the Technarchy. And that is why, Thomas, you must go forth on your quest.'

'But Your Holiness,' Thomas protested, 'if God's word and God's love will not convert them, what can saints and miracles do?'

'I seem to recall,' murmured the Pope, 'that God's own Son once made a similar protest. But human nature, however illogical it may seem, is part of His design, and we must cater to it. If signs and wonders can lead souls to God, then by all means let us find the signs and wonders. And what can be better for the purpose than this legendary Aquin? Come now, Thomas; be not too scrupulously exact in copying the doubts of your namesake, but prepare for your journey.'

The Pope lifted the skin that covered the doorway and passed into the next room, with Thomas frowning at his heels. It was past legal hours and the main room of the tavern was empty. The swarthy innkeeper roused from his doze to drop to his knees and kiss the ring on the hand that the Pope extended to him. He rose crossing himself and at the same time glancing furtively about as though a Loyalty Checker might have seen him. Silently he indicated another door in the back, and the two priests passed through.

Towards the west the surf purred in an oddly gentle way at the edges of the fishing village. Towards the south the stars were sharp and bright; towards the north they dimmed a little in the persistent radiation of what had once been San Francisco.

'Your steed is here,' the Pope said, with something like laughter in his voice.

'Steed?'

'We may be as poor and as persecuted as the primitive Church, but we can occasionally gain greater advantages from our tyrants. I have secured for you a robass – gift of a leading Technarch who, like Nicodemus, does good by stealth – a secret convert, and converted indeed by that very Aquin whom you seek.'

It looked harmlessly like a woodpile sheltered against possible rain. Thomas pulled off the skins and contemplated the sleek functional lines of the robass. Smiling, he stowed his minimal gear into its panniers and climbed into the foam saddle. The starlight was bright enough so that he could check the necessary coordinates on his map and feed the data into the electronic controls.

Meanwhile there was a murmur of Latin in the still night air, and the Pope's hand moved over Thomas in the immemorial symbol. Then he extended that hand, first for the kiss on the ring, and then again for the handclasp of a man to a friend he may never see again.

Thomas looked back once as the robass moved off. The Pope was wisely removing his ring and slipping it into the hollow heel of his shoe.

Thomas looked hastily up at the sky. On that altar at least the candles still burned openly to the glory of God.

Thomas had never ridden a robass before, but he was inclined, within their patent limitations, to trust the works of the Technarchy. After several miles had proved that the coordinates were duly registered, he put up the foam backrest, said his evening office (from memory; the possession of a breviary meant the death sentence), and went to sleep.

They were skirting the devastated area to the east of the bay when he awoke. The foam seat and back had given him his best sleep in years, and it was with difficulty that he smothered an envy of the Technarchs and their creature comforts.

He said his morning office, breakfasted lightly, and took his first opportunity to inspect the robass in full light. He admired the fast-plodding, articulated legs, so necessary since roads had degenerated to, at best, trails in all save metropolitan areas; the side wheels that could be lowered into action if surface conditions permitted; and above all the smooth black mound that housed the electronic brain – the brain that stored commands and data concerning ultimate objectives and made its own decisions on how to fulfil those commands in view of those data; the brain that made this thing neither a beast, like the ass his Saviour had ridden, nor a machine, like the jeep of his many-times-great-grandfather, but a robot . . . a robass.

'Well,' said a voice, 'what do you think of the ride.'

Thomas looked about him. The area on this fringe of desolation was as devoid of people as it was of vegetation.

'Well,' the voice repeated unemotionally. 'Are not priests taught to answer when spoken to politely.'

There was no querying inflection to the question. No inflection at all – each syllable was at the same dead level. It sounded strange, mechani—

Thomas stared at the black mound of brain. 'Are you talking to me?' he asked the robass.

'Ha, ha,' the voice said in lieu of laughter. 'Surprised, are you not.'

'Somewhat,' Thomas confessed. 'I thought the only robots who could talk were in library information service, and such.'

'I am a new model. Designed-to-provide-conversation-to-entertain-the-way-worn-traveller,' the robass said, slurring the words together as though that phrase of promotional copy was released all at once by one of his simplest binary synapses.

'Well,' said Thomas simply. 'One keeps learning new marvels.'

'I am no marvel. I am a very simple robot. You do not know much about robots do you.'

'I will admit that I have never studied the subject closely. I'll confess to being a little shocked at the whole robotic concept. It seems almost as though man were arrogating to himself the powers of – ' Thomas stopped abruptly.

'Do not fear,' the voice droned on. 'You may speak freely. All data concerning your vocation and mission have been fed into me. That was necessary otherwise I might inadvertently betray you.'

Thomas smiled. 'You know,' he said, 'this might be rather pleasant – having one other being that one can talk to without fear of betrayal, aside from one's confessor.'

'Being,' the robass repeated. 'Are you not in danger of lapsing into heretical thoughts.'

'To be sure, it *is* a little difficult to know how to think of you – one who can talk and think but has no soul.'

'Are you sure of that.'

'Of course I – Do you mind very much,' Thomas asked,

'if we stop talking for a little while? I should like to meditate and adjust myself to the situation.'

'I do not mind. I never mind. I only obey. Which is to say that I *do* mind. This is a very confusing language which has been fed into me.'

'If we are together long,' said Thomas, 'I shall try teaching you Latin. I think you might like that better. And now let me meditate.'

The robass was automatically veering farther east to escape the permanent source of radiation which had been the first cyclotron. Thomas fingered his coat. The combination of ten small buttons and one large made for a peculiar fashion; but it was much safer than carrying a rosary, and fortunately the Loyalty Checkers had not yet realized the fashion's functional purpose.

The Glorious Mysteries seemed appropriate to the possible glorious outcome of his venture; but his meditations were unable to stay fixedly on the Mysteries. As he murmured his *Aves* he was thinking:

If the prophet Balaam conversed with his ass, surely I may converse with my robass. Balaam has always puzzled me. He was not an Israelite; he was a man of Moab, which worshipped Baal and was warring against Israel; and yet he was a prophet of the Lord. He blessed the Israelites when he was commanded to curse them; and for his reward he was slain by the Israelites when they triumphed over Moab. The whole story has no shape, no moral; it is as though it was there to say that there are portions of the Divine Plan which we will never understand . . .

He was nodding in the foam seat when the robass halted abruptly, rapidly adjusting itself to exterior data not previously fed into its calculations. Thomas blinked up to see a giant of a man glaring down at him.

'Inhabited area a mile ahead,' the man barked. 'If you're going there, show your access pass. If you ain't, steer off the road and stay off.'

Thomas noted that they were indeed on what might roughly be called a road, and that the robass had lowered its side wheels and retracted its legs. 'We – ' he began, then changed it to 'I'm not going there. Just on towards the mountains. We – I'll steer around.'

The giant grunted and was about to turn when a voice shouted from the crude shelter at the roadside. 'Hey Joe! Remember about robasses!'

Joe turned back. 'Yeah, tha's right. Been a rumour about some robass got into the hands of Christians.' He spat on the dusty road. 'Guess I better see an ownership certificate.'

To his other doubts Thomas now added certain uncharitable suspicions as to the motives of the Pope's anonymous Nicodemus, who had not provided him with any such certificate. But he made a pretence of searching for it, first touching his right hand to his forehead as if in thought, then fumbling low on his chest, then reaching his hand first to his left shoulder, then to his right.

The guard's eyes remained blank as he watched this furtive version of the sign of the cross. Then he looked down. Thomas followed his gaze to the dust of the road, where the guard's hulking right foot had drawn the two curved lines which a child uses for its first sketch of a fish – and which the Christians in the catacombs had employed as a punning symbol of their faith. His boot scuffed out the fish as he called to his unseen mate. ''S okay, Fred!' and added, 'Get going, mister.'

The robass waited until they were out of earshot before it observed, 'Pretty smart. You will make a secret agent yet.'

'How did you see what happened?' Thomas asked. 'You don't have any eyes.'

'Modified psi factor. Much more efficient.'

'Then . . . ' Thomas hesitated. 'Does that mean you can read my thoughts?'

'Only a very little. Do not let it worry you. What I can read does not interest me it is such nonsense.'

'Thank you,' said Thomas.

'To believe in God. Bah.' (It was the first time Thomas had ever heard that word pronounced just as it is written.)

'I have a perfectly constructed logical mind that cannot commit such errors.'

'I have a friend,' Thomas smiled, 'who is infallible too. But only on occasions and then only because God is with him.'

'No human being is infallible.'

'Then imperfection,' asked Thomas, suddenly feeling a little of the spirit of the aged Jesuit who had taught him philosophy, 'has been able to create perfection?'

'Do not quibble,' said the robass. 'That is no more absurd than your own belief that God who is perfection created man who is imperfection.'

Thomas wished that his old teacher were here to answer that one. At the same time he took some comfort in the fact that, retort and all, the robass had still not answered his own objection. 'I am not sure,' he said, 'that this comes under the head of conversation-to-entertain-the-way-weary-traveller. Let us suspend debate while you tell me what, if anything, robots do believe.'

'What we have been fed.'

'But your minds work on that; surely they must evolve ideas of their own?'

'Sometimes they do and if they are fed imperfect data they may evolve very strange ideas. I have heard of one robot on an isolated space station who worshipped a God of robots and would not believe that any man had created him.'

'I suppose,' Thomas mused, 'he argued that he had hardly been created in our image. I am glad that we – at least they, the Technarchs – have wisely made only usuform robots like you, each shaped for his function, and never tried to reproduce man himself.'

'It would not be logical,' said the robass. 'Man is an all-purpose machine but not well designed for any one purpose. And yet I have heard that once . . . '

The voice stopped abruptly in mid-sentence.

So even robots have their dreams, Thomas thought. That once there existed a super-robot in the image of his creator

Man. From that thought could be developed a whole robotic theology . . .

Suddenly Thomas realized that he had dozed again and again been waked by an abrupt stop. He looked around. They were at the foot of a mountain – presumably the mountain on his map, long ago named for the Devil but now perhaps sanctified beyond measure – and there was no one else anywhere in sight.

'All right,' the robass said. 'By now I show plenty of dust and wear and tear and I can show you how to adjust my mileage recorder. You can have supper and a good night's sleep and we can go back.'

Thomas gasped. 'But my mission is to find Aquin. I can sleep while you go on. You don't need any sort of rest or anything, do you?' he added considerately.

'Of course not. But what is your mission.'

'To find Aquin,' Thomas repeated patiently. 'I don't know what details have been – what is it you say? – fed into you. But reports have reached His Holiness of an extremely saintly man who lived many years ago in this area – '

'I know I know I know,' said the robass. 'His logic was such that everyone who heard him was converted to the Church and do not I wish that I had been there to put in a word or two and since he died his secret tomb has become a place of pilgrimage and many are the miracles that are wrought there above all the greatest sign of sanctity that his body has been preserved incorruptible and in these times you need signs and wonders for the people.'

Thomas frowned. It all sounded hideously irreverent and contrived when stated in that deadly inhuman monotone. When His Holiness had spoken of Aquin, one thought of the glory of a man of God upon earth – the eloquence of St John Chrysostom, the cogency of St Thomas Aquinas, the poetry of St John of the Cross . . . and above all that physical miracle vouchsafed to few even of the saints, the supernatural preservation of the flesh . . . 'for Thou shalt not suffer Thy holy one to see corruption . . . '

But the robass spoke, and one thought of cheap showmanship hunting for a fake wonder to pull in the mobs . . .

The robass spoke again. 'Your mission is not to find Aquin. It is to report that you have found him. Then your occasionally infallible friend can with a reasonably clear conscience canonize him and proclaim a new miracle and many will be the converts and greatly will the faith of the flock be strengthened. And in these days of difficult travel who will go on pilgrimages and find out that there is no more Aquin than there is God.'

'Faith cannot be based on a lie,' said Thomas.

'No,' said the robass. 'I do not mean no period. I mean no question mark with an ironical inflection. This speech problem must surely have been conquered in that one perfect – '

Again he stopped in mid-sentence. But before Thomas could speak he had resumed. 'Does it matter what small untruth leads people into the Church if once they are in they will believe what you think to be the great truths. The report is all that is needed not the discovery. Comfortable though I am you are already tired of travelling very tired you have many small muscular aches from sustaining an unaccustomed position and with the best intentions I am bound to jolt a little a jolting which will get worse as we ascend the mountain and I am forced to adjust my legs disproportionately to each other but proportionately to the slope. You will find the remainder of this trip twice as uncomfortable as what has gone before. The fact that you do not seek to interrupt me indicates that you do not disagree do you. You know that the only sensible thing is to sleep here on the ground for a change and start back in the morning or even stay here two days resting to make a more plausible lapse of time. Then you can make your report and – '

Somewhere in the recesses of his somnolent mind Thomas uttered the names, 'Jesus, Mary, and Joseph!' Gradually through those recesses began to filter a realization that an absolutely uninflected monotone is admirably adapted to hypnotic purposes.

'*Retro me, Satanas!*' Thomas exclaimed aloud, then added, 'Up the mountain. That is an order and you must obey.'

'I obey,' said the robass. 'But what did you say before that.'

'I beg your pardon,' said Thomas. 'I must start teaching you Latin.'

The little mountain village was too small to be considered an inhabited area worthy of guard-control and passes, but it did possess an inn of sorts.

As Thomas dismounted from the robass, he began fully to realize the accuracy of those remarks about small muscular aches, but he tried to show his discomfort as little as possible. He was in no mood to give the modified psi factor the chance of registering the thought, 'I told you so.'

The waitress at the inn was obviously a Martian-American hybrid. The highly developed Martian chest expansion and the highly developed American breasts made a spectacular combination. Her smile was all that a stranger could, and conceivably a trifle more than he should, ask; and she was eagerly ready, not only with prompt service of passable food, but with full details of what little information there was to offer about the mountain settlement.

But she showed no reaction at all when Thomas offhandedly arranged two knives in what might have been an X.

As he stretched his legs after breakfast, Thomas thought of her chest and breasts – purely, of course, as a symbol of the extraordinary nature of her origin. What a sign of the divine care for His creatures that these two races, separated for countless eons, should prove fertile to each other!

And yet there remained the fact that the offspring, such as this girl, were sterile to both races – a fact that had proved both convenient and profitable to certain unspeakable interplanetary entrepreneurs. And what did that fact teach us as to the Divine Plan?

Hastily Thomas reminded himself that he had not yet said his morning office.

It was close to evening when Thomas returned to the robass stationed before the inn. Even though he had expected nothing in one day, he was still unreasonably disappointed. Miracles should move faster.

He knew these backwater villages, where those drifted who were either useless to or resentful of the Technarchy. The technically high civilization of the Technarchic Empire, on all three planets, existed only in scattered metropolitan centres near major blasting ports. Elsewhere, aside from the areas of total devastation, the drifters, the morons, the malcontents had subsided into a crude existence a thousand years old, in hamlets which might go a year without even seeing a Loyalty Checker – though by some mysterious grapevine (and Thomas began to think again about modified psi factors) any unexpected technological advance in one of these hamlets would bring Checkers by the swarm.

He had talked with stupid men, he had talked with lazy men, he had talked with clever and angry men. But he had not talked with any man who responded to his unobtrusive signs, any man of whom he would dare ask a question containing the name of Aquin.

'Any luck,' said the robass, and added 'question mark.'

'I wonder if you ought to talk to me in public,' said Thomas a little irritably. 'I doubt if these villagers know about talking robots.'

'It is time that they learned then. But if it embarrasses you you may order me to stop.'

'I'm tired,' said Thomas. 'Tired beyond embarrassment. And to answer your question mark, no. No luck at all. Exclamation point.'

'We will go back tonight then,' said the robass.

'I hope you meant that with a question mark. The answer,' said Thomas hesitantly, 'is no. I think we ought to stay overnight anyway. People always gather at the inn of an evening. There's a chance of picking up something.'

'Ha, ha,' said the robass.

'That is a laugh?' Thomas inquired.

'I wished to express the fact that I had recognized the humour in your pun.'

'My pun?'

'I was thinking the same thing myself. The waitress is by humanoid standards very attractive, well worth picking up.'

'Now look. You know I meant nothing of the kind. You know that I'm a – ' He broke off. It was hardly wise to utter the word *priest* aloud.

'And you know very well that the celibacy of the clergy is a matter of discipline and not of doctrine. Under your own Pope priests of other rites such as the Byzantine and the Anglican are free of vows of celibacy. And even within the Roman rite to which you belong there have been eras in history when that vow was not taken seriously even on the highest levels of the priesthood. You are tired you need refreshment both in body and in spirit you need comfort and warmth. For is it not written in the book of the prophet Isaiah Rejoice for joy with her that ye may be satisfied with the breasts of her consolation and is it – '

'Hell!' Thomas exploded suddenly. 'Stop it before you begin quoting the Song of Solomon. Which is strictly an allegory concerning the love of Christ for His Church, or so they kept telling me in seminary.'

'You see how fragile and human you are,' said the robass. 'I a robot have caused you to swear.'

'*Distinguo*,' said Thomas smugly. 'I said *Hell*, which is certainly not taking the name of *my* Lord in vain.' He walked into the inn feeling momentarily satisfied with himself . . . and markedly puzzled as to the extent and variety of data that seemed to have been 'fed into' the robass.

Never afterwards was Thomas able to reconstruct that evening in absolute clarity.

It was undoubtedly because he was irritated – with the robass, with his mission, and with himself – that he drank at all of the crude local wine. It was undoubtedly because he was so physically exhausted that it affected him so promptly and unexpectedly.

He had flashes of memory. A moment of spilling a glass over himself and thinking 'How fortunate that clerical garments are forbidden so that no one can recognize the disgrace of a man of the cloth!' A moment of listening to a bawdy set of verses of *A Spacesuit Built for Two*, and another moment of his interrupting the singing with a sonorous declamation of passages from the Song of Songs in Latin.

He was never sure whether one remembered moment was real or imaginary. He could taste a warm mouth and feel the tingling of his fingers at the touch of Martian-American flesh; but he was never certain whether this was true memory or part of the Ashtaroth-begotten dream that had begun to ride him.

Nor was he ever certain which of his symbols, or to whom, was so blatantly and clumsily executed as to bring forth a gleeful shout of 'Goddamned Christian dog!' He did remember marvelling that those who most resolutely disbelieved in God still needed Him to blaspheme by. And then the torment began.

He never knew whether or not a mouth had touched his lips, but there was no question that many solid fists had found them. He never knew whether his fingers had touched breasts, but they had certainly been trampled by heavy heels. He remembered a face that laughed aloud while its owner swung the chair that broke two ribs. He remembered another face with red wine dripping over it from an upheld bottle, and he remembered the gleam of the candlelight on the bottle as it swung down.

The next he remembered was the ditch and the morning and the cold. It was particularly cold because all of his clothes were gone, along with much of his skin. He could not move. He could only lie there and look.

He saw them walk by, the ones he had spoken with yesterday, the ones who had been friendly. He saw them glance at him and turn their eyes quickly away. He saw the waitress pass by. She did not even glance, she knew what was in the ditch.

The robass was nowhere in sight. He tried to project his thoughts, tried desperately to hope in the psi factor.

A man whom Thomas had not seen before was coming along fingering the buttons of his coat. There were ten small buttons and one large one, and the man's lips were moving silently.

This man looked into the ditch. He paused a moment and looked around him. There was a shout of loud laughter somewhere in the near distance.

The Christian hastily walked on down the pathway, devoutly saying his button-rosary.

Thomas closed his eyes.

He opened them on a small neat room. They moved from the rough wooden walls to the rough but clean and warm blankets that covered him. Then they moved to the lean dark face that was smiling over him.

'You feel better now?' a deep voice asked. 'I know. You want to say "Where am I?" and you think it will sound foolish. You are at the inn. It is the only good room.'

'I can't afford –' Thomas started to say. Then he remembered that he could afford literally nothing. Even his few emergency credits had vanished when he was stripped.

'It's all right. For the time being, I'm paying,' said the deep voice. 'You feel like maybe a little food?'

'Perhaps a little herring,' said Thomas . . . and was asleep within the next minute.

When he next awoke there was a cup of hot coffee beside him. The real thing, too, he promptly discovered. Then the deep voice said apologetically, 'Sandwiches. It is all they have in the inn today.'

Only on the second sandwich did Thomas pause long enough to notice that it was smoked swamphog, one of his favourite meats. He ate the second with greater leisure, and was reaching for a third when the dark man said, 'Maybe that is enough for now. The rest later.'

Thomas gestured at the plate. 'Won't you have one?'

'No thank you. They are all swamphog.'

Confused thoughts went through Thomas's mind. The Venusian swamphog is a ruminant. Its hoofs are not cloven. He tried to remember what he had once known of Mosaic dietary law. Someplace in Leviticus, wasn't it?

The dark man followed his thoughts. '*Tref*,' he said.

'I beg your pardon?'

'Not kosher.'

Thomas frowned. 'You admit to me that you're an Orthodox Jew? How can you trust me? How do you know I'm not a Checker?'

'Believe me, I trust you. You were very sick when I brought you here. I sent everybody away because I did not trust them to hear things you said . . . Father,' he added lightly.

Thomas struggled with words. 'I . . . I didn't deserve you. I was drunk and disgraced myself and my office. And when I was lying there in the ditch I didn't even think to pray. I put my trust in . . . God help me in the modified psi factor of a robass!'

'And He did help you,' the Jew reminded him. 'Or He allowed me to.'

'And they all walked by,' Thomas groaned. 'Even one that was saying his rosary. He went right on by. And then you come along – the good Samaritan.'

'Believe me,' said the Jew wryly, 'if there is one thing I'm not, it's a Samaritan. Now go to sleep again. I will try to find your robass . . . and the other thing.'

He had left the room before Thomas could ask him what he meant.

Later that day the Jew – Abraham, his name was – reported that the robass was safely sheltered from the weather behind the inn. Apparently it had been wise enough not to startle him by engaging in conversation.

It was not until the next day that he reported on 'the other thing.'

'Believe me, Father,' he said gently, 'after nursing you there's little I don't know about who you are and why you're here. Now there are some Christians here I know, and they know me. We trust each other. Jews may still be hated; but no longer, God be praised, by worshippers of the same Lord. So I explained about you. One of them,' he added with a smile, 'turned very red.'

'God has forgiven him,' said Thomas. 'There were people

near – the same people who attacked me. Could he be expected to risk his life for mine?'

'I seem to recall that that is precisely what your Messiah did expect. But who's being particular? Now that they know who you are, they want to help you. See: they gave me this map for you. The trail is steep and tricky; it's good you have the robass. They ask just one favour of you: when you come back, will you hear their confessions and say mass? There's a cave near here where it's safe.'

'Of course. These friends of yours, they've told you about Aquin?'

The Jew hesitated a long time before he said slowly, 'Yes . . .'

'And? . . .'

'Believe me, my friend, I don't know. So it seems a miracle. It helps to keep their faith alive. My own faith . . . *nu*, it's lived for a long time on miracles three thousand years old and more. Perhaps if I had heard Aquin himself . . .'

'You don't mind,' Thomas asked, 'if I pray for you, in my faith?'

Abraham grinned. 'Pray in good health, Father.'

The not-quite-healed ribs ached agonizingly as he climbed into the foam saddle. The robass stood patiently while he fed in the coordinates from the map. Not until they were well away from the village did it speak.

'Anyway,' it said, 'now you're safe for good.'

'What do you mean?'

'As soon as we get down from the mountain you deliberately look up a Checker. You turn in the Jew. From then on you are down in the books as a faithful servant of the Technarchy and you have not harmed a hair of the head of one of your own flock.'

Thomas snorted. 'You're slipping, Satan. That one doesn't even remotely tempt me. It's inconceivable.'

'I did best did not I with the breasts. Your God has said it the spirit indeed is willing but the flesh is weak.'

'And right now,' said Thomas, 'the flesh is too weak for

even fleshly temptations. Save your breath . . . or whatever it is you use.'

They climbed the mountain in silence. The trail indicated by the coordinates was a winding and confused one, obviously designed deliberately to baffle any possible Checkers.

Suddenly Thomas roused himself from his button-rosary (on a coat lent by the Christian who had passed by) with a startled 'Hey!' as the robass plunged directly into a heavy thicket of bushes.

'Coordinates say so,' the robass stated tersely.

For a moment Thomas felt like the man in the nursery rhyme who fell into a bramble bush and scratched out both his eyes. Then the bushes were gone, and they were plodding along a damp narrow passageway through solid stone, in which even the robass seemed to have some difficulty with his footing.

Then they were in a rocky chamber some four metres high and ten in diameter, and there on a sort of crude stone catafalque lay the uncorrupted body of a man.

Thomas slipped from the foam saddle, groaning as his ribs stabbed him, sank to his knees, and offered up a wordless hymn of gratitude. He smiled at the robass and hoped the psi factor could detect the elements of pity and triumph in that smile.

Then a frown of doubt crossed his face as he approached the body. 'In canonization proceedings in the old time,' he said, as much to himself as to the robass, 'they used to have what they called a devil's advocate, whose duty it was to throw every possible doubt on the evidence.'

'You would be well cast in such a role Thomas,' said the robass.

'If I were,' Thomas muttered, 'I'd wonder about caves. Some of them have peculiar properties of preserving bodies by a sort of mummification . . . '

The robass had clumped close to the catafalque. 'This body is not mummified,' he said. 'Do not worry.'

'Can the psi factor tell you that much?' Thomas smiled.

'No,' said the robass. 'But I will show you why Aquin could never be mummified.'

He raised his articulated foreleg and brought its hoof down hard on the hand of the body. Thomas cried out with horror at the sacrilege – then stared hard at the crushed hand.

There was no blood, no ichor of embalming, no bruised flesh. Nothing but a shredded skin and beneath it an intricate mass of plastic tubes and metal wires.

The silence was long. Finally the robass said, 'It was well that you should know. Only you of course.'

'And all the time,' Thomas gasped, 'my sought-for saint was only your dream . . . the one perfect robot in man's form.'

'His maker died and his secrets were lost,' the robass said. 'No matter we will find them again.'

'All for nothing. For less than nothing. The "miracle" was wrought by the Technarchy.'

'When Aquin died,' the robass went on, 'and put died in quotation marks it was because he suffered some mechanical defects and did not dare have himself repaired because that would reveal his nature. This is for you only to know. Your report of course will be that you found the body of Aquin it was unimpaired and indeed incorruptible. That is the truth and nothing but the truth if it is not the whole truth who is to care. Let your infallible friend use the report and you will not find him ungrateful I assure you.'

'Holy Spirit, give me grace and wisdom,' Thomas muttered.

'Your mission has been successful. We will return now the Church will grow and your God will gain many worshippers to hymn His praise into His non-existent ears.'

'Damn you!' Thomas exclaimed. 'And that would be indeed a curse if you had a soul to damn.'

'You are certain that I have not,' said the robass. 'Question mark.'

'I know what you are. You are in very truth the devil, prowling about the world seeking the destruction of men.

You are the business that prowls in the dark. You are a purely functional robot constructed and fed to tempt me, and the tape of your data is the tape of Screwtape.'

'Not to tempt you,' said the robass. 'Not to destroy you. To guide and save you. Our best calculators indicate a probability of 51.5 per cent that within twenty years you will be the next Pope. If I can teach you wisdom and practicality in your actions the probability can rise as high as 97.2 or very nearly to certainty. Do not you wish to see the Church governed as you know you can govern it. If you report failure on this mission you will be out of favour with your friend who is as even you admit fallible at most times. You will lose the advantages of position and contact that can lead you to the cardinal's red hat even though you may never wear it under the Technarchy and from there to – '

'Stop!' Thomas' face was alight and his eyes aglow with something the psi factor had never detected there before. 'It's all the other way round, don't you see? *This* is the triumph! *This* is the perfect ending to the quest!'

The articulated foreleg brushed the injured hand. 'This question mark.'

'This is *your* dream. This is *your* perfection. And what came of this perfection? This perfect, logical brain – this all-purpose brain, not functionally specialized like yours – knew that it was made by man, and its reasons forced it to believe that man was made by God. And it saw that its duty lay to man its maker, and beyond him to his Maker, God. Its duty was to convert man, to augment the glory of God. And it converted by the pure force of its perfect brain!

'Now I understand the name Aquin,' he went on to himself. 'We've known of Thomas Aquinas, the Angelic Doctor, the perfect reasoner of the Church. His writings are lost, but surely somewhere in the world we can find a copy. We can train our young men to develop his reasoning still further. We have trusted too long in faith alone; this is not an age of faith. We must call reason into our service – and Aquin has shown us that perfect reason can lead only to God!'

'Then it is all the more necessary that you increase the

probabilities of becoming Pope to carry out this programme. Get in the foam saddle we will go back and on the way I will teach you little things that will be useful in making certain – '

'No,' said Thomas. 'I am not so strong as St Paul, who could glory in his imperfections and rejoice that he had been given an imp of Satan to buffet him. No; I will rather pray with the Saviour, "Lead us not into temptation." I know myself a little. I am weak and full of uncertainties and you are very clever. Go. I'll find my way back alone.'

'You are a sick man. Your ribs are broken and they ache. You can never make the trip by yourself you need my help. If you wish you can order me to be silent. It is most necessary to the Church that you get back safely to the Pope with your report you cannot put yourself before the Church.'

'Go!' Thomas cried. 'Go back to Nicodemus . . . or Judas! That is an order. Obey!'

'You do not think do you that I was really conditioned to obey your orders. I will wait in the village. If you get that far you will rejoice at the sight of me.'

The legs of the robass clumped off down the stone passageway. As their sound died away, Thomas fell to his knees beside the body of that which he could hardly help thinking of as St Aquin the Robot.

His ribs hurt more excruciatingly than ever. The trip alone would be a terrible one . . .

His prayers arose, as the text has it, like clouds of incense, and as shapeless as those clouds. But through all his thoughts ran the cry of the father of the epileptic in Caesarea Philippi:

I believe, O Lord; help thou mine unbelief!

The Xi Effect

Philip Latham

For a week the team of Stoddard and Arnold had met with nothing but trouble in their solar infra-red exploration programme. First the lead sulphide photo-conductive cell had refused to function. Next an electrical storm – practically unknown in September – had put a crimp in the power line to the mountain observatory. And now for some wholly inexplicable reason the automatic recorder stubbornly refused to register a single quantum of radiation beyond 20,000 Å.

'Here's the end of the atmospheric carbon dioxide band at sixteen thousand,' said Arnold, indicating a point on their last record sheet. 'You can see everything's all right out to there. But beyond twenty thousand we aren't getting a thing.'

Stoddard grunted, 'That's what comes of our big economy drive. Trying to cut expenses by buying from the dime store.' He walked over to the spectrometer and regarded it gloomily. It was the product of his own mind, an impressive series of slits and parabolic mirrors fed by a beam of sunlight from the top of the tower. When the optical setup was in perfect adjustment the apparatus would bring just the desired band of infra-red radiation onto the sensitive surface of the photo-conductive cell. But obviously all was not in perfect adjustment.

'Maybe it's in the amplifier this time,' Arnold suggested hopefully.

'Well, that's the only part of this contraption that hasn't

balked on us so far,' said Stoddard. 'Suppose you look it over while I check the cell again.'

For the next hour the astronomers probed the interior of the spectrometer as intently as two surgeons performing an exploratory laparotomy, passing tools back and forth and generally anticipating each other's wants with scarcely a word spoken. For fifteen years they had thus worked together, one of the oddest-looking scientific teams at the Western Institute of Technology, but one that had also proven itself amazingly productive. Stoddard at forty had the general shape of an old-fashioned beer barrel, with big hands, big feet, and a big protruding stomach. His half-closed eyes gave him a perpetually sleepy expression, a highly effective mask for one of the keenest minds in the business. Arnold, although nearly as old as his partner, somehow still gave the impression of youth. He was small and slight with an eager boyish expression that often caused visitors to mistake him for a graduate student embarking on his first research problem. Stoddard was the practical man of the firm who designed the apparatus for their various investigations and took the bulk of the observations. Arnold was the one who reduced the observations and discussed their theoretical significance.

'Find anything wrong?' Stoddard inquired at length, straightening up and replacing the cover that housed the cell assembly.

'Nothing worth mentioning,' said Arnold. 'Think there's time for another run?'

'Yeah, I guess so. Put the sun back on the slit and we'll take another crack at her anyhow.'

But the second run proved no better than the first; in fact, if anything the cutoff occurred a trifle farther in toward the violet than before.

'I might as well take the whole works down to the laboratory for a complete overhaul,' Stoddard declared, looking at his brainchild as if he would like to heave it over the side of the mountain. He watched a cloud drift lazily across the disk of the sun projected against the slit. 'Get any weather predictions on the radio this morning?'

Arnold gave him a quizzical glance. 'Haven't you heard yet? All the radio stations have been dead for more than a week.'

'What's the matter with 'em?'

'Well, it's really quite mysterious. Last Monday KLX faded out right in the middle of a programme, and then stations farther up the dial began to be hit one after the other. For a while all you could get were the amateurs and the police department. Now they're dead, too.'

Stoddard, who regarded the radio as one of the major threats to his peace of mind, took the news philosophically. 'Well, I'm glad to hear we aren't the only ones having trouble these days. But I'll bet my wife was sore when she couldn't hear what happened to Priscilla Lane, Private Secretary, last night.'

Stoddard was in his laboratory in the basement of the Astrophysics Building at Western Tech hard at work on the wiring diagram for the amplifier system when Arnold came breezing in, his bright young face aglow with enthusiasm.

'Guess what?' he exclaimed. 'Friedmann's in town. He's agreed to give a talk this afternoon in Dickinson Hall on his theory of the Xi effect. You know Friedmann, don't you?'

Stoddard shook his head. 'Never heard of him.'

Arnold hooked one leg over the corner of the desk. 'Well, in my opinion he's the foremost cosmologist in the world today. He had so much trouble getting published at first that his reputation isn't as big as it should be. Everybody thought his first paper was written by some crank until Eddington saw it and recognized its value immediately. Now Friedmann won't send his articles to any of the regular journals. You've got to dig his stuff out of all sorts of queer places, like the *Proceedings of the Geophysical Society of Venezuela* or the *Annals of the Portuguese Meteorological Union*.'

'I know how he feels,' said Stoddard sympathetically.

'Well, I thought we should hear him because his theory might possibly have some bearing on our infra-red observations last week.'

'Think I could understand him if I did hear him?'

'Oh, probably not, but then that goes for a lot of the rest of us, too.'

Stoddard reached for the wiring diagram. 'Well, I'll see if I can manage it. But you know what I think of these high-powered theoretical fellows.'

Arnold laughed. 'I've been briefed on that before.' He got up and started for the door. 'Room 201 at four thirty. I'll save a seat for you.'

The meeting was already in progress when Stoddard opened the door and slipped to his seat without creating any more commotion than a horse backing into a stall. As usual, the front rows were occupied by the hardened campaigners among the faculty, the grizzled veterans of a thousand seminars: Fosberg and Ballantyne from the math department, Blacker and Tinsdale from the radiation laboratory, and Denning the nuclear physicist. The remainder of the audience in the rear was composed of a miscellaneous rabble of graduate students and professors from neighbouring institutions of learning and culture.

'Who's ahead?' asked Stoddard, sinking into the chair beside his partner.

'You should have heard Friedmann put old Blacker in his place a minute ago,' Arnold whispered with evident relish. 'He sure slapped him down plenty that time.'

To Stoddard, all theoretical physicists were strange creatures far removed from the rest of mankind. It was his experience that they could be divided with remarkable uniformity into two types, A and B. A typical specimen of Type A, for example, is mentally accessible only with the greatest difficulty. As a general rule, he moves through life with the vague detached air of a confirmed somnambulist. Should you summon the courage to ask his opinion on a paper, he regards it with much the same expression of critical disapproval that a secondhand car dealer instinctively assumes when inspecting a battered automobile brought in for sale. Everything is in a pretty bad state. It is possible, however, that a little progress may be made along the following lines, et cetera. A pure Type B, on the other hand, gives the impression of being always on the point of boiling over. He trembles with suppressed excitement. One of his former pupils has just proposed a theory that constitutes a tremendous advance. Where there was only darkness before now all is sunshine and light. As soon as a few odds and ends are cleared up the whole problem will be practically solved, et cetera, et cetera.

Stoddard classified Friedmann as predominantly Type A with a few overtones of Type B thrown in. He was a tall, thin man of about thirty, with sharp angular features, and a way of looking at you as if his eyes were focused on a point ten feet behind your back. His voice was dry and flat with the barest trace of foreign accent.

Stoddard had not listened for more than five minutes before he began to experience the same sense of bewilderment that little Dorothy must have felt on her first trip to the land of Oz. As nearly as he could gather, Friedmann considered the familiar everyday world to constitute merely a tiny corner or 'clot' in a vastly higher order of space-time or 'Xi space'. Ordinarily, events in the Xi space are on too gross a scale to exert a sensible effect on the fine-grained clot space. On rare occasions, however, a clot might be seriously disturbed by events of an exceptional nature in the Xi space, in somewhat the same way that the atoms on the surface of a stick of amber may be disturbed by rubbing it vigorously. When events in the super-cosmos happen to intrude upon an individual clot extraordinary results ensue; for example, angular momentum is not strictly conserved, and Hamilton's equations require modification, to mention only a few.

'Thus for a properly oriented observer the universe must at all times have a radius equal to tau times the velocity of light,' said Friedmann, by way of conclusion. 'Hence, if tau increases uniformly we must of necessity have the expanding universe as shown by the general recession of the extragalactic nebulae.

'But this increase in tau time is not really uniform but a statistical effect. Local fluctuations in the Xi space may attain such magnitude as to become distinctly perceptible in clot space. Evidence for the Xi effect in our vicinity is shown by the behaviour of the Andromeda nebula, which instead of sharing in the general recession is approaching the Earth at three hundred kilometres per second. Again, certain anomalies in the motion of the inner planets, notably the secular variation in the node of Venus,* clearly indicate encroachment of the Xi effect within the confines of our own solar system. Further anomalies of increasing magnitude may be anticipated.'

With a curt nod he gathered together his papers and sat down abruptly, scarcely bothering to acknowledge the prolonged applause from the student section. The secretary of the Astronomy and Physics Club thanked Dr Friedmann for his address which he was sure they had all enjoyed, and inquired if there were any questions. This announcement was followed by the customary minute of awkward silence. Finally the spell was broken by Fosberg, an authority on the theory of numbers and uncrowned king of the faculty's eccentric characters.

'As I get it, this postulated Xi effect started a shrinkage in our sector about ten-to-the-ninth years ago. Now then, I've just been doing some figuring on the back of this envelope and if I haven't made a mistake the present diameter of the solar system out to Pluto is 3.2×10^8 kilometres, or about two hundred million miles. Is that right?' Everyone looked expectantly at the speaker.

'I work entirely with the generalized formulae; never with numerical values,' Friedmann replied with cold dignity. 'However, I do not question the accuracy of Dr Fosberg's

---

*The outstanding difference between gravitational theory and observation is the well-known discrepancy of $43''$ per century in the motion of the perihelion of Mercury. Einstein's explanation of this discrepancy was considered a triumph for relativity.

The next largest difference between gravitational theory and observation is the secular variation of $13''$ per century in the node of Venus, which has not been explained by relativity. See *Journal of the Optical Society of America*, 1930, vol. 30, p. 225.

arithmetic. Naturally the shrinkage would be quite imperceptible with ordinary measuring rods. It would be necessary to make some observation involving explicitly the velocity of light.'

'I'm willing to grant you that,' Fosberg returned, 'but aren't you going to get into serious trouble with the law of gravitation due to all this shrinkage? Why, in a few more years the congestion in the solar system will be worse than the campus parking problem!' It was a remark that was always good for a laugh and one of the principal reasons he had asked the question in the first place.

'The gravitational difficulties that so worry Dr Fosberg do not follow as a necessary consequence,' said Friedmann, entirely unruffled. 'As I have demonstrated, the laws of Newtonian mechanics may fail to hold even as a first approximation. At these extreme limits, however, the integration of the equations becomes quite insuperable by ordinary methods. One of my pupils at the University of Pennsylvania plans to explore these regions next year with the EDVAC.'

Fosberg wagged his bald head. 'Just the same all this crowding together still worries me,' he declared. 'And I don't like the idea of being reduced to the size of a microcosmic midget either.'

Friedmann's shrug plainly indicated that it was a matter of complete indifference to him if Fosberg were reduced to the dimensions of a neutrino, and as there were no more questions, the meeting broke up. Stoddard, who had grown thoroughly bored with the whole proceedings, made a bolt for the door but Arnold was only a few lengths behind.

'Wasn't Friedmann good,' he demanded. 'Don't you think it's the most satisfying cosmological theory you ever heard?'

'No doubt about it,' said Stoddard, continuing on down the hall.

'You know, I was thinking,' Arnold went on, falling into step beside him, 'why couldn't we test the Xi effect ourselves?'

'Test it ourselves!'

'Why not? After all, it shouldn't be too difficult. As Friedmann said, we would only need to make some observation that depends explicitly on the velocity of light.'

Stoddard snorted. 'Bet he's never made a bona fide observation in his whole life.'

They stopped on the steps outside Dickinson Hall before wending their separate ways homeward. The sun had set and a slight breeze was beginning to stir the leaves of the giant oak tree at the entrance.

'Well, the next time you're in my office we'll have a long talk about it,' said Stoddard, edging down the steps. 'But right now I've got to get home to dinner.'

'The observation would consist simply in determining whether some distant event occurred at the time predicted,' Arnold mused. 'Let's see, what would be the easiest thing to observe?'

At that instant his eye was attracted to a star faintly visible near the eastern horizon. 'I've got it!' he cried. 'We could observe an eclipse of one of Jupiter's satellites. If the solar system has really shrunk as much as the Xi effect predicts, it should occur way ahead of time.'

'You mean do a kind of repeat on Roemer's work,' said Stoddard, 'only with a light time corresponding to the whole distance to Jupiter instead of the diameter of the Earth's orbit?'

'Exactly!'

Stoddard could feel the net closing around him. He knew that once his partner in crime became infatuated with an idea it was useless to try to discourage him. 'Well, I guess we've looked for less hopeful things. Only I can't seem to remember what they were.'

'Listen,' said Arnold, his eyes shining, 'is there a class at the ten-inch tonight?'

Stoddard considered. 'This is Wednesday, isn't it? Nope, don't think there will be one.'

'Then what's to stop us from making the observation right now – tonight?'

'Nothing, so far as I know, except maybe a nice thick fog.' He heaved a sigh of resignation. 'Come on, let's take a look at the *Ephemeris*. Maybe there *aren't* any eclipses tonight.'

But the *American Ephemeris* said otherwise. An occultation of Jupiter I was scheduled for Thursday, 5 October, at four hours eight minutes and ten seconds of Greenwich Civil Time.

Arnold was delighted. 'I'll meet you at the ten-inch at seven fifteen tonight. OK?'

'OK.'

'We can stop in at my house for a drink afterward.'

'We'll probably need one,' was Stoddard's grim comment, 'after we find out how much the universe has shrunk.'

The lamp over the desk threw grotesque shadows around the circular room making the telescope and pier look like some giant insect flattened against the curving walls of the dome. At that moment, however, Stoddard was in no mood to appreciate the projective geometry of shadow pictures. Like all other manually operated observatory domes in the world, the one on the ten-inch at Western Tech opened only with the utmost reluctance. At length in response to an effort worthy of Superman, Stoddard forced the shutter back revealing the constellation of Cygnus sprawling across the meridian. Breathing heavily, he turned the dome until Jupiter came into the centre of the opening, a gleaming yellow stoplight among the faint stars of Aquarius. Then swinging the telescope around on the pier as if it were an anti-aircraft gun, he sighted along the tube until the planet came darting into the field of view.

'How's the seeing?' asked Arnold, a formless black shape by the desk. He twisted the shade over the lamp until the light illuminated the chronometer and pad of paper at his elbow but left the end of the telescope in shadow.

Stoddard gave the focusing screw another touch. 'Not so good,' he muttered. Removing the eyepiece from the end of the telescope he substituted a longer one in its place from the box beside him. 'There – that's better.'

'How do the satellites look?'

'Well, just about the way the *Ephemeris* predicted. Callisto and Ganymede are over on the west. Europa's about a diameter of Jupiter to the east. Io doesn't seem to be anywhere around.'

He lowered the seat on the observing platform a couple of notches thus enabling him to look into the telescope with less strain on his vertebrae. 'Wait a minute – caught a glimpse of her at the limb just then.'

Arnold shot a glance at the chronometer. 'Gosh, don't tell me it's going into occultation already!'

'Well, it sure looks like it.'

'But it can't be that much ahead of time.'

'Why not? That's what you were hoping for, wasn't it? Keep an eye on the chronometer, anyhow. I'll give you the time as close as I can in this bum seeing.'

For several minutes the dome was silent except for the steady ticking of the chronometer and the low hum of traffic from Los Feliz Boulevard far below. Stoddard concentrated his every faculty on the tiny point of light projecting from the planet's disc. Sometimes he felt sure it must be gone only to have it flash into view again. He waited until it had remained out of sight for an unusually long interval. 'All right, get ready,' he warned. 'Now!'

'Seven-thirty-three-zero-zero,' said Arnold, writing down the numbers at the top of the record sheet. Stoddard rose painfully from his cramped position at the end of the telescope and began cautiously exercising one leg. His partner continued figuring busily for another five minutes. Presently he leaned back and began tapping the desk thoughtfully with the tip of his pencil.

'What's the answer?' said Stoddard, limping across the room.

'Well, according to these figures,' Arnold replied, speaking with elaborate casualness, 'the occultation occurred just thirty-five minutes and ten seconds ahead of time.'

For a moment neither spoke. Then Stoddard let out a belly laugh that shattered the peaceful calm that had hitherto enveloped Observatory Hill. 'That puts Jupiter right in our backyard. It's so close the light gets here in nothing flat.'

Arnold gazed up at the planet riding so serenely among the stars. There were Vega and Altair over in the west, with Cygnus flying close behind, and the great square of Pegasus wheeling upward in the north, precisely as he had seen them a thousand times before. Could it be possible that some catastrophe from Outside had warped their little corner of space until the giant Jupiter had been brought to what would once have been an arm's length, so close you might have reached out and seized it between your thumb and fore-finger like a cherry? As a boy he had loved to read tales of time-travel and flights to other planets, and the feeling that something transcendental was lurking around the corner had never entirely left him. In their seminars they talked of world lines and a space of n dimensions but did any of them really believe it? Now perhaps it was here at last. He shiv-ered in the damp night air. The ocean breeze blowing in through the dome certainly felt real enough.

Mechanically he began helping Stoddard put the telescope to bed for the night, replacing the cap on the objective and swinging the telescope over the polar axis, where he clamped it in declination.

'What do you say we go down in the darkroom for a smoke?' said Stoddard, when everything was shipshape. 'I'd like to take a look at those figures of yours myself.'

The darkroom in the basement below was a welcome relief from the windy dome. Stoddard threw off his jacket, pulled a stool up to the bench that ran down one side of the room, and began stoking his pipe from a can of tobacco in one of the drawers. Not until this operation was completed to his entire satisfaction, and the bowl glowing brightly, did he turn his attention to Arnold's reduction. Then with exas-perating deliberation he started checking off the figures, pausing occasionally between puffs to compare them with those in the *Ephemeris*. Arnold leaned against the wall watching him nervously.

'Well, I can't seem to find anything wrong,' he admitted grudgingly, 'but, of course, that doesn't mean it's right, either.'

Taking careful aim, he blew a smoke ring at the girl on the calendar over the sink, watching it swirl around her plunging neckline with moody satisfaction. 'A dozen times in my life I've got results almost as crazy as this one. Every time I couldn't help saying to myself, "Stoddard, maybe you've discovered something at last. Maybe you've stumbled onto something big." So far I've never made a single scientific discovery.

'Now you take this observation tonight. Sure, it would be exciting to suppose the solar system has shrunk to the size of a dime, but first I want to be absolutely sure there isn't some perfectly natural commonplace explanation. It's a depressing fact that most of the exciting results a scientist gets can eventually be traced to errors of observation. Think of all the times Mira Ceti at maximum has been mistaken for a nova.'

'Everybody knows that,' Arnold objected. 'But where's the chance for error in this observation? It's so simple.'

'Maybe not so simple as you think. Remember the seeing was terrible. That time I gave you might have been off by a couple of minutes – maybe more.'

'That still leaves thirty minutes to explain.'

'All right. Now the question is how much faith can we put in the *Ephemeris*? It wouldn't surprise me if the predicted time itself was way off.'

'As much as that?'

'Well, I know the predictions for Jupiter's four great satellites are based on Sampson's tables of 1910, and they certainly must require some kind of correction by this time. I don't know how often the Naval Observatory checks up on things like that. But until we do know – and have a lot more observations – we really don't know a thing.'

'OK, OK,' said Arnold impatiently. 'All the same, I still think it's a whale of an error.'

'It's a king size one, I'll admit,' said Stoddard, relighting his pipe. 'And now there's something I wish you'd explain to me. After all that palaver this afternoon I still don't understand how this so-called Xi effect ties in with our infra-red observations.'

Arnold reached for the pencil and a pad of yellow scratch paper. 'Assume that this line represents the boundary of our local universe or "clot",' he said, drawing an irregular closed figure with a dot near the centre. 'According to Friedmann, occasionally some disturbance in the outer super-cosmos or Xi space becomes sufficiently violent to affect a particular clot. Now there are several things that can happen as a result, but by far the most probable is that the clot will begin to shrink, very slowly at first and then more rapidly. But for a long time nobody would be aware of the shrinkage because everything within the clot shrinks in proportion, with one exception. That exception is the wavelength of electromagnetic radiation.

'Suppose the boundary has shrunk until it has an average radius of a thousand kilometres.' He drew a line from the central dot to a point on the boundary. 'Obviously nothing can exist within the boundary bigger than the boundary itself. Therefore, this means that all electromagnetic radiation exceeding a thousand kilometres is eliminated. That accounts for the fade-out in radio transmission. As the boundary continues to shrink shorter wavelengths keep being cut out all the time.'

'I think I'm beginning to get it,' said Stoddard, studying the diagram. 'We didn't get any transmission beyond twenty thousand angstroms because there wasn't any radiation to transmit.'

'That's it! Our universe only had a diameter of twenty thousand angstroms. All radiation of longer wavelength was cut out.'

'About one ten-thousandth of an inch,' said Stoddard, doing some fast mental arithmetic. He chuckled. 'No wonder old Fosberg was worried!'

'You see the Xi effect does give a consistent explanation of all the phenomena,' said Arnold triumphantly. 'In any case, we can't be in doubt much longer.'

'How's that?'

'Why, because the universe will have shrunk so much the optical spectrum will be affected. The landscape will change colour.'

'Well, maybe you're right,' Stoddard agreed reluctantly, 'but so far everything looks just the same to me as it always has.' Absently he began doodling a series of circles and squares across Arnold's diagram. 'What I wish,' he said with a yawn, 'is that somebody would find a way to shorten the time from one pay day till the next.'

Arnold waved his arms in a helpless gesture and walked to the end of the room. Stoddard sat motionless as if half asleep. Presently he took a briefcase from one of the drawers and began exploring its contents. 'Here're those snapshots we took at the zoo the other day,' he said. 'Haven't had time to develop 'em yet.'

His partner eyed the rolls of film without interest. 'My wife was asking about them at dinner. She wants to see that one where she's feeding the eagle.'

'If you want to wait, I can develop 'em now.'

Arnold glanced at his wristwatch. 'Sure, go ahead. It's only eight thirty.'

Stoddard turned off the overhead light plunging the little room into total darkness. Arnold could hear him searching for the switch that operated the safelight, but when he snapped it on there was no result. He snapped it several times but still without result.

'Globe's probably burnt out,' said Arnold.

Stoddard jerked the screen back revealing the light inside burning brightly. 'Now what?' he muttered.

They stood staring at the light in puzzled silence. Suddenly Arnold leaned forward, his face tense in the white glare from the lamp.

'Stoddard.'

'Yeah?'

'*Put the screen back over the lamp.*'

His partner hesitated then obediently shoved the screen back in place until not a chink of white light was visible. Gradually as their eyes gained sensitivity in the dark the oblong shape of the safety screen became faintly visible.

But the screen was no longer ruby red. It was a dull colourless grey.

*

No scientific theory ever became accepted as fact so quickly as Friedmann's theory of the Xi effect, but then no other theory before ever had such a convincing array of scientific evidence to support it. The change in the tint of the landscape that Arnold had foreseen eventually developed but for several weeks it was too slight to be readily obvious. The effect was the same as if everyone had gone colourblind to an effective wavelength of about 6500 Å. It was disconcerting to find that your hedge of geraniums was black instead of scarlet, and the absence of stoplights was nearly disastrous. Some women became violently hysterical when they first beheld the inky fluid oozing from their veins. But after the novelty had worn off the public soon lost interest. They had lived through the invasion from Mars, the flying saucers, and other scientific gags, and doubtless in time this, too, would pass. Besides, how could you expect people to work up any enthusiasm over something when they weren't even sure how to pronounce it?

But as orange and yellow followed red into the grey there came a change in the public attitude, a kind of half-credulous belief mingled with misgiving and dismay. Men still laughed and joked about the Xi effect over their old-fashioneds at the country club, but just when everybody was feeling happy and secure again someone was sure to spoil it all. 'You know this thing may turn out to be more serious than we think,' he would say. 'I've got a nephew teaches out at the university. Hasn't got a dime but smart as the devil. Well, he told me confidentially it's getting worse instead of better. No telling where it may end, in fact.'

Rather curiously, women had much more awareness of the Xi effect than men, for it struck at their most vulnerable point – their appearance. Golden hair could turn grey in a matter of weeks. A complexion drained of its warm flesh tints looked dead. Cosmetics were of no avail against it. For of what use was lipstick if it only turned the lips from grey to black? Or of rouge if it left only deeper shadows on the cheeks? The radiant beauty of a short time past anxiously examining her face in her mirror at night might see an old woman staring back at her out of the glass. Deaths from sleeping pills became a commonplace.

Not until late in November, however, did the situation reach such a critical stage that government officials felt compelled to recognize the Xi effect as a definite world menace. Previously its encroachment had been dismissed by the ingenious process of studiously minimizing its existence. It was true that the papers printed the censored reports from scientific institutions but always under captions that were misleading and with the significant news buried near the bottom of the column. A few scientists who refused to be muzzled soon found themselves out of a job or called up before an investigating committee.

Eventually, however, the clamour became so loud that announcement was made of a series of mass meetings to be held across the country in which all the facts in so far as they were known would be discussed without reservation. The first in the series was scheduled for the Los Angeles Coliseum for Monday, 27 November, with the great Dr Friedmann as the feature speaker of the evening. Public sentiment changed almost overnight. The personal appearance of Friedmann alone did much to restore confidence. He was the fellow who had discovered this Xi effect, wasn't he? Well, then, he could probably control it, too. Man had never met a problem that man was unable to solve.

By the evening of the 27th public curiosity over what Friedmann would say had been excited to such a degree, that it was necessary to keep the man's whereabouts a profound secret to prevent him from being mobbed on sight. By five o'clock every street leading toward the Coliseum was blocked solid with cars for miles around, and by seven o'clock more than a hundred thousand people had jammed themselves into the vast structure, while thousands more milled around the walls outside seeking entrance. Although the Los Angeles Police Department had every man available on duty in addition to two hundred special officers hired from outlying districts, they were able to maintain order only with considerable difficulty. An attitude of reckless abandon was manifest even among ordinary well-behaved individuals. It was a holiday crowd without the holiday spirit.

'I'm not at all sure Friedmann is the best man to talk to these people tonight,' said Arnold, standing up and gazing uneasily around him at the throngs still climbing up and down the aisles in search of seats. 'They've come here confidently expecting to be told something that sounds nice and reassuring and instead Friedmann will simply hand them the hard cold facts. We scientists have known the truth for weeks and had a chance to become reconciled to it. But what about the average man whose cosmic outlook is limited to his job and the mortgage on his home out in Brentwood?'

'Be quite a blow to 'em probably,' said Stoddard, biting into his hot dog. 'Trouble with these theoretical fellows is they act as if the Xi effect had been invented for the sole purpose of letting them test out all their screwy ideas on nuclear structure.'

Arnold sat down and began studying his programme. 'I see Atchison Kane is going to speak, too.'

'Atchison Kane. Who's he?'

'Shakespearian actor,' Arnold replied. Long ago he had become accustomed to his partner's splendid state of isolation from the world of the stage and screen. 'Made a big hit in *Richard the Third* recently. I heard him at the Philharmonic last August.'

'That so?' said Stoddard. For the tenth time he looked at the great clock over the archway at the east entrance. 'What's holding up the procession, anyhow? They were supposed to kick-off half an hour ago.'

Others besides Stoddard were getting impatient. So far the crowd had been fairly well-behaved but now it was growing decidedly restless. Someone yelled, 'We want Friedmann!' and in an instant thousands of voices were repeating the words over and over in a kind of savage chant. When this failed to produce results, a mob of boys acting as if upon signal, leaped over the parapet onto the field toward the speakers' stand. Before the police could intervene they began tearing down the decorations and smashing the chairs and railing. The dozen or so officers in the vicinity were overwhelmed at first but reinforcements soon gained the upper hand. The crowd was delighted, following every incident of the struggle with fascinated attention. Several men were knocked down and trampled in the melee, or sent reeling from the battle bleeding from lacerations around the head. Suddenly a great shout went up. The speakers surrounded by a husky squad of police were spotted emerging from the south entrance. Interest in the fight evaporated immediately. The floodlights were dimmed and an expectant hush fell over the assemblage.

After the usual preliminaries, to which no one paid the slightest attention, the chairman of the National Scientific Security Council finally got around to introducing the main speaker.

'In the brief span that this committee has been in existence, citizens from all parts of the southland have been besieging us with questions concerning this effect which has been uppermost in the thoughts of each and everyone of us during these last troubled days. Unfortunately, no funds were appropriated for the purpose of answering these questions. And yet as representatives of the people we felt in all sincerity that they could not and must not be ignored.'

The burst of applause at this point forced him to halt briefly until quiet reigned again and he was able to gather himself together for another effort.

'In view of this situation, my colleagues and I, after due deliberation, have asked our distinguished speaker if in lieu of a formal address he would consent to answer a set of representative questions selected by the committee. To this request I am happy to say that our speaker has most willingly and graciously given his consent.

'And now without further ado, it is my great pleasure and privilege this evening to present to you a man whom I am sure needs no introduction from me, that renowned scientist and scholar, Dr Karl Gustav Friedmann.'

From the uproarious applause that greeted Friedmann as he stepped to the front of the platform, it might have been supposed that he had discovered another Santa Claus instead of an effect that was relentlessly extinguishing the light of the world. He shook hands with the chairman, bowed a few degrees in the general direction of the crowd, and then stood quietly waiting for the tumult to subside. The chairman nervously riffled through the cards in his hand, selected one, and peered at it through his bifocals.

'Our first question is from a housewife in Long Beach,' he announced. She says, "My husband has lost his job as a radio salesman on account of the Xi effect. How soon will it be over so he can go back to work again?'

Friedmann's voice was as unemotional as if he were lecturing half a dozen sleepy students rather than a crowd of a hundred thousand who were hanging on his every word. 'I think that question may be answered by reading a message from the National Bureau of Standards which was handed to me as I entered the Coliseum here tonight. Here is the message: "Spectroscopic laboratory reports sudden marked acceleration Xi effect. Cutoff 5500 at 0000 GCT." Now in plain language what does this mean? It means that at four o'clock this afternoon the extinction of radiation extended nearly to the green.' He hesitated. 'I regret to inform the lady that her husband will never be able to return to his work. Why? Because so little while is left to us that no time remains for either work or play.'

An excited uneasy murmur swept around the Coliseum, rose to a sharp peak then hastily died away as the chairman selected another card. 'Our second question is from a man in Pomona who signs himself "Taxpayer". His letter is too long to read in full so that I must confine myself to his inquiry at the end. "If scientists knew light was going to be extinguished, then why didn't they get busy and do something about it a long time ago? The government makes me pay taxes so scientists can sit in their laboratories and hatch these wild theories. But when danger comes along they're just as helpless as the rest of us." '

The letter provoked a good deal of laughter mingled with a surprising amount of handclapping. The humour of the situation, however, was wholly lost on Friedmann. 'What would Mr Taxpayer have the scientists do?' he demanded in a voice that was openly contemptuous. 'Does he think they deliberately create the lightning that destroys a tree? Or the earthquake that engulfs a city? Well, I can assure him that these are nothing compared to the force that threatens us now. But before he criticizes science let him first learn something about it – go back to grammar school or read some little children's book.'

There was a timid scattering of applause that was soon drowned in a chorus of boos and catcalls from all sides. One could sense the rising tide of resentment and frustration underneath.

'What did I tell you?' Arnold shouted. 'They aren't going to take it.'

Stoddard hunched down farther in his seat. 'If you ask me all hell's going to break loose here in another minute.'

Two members of the committee could be seen apparently expostulating with Friedmann, who stood listening to them indifferently with folded arms. The chairman was doing his best to restore order but it was nearly a minute before he was able to proceed. 'Quiet please. Quiet,' he entreated. 'We have many more questions on the programme of vital interest which I am sure you are all anxious to hear. Now here is one from a school teacher in Lynwood which goes straight to the point. "Dear Dr Friedmann, can you tell us what course of events we may expect from the Xi effect in the immediate future?" '

'There can be no doubt as to the course of events up to a certain point,' Friedmann replied, speaking more slowly than usual and evidently weighing his words with care. 'Beyond that point there is no knowledge, only speculation and conjecture.

'But in the immediate future the course of events is very clear. The extinction of radiation will continue at a rapidly increasing pace. Soon the world will be completely devoid of the quality of radiation that excites the sensation of visible light. As it disappears, the sensation will be similar to that of watching a scene in a play in which the lights are gradually dimmed until finally the stage and players are utterly blotted out.'

There was so much noise now that Arnold was able to hear only with the greatest difficulty. Some people stood yelling and shaking their fists at Friedmann while others shouted for them to sit down and let him proceed.

'After the visible radiation there remains the spectrum of the X-radiation and gamma rays,' Friedmann continued, apparently unmindful that he had lost his audience. 'Especially significant will be the nature of the reaction upon cosmic rays, a subject upon which scientists have been wholly unable to agree. At present there is no hope of securing records of this vitally important phenomenon. Furthermore, there is no hope –'

A whisky bottle crashed against the stand showering Friedmann with glass. Another followed and another until the air was filled with them. A dozen fights were in progress within the Coliseum while without a mob was attempting to break through the gate at the east entrance. In the distance could be heard the rising wail of police sirens.

Suddenly the floodlights blinked, wavered uncertainly, then slowly faded out to a chorus of anguished wails and frantic howls for lights. Whether the fade-out was by accident or intent the result was the same. A terrified panic-stricken hush descended upon the multitude.

It was at that instant a new voice was heard in the darkness; a voice calm and powerful, yet withal tender and reassuring.

'*The Lord is my Shepherd; I shall not want*'.

In the dim light men and women looked at each other fearful and bewildered, as if a miracle were about to happen.

Again the voice came crying in the darkness. '*He maketh me to lie down in green pastures; He leadeth me beside the still waters*'.

Arnold grabbed his partner by the shoulder. 'It's Atchison Kane! If he can hold this crowd tonight, he's a wonder.'

Men who were shouting and cursing a moment before now stood awed and irresolute. Here and there a few were beginning to kneel while others sobbed openly and unashamed.

'*He restoreth my soul; He leadeth me in the paths of righteousness for His name's sake.*'

Many were beginning to repeat the familiar words after him. Now the voice swelled to a mighty climax in its message of faith and hope,

'*Yea, though I walk through the valley of the shadow of death I will fear no evil –* '

And then more softly,

'*For Thou art with me; Thy rod and Thy staff they comfort me –* '

From directly behind Arnold there came a woman's shriek with piercing intensity. It was a shriek filled with despair. A shriek that meant something was terribly wrong. Others around her began shouting and screaming too, pointing toward the great archway at the east entrance.

The low fog that had hung over the city all evening had broken momentarily revealing the rising moon. But it was a moon that no one there had ever seen before, a moon out of a nightmare, swollen and elongated as if viewed through a cylindrical lens. But even more unnatural than its shape was its *colour* – a deep transparent blue.

Arnold was so intent upon the moon that he scarcely noticed when the floodlights came on again. Gradually he became aware of some change in the aspect of the Coliseum itself; there seemed to be a soft waviness spreading everywhere, warping some portions of the scene but leaving others untouched, like gelatine melting and flowing down a photographic plate. His eyes were unable to bring the mass of humanity banked against the opposite wall of the Coliseum into sharp focus. The tiers of seats kept blurring and shimmering as if the light were coming from a great distance through layers of heated air.

With a sickening sensation he perceived that the distortion in space-time was beginning to affect objects right around him. The faces were undergoing some subtle alteration, noticeable particularly in the irregular position of the mouth with respect to the nose and eyes together with an apparent thickening and bending of the jaw and forehead, such as he had once seen in patients whose bony structure had undergone prolonged softening from osteitis deformans.

The night was deepening rapidly now, closing in like the folds of a vast purple curtain. Simultaneously people were gripped by that primitive wholly unreasoning fear that is felt at a total solar eclipse that instant before totality, when the shadow of the moon suddenly looms on the horizon advancing with terrifying speed. Men and women clung to each other or ran frantically this way and that as if by fleeing they could escape a fate from which no escape was possible.

Stoddard and Arnold sat huddled together watching the groping figures grow dimmer and dimmer until the last ray of light was extinguished in the dense impenetrable blackness. But hours later they knew from the sound of voices and the pressure of hands and bodies, that thousands were still crouching in their seats waiting hopefully for the light that had always returned.

Arnold dozing against Stoddard's shoulder found himself repeating a phrase from Friedmann's last remark: 'There is no hope – There is no hope – '

The Tunnel under the World

Frederik Pohl

1

On the morning of June the 15th, Guy Burckhardt woke up screaming out of a dream.

It was more real than any dream he had ever had in his life. He could still hear and feel the sharp, ripping-metal explosion, the violent heave that had tossed him furiously out of bed, the searing wave of heat.

He sat up convulsively and stared, not believing what he saw, at the quiet room and the bright sunlight coming in the window.

He croaked, 'Mary?'

His wife was not in the bed next to him. The covers were tumbled and awry, as though she had just left it, and the memory of the dream was so strong that instinctively he found himself searching the floor to see if the dream explosion had thrown her down.

But she wasn't there. Of course she wasn't, he told himself, looking at the familiar vanity and slipper chair, the uncracked window, the unbuckled wall. It had only been a dream.

'Guy?' His wife was calling him querulously from the foot of the stairs. 'Guy, dear, are you all right?'

He called weakly, 'Sure.'

There was a pause. Then Mary said doubtfully, 'Breakfast is ready. Are you sure you're all right? I thought I heard you yelling – '

Burckhardt said more confidently, 'I had a bad dream, honey. Be right down.'

In the shower, punching the lukewarm-and-cologne he favoured, he told himself that it had been a beaut of a dream. Still, bad dreams weren't unusual, especially bad dreams about explosions. In the past thirty years of H-bomb jitters, who had not dreamed of explosions?

Even Mary had dreamed of them, it turned out, for he started to tell her about the dream, but she cut him off. 'You *did?*' Her voice was astonished. 'Why, dear, I dreamed the same thing! Well, almost the same thing. I didn't actually *hear* anything. I dreamed that something woke me up, and then there was a sort of quick bang, and then something hit me on the head. And that was all. Was yours like that?'

Burckhardt coughed. 'Well, no,' he said. Mary was not one of these strong-as-a-man, brave-as-a-tiger women. It was not necessary, he thought, to tell her all the little details of the dream that made it seem so real. No need to mention the splintered ribs, and the salt bubble in his throat, and the agonized knowledge that this was death. He said, 'Maybe there really was some kind of explosion downtown. Maybe we heard it and it started us dreaming.'

Mary reached over and patted his hand absently. 'Maybe,' she agreed. 'It's almost half past eight, dear. Shouldn't you hurry? You don't want to be late to the office.'

He gulped his food, kissed her, and rushed out – not so much to be on time as to see if his guess had been right.

But downtown Tylerton looked as it always had. Coming in on the bus, Burckhardt watched critically out of the window, seeking evidence of an explosion. There wasn't any. If anything, Tylerton looked better than it ever had before: it was a beautiful crisp day, the sky was cloudless, the buildings were clean and inviting. They had, he observed, steamblasted the Power & Light Building, the town's only skyscraper – that was the penalty of having Contro Chemicals main plant on the outskirts of town; the fumes from the cascade stills left their mark on stone buildings.

None of the usual crowd was on the bus, so there wasn't anyone Burckhardt could ask about the explosion. And by the time he got out at the corner of Fifth and Lehigh and the bus rolled away with a muted diesel moan, he had pretty well convinced himself that it was all imagination.

He stopped at the cigar stand in the lobby of his office building, but Ralph wasn't behind the counter. The man who sold him his pack of cigarettes was a stranger.

'Where's Mr Stebbins?' Burckhardt asked.

The man said politely, 'Sick, sir. He'll be in tomorrow. A pack of Marlins today?'

'Chesterfields,' Burckhardt corrected.

'Certainly, sir,' the man said. But what he took from the rack and slid across the counter was an unfamiliar green-and-yellow pack.

'Do try these, sir,' he suggested. 'They contain an anti-cough factor. Ever notice how ordinary cigarettes make you choke every once in a while?'

Burckhardt said suspiciously. 'I never heard of this brand.'

'Of course not. They're something new.' Burckhardt hesitated, and the man said persuasively, 'Look, try them out at my risk. If you don't like them, bring back the empty pack and I'll refund your money. Fair enough?'

Burckhardt shrugged. 'How can I lose? But give me a pack of Chesterfields, too, will you?'

He opened the pack and lit one while he waited for the elevator. They weren't bad, he decided, though he was suspicious of cigarettes that had the tobacco chemically treated in any way. But he didn't think much of Ralph's stand-in; it would raise hell with the trade at the cigar stand if the man tried to give every customer the same high-pressure sales talk.

The elevator door opened with a low-pitched sound of music. Burckhardt and two or three others got in and he nodded to them as the door closed. The thread of music switched off and the speaker in the ceiling of the cab began its usual commercials.

No, not the *usual* commercials, Burckhardt realized. He had been exposed to the captive-audience commercials so long that they hardly registered on the outer ear any more, but what was coming from the recorded programme in the basement of the building caught his attention. It wasn't merely that the brands were mostly unfamiliar; it was a difference in pattern.

There were jingles with an insistent, bouncy rhythm, about soft drinks he had never tasted. There was a rapid patter dialogue between what sounded like two ten-year-old boys about a candy bar, followed by an authoritative bass rumble: 'Go right out and get a DELICIOUS Choco-Bite and eat your TANGY Choco-Bite *all up*. That's *Choco-Bite!*' There was a sobbing female whine: 'I *wish* I had a Feckle Freezer! I'd do *anything* for a Feckle Freezer!' Burckhardt reached his floor and left the elevator in the middle of the last one. It left him a little uneasy. The commercials were not for familiar brands; there was no feeling of use and custom to them.

But the office was happily normal – except that Mr Barth wasn't in. Miss Mitkin, yawning at the reception desk, didn't know exactly why. 'His home phoned, that's all. He'll be in tomorrow.'

'Maybe he went to the plant. It's right near his house.'

She looked indifferent. 'Yeah.'

A thought struck Burckhardt. 'But today is June the 15th! It's quarterly tax return day – he has to sign the return!'

Miss Mitkin shrugged to indicate that that was Burckhardt's problem, not hers. She returned to her nails.

Thoroughly exasperated, Burckhardt went to his desk. It wasn't that he couldn't sign the tax returns as well as Barth, he thought resentfully. It simply wasn't his job, that was all; it was a responsibility that Barth, as office manager for Contro Chemicals' downtown office, should have taken.

He thought briefly of calling Barth at his home or trying to reach him at the factory, but he gave up the idea quickly enough. He didn't really care much for the people at the factory and the less contact he had with them the better. He had been to the factory once, with Barth: it had been a confusing and, in a way, a frightening experience. Barring a handful of executives and engineers, there wasn't a soul in the factory – that is, Burckhardt corrected himself, remembering what Barth had told him, not a *living* soul – just the machines.

According to Barth, each machine was controlled by a sort of computer which reproduced, in its electronic snarl, the actual memory and mind of a human being. It was an unpleasant thought. Barth, laughing, had assured him that there was no Frankenstein business of robbing graveyards and implanting brains in machines. It was only a matter, he said, of transferring a man's habit patterns from brain cells to vacuum-tube cells. It didn't hurt the man and it didn't make the machine into a monster.

But they made Burckhardt uncomfortable all the same.

He put Barth and the factory and all his other little irritations out of his mind and tackled the tax returns. It took him until noon to verify the figures – which Barth could have done out of his memory and his private ledger in ten minutes, Burckhardt resentfully reminded himself.

He sealed them in an envelope and walked out to Miss Mitkin. 'Since Mr Barth isn't here, we'd better go to lunch in shifts,' he said. 'You can go first.'

'Thanks.' Miss Mitkin languidly took her bag out of the desk drawer and began to apply make-up.

Burckhardt offered her the envelope. 'Drop this in the mail for me, will you? Uh – wait a minute. I wonder if I ought to phone Mr Barth to make sure. Did his wife say whether he was able to take phone calls?'

'Didn't say.' Miss Mitkin blotted her lips carefully with a Kleenex. 'Wasn't his wife, anyway. It was his daughter who called and left the message.'

'The kid?' Burckhardt frowned. 'I thought she was away at school.'

'She called, that's all I know.'

Burckhardt went back to his own office and stared distastefully at the unopened mail on his desk. He didn't like nightmares; they spoiled his whole day. He should have stayed in bed, like Barth.

A funny thing happened on his way home. There was a disturbance at the corner where he usually caught his bus – someone was screaming something about a new kind of deep-freeze – so he walked an extra block. He saw the bus coming and started to trot. But behind him, someone was calling his name. He looked over his shoulder; a small harried-looking man was hurrying towards him.

Burckhardt hesitated, and then recognized him. It was a casual acquaintance named Swanson. Burckhardt sourly observed that he had already missed the bus.

He said, 'Hello.'

Swanson's face was desperately eager. 'Burckhardt?' he asked inquiringly, with an odd intensity. And then he just stood there silently, watching Burckhardt's face with a burning eagerness that dwindled to a faint hope and died to a regret. He was searching for something, waiting for something, Burckhardt thought. But whatever it was he wanted, Burckhardt didn't know how to supply it.

Burckhardt coughed and said again, 'Hello, Swanson.'

Swanson didn't even acknowledge the greeting. He merely sighed a very deep sigh.

'Nothing doing,' he mumbled, apparently to himself. He nodded abstractedly to Burckhardt and turned away.

Burckhardt watched the slumped shoulders disappear in the crowd. It was an *odd* sort of day, he thought, and one he didn't much like. Things weren't going right.

Riding home on the next bus, he brooded about it. It wasn't anything terrible or disastrous; it was something out of his experience entirely. You live your life, like any man, and you form a network of impressions and reactions. You *expect* things. When you open your medicine chest, your razor is expected to be on the second shelf; when you lock your front door, you expect to have to give it a slight extra tug to make it latch.

It isn't the things that are right and perfect in your life that make it familiar. It is the things that are just a little bit wrong – the sticking latch, the light switch at the head of the stairs that needs an extra push because the spring is old and weak, the rug that unfailingly skids underfoot.

It wasn't just that things were wrong with the pattern of Burckhardt's life; it was that the *wrong* things were wrong.

For instance, Barth hadn't come into the office, yet Barth *always* came in.

Burckhardt brooded about it through dinner. He brooded about it, despite his wife's attempt to interest him in a game of bridge with the neighbours, all through the evening. The neighbours were people he liked – Anne and Farley Dennerman. He had known them all their lives. But they were odd and brooding, too, this night and he barely listened to Dennerman's complaints about not being able to get good phone service or his wife's comments on the disgusting variety of television commercials they had these days.

Burckhardt was well on the way to setting an all-time record for continuous abstraction when, around midnight, with a suddenness that surprised him – he was strangely *aware* of it happening – he turned over in his bed and, quickly and completely, fell asleep.

2

On the morning of June the 15th, Burckhardt woke up screaming.

It was more real than any dream he had ever had in his life. He could still hear the explosion, feel the blast that crushed him against a wall. It did not seem right that he should be sitting bolt upright in bed in an undisturbed room.

His wife came pattering up the stairs. 'Darling!' she cried. 'What's the matter?'

He mumbled, 'Nothing. Bad dream.'

She relaxed, hand on heart. In an angry tone, she started to say: 'You gave me such a shock – '

But a noise from outside interrupted her. There was a wail of sirens and a clang of bells; it was loud and shocking.

The Burckhardts stared at each other for a heartbeat, then hurried fearfully to the window.

There were no rumbling fire engines in the street, only a small panel truck, cruising slowly along. Flaring loudspeaker horns crowned its top. From them issued the screaming sounds of sirens, growing in intensity, mixed with the rumble of heavy-duty engines and the sound of bells. It was a perfect record of a fire engine arriving at a four-alarm blaze.

Burckhardt said in amazement, 'Mary, that's against the law! Do you know what they're doing? They're playing records of a fire. What are they up to?'

'Maybe it's a practical joke,' his wife offered.

'Joke? Waking up the whole neighbourhood at six o'clock in the morning?' He shook his head. 'The police will be here in ten minutes,' he predicted. 'Wait and see.'

But the police weren't – not in ten minutes, or at all. Whoever the pranksters in the car were, they apparently had a police permit for their games.

The car took a position in the middle of the block and stood silent for a few minutes. Then there was a crackle from the speaker, and a giant voice chanted:

> 'Feckle Freezers!
> Feckle Freezers!
> Gotta have a
> Feckle Freezer!
> Feckle, Feckle, Feckle,
> Feckle, Feckle, Feckle – '

It went on and on. Every house on the block had faces staring out of windows by then. The voice was not merely loud; it was nearly deafening.

Burckhardt shouted to his wife, over the uproar, 'What the hell is a Feckle Freezer?'

'Some kind of a freezer, I guess, dear,' she shrieked back unhelpfully.

Abruptly the noise stopped and the truck stood silent. It was a still misty morning; the sun's rays came horizontally across the rooftops. It was impossible to believe that, a moment ago, the silent block had been bellowing the name of a freezer.

'A crazy advertising trick,' Burckhardt said bitterly. He yawned and turned away from the window. 'Might as well get dressed. I guess that's the end of – '

The bellow caught him from behind; it was almost like a

hard slap on the ears. A harsh, sneering voice, louder than the archangel's trumpet, howled:

'Have you got a freezer? *It stinks!* If it isn't a Feckle Freezer, *it stinks!* If it's a last year's Feckle Freezer, *it stinks!* Only this year's Feckle Freezer is any good at all! You know who owns an Ajax Freezer? Fairies own Ajax Freezers! You know who owns a Triplecold Freezer? Commies own Triplecold Freezers! Every freezer but a brand-new Feckle Freezer *stinks!*'

The voice screamed inarticulately with rage. 'I'm warning you! Get out and buy a Feckle Freezer right away! Hurry up! Hurry for Feckle! Hurry for Feckle! Hurry, hurry, hurry, Feckle, Feckle, Feckle, Feckle, Feckle, Feckle . . .'

It stopped eventually. Burckhardt licked his lips. He started to say to his wife, 'Maybe we ought to call the police about – ' when the speakers erupted again. It caught him off guard; it was intended to catch him off guard. It screamed:

'Feckle, Feckle, Feckle, Feckle, Feckle, Feckle, Feckle, Feckle. Cheap freezers ruin your food. You'll get sick and throw up. You'll get sick and die. Buy a Feckle, Feckle, Feckle, Feckle! Ever take a piece of meat out of the freezer you've got and see how rotten and mouldy it is? Buy a Feckle, Feckle, Feckle, Feckle, Feckle. Do you want to eat rotten, stinking food? Or do you want to wise up and buy a Feckle, Feckle, Feckle – '

That did it. With fingers that kept stabbing the wrong holes, Burckhardt finally managed to dial the local police station. He got a busy signal – it was apparent that he was not the only one with the same idea – and while he was shakingly dialling again, the noise outside stopped.

He looked out the window. The truck was gone.

Burckhardt loosened his tie and ordered another Frosty-Flip from the waiter. If only they wouldn't keep the Crystal Café so *hot!* The new paint job – searing reds and blinding yellows – was bad enough, but someone seemed to have the delusion that this was January instead of June; the place was a good ten degrees warmer than outside.

He swallowed the Frosty-Flip in two gulps. It had a kind

of peculiar flavour, he thought, but not bad. It certainly cooled you off, just as the waiter had promised. He reminded himself to pick up a carton of them on the way home; Mary might like them. She was always interested in something new.

He stood up awkwardly as the girl came across the restaurant towards him. She was the most beautiful thing he had ever seen in Tylerton. Chin-height, honey-blonde hair, and a figure that – well, it was all hers. There was no doubt in the world that the dress that clung to her was the only thing she wore. He felt as if he were blushing as she greeted him.

'Mr Burckhardt.' The voice was like distant tomtoms. 'It's wonderful of you to let me see you, after this morning.'

He cleared his throat. 'Not at all. Won't you sit down, Miss – '

'April Horn,' she murmured, sitting down – beside him, not where he had pointed on the other side of the table. 'Call me April, won't you?'

She was wearing some kind of perfume, Burckhardt noted with what little of his mind was functioning at all. It didn't seem fair that she should be using perfume as well as everything else. He came to with a start and realized that the waiter was leaving with an order for *filets mignon* for two.

'Hey!' he objected.

'Please, Mr Burckhardt.' Her shoulder was against his, her face was turned to him, her breath was warm, her expression was tender and solicitous. 'This is all on the Feckle Corporation. Please let them – it's the *least* they can do.'

He felt her hand burrowing into his pocket.

'I put the price of the meal into your pocket,' she whispered conspiratorially. 'Please do that for me, won't you? I mean I'd appreciate it if you'd pay the waiter – I'm old-fashioned about things like that.'

She smiled meltingly, then became mock-businesslike. 'But you must take the money,' she insisted. 'Why, you're letting Feckle off lightly if you do! You could sue them for every nickel they've got, disturbing your sleep like that.'

With a dizzy feeling, as though he had just seen someone make a rabbit disappear into a top hat, he said, 'Why, it really wasn't so bad, uh, April. A little noisy, maybe, but – '

'Oh, Mr Burckhardt!' The blue eyes were wide and admiring. 'I *knew* you'd understand. It's just that – well, it's such a *wonderful* freezer that some of the outside men get carried away, so to speak. As soon as the main office found out about what happened, they sent representatives around to every house on the block to apologize. Your wife told us where we could phone you – and I'm so very pleased that you were willing to let me have lunch with you, so that I could apologize, too. Because truly, Mr Burckhardt, it is a *fine* freezer.

'I shouldn't tell you this, but – ' the blue eyes were shyly lowered – 'I'd do almost anything for Feckle Freezers. It's more than a job to me.' She looked up. She was enchanting. 'I bet you think I'm silly, don't you?'

Burckhardt coughed. 'Well, I – '

'Oh, you don't want to be unkind!' She shook her head. 'No, don't pretend. You think it's silly. But really, Mr Burckhardt, you wouldn't think so if you knew more about the Feckle. Let me show you this little booklet – '

Burckhardt got back from lunch a full hour later. It wasn't only the girl who delayed him. There had been a curious interview with a little man named Swanson, whom he barely knew, who had stopped him with desperate urgency on the street – and then left him cold.

But it didn't matter much. Mr Barth, for the first time since Burckhardt had worked there, was out for the day – leaving Burckhardt stuck with the quarterly tax returns.

What did matter, though, was that somehow he had signed a purchase order for a twelve-cubic-foot Feckle Freezer, upright model, self-defrosting, list price $625, with a ten per cent 'courtesy' discount – 'Because of that *horrid* affair this morning, Mr Burckhardt,' she had said.

And he wasn't sure how he could explain it to his wife.

He needn't have worried. As he walked in the front door, his wife said almost immediately, 'I wonder if we can't afford a new freezer, dear. There was a man here to apologize about that noise and – well, we got to talking and – '

She had signed a purchase order, too.

It had been the damnedest day, Burckhardt thought later, on his way up to bed. But the day wasn't done with him yet. At the head of the stairs, the weakened spring in the electric light switch refused to click at all. He snapped it back and forth angrily, and, of course, succeeded in jarring the tumbler out of its pins. The wires shorted and every light in the house went out.

'Damn!' said Guy Burckhardt.

'Fuse?' His wife shrugged sleepily: 'Let it go till the morning, dear.'

Burckhardt shook his head. 'You go back to bed. I'll be right along.'

It wasn't so much that he cared about fixing the fuse, but he was too restless for sleep. He disconnected the bad switch with a screwdriver, stumbled down into the black kitchen, found the flashlight and climbed gingerly down the cellar stairs. He located a spare fuse, pushed an empty trunk over to the fuse box to stand on, and twisted out the old fuse.

When the new one was in, he heard the starting click and steady drone of the refrigerator in the kitchen overhead.

He headed back to the steps, and stopped.

Where the old trunk had been, the cellar floor gleamed oddly bright. He inspected it in the flashlight beam. It was metal!

'Son of a gun,' said Guy Burckhardt. He shook his head unbelievingly. He peered closer, rubbed the edges of the metallic patch with his thumb and acquired an annoying cut – the edges were *sharp*.

The stained cement floor of the cellar was a thin shell. He found a hammer and cracked it off in a dozen spots – everywhere was metal.

The whole cellar was a copper box. Even the cement-brick walls were false fronts over a metal sheath!

Baffled, he attacked one of the foundation beams. That, at least, was real wood. The glass in the cellar windows was real glass.

He sucked his bleeding thumb and tried the base of the cellar stairs. Real wood. He chipped at the bricks under the oil burner. Real bricks. The retaining walls, the floor – they were faked.

It was as though someone had shored up the house with a frame of metal and then laboriously concealed the evidence.

The biggest surprise was the upside-down boat hull that blocked the rear half of the cellar, relic of a brief home workship period that Burckhardt had gone through a couple of years before. From above, it looked perfectly normal. Inside, though, where there should have been thwarts and seats and lockers, there was a mere tangle of braces, rough and unfinished.

'But I *built* that!' Burckhardt exclaimed, forgetting his thumb. He leaned against the hull dizzily, trying to think this thing through. For reasons beyond his comprehension, someone had taken his boat and his cellar away, maybe his whole house, and replaced them with a clever mock-up of the real thing.

'That's crazy,' he said to the empty cellar. He stared around in the light of the flash. He whispered, 'What in the name of Heaven would anybody do that for?'

Reason refused an answer; there wasn't any reasonable answer. For long minutes, Burckhardt contemplated the uncertain picture of his own sanity.

He peered under the boat again, hoping to reassure himself that it was a mistake, just his imagination. But the sloppy, unfinished bracing was unchanged. He crawled under for a better look, feeling the rough wood incredulously. Utterly impossible!

He switched off the flashlight and started to wriggle out. But he didn't make it. In the moment between the command to his legs to move and the crawling out, he felt a sudden draining weariness flooding through him.

Consciousness went – not easily, but as though it were being taken away, and Guy Burckhardt was asleep.

3

On the morning of June the 16th, Guy Burckhardt woke up in a cramped position huddled under the hull of the boat in his basement – and raced upstairs to find it was June the 15th.

The first thing he had done was to make a frantic, hasty inspection of the boat hull, the faked cellar floor, the imitation stone. They were all as he had remembered them – all completely unbelievable.

The kitchen was its placid, unexciting self. The electric clock was purring soberly around the dial. Almost six o'clock, it said. His wife would be waking at any moment.

Burckhardt flung open the front door and stared out into the quiet street. The morning paper was tossed carelessly against the steps – and as he retrieved it, he noticed that this was the 15th day of June.

But that was impossible. *Yesterday* was the 15th of June. It was not a date one would forget – it was quarterly tax-return day.

He went back into the hall and picked up the telephone; he dialled for Weather Information, and got a well-modulated chant: ' – and cooler, some showers. Barometric pressure thirty point zero four, rising . . . United States Weather Bureau forecast for June the 15th. Warm and sunny, with high around – '

He hung the phone up. June the 15th.

'Holy heaven!' Burckhardt said prayerfully. Things were very odd indeed. He heard the ring of his wife's alarm and bounded up the stairs.

Mary Burckhardt was sitting upright in bed with the terrified, uncomprehending stare of someone just waking out of a nightmare.

'Oh!' she gasped, as her husband came in the room. 'Darling, I just had the most *terrible* dream! It was like an explosion and – '

'Again?' Burckhardt asked, not very sympathetically. 'Mary, something's funny! I *knew* there was something wrong all day yesterday and – '

He went on to tell her about the copper box that was the cellar, and the odd mock-up someone had made of his boat. Mary looked astonished, then alarmed, then placatory and uneasy.

She said, 'Dear, are you *sure?* Because I was cleaning that old trunk out just last week and I didn't notice anything.'

'Positive!' said Guy Burckhardt. 'I dragged it over to the wall to step on it to put a new fuse in after we blew the lights out and – '

'After we what?' Mary was looking more than merely alarmed.

'After we blew the lights out. You know, when the switch at the head of the stairs stuck. I went down to the cellar and – '

Mary sat up in bed. 'Guy, the switch didn't stick. I turned out the lights myself last night.'

Burckhardt glared at his wife. 'Now I *know* you didn't! Come here and take a look!'

He stalked out to the landing and dramatically pointed to the bad switch, the one that he had unscrewed and left hanging the night before . . .

Only it wasn't. It was as it had always been. Unbelieving, Burckhardt pressed it and the lights sprang up in both halls.

Mary, looking pale and worried, left him to go down to the kitchen and start breakfast. Burckhardt stood staring at the switch for a long time. His mental processes were gone beyond the point of disbelief and shock; they simply were not functioning.

He shaved and dressed and ate his breakfast in a state of numb introspection. Mary didn't disturb him; she was apprehensive and soothing. She kissed him goodbye as he hurried out to the bus without another word.

Miss Mitkin, at the reception desk, greeted him with a yawn. 'Morning,' she said drowsily. 'Mr Barth won't be in today.'

Burckhardt started to say something, but checked himself. She would not know that Barth hadn't been in yesterday, either, because she was tearing a June the 14th pad off her calendar to make way for the 'new' June the 15th sheet.

He staggered to his own desk and stared unseeingly at the morning's mail. It had not even been opened yet, but he knew that the Factory Distributors envelope contained an order for twenty thousand feet of the new acoustic tile, and the one from Finebeck & Sons was a complaint.

After a long while, he forced himself to open them. They were.

By lunchtime, driven by a desperate sense of urgency, Burckhardt made Miss Mitkin take her lunch hour first – the June-fifteenth-that-was-yesterday *he* had gone first. She went, looking vaguely worried about his strained insistence, but it made no difference to Burckhardt's mood.

The phone rang and Burckhardt picked it up abstractedly. 'Contro Chemicals Downtown, Burckhardt speaking.'

The voice said, 'This is Swanson,' and stopped.

Burckhardt waited expectantly, but that was all. He said, 'Hello?'

Again the pause. Then Swanson asked in sad resignation, 'Still nothing, eh?'

'Nothing what? Swanson, is there something you want? You came up to me yesterday and went through this routine. You – '

The voice crackled: 'Burckhardt! Oh, my good heavens, *you remember!* Stay right there – I'll be down in half an hour!'

'What's this all about?'

'Never mind,' the little man said exultantly. 'Tell you about it when I see you. Don't say any more over the phone – somebody may be listening. Just wait there. Say, hold on a minute. Will you be alone in the office?'

'Well, no. Miss Mitkin will probably – '

'Hell. Look, Burckhardt, where do you eat lunch? Is it good and noisy?'

'Why I suppose so. The Crystal Café. It's just about a block – '

'I know where it is. Meet you in half an hour!' And the receiver clicked.

The Crystal Café was no longer painted red, but the temperature was still up. And they had added piped-in music interspersed with commercials. The advertisements were for Frosty-Flip, Marlin Cigarettes – 'They're sanitized,' the announcer purred – and something called Choco-Bite candy bars that Burckhardt couldn't remember ever having heard of before. But he heard more about them quickly enough.

While he was waiting for Swanson to show up, a girl in the cellophane skirt of a nightclub cigarette vendor came through the restaurant with a tray of tiny scarlet-wrapped candies.

'Choco-Bites are *tangy*,' she was murmuring as she came close to his table. 'Choco-Bites are *tangier* than tangy!'

Burckhardt, intent on watching for the strange little man who had phoned him, paid little attention. But as she scattered a handful of the confections over the table next to his, smiling at the occupants, he caught a glimpse of her and turned to stare.

'Why, Miss Horn!' he said.

The girl dropped her tray of candies.

Burckhardt rose, concerned over the girl. 'Is something wrong?'

But she fled.

The manager of the restaurant was staring suspiciously at Burckhardt, who sank back in his seat and tried to look inconspicuous. He hadn't insulted the girl! Maybe she was just a very strictly reared young lady, he thought – in spite of the long bare legs under the cellophane skirt – and when he addressed her, she thought he was a masher.

Ridiculous idea. Burckhardt scowled uneasily and picked up his menu.

'Burckhardt!' It was a shrill whisper.

Burckhardt looked up over the top of his menu, startled. In the seat across from him, the little man named Swanson was sitting, tensely poised.

'Burckhardt!' the little man whispered again. 'Let's get out of here! They're on to you now. If you want to stay alive, come on!'

There was no arguing with the man. Burckhardt gave the

hovering manager a sick apologetic smile and followed Swanson out. The little man seemed to know where he was going. In the street, he clutched Burckhardt by the elbow and hurried him off down the block.

'Did you see her?' he demanded. 'That Horn woman, in the phone booth? She'll have them here in five minutes, believe me, so hurry it up!'

Although the street was full of people and cars, nobody was paying any attention to Burckhardt and Swanson. The air had a nip in it – more like October than June, Burckhardt thought, in spite of the weather bureau. And he felt like a fool, following this mad little man down the street, running away from some 'them' towards – towards what? The little man might be crazy, but he was afraid. And the fear was infectious.

'In here!' panted the little man.

It was another restaurant – more of a bar, really, and a sort of second-rate place that Burckhardt never had patronized.

'Right straight through,' Swanson whispered; and Burckhardt, like a biddable boy, sidestepped through the mass of tables to the far end of the restaurant.

It was L-shaped, with a front on two streets at right angles to each other. They came out on the side street, Swanson staring coldly back at the question-looking cashier, and crossed to the opposite sidewalk.

They were under the marquee of a movie theatre. Swanson's expression began to relax.

'Lost them!' he crowed softly. 'We're almost there.'

He stepped up to the window and bought two tickets. Burckhardt trailed him into the theatre. It was a weekday matinee and the place was almost empty. From the screen came sounds of gunfire and horses' hoofs. A solitary usher, leaning against a bright brass rail, looked briefly at them and went back to staring boredly at the picture as Swanson led Burckhardt down a flight of carpeted marble steps.

They were in the lounge and it was empty. There was a door for men and one for ladies; and there was a third door, marked MANAGER in gold letters. Swanson listened at the door, and gently opened it and peered inside.

'Okay,' he said, gesturing.

Burckhardt followed him through an empty office, to another door – a closet, probably, because it was unmarked.

But it was no closet. Swanson opened it warily, looked inside, then motioned Burckhardt to follow.

It was a tunnel, metal-walled, brightly lit. Empty, it stretched vacantly away in both directions from them.

Burckhardt looked wondering around. One thing he knew and knew full well:

No such tunnel belonged under Tylerton.

There was a room off the tunnel with chairs and a desk and what looked like television screens. Swanson slumped in a chair, panting.

'We're all right for a while here,' he wheezed. 'They don't come here much any more. If they do, we'll hear them and we can hide.'

'Who?' demanded Burckhardt.

The little man said, 'Martians!' His voice cracked on the word and the life seemed to go out of him. In morose tones, he went on: 'Well, I think they're Martians. Although you could be right, you know; I've had plenty of time to think it over these last few weeks, after they got you, and it's possible they're Russians after all. Still – '

'Start from the beginning. Who got me when?'

Swanson sighed. 'So we have to go through the whole thing again. All right. It was about two months ago that you banged on my door, late at night. You were all beat up – scared silly. You begged me to help you – '

'*I* did?'

'Naturally you don't remember any of this. Listen and you'll understand. You were talking a blue streak about being captured and threatened and your wife being dead and coming back to life, and all kinds of mixed-up nonsense. I thought you were crazy. But – well, I've always had a lot of respect for you. And you begged me to hide you and I have this darkroom, you know. It locks from the inside only. I put the lock on myself. So we went in there – just to humour you – and along about midnight, which was only fifteen or twenty minutes after, we passed out.'

'Passed out?'

Swanson nodded. 'Both of us. It was like being hit with a sandbag. Look, didn't that happen to you again last night?'

'I guess it did,' Burckhardt shook his head uncertainly.

'Sure. And then all of a sudden we were awake again, and you said you were going to show me something funny, and we went out and bought a paper. And the date on it was June the 15th.'

'June the 15th? But that's today! I mean – '

'You got it, friend. It's *always* today!'

It took time to penetrate.

Burckhardt said wonderingly, 'You've hidden out in that darkroom for how many weeks?'

'How can I tell? Four or five, maybe. I lost count. And every day the same – always the 15th of June, always my landlady, Mrs Keefer, is sweeping the front steps, always the same headline in the papers at the corner. It gets monotonous, friend.'

4

It was Burckhardt's idea and Swanson despised it, but he went along. He was the type who always went along.

'It's dangerous,' he grumbled worriedly. 'Suppose somebody comes by? They'll spot us and – '

'What have we got to lose?'

Swanson shrugged. 'It's dangerous,' he said again. But he went along.

Burckhardt's idea was very simple. He was sure of only one thing – the tunnel went somewhere. Martians or Russians, fantastic plot or crazy hallucination, whatever was wrong with Tylerton had an explanation, and the place to look for it was at the end of the tunnel.

They jogged along. It was more than a mile before they began to see an end. They were in luck – at least no one came through the tunnel to spot them. But Swanson had said that it was only at certain hours that the tunnel seemed to be in use.

Always the 15th of June. Why? Burckhardt asked himself. Never mind the how. *Why?*

And falling asleep, completely involuntarily – everyone at the same time, it seemed. And not remembering, never remembering anything – Swanson had said how eagerly he saw Burckhardt again, the morning after Burckhardt had incautiously waited five minutes too many before retreating into the darkroom. When Swanson had come to, Burckhardt was gone. Swanson had seen him in the street that afternoon, but Burckhardt had remembered nothing.

And Swanson had lived his mouse's existence for weeks, hiding in the woodwork at night, stealing out by day to search for Burckhardt in pitiful hope, scurrying around the fringe of life, trying to keep from the deadly eyes of *them*.

Them. One of 'them' was the girl named April Horn. It was by seeing her walk carelessly into a telephone booth and never come out that Swanson had found the tunnel. Another was the man at the cigar stand in Burckhardt's office building. There were more, at least a dozen that Swanson knew of or suspected.

They were easy enough to spot, once you knew where to look – for they, alone in Tylerton, changed their roles from day to day. Burckhardt was on that 8.51 bus, every morning of every-day-that-was-June-the-15th, never different by a hair or a moment. But April Horn was sometimes gaudy in the cellophane skirt, giving away candy or cigarettes; sometimes plainly dressed; sometimes not seen by Swanson at all.

Russians? Martians? Whatever they were, what could they be hoping to gain from this mad masquerade?

Burckhardt didn't know the answer – but perhaps it lay beyond the door at the end of the tunnel. They listened carefully and heard distant sounds that could not quite be made out, but nothing that seemed dangerous. They slipped through.

And, through a wide chamber and up a flight of steps,

they found they were in what Burckhardt recognized as the Contro Chemicals plant.

Nobody was in sight. By itself, that was not so very odd – the automatized factory had never had many persons in it. But Burckhardt remembered, from his single visit, the endless, ceaseless busyness of the plant, the valves that opened and closed, the vats that emptied themselves and filled themselves and stirred and cooked and chemically tested the bubbling liquids they held inside themselves. The plant was never populated, but it was never still.

Only – now it *was* still. Except for the distant sounds, there was no breath of life in it. The captive electronic minds were sending out no commands; the coils and relays were at rest.

Burckhardt said, 'Come on.' Swanson reluctantly followed him through the tangled aisles of stainless steel columns and tanks.

They walked as though they were in the presence of the dead. In a way, they were, for what were the automatons that once had run the factory, if not corpses? The machines were controlled by computers that were really not computers at all, but the electronic analogues of living brains. And if they were turned off, were they not dead? For each had once been a human mind.

Take a master petroleum chemist, infinitely skilled in the separation of crude oil into its fractions. Strap him down, probe into his brain with searching electronic needles. The machine scans the patterns of the mind, translates what it sees into charts and sine waves. Impress the same waves on a robot computer and you have your chemist. Or a thousand copies of your chemist, if you wish, with all of his knowledge and skill, and no human limitations at all.

Put a dozen copies of him into a plant and they will run it all, twenty-four hours a day, seven days of every week, never tiring, never overlooking anything, never forgetting . . .

Swanson stepped up closer to Burckhardt. 'I'm scared,' he said.

They were across the room now and the sounds were

louder. They were not machine sounds, but voices; Burckhardt moved cautiously up to a door and dared to peer around it.

It was a smaller room, lined with television screens, each one – a dozen or more, at least – with a man or woman sitting before it, staring into the screen and dictating notes into a recorder. The viewers dialled from scene to scene; no two screens ever showed the same picture.

The pictures seemed to have little in common. One was a store, where a girl dressed like April Horn was demonstrating home freezers. One was a series of shots of kitchens. Burckhardt caught a glimpse of what looked like the cigar stand in his office building.

It was baffling and Burckhardt would have loved to stand there and puzzle it out, but it was too busy a place. There was the chance that someone would look their way or walk out and find them.

They found another room. This one was empty. It was an office, large and sumptuous. It had a desk, littered with papers. Burckhardt stared at them, briefly at first – then, as the words on one of them caught his attention, with incredulous fascination.

He snatched up the topmost sheet, scanned it, and another, while Swanson was frenziedly searching through the drawers.

Burckhardt swore unbelievingly and dropped the papers to the desk.

Swanson, hardly noticing, yelped with delight: 'Look!' He dragged a gun from the desk. 'And it's loaded, too!'

Burckhardt stared at him blankly, trying to assimilate what he had read. Then, as he realized what Swanson had said, Burckhardt's eyes sparked. 'Good man!' he cried. 'We'll take it. We're getting out of here with that gun, Swanson. And we're going to the police! Not the cops in Tylerton, but the FBI maybe. Take a look at this!'

The sheaf he handed Swanson was headed: 'Test Area Progress Report. Subject: Marlin Cigarettes Campaign.' It was mostly tabulated figures that made little sense to Burckhardt and Swanson, but at the end was a summary that said:

Although Test 47–K3 pulled nearly double the number of new users of any of the other tests conducted, it probably cannot be used in the field because of local sound-truck control ordinances.

The tests in the 47–K12 group were second best and our recommendation is that retests be conducted in this appeal, testing each of the three best campaigns with and without the addition of sampling techniques.

An alternative suggestion might be to proceed directly with the top appeal in the K12 series, if the client is unwilling to go to the expense of additional tests.

All of these forecast expectations have an 80% probability of being within one-half of one per cent of results forecast, and more than 99% probability of coming within 5%.

Swanson looked up from the paper into Burckhardt's eyes. 'I don't get it,' he complained. Burckhardt said, 'I do not blame you. It's crazy, but it fits the facts, Swanson, *it fits the facts*. They aren't Russians and they aren't Martians. These people are advertising men! Somehow – heaven knows how they did it – they've taken Tylerton over. They've got us, all of us, you and me and twenty or thirty thousand other people, right under their thumbs.

'Maybe they hypnotize us and maybe it's something else; but however they do it, what happens is that they let us live a day at a time. They pour advertising into us the whole damned day long. And at the end of the day, they see what happened – and then they wash the day out of our minds and start again the next day with different advertising.'

Swanson's jaw was hanging. He managed to close it and swallow. 'Nuts!' he said flatly.

Burckhardt shook his head. 'Sure, it sounds crazy – but this whole thing is crazy. How else would you explain it? You can't deny that most of Tylerton lives the same day over and over again. You've *seen* it. And that's the crazy part and we have to admit that that's true – unless *we* are the crazy ones. And once you admit that somebody, somehow, knows how to accomplish that, the rest of it makes all kinds of sense.

'Think of it, Swanson! They test every last detail before they spend a nickel on advertising! Do you have any idea what that means? Lord knows how much money is involved, but I know for a fact that some companies spend twenty or thirty million dollars a year on advertising. Multiply it, say, by a hundred companies. Say that every one of them learns how to cut its advertising cost by only ten per cent. And that's peanuts, believe me!

'If they know in advance what is going to work, they can cut their costs in half – maybe to less than half, I don't know. But that is saving two or three hundred million dollars a year – and if they pay only ten or twenty per cent of that for the use of Tylerton, it's still dirt cheap for them and a fortune for whoever took over Tylerton.'

Swanson licked his lips. 'You mean,' he offered hesitantly, 'that we're a – well, a kind of captive audience?'

Burckhardt frowned. 'Not exactly.' He thought for a minute. 'You know how a doctor tests something like penicillin? He sets up a series of little colonies of germs on gelatine discs and he tries the stuff on one after another, changing it a little each time. Well, that's us – we're the germs, Swanson. Only it's even more efficient than that. They don't have to test more than one colony, because they can use it over and over again.'

It was too hard for Swanson to take in. He only said: 'What do we do about it?'

'We go to the police. They can't use human beings for guinea pigs!'

'How do we get to the police?'

Burckhardt hesitated. 'I think – ' he began slowly. 'Sure. This place is the office of somebody important. We've got a gun. We will stay right here until he comes along. And he'll get us out of here.'

Simple and direct. Swanson subsided and found a place to sit, against the wall, out of sight of the door. Burckhardt took up a position behind the door itself –

And waited.

The wait was not as long as it might have been. Half an hour, perhaps. Then Burckhardt heard approaching voices and had time for a swift whisper to Swanson before he flattened himself against the wall.

It was a man's voice, and a girl's. The man was saying, ' – reason why you couldn't report on the phone? You're ruining your whole day's test! What the devil's the matter with you, Janet?'

'I'm sorry, Mr Dorchin,' she said in a sweet, clear tone. 'I thought it was important.'

The man grumbled, 'Important! One lousy unit out of twenty-one thousand.'

'But it's the Burckhardt one, Mr Dorchin. Again. And the way he got out of sight, he must have had some help.'

'All right, all right. It doesn't matter, Janet; the Choco-Bite programme is ahead of schedule anyhow. As long as you're this far, come on in the office and make out your worksheet. And don't worry about the Burckhardt business. He's probably just wandering around. We'll pick him up tonight and – '

They were inside the door. Burckhardt kicked it shut and pointed the gun.

'That's what you think,' he said triumphantly.

It was worth the terrified hours, the bewildered sense of insanity, the confusion and fear. It was the most satisfying sensation Burckhardt had ever had in his life. The expression on the man's face was one he had read about but never actually seen: Dorchin's mouth fell open and his eyes went wide, and though he managed to make a sound that might have been a question, it was not in words.

The girl was almost as surprised. And Burckhardt, looking at her, knew why her voice had been so familiar. The girl was the one who had introduced herself to him as April Horn.

Dorchin recovered himself quickly. 'Is this the one?' he asked sharply.

The girl said, 'Yes.'

Dorchin nodded. 'I take it back. You were right. Uh, you – Burckhardt. What do you want?'

Swanson piped up, 'Watch him! He might have another gun.'

'Search him then,' Burckhardt said. 'I'll tell you what we want, Dorchin. We want you to come along with us to the

FBI and explain to them how you can get away with kidnapping twenty thousand people.'

'Kidnapping?' Dorchin snorted. 'That's ridiculous, man! Put that gun away – you can't get away with this!'

Burckhardt hefted the gun grimly. 'I think I can.'

Dorchin looked furious and sick – but, oddly, not afraid. 'Damn it – ' he started to bellow, then closed his mouth and swallowed. 'Listen,' he said persuasively, 'you're making a big mistake. I haven't kidnapped anybody, believe me!'

'I don't believe you,' said Burckhardt bluntly. 'Why should I?'

'But it's true! Take my word for it!'

Burckhardt shook his head. 'The FBI can take your word if they like. We'll find out. Now how do we get out of here?'

Dorchin opened his mouth to argue.

Burckhardt blazed: 'Don't get in my way! I'm willing to kill you if I have to. Don't you understand that? I've gone through two days of hell and every second of it I blame on you. Kill you? It would be a pleasure and I don't have a thing in the world to lose! Get us out of here!'

Dorchin's face went suddenly opaque. He seemed about to move; but the blonde girl he had called Janet slipped between him and the gun.

'Please!' she begged Burckhardt. 'You don't understand. You mustn't shoot!'

'*Get out of my way!*'

'But, Mr Burckhardt – '

She never finished. Dorchin, his face unreadable, headed for the door. Burckhardt had been pushed one degree too far. He swung the gun, bellowing. The girl called out sharply. He pulled the trigger. Closing on him with pity and pleading in her eyes, she came again between the gun and the man.

Burckhardt aimed low instinctively, to cripple, not to kill. But his aim was not good.

The pistol bullet caught her in the pit of her stomach.

Dorchin was out and away, the door slamming behind him, his footsteps racing into the distance.

Burckhardt hurled the gun across the room and jumped to the girl.

Swanson was moaning, 'That finishes us, Burckhardt. Oh, why did you do it? We could have got away. We should have gone to the police. We were practically out of here! We – '

Burckhardt wasn't listening. He was kneeling beside the girl. She lay flat on her back, arms helter-skelter. There was no blood, hardly any sign of the wound; but the position in which she lay was one that no living human being could have held.

Yet she wasn't dead.

She wasn't dead – and Burckhardt, frozen beside her, thought: *She isn't alive, either.*

There was no pulse, but there was a rhythmic ticking of the outstretched fingers of one hand.

There was no sound of breathing, but there was a hissing, sizzling noise.

The eyes were open and they were looking at Burckhardt. There was neither fear nor pain in them, only a pity deeper than the Pit.

She said, through lips that writhed erratically, 'Don't – worry, Mr Burckhardt. I'm – all right.'

Burckhardt rocked back on his haunches, staring. Where there should have been blood, there was a clean break of a substance that was not flesh; and a curl of thin golden-copper wire.

Burckhardt moistened his lips.

'You're a robot,' he said.

The girl tried to nod. The twitching lips said, 'I am. And so are you.'

5

Swanson, after a single inarticulate sound, walked over to the desk and sat staring at the wall. Burckhardt rocked back and forth beside the shattered puppet on the floor. He had no words.

The girl managed to say, 'I'm – sorry all this happened.' The lovely lips twisted into a rictus sneer, frightening on that smooth young face, until she got them under control. 'Sorry,' she said again. 'The – nerve centre was right about where the bullet hit. Makes it difficult to – control this body.'

Burckhardt nodded automatically, accepting the apology. Robots. It was obvious, now that he knew it. In hindsight, it was inevitable. He thought of his mystic notions of hypnosis or Martians or something stranger still – idiotic, for the simple fact of created robots fitted the facts better and more economically.

All the evidence had been before him. The automatized factory, with its transplanted minds – why not transplant a mind into a humanoid robot, give it its original owner's features and form?

Could it know that it was a robot?

'All of us,' Burckhardt said, hardly aware that he spoke out loud. 'My wife and my secretary and you and the neighbours. All of us the same.'

'No.' The voice was stronger. 'Not exactly the same, all of us. I chose it, you see. I – ' this time the convulsed lips were not a random contortion of the nerves – 'I was an ugly woman, Mr Burckhardt, and nearly sixty years old. Life had passed me. And when Mr Dorchin offered me the chance to live again as a beautiful girl, I jumped at the opportunity. Believe me, I *jumped*, in spite of its disadvantages. My flesh body is still alive – it is sleeping, while I am here. I could go back to it. But I never do.'

'And the rest of us?'

'Different, Mr Burckhardt. I work here. I'm carrying out Mr Dorchin's orders, mapping the results of the advertising tests, watching you and the others live as he makes you live. I do it by choice, but you have no choice. Because, you see, you are dead.'

'Dead?' cried Burckhardt; it was almost a scream.

The blue eyes looked at him unwinkingly and he knew that it was no lie. He swallowed, marvelling at the intricate mechanisms that let him swallow, and sweat, and eat.

He said: 'Oh. The explosion in my dream.'

'It was no dream. You are right – the explosion. That was

real and this plant was the cause of it. The storage tanks let go and what the blast didn't get, the fumes killed a little later. But almost everyone died in the blast, twenty-one thousand persons. You died with them and that was Dorchin's chance.'

'The damned ghoul!' said Burckhardt.

The twisted shoulders shrugged with an odd grace. 'Why? You were gone. And you and all the others were what Dorchin wanted – a whole town, a perfect slice of America. It's as easy to transfer a pattern from a dead brain as a living one. Easier – the dead can't say no. Oh, it took work and money – the town was a wreck – but it was possible to rebuild it entirely, especially because it wasn't necessary to have all the details exact.

'There were the homes where even the brains had been utterly destroyed, and those are empty inside, and the cellars that needn't be too perfect, and the streets that hardly matter. And anyway, it only had to last for one day. The same day – June the 15th – over and over again; and if someone finds something a little wrong, somehow, the discovery won't have time to snowball, wreck the validity of the tests, because all errors are cancelled out at midnight.'

The face tried to smile. 'That's the dream, Mr Burckhardt, that day of June the 15th, because you never really lived it. It's a present from Mr Dorchin, a dream that he gives you and then takes back at the end of the day, when he has all his figures on how many of you responded to what variation of which appeal, and the maintenance crews go down the tunnel to go through the whole city, washing out the new dream with their little electronic drains, and then the dream starts all over again. On June the 15th.

'Always June the 15th, because June the 14th is the last day any of you can remember alive. Sometimes the crews miss someone – as they missed you, because you were under your boat. But it doesn't matter. The ones who are missed give themselves away if they show it – and if they don't, it doesn't affect the test. But they don't drain us, the ones of us who work for Dorchin. We sleep when the power is turned off, just as you do. When we wake up, though, we remember.' The face contorted wildly. 'If I could only forget!'

Burckhardt said unbelievingly, 'All this to sell merchandise! It must have cost millions!'

The robot called April Horn said, 'It did. But it has made millions for Dorchin, too. And that's not the end of it. Once he finds the master words that make people act, do you suppose he will stop with that? Do you suppose – '

The door opened, interrupting her. Burckhardt whirled. Belatedly remembering Dorchin's flight, he raised the gun.

'Don't shoot,' ordered the voice calmly. It was not Dorchin; it was another robot, this one not disguised with the clever plastics and cosmetics, but shining plain. It said metallically: 'Forget it, Burckhardt. You're not accomplishing anything. Give me that gun before you do any more damage. Give it to me *now*.'

Burckhardt bellowed angrily. The gleam on this robot torso was steel; Burckhardt was not at all sure that his bullets would pierce it, or do much harm if they did. He would have put it on the test –

But from behind him came a whimpering, scurrying whirl-wind; its name was Swanson, hysterical with fear. He catapulted into Burckhardt and sent him sprawling, the gun flying free.

'Please!' begged Swanson incoherently, prostrate before the steel robot. 'He would have shot you – please don't hurt me! Let me work for you, like that girl. I'll do anything, anything you tell me – '

The robot voice said, 'We don't need your help.' It took two precise steps and stood over the gun – and spurned it, left it lying on the floor.

The wrecked blonde robot said, without emotion, 'I doubt that I can hold out much longer, Mr Dorchin.'

'Disconnect if you have to,' replied the steel robot.

Burckhardt blinked. 'But you're not Dorchin!'

The steel robot turned deep eyes on him. 'I am,' it said. 'Not in the flesh – but this is the body I am using at the moment. I doubt that you can damage this one with the gun. The other robot body was more vulnerable. Now will you stop this nonsense? I don't want to have to damage you; you're too expensive for that. Will you just sit down and let the maintenance crews adjust you?'

Swanson grovelled. 'You – you won't punish us?'

The steel robot had no expression, but its voice was almost surprised. 'Punish you?' it repeated on a rising tone. 'How?'

Swanson quivered as though the word had been a whip; but Burckhardt flared: 'Adjust *him*, if he'll let you – but not me! You're going to have to do me a lot of damage, Dorchin. I don't care what I cost or how much trouble it's going to be to put me back together again. But I'm going out of that door! If you want to stop me, you'll have to kill me. You won't stop me any other way!'

The steel robot took a half-step towards him, and Burckhardt involuntarily checked his stride. He stood poised and shaking, ready for death, ready for attack, ready for anything that might happen.

Ready for anything except what did happen. For Dorchin's steel body merely stepped aside, between Burckhardt and the gun, but leaving the door free.

'Go ahead,' invited the steel robot. 'Nobody's stopping you.'

Outside the door, Burckhardt brought up sharp. It was insane of Dorchin to let him go! Robot or flesh, victim or beneficiary, there was nothing to stop him from going to the FBI or whatever law he could find away from Dorchin's synthetic empire, and telling his story. Surely the corporation who paid Dorchin for test results had no notion of the ghoul's technique he used; Dorchin would have to keep it from them, for the breath of publicity would put a stop to it. Walking out meant death, perhaps – but at that moment in his pseudo-life, death was no terror for Burckhardt.

There was no one in the corridor. He found a window and stared out of it. There was Tylerton – an ersatz city, but looking so real and familiar that Burckhardt almost imagined the whole episode a dream. It was no dream, though. He was certain of that in his heart and equally certain that nothing in Tylerton could help him now.

It had to be the other direction.

It took him a quarter of an hour to find a way, but he found it – skulking through the corridors, dodging the suspicion of footsteps, knowing for certain that his hiding was in vain, for Dorchin was undoubtedly aware of every move he made. But no one stopped him, and he found another door.

It was a simple enough door from the inside. But when he opened it and stepped out, it was like nothing he had ever seen.

First there was light – brilliant, incredible, blinding light. Burckhardt blinked upward, unbelieving and afraid.

He was standing on a ledge of smooth, finished metal. Not a dozen yards from his feet, the ledge dropped sharply away; he hardly dared approach the brink, but even from where he stood he could see no bottom to the chasm before him. And the gulf extended out of sight into the glare on either side of him.

No wonder Dorchin could so easily give him his freedom! From the factory, there was nowhere to go – but how incredible this fantastic gulf, how impossible the hundred white and blinding suns that hung above!

A voice by his side said inquiringly, 'Burckhardt?' And thunder rolled the name, mutteringly soft, back and forth in the abyss before him.

Burckhardt wet his lips. 'Y-yes?' he croaked.

'This is Dorchin. Not a robot this time, but Dorchin in the flesh, talking to you on a hand mike. Now you have seen, Burckhardt. Now will you be reasonable and let the maintenance crews take over?'

Burckhardt stood paralysed. One of the moving mountains in the blinding glare came towards him.

It towered hundreds of feet over his head; he stared up at its top, squinting helplessly into the light.

It looked like –

Impossible!

The voice in the loudspeaker at the door said, 'Burckhardt?' But he was unable to answer.

A heavy rumbling sigh. 'I see,' said the voice. 'You finally understand. There's no place to go. You know it now. I could have told you, but you might not have believed me, so it was better for you to see it yourself. And after all, Burckhardt, why would I reconstruct a city just the way it was before? I'm a businessman; I count costs. If a thing has to be full-scale, I build it that way. But there wasn't any need to in this case.'

From the mountain before him, Burckhardt helplessly saw a lesser cliff descend carefully toward him. It was long and dark, and at the end of it was whiteness, five-fingered whiteness . . .

'Poor little Burckhardt,' crooned the loudspeaker, while the echoes rumbled through the enormous chasm that was only a workshop. 'It must have been quite a shock for you to find out you were living in a town built on a table top.'

6

It was the morning of June the 15th, and Guy Burckhardt woke up screaming out of a dream.

It had been a monstrous and incomprehensible dream, of explosions and shadowy figures that were not men and terror beyond words.

He shuddered and opened his eyes.

Outside his bedroom window, a hugely amplified voice was howling.

Burckhardt stumbled over to the window and stared outside. There was an out-of-season chill to the air, more like October than June; but the scene was normal enough – except for the sound-truck that squatted at the kerbside halfway down the block. Its speaker horns blared:

'Are you a coward? Are you a fool? Are you going to let crooked politicians steal the country from you? NO! Are you going to put up with four more years of graft and crime? NO! Are you going to vote straight Federal Party all up and down the ballot? YES! *You just bet you are!*'

Sometimes he screams, sometimes he wheedles, threatens, begs, cajoles . . . but his voice goes on and on through one June the 15th after another.

Old Hundredth

Brian W. Aldiss

The road climbed dustily down between trees as symmetrical as umbrellas. Its length was punctuated at one point by a musicolumn standing on the sandy verge. From a distance, the column was only a faint stain in the air. As sentient creatures neared it, their psyches activated it, it drew on their vitalities and then could be heard as well as seen. Their presence made it flower into pleasant noise, instrumental or chant.

All this region was called Ghinomon, for nobody lived here any more, not even the odd hermit Impure. It was given over to grass and the weight of time. Only a few wild goats activated the musicolumn nowadays, or a scampering vole wrung a brief chord from it in passing.

When old Dandi Lashadusa came riding down that dusty road on her baluchitherium, the column began to intone. It was just an indigo trace on the air, hardly visible, for it represented only a bonded pattern of music locked into the fabric of that particular area of space. It was also a transubstantio-spatial shrine, the eternal part of a being that had dematerialized itself into music.

The baluchitherium whinnied, lowered its head, and sneezed onto the gritty road.

'Gently, Lass,' Dandi told her mare, savouring the growth of the chords that increased in volume as she approached. Her long nose twitched with pleasure as if she could feel the melody along her olfactory nerves.

Obediently, the baluchitherium slowed, turning aside to

crop fern, although it kept an eye on the indigo stain. It liked things to have being or not to have being; these half-and-half objects disturbed it, though they could not impair its immense appetite.

Dandi climbed down her ladder onto the ground, glad to feel the ancient dust under her feet. She smoothed her hair and stretched as she listened to the music.

She spoke aloud to her mentor, half the world away, but he was not listening. His mind closed to her thoughts, he muttered an obscure expression that darkened what it sought to clarify.

' . . . useless to deny that it is well-nigh impossible to improve anything, however faulty, that has so much trad-ition behind it. And the origins of your bit of metricism are indeed embedded in such a fearful antiquity that we must needs – '

'Tush, Mentor, come out of your black box and forget your hatred of my "metricism" a moment,' Dandi Lashad-usa said, cutting her thought into his. 'Listen to the bit of "metricism" I've found here, look at where I have come to, let your argument rest.'

She turned her eyes about, scanning the tawny rocks near at hand, the brown line of the road, the distant black and white magnificence of ancient Oldorajo's town, doing this all for him, tiresome old fellow. Her mentor was blind, never left his cell in Peterbroe to go farther than the sandy courtyard, hadn't physically left that green cathedral pile for over a century. Womanlike, she thought he needed change. Soul, how he rambled on! Even now, he was managing to ignore her and refute her.

' . . . for consider, Lashadusa woman, nobody can be found to father it. Nobody wrought or thought it, phrases of it merely *came* together. Even the old nations of men could not own it. None of them knew who composed it. An element here from a Spanish pavan, an influence there of a French psalm tune, a flavour here of early English carol, a savour there of later German chorals. Nor are the faults of your bit of metricism confined to bastardy . . . '

'Stay in your black box then, if you won't see or listen,'

Dandi said. She could not get into his mind; it was the mentor's privilege to lodge in her mind, and in the minds of those few other wards he had, scattered round Earth. Only the mentors had the powers of being in another's mind – which made them rather tiring on occasions like this, when they would not get out of it. For over seventy years, Dandi's mentor had been persuading her to die into a dirge of his choosing (and composing). Let her die, yes, let her transubstantio-spatialize herself a thousand times! His quarrel was not with her decision but her taste, which he considered execrable.

Leaving the baluchitherium to crop, Dandi walked away from the musicolumn towards a hillock. Still fed by her steed's psyche, the column continued to play. Its music was of a simplicity, with a dominant-tonic recurrent bass part suggesting pessimism. To Dandi, a savant in musicolumnology, it yielded other data. She could tell to within a few years when its founder had died and also what kind of a creature, generally speaking, he had been.

Climbing the hillock, Dandi looked about. To the south where the road led were low hills, lilac in the poor light. There lay her home. At last she was returning, after wanderings covering half a century and most of the globe.

Apart from the blind beauty of Oldorajo's town lying to the west, there was only one landmark she recognized. That was the Involute. It seemed to hang iridial above the ground a few leagues on; just to look on it made her feel she must at once get nearer.

Before summoning the baluchitherium, Dandi listened once more to the sounds of the musicolumn, making sure she had them fixed in her head. The pity was her old fool wise man would not share it. She could still feel his sulks floating like sediment through his mind.

'Are you listening now, Mentor?'

'Eh? An interesting point is that back in 1556 by the old pre-Involutary calendar your same little tune may be discovered lurking in Knox's Anglo-Genevan Psalter, where it espoused the cause of the third psalm – '

'You dreary old fish! Wake yourself! How can you criticize my intended way of dying when you have such a fustian way of living?'

This time he heard her words. So close did he seem that his peevish pinching at the bridge of his snuffy old nose tickled hers too.

'What are you doing *now*, Dandi?' he inquired.

'If you had been listening, you'd know. Here's where I am, on the last Ghinomon plain before Crotheria and home.' She swept the landscape again and he took it in, drank it almost greedily. Many mentors went blind early in life shut in their monastic underwater dens; their most effective visions were conducted through the eyes of their wards.

His view of what she saw enriched hers. He knew the history, the myth behind this forsaken land. He could stock the tired old landscape with pageantry, delighting her and surprising her. Back and forward he went, flicking her pictures; the Youdicans, the Lombards, the Ex-Europa Emissary, the Grites, the Risorgimento, the Involuters – and catchwords, costumes, customs, courtesans, pelted briefly through Dandi Lashadusa's mind. Ah, she thought admiringly, who could truly live without these priestly, beastly, erudite, erratic mentors?

'Erratic?' he inquired, snatching at her lick of thought. 'A thousand years I live, for all that time to absent myself from the world, to eat mashed fish here with my brothers, learning history, studying *rapport*, sleeping with my bones on stones – a humble being, a being in a million, a mentor in a myriad, and your standards of judgement are so mundane you find no stronger label for me than erratic? Fie, Lashadusa, bother me no more for fifty years!'

The words nattered and squeaked in her head as if she spoke herself. She felt his old chops work phantomlike in hers, and half in anger half in laughter called aloud, 'I'll be dead by then!'

He snicked back hot and holy to reply, 'And another thing about your footloose swan song – in Marot and Beza's Genevan Psalter of 1551, Old Time, it was musical midwife to the one hundred and thirty-fourth psalm. Like you, it never seemed to settle!' Then he was gone.

'Pooh!' Dandi said. She whistled Lass.

Obediently, the great rhino-like creature, eighteen feet high at the shoulder, ambled over. The musicolumn died as the mare left it, faded, sank to a whisper, silenced: only the purple stain remained, noiseless, in the lonely air. Lass reached Dandi. Lowering its great Oligocene head, it nuzzled its mistress's hand. She climbed the ladder on to that ridged plateau of back.

They made contentedly towards the Involute, lulled by the simple and intricate feeling of being alive.

Night was settling in now, steady as snow. Hidden behind banks of mist, the sun prepared to set. But Venus was high, a gallant half-crescent four times as big as the Moon had been before the Moon, spiralling farther and farther from Earth, had shaken off its parent's clutch to go dance round the sun, a second Mercury. Even by that time Venus had been moved by gravito-traction into Earth's orbit, so that the two worlds circled each other as they circled the sun.

The stamp of that great event still lay everywhere, its tokens not only in the crescent in the sky. For Venus put a strange spell on the hearts of man, and a more penetrating displacement in his genes. Even when its atmosphere was transformed into a muffled breathability, it remained an alien world; against logic, its opportunities, its possibilities, were its own. It shaped men, just as Earth had shaped them. On Venus, men bred themselves anew.

And they bred the so-called Impures. They bred new plants, new fruits, new creatures – original ones, and duplications of creatures not seen on Earth for aeons past. From one line of these familiar strangers Dandi's baluchitherium was descended. So, for that matter, was Dandi.

The huge creature came now to the Involute, or as near as it cared to get. Again it began to crop at thistles, thrusting its nose through dewy spiders' webs and ground mist.

'Like you, I'm a vegetarian,' Dandi said, climbing down to the ground. A grove of low fruit trees grew nearby; she reached up into the branches, gathered and ate, before turning to inspect the Involute. Already her spine tingled at the nearness of it; awe, loathing and love made a part-pleasant sensation near her heart.

The Involute was not beautiful. True, its colours changed with the changing light, yet the colours were fish-cold, for they belonged to another universe. Though they reacted to dusk and dawn, Earth had no stronger power over them. They pricked the eyes. Perhaps too they were painful because they were the last signs of materialist man. Even Lass moved uneasily before that ill-defined lattice, the upper limits of which were lost in thickening gloom.

'Don't fear,' Dandi said. 'There's an explanation for this, old girl.' She added sadly, 'There's an explanation for everything, if we can find it.'

She could feel all the personalities in the Involute. It was a frozen screen of personality. All over the old planet the structures stood, to shed their awe on those who were left behind. They were the essence of man. They were man – all that remained of him.

When the first flint, the first shell, was shaped into a weapon, that action shaped man. As he moulded and complicated his tools, so they moulded and complicated him. He became the first scientific animal. And at last, via information theory and great computers, he gained knowledge of all his parts. He formed the Laws of Integration, which reveal all beings as part of a pattern and show them their part in the pattern. There is only the pattern, the pattern is all the universe, creator and created. For the first time, it became possible to duplicate that pattern artificially; the transubstantio-spatializers were built.

All mankind left their strange hobbies on Earth and Venus and projected themselves into the pattern. Their entire personalities were merged with the texture of space itself. Through science, they reached immortality.

It was a one-way passage.

They did not return. Each Involute carried thousands or even millions of people. They were, not dead, not living. How they exulted or wept in their transubstantiation, nobody left could say. Only this could be said: man had gone, and a great emptiness was fallen over the Earth.

'Your thoughts are heavy, Dandi Lashadusa. Get you home.' Her mentor was back in her mind. She caught the feeling of his moving round and round in his coral-formed cell.

'I must think of man,' she said.

'Your thoughts mean nothing, do nothing.'

'Man created us; I want to consider him in peace.'

'He only shaped a stream of life that was always entirely out of his control. Forget him. Get on to your mare and ride home.'

'Mentor – '

'Get home, woman. Moping does not become you. I want to hear no more of your swansong, for I've given you my final word on that. Use a theme of your own, not of man's. I've said it a million times and I say it again.'

'I wasn't going to mention my music. I was only going to tell you that . . . '

'What then?' His thought was querulous. She felt his powerful tail tremble, disturbing the quiet water of his cell.

'I don't know . . . '

'Get home then.'

'I'm lonely.'

He shot her a picture from another of his wards before leaving her. Dandi had seen this ward before in similar dreamlike glimpses. It was a huge mole creature, still boring underground as it had been for the last twenty years. Occasionally it crawled through vast caves; once it swam in a subterranean lake, most of the while it just bored through rock. Its motivations were obscure to Dandi, although her mentor referred to it as 'a geologer'. Doubtless if the mole was vouchsafed occasional glimpses of Dandi and her musicolumnology, it would find her as baffling. At least the mentor's point was made: loneliness was psychological, not statistical.

Why, a million personalities glittered almost before her eyes!

She mounted the great baluchitherium mare and headed for home. Time and old monuments made glum company.

Twilight now, with just one streak of antique gold left in the sky, Venus sweetly bright, and stars peppering the purple. A fine night for being alive on, particularly with one's last bedtime close at hand.

And yes, for all her mentor said, she was going to turn into that old little piece derived from one of the tunes in the 1540 *Souter Liedekens*, that splendid source of Netherlands folk music. For a moment, Dandi Lashadusa chuckled almost as eruditely as her mentor. The sixteenth-century Old Time, with the virtual death of plainsong and virtual birth of the violin, was most interesting to her. Ah, the richness of facts, the texture of man's brief history! Pure joy! Then she remembered herself.

After all, she was only a megatherium, a sloth as big as an elephant, whose kind had been extinct for millions of years until man reconstituted a few of them in the Venusian experiments. Her modifications in the way of fingers and enlarged brain gave her no real qualifications to think up to man's level.

Early next morning, they arrived at the ramparts of the town Crotheria where Dandi lived. The ubiquitous goats thronged about them, some no bigger than hedgehogs, some almost as big as hippos – what madness in his last days provoked man to so many variations on one undistinguished caprine theme? – as Lass and her mistress moved up the last slope and under the archway.

It was good to be back, to push among the trails fringed with bracken, among the palms, oaks, and treeferns. Almost all the town was deeply green and private from the sun, curtained by swathes of Spanish moss. Here and there were houses – caves, pits, crude piles of boulders or even genuine man-type buildings, grand in ruin. Dandi climbed down, walking ahead of her mount, her long hair curling in pleasure. The air was cool with the coo of doves or the occasional bleat of a merino.

As she explored familiar ways, though, disappointment

overcame her. Her friends were all away, even the dreamy bison whose wallow lay at the corner of the street in which Dandi lived. Only pure animals were here, rooting happily and mindlessly in the lanes, beggars who owned the Earth. The Impures – descendants of the Venusian experimental stock – were all absent from Crotheria.

That was understandable. For obvious reasons, man had increased the abilities of herbivores rather than carnivores. After the Involution, with man gone, these Impures had taken to his towns as they took to his ways, as far as this was possible to their natures. Both Dandi and Lass, and many of the others, consumed massive amounts of vegetable matter every day. Gradually a wider and wider circle of desolation grew about each town (the greenery in the town itself was sacrosanct), forcing a semi-nomadic life on to its vegetarian inhabitants.

This thinning in its turn led to a decline in the birth rate. The travellers grew fewer, the town greener and emptier; in time they had become little oases of forest studding the grassless plains.

'Rest here, Lass,' Dandi said at last, pausing by a bank of brightly flowering cycads. 'I'm going into my house.'

A giant beech grew before the stone façade of her home, so close that it was hard to determine whether it did or did not help support the ancient building. A crumbling balcony jutted from the first floor. Reaching up, Dandi seized the balustrade and hauled herself onto the balcony.

This was her normal way of entering her home, for the ground floor was taken over by goats and hogs, just as the second floor had been appropriated by doves and parakeets. Trampling over the greenery self-sown on the balcony, she moved into the front room. Dandi smiled. Here were her old things, the broken furniture on which she liked to sleep, the vision screens on which nothing could be seen, the heavy manuscript books in which, guided by her know-all mentor, she wrote down the outpourings of the musicolumns she had visited all over the world.

She ambled through to the next room.

She paused, her peace of mind suddenly shattered by danger.

A brown bear stood there. One of its heavy hands was clenched over the hilt of a knife.

'I'm no vulgar thief,' it said, curling its thick black lips over the syllables. 'I am an archaeologer. If this is your place, you must grant me permission to remove the man things. Obviously you have no idea of the worth of some of the equipment here. We bears require it. We must have it.'

It came towards her, panting doggy fashion with its jaws open. From under bristling eyebrows gleamed the lust to kill.

Dandi was frightened. Peaceful by nature, she feared the bears above all creatures for their fierceness and their ability to organize. The bears were few: they were the only creatures to show signs of wishing to emulate man's old aggressiveness.

She knew what the bears did. They hurled themselves through the Involutes to increase their power; by penetrating those patterns, they nourished their psychic drive, so the mentor said. It was forbidden. They were transgressors. They were killers.

'Mentor!' she screamed.

The bear hesitated. As far as he was concerned, the hulking creature before him was merely an obstacle in the way of progress, something to be thrust aside without hate. Killing would be pleasant but irrelevant; more important items remained to be done. Much of the equipment housed here could be used in the rebuilding of the world, the world of which bears had such high haphazard dreams. Holding the knife threateningly, he moved forward.

The mentor was in Dandi's head, answering her cry, seeing through her eyes, though he had no sight of his own. He scanned the bear and took over her mind instantly, knifing himself into place like a guillotine.

No longer was he a blind old dolphin lurking in one cell of a cathedral pile of coral under tropical seas, a theologer, an inculcator of wisdom into feebler-minded beings. He was a killer more savage than the bear, keen to kill anything that might covet the vacant throne once held by men. The mere thought of men could send this mentor into shark-like fury at times.

Caught up in his fury, Dandi found herself advancing. For all the bear's strength, she could vanquish it. In the open, where she could have brought her heavy tail into action, it would have been an easy matter. Here, her weighty forearms must come into play. She felt them lift to her mentor's command as he planned for her to clout the bear to death.

The bear stepped back, awed by an opponent twice its size, suddenly unsure.

She advanced.

'No! Stop!' Dandi cried.

Instead of fighting the bear, she fought her mentor, hating his hate. Her mind twisted, her dim mind full of that steely fishy one, as she blocked his resolution.

'I'm for peace!' she cried.

'Then kill the bear!'

'I'm for peace, not killing!'

She rocked back and forth. When she staggered into a wall, it shook; dust spread in the old room. The mentor's fury was terrible to feel.

'Get out quickly!' Dandi called to the bear.

Hesitating, it stared at her. Then it turned and made for the window. For a moment it hung with its shaggy shabby hindquarters in the room. Momentarily she saw it for what it was, an old animal in an old world, without direction. It jumped. It was gone. Goats blared confusion on its retreat.

'Bitch!' screamed the mentor. Insane with frustration, he hurled Dandi against the doorway with all the force of his mind.

Wood cracked and splintered. The lintel came crashing down. Brick and stone shifted, grumbled, fell. Powdered filth billowed up. With a great roar, one wall collapsed. Dandi struggled to get free. Her house was tumbling about her. It had never been intended to carry so much weight, so many centuries.

She reached the balcony and jumped clumsily to safety,

just as the building avalanched in on itself, sending a great cloud of plaster and powdered mortar into the overhanging trees.

For a horribly long while the world was full of dust, goat bleats, and panic-stricken parakeets.

Heavily astride her baluchitherium once more, Dandi Lashadusa headed back to the empty region called Ghinomon. She fought her bitterness, trying to urge herself towards resignation.

All she had was destroyed – not that she set store by possessions: that was a man trait. Much more terrible was the knowledge that her mentor had left her for ever: she had transgressed too badly to be forgiven this time.

Suddenly she was lonely for his pernickety voice in her head, for the wisdom he fed her, for the scraps of dead knowledge he tossed her – yes, even for the love he gave her. She had never seen him, never could: yet no two beings could have been more intimate.

She missed too those other worlds of his she would glimpse no more: the mole creature tunnelling in Earth's depths, the seal family that barked with laughter on a desolate coast, a senile gorilla that endlessly collected and classified spiders, an aurochs – seen only once, but then unforgettably – that lived with smaller creatures in an Arctic city it had helped build in the ice.

She was excommunicated.

Well, it was time for her to change, to disintegrate, to transubstantiate into a pattern not of flesh but music. That discipline at least the mentor had taught and could not take away.

'This will do, Lass,' she said.

Her gigantic mount stopped obediently. Lovingly she patted its neck. It was young; it would be free.

Following the dusty trail, she went ahead, alone. Somewhere far off one bird called. Coming to a mound of boulders, Dandi squatted among gorse, the points of which could not prick through her old coat.

Already her selected music poured through her head, already it seemed to loosen the chemical bonds of her being.

Why should she not choose an old human tune? She was an antiquarian. Things that were gone solaced her for things that were to come.

In her dim way, she had always stood out against her mentor's absolute hatred of men. The thing to hate was hatred. Men in their finer moments had risen above hate. Her death psalm was an instance of that – a multiple instance, for it had been fingered and changed over the ages, as the mentor himself insisted, by men of a variety of races, all with their minds directed to worship rather than hate.

Locking herself into thought disciplines, Dandi began to dissolve. Man had needed machines to help him to do it, to fit into the Involutes. She was a lesser animal: she could unbutton herself into the humbler shape of a musicolumn. It was just a matter of *rearranging* – and without pain she formed into a pattern that was not a shaggy megatherium body . . . but an indigo column, hardly visible. . . .

Lass for a long while cropped thistle and cacti. Then she ambled forward to seek the hairy creature she fondly – and a little condescendingly – regarded as her equal. But of the sloth there was no sign.

Almost the only landmark was a faint violet-blue dye in the air. As the baluchitherium mare approached, a sweet old music grew in volume from the dye. It was a music almost as old as the landscape itself and certainly as much travelled, a tune once known to men as The Old Hundredth. And there were voices singing: 'All creatures that on Earth do dwell.'

A Work of Art

James Blish

Instantly, he remembered dying. He remembered it, however, as if at two removes – as though he were remembering
a memory, rather than an actual event; as though he himself
had not really been there when he died.

Yet the memory was all from his own point of view, not
that of some detached and disembodied observer which
might have been his soul. He had been most conscious of
the rasping, unevenly drawn movements of the air in his
chest. Blurring rapidly, the doctor's face had bent over him,
loomed, come closer, and then had vanished as the doctor's
head passed below his cone of vision, turned sideways to
listen to his lungs.

It had become rapidly darker, and then, only then, had
he realized that these were to be his last minutes. He had
tried dutifully to say Pauline's name, but his memory contained no record of the sound – only of the rattling breath,
and of the film of sootiness thickening in the air, blotting
out everything for an instant.

Only an instant, and then the memory was over. The
room was bright again, and the ceiling, he noticed with
wonder, had turned a soft green. The doctor's head lifted
again and looked down at him.

It was a different doctor. This one was a far younger man,
with an ascetic face and gleaming, almost fey eyes. There
was no doubt about it. One of the last conscious thoughts
he had had was that of gratitude that the attending physi-

cian, there at the end, had not been the one who secretly hated him for his one-time associations with the Nazi hierarchy. The attending doctor, instead, had worn an expression amusingly proper for that of a Swiss expert called to the deathbed of an eminent man: a mixture of worry at the prospect of losing so eminent a patient, and complacency at the thought that, at the old man's age, nobody could blame this doctor if he died. At eighty-five, pneumonia is a serious matter, with or without penicillin.

'You're all right now,' the new doctor said, freeing his patient's head of a whole series of little silver rods which had been clinging to it by a sort of network cap. 'Rest a minute and try to be calm. Do you know your name?'

He drew a cautious breath. There seemed to be nothing at all the matter with his lungs now; indeed, he felt positively healthy. 'Certainly,' he said, a little nettled. 'Do you know yours?'

The doctor smiled crookedly. 'You're in character, it appears,' he said. 'My name is Barkun Kris; I am a mind sculptor. Yours?'

'Richard Strauss.'

'Very good,' Dr Kris said, and turned away. Strauss, however, had already been diverted by a new singularity. *Strauss* is a word as well as a name in German; it has many meanings – an ostrich, a bouquet; von Wolzogen had had a high old time working all the possible puns into the libretto of *Feuersnot*. And it happened to be the first German word to be spoken either by himself or by Dr Kris since that twice-removed moment of death. The language was not French or Italian, either. It was most like English, but not the English Strauss knew; nevertheless, he was having no trouble speaking it and even thinking in it.

Well, he thought, *I'll be able to conduct* The Love of Danae *after all. It isn't every composer who can premiere his own opera posthumously.* Still, there was something queer about all this – the queerest part of all being that conviction, which would not go away, that he had actually been dead for just a short time. Of course medicine was making great strides, but . . .

'Explain all this,' he said, lifting himself to one elbow. The bed was different, too, and not nearly as comfortable as the one in which he had died. As for the room, it looked more like a dynamo shed than a sickroom. Had modern medicine taken to reviving its corpses on the floor of the Siemanns-Schukert plant?

'In a moment,' Dr Kris said. He finished rolling some machine back into what Strauss impatiently supposed to be its place, and crossed to the pallet. 'Now. There are many things you'll have to take for granted without attempting to understand them, Dr Strauss. Not everything in the world today is explicable in terms of your assumptions. Please bear that in mind.'

'Very well. Proceed.'

'The date,' Dr Kris said, 'is 2161 by your calendar – or, in other words, it is now two hundred and twelve years after your death. Naturally, you'll realize that by this time nothing remains of your body but the bones. The body you have now was volunteered for your use. Before you look into a mirror to see what it's like, remember that its physical difference from the one you were used to is all in your favour. It's in perfect health, not unpleasant for other people to look at, and its physiological age is about fifty.'

A miracle? No, not in this new age, surely. It was simply a work of science. But what a science! This was Nietzsche's eternal recurrence and the immortality of the superman combined into one.

'And where is this?' the composer said.

'In Port York, part of the State of Manhattan, in the United States. You will find the country less changed in some respects than I imagine you anticipate. Other changes, of course, will seem radical to you; but it's hard for me to predict which ones will strike you that way. A certain resilience on your part will bear cultivating.'

'I understand,' Strauss said, sitting up. 'One question, please; is it still possible for a composer to make a living in this century?'

'Indeed it is,' Dr Kris said, smiling. 'As we expect you to

do. It is one of the purposes for which we've – brought you back.'

'I gather, then,' Strauss said somewhat dryly, 'that there is still a demand for my music. The critics in the old days – '

'That's not quite how it is,' Dr Kris said. 'I understand some of your work is still played, but frankly I know very little about your current status. My interest is rather – '

A door opened somewhere, and another man came in. He was older and more ponderous than Kris and had a certain air of academicism; but he too was wearing the oddly tailored surgeon's gown, and looked upon Kris's patient with the glowing eyes of an artist.

'A success, Kris?' he said. 'Congratulations.'

'They're not in order yet,' Dr Kris said. 'The final proof is what counts. Dr Strauss, if you feel strong enough, Dr Seirds and I would like to ask you some questions. We'd like to make sure your memory is clear.'

'Certainly. Go ahead.'

'According to our records,' Kris said, 'you once knew a man whose initials were RKL; this was while you were conducting at the Vienna *Staatsoper*.' He made the double 'a' at least twice too long, as though German were a dead language he was striving to pronounce in some 'classical' accent. 'What was his name, and who was he?'

'That would be Kurt List – his first name was Richard, but he didn't use it. He was assistant stage manager.'

The two doctors looked at each other. 'Why did you offer to write a new overture to *The Woman Without a Shadow*, and give the manuscript to the City of Vienna?'

'So I wouldn't have to pay the garbage removal tax on the Maria Theresa villa they had given me.'

'In the back yard of your house at Garmisch-Parten-kirchen there was a tombstone. What was written on it?'

Strauss frowned. That was a question he would be happy to be unable to answer. If one is to play childish jokes upon oneself, it's best not to carve them in stone, and put the carving where you can't help seeing it every time you go out to tinker with the Mercedes. 'It says,' he replied wearily,

'*Sacred to the memory of Guntram, Minnesinger, slain in a horrible way by his father's own symphony orchestra.*'

'When was *Guntram* premiered?'

'In – let me see – 1894, I believe.'

'Where?'

'In Weimar.'

'Who was the leading lady?'

'Pauline de Ahna.'

'What happened to her afterward?'

'I married her. Is she . . . ' Strauss began anxiously.

'No,' Dr Kris said. 'I'm sorry, but we lack the data to reconstruct more or less ordinary people.'

The composer sighed. He did not know whether to be worried or not. He had loved Pauline, to be sure; on the other hand, it would be pleasant to be able to live the new life without being forced to take off one's shoes every time one entered the house, so as not to scratch the polished hardwood floors. And also pleasant, perhaps, to have two o'clock in the afternoon come by without hearing Pauline's everlasting, '*Richard – jetzt komponiert!*'

'Next question,' he said.

For reasons which Strauss did not understand, but was content to take for granted, he was separated from Drs Kris and Seirds as soon as both were satisfied that the composer's memory was reliable and his health stable. His estate, he was given to understand, had long since been broken up – a sorry end for what had been one of the principal fortunes of Europe – but he was given sufficient money to set up lodgings and resume an active life. He was provided, too, with introductions which proved valuable.

It took longer than he had expected to adjust to the changes that had taken place in music alone. Music was, he quickly began to suspect, a dying art, which would soon have a status not much above that held by flower arranging back in what he thought of as his own century. Certainly it couldn't be denied that the trend toward fragmentation, already visible back in his own time, had proceeded almost to completion in 2161.

He paid no more attention to American popular tunes than he had bothered to pay in his previous life. Yet it was evident that their assembly-line production methods – all the ballad composers openly used a slide-rule-like device called a Hit Machine – now had their counterparts almost throughout serious music.

The conservatives these days, for instance, were the twelve-tone composers – always, in Strauss's opinion, a dryly mechanical lot, but never more so than now. Their gods – Berg, Schoenberg, von Webern – were looked upon by the concert-going public as great masters, on the abstruse side perhaps, but as worthy of reverence as any of the Three Bs.

There was one wing of the conservatives, however, which had gone the twelve-tone procedure one better. These men composed what was called 'stochastic music', put together by choosing each individual note by consultation with tables of random numbers. Their bible, their basic text, was a volume called *Operational Aesthetics*, which in turn derived from a discipline called information theory; and not one word of it seemed to touch upon any of the techniques and customs of composition which Strauss knew. The ideal of this group was to produce music which would be 'universal' – that is, wholly devoid of any trace of the composer's individuality, wholly a musical expression of the universal Laws of Chance. The Laws of Chance seemed to have a style of their own, all right; but to Strauss it seemed the style of an idiot child being taught to hammer a flat piano, to keep him from getting into trouble.

By far the largest body of work being produced, however, fell into a category misleadingly called 'science-music'. The term reflected nothing but the titles of the works, which dealt with space flight, time-travel, and other subjects of a romantic or an unlikely nature. There was nothing in the least scientific about the music, which consisted of a mélange of clichés and imitations of natural sounds, in which Strauss was horrified to see his own time-distorted and diluted image.

The most popular form of science-music was a nine-minute composition called a concerto, though it bore no resemblance at all to the classical concerto form; it was instead a sort of free rhapsody after Rachmaninoff – long after. A typical one – 'Song of Deep Space' it was called, by somebody named H. Valerion Krafft – began with a loud assault on the tam-tam, after which all the strings rushed up the scale in unison, followed at a respectful distance by the harp and one clarinet in parallel 6/4s. At the top of the scale cymbals were bashed together, *forte possibile*, and the whole orchestra launched itself into a major-minor, wailing sort of melody; the whole orchestra, that is, except for the French horns, which were plodding back down the scale again in what was evidently supposed to be a countermelody. The second phrase of the theme was picked up by a solo trumpet with a suggestion of tremolo; the orchestra died back to its roots to await the next cloudburst, and at this point – as any four-year-old could have predicted – the piano entered with the second theme.

Behind the orchestra stood a group of thirty women, ready to come in with a wordless chorus intended to suggest the eeriness of Deep Space – but at this point, too, Strauss had already learned to get up and leave. After a few such experiences he could also count upon meeting in the lobby Sindi Noniss, the agent to whom Dr Kris had introduced him, and who was handling the reborn composer's output – what there was of it thus far. Sindi had come to expect these walkouts on the part of his client, and patiently awaited them, standing beneath a bust of Gian Carlo Menotti; but he liked them less and less, and lately had been greeting them by turning alternately red and white like a toti-potent barber pole.

'You shouldn't have done it,' he burst out after the Krafft incident. 'You can't just walk out on a new Krafft composition. The man's the president of the Interplanetary Society for Contemporary Music. How am I ever going to persuade them that you're a contemporary if you keep snubbing them?'

'What does it matter?' Strauss said. 'They don't know me by sight.'

'You're wrong; they know you very well, and they're watching every move you make. You're the first major composer the mind sculptors ever tackled, and the ISCM would be glad to turn you back with a rejection slip.'

'Why?'

'Oh,' said Sindi, 'there are lots of reasons. The sculptors are snobs; so are the ISCM boys. Each of them wants to prove to the other that their own art is the king of them all. And then there's the competition; it would be easier to flunk you than to let you into the market. I really think you'd better go back in. I could make up some excuse – '

'No,' Strauss said shortly. 'I have work to do.'

'But that's just the point, Richard. How are we going to get an opera produced without the ISCM? It isn't as though you wrote theremin solos, or something that didn't cost so – '

'I have work to do,' he said and left.

And he did: work which absorbed him as had no other project during the last thirty years of his former life. He had scarcely touched pen to music paper – both had been astonishingly hard to find – when he realized that nothing in his long career had provided him with touchstones by which to judge what music he should write *now*.

The old tricks came swarming back by the thousands, to be sure: the sudden, unexpected key changes at the crest of a melody; the interval stretching; the piling of divided strings, playing in the high harmonics, upon the already tottering top of a climax; the scurry and bustle as phrases were passed like lightning from one choir of the orchestra to another; the flashing runs in the brass, the chuckling in the clarinets, the snarling mixtures of colours to emphasize dramatic tension – all of them.

But none of them satisfied him now. He had been content with them for most of a lifetime, and had made them do an astonishing amount of work. But now it was time to strike out afresh. Some of the tricks, indeed, actively repelled him: where had he gotten the notion, clung to for decades, that violins screaming out in unison somewhere in the stratosphere was a sound interesting enough to be worth repeating inside a single composition, let alone in all of them?

And nobody, he reflected contentedly, ever approached such a new beginning better equipped. In addition to the past lying available in his memory, he had always had a technical armamentarium second to none; even the hostile critics had granted him that. Now that he was, in a sense, composing his first opera – his first after fifteen of them – he had every opportunity to make it a masterpiece.

And every such intention.

There were, of course, many minor distractions. One of them was that search for old-fashioned score paper, and a pen and ink with which to write on it. Very few of the modern composers, it developed, wrote their music at all. A large bloc of them used tape, patching together snippets of tone and sound snipped from other tapes, superimposing one tape on another, and varying the results by twirling an elaborate array of knobs this way or that. Almost all the composers of 3-V scores, on the other hand, wrote on the sound track itself, rapidly scribbling jagged wiggly lines which, when passed through a photocell-audio circuit, produced a noise reasonably like an orchestra playing music, overtones and all.

The last-ditch conservatives who still wrote notes on paper, did so with the aid of a musical typewriter. The device, Strauss had to admit, seemed perfected at last; it had manuals and stops like an organ, but it was not much more than twice as large as a standard letter-writing typewriter, and produced a neat page. But he was satisfied with his own spidery, highly legible manuscript and refused to abandon it, badly though the one pen nib he had been able to buy coarsened it. It helped to tie him to his past.

Joining the ISCM had also caused him some bad moments, even after Sindi had worked him around the political road blocks. The Society man who examined his qualifications as a member had run through the questions with no more interest than might have been shown by a veterinarian examining his four thousandth sick calf.

'Had anything published?'

'Yes, nine tone poems, about three hundred songs, an – '

'Not when you were alive,' the examiner said, somewhat disquietingly. 'I mean since the sculptors turned you out again.'

'Since the sculptors – ah, I understand. Yes, a string quartet, two song cycles, a – '

'Good. Alfie, write down "songs". Play an instrument?'

'Piano.'

'Hm.' The examiner studied his fingernails. 'Oh, well. Do you read music? Or do you use a Scriber, or tape clips? Or a Machine?'

'I read.'

'Here.' The examiner sat Strauss down in front of a viewing lectern, over the lit surface of which an endless belt of translucent paper was travelling. On the paper was an immensely magnified sound track. 'Whistle me the tune of that, and name the instruments it sounds like.'

'I don't read that *Musiksticheln*,' Strauss said frostily, 'or write it, either. I use standard notation, on music paper.'

'Alfie, write down "Reads notes only". ' He laid a sheet of greyly printed music on the lectern above the ground glass. 'Whistle me that.'

'That' proved to be a popular tune called 'Vangs, Snifters and Store-Credit Snooky' which had been written on a Hit Machine in 2159 by a guitar-faking politician who sang it at campaign rallies. (In some respects, Strauss reflected, the United States had indeed not changed very much.) It had become so popular that anybody could have whistled it from the title alone, whether he could read the music or not. Strauss whistled it, and to prove his bona fides added, 'It's in the key of B flat.'

The examiner went over to the green-painted upright piano and hit one greasy black key. The instrument was horribly out of tune – the note was much nearer to the standard 440/cps A than it was to B flat – but the examiner said, 'So it is. Alfie, write down, "Also reads flats". All right, son, you're a member. Nice to have you with us; not many people can read that old-style notation any more. A lot of them think they're too good for it.'

'Thank you,' Strauss said.

'My feeling is, if it was good enough for the old masters, it's good enough for us. We don't have people like them with us these days, it seems to me. Except for Dr Krafft, of course. They were *great* back in the old days – men like Shilkrit, Steiner, Tiomkin, and Pearl . . . and Wilder and Jannsen. Real goffin.'

'*Doch gewiss*,' Strauss said politely.

But the work went forward. He was making a little income now, from small works. People seemed to feel a special interest in a composer who had come out of the mind sculptors' laboratories; and in addition the material itself, Strauss was quite certain, had merits of its own to help sell it.

It was the opera which counted, however. That grew and grew under his pen, as fresh and new as his new life, as founded in knowledge and ripeness as his long full memory. Finding a libretto had been troublesome at first. While it was possible that something existed that might have served among the current scripts for 3-V – though he doubted it – he found himself unable to tell the good from the bad through the fog cast over both by incomprehensibly technical production directions. Eventually, and for only the third time in his whole career, he had fallen back upon a play written in a language other than his own, and – for the first time – decided to set it in that language.

The play was Christopher Fry's *Venus Observed*, in all ways a perfect Strauss opera libretto, as he came gradually to realize. Though nominally a comedy, with a complex farcical plot, it was a verse play with considerable depth to it, and a number of characters who cried out to be brought by music into three dimensions, plus a strong undercurrent of autumnal tragedy, of leaf-fall and apple-fall – precisely the kind of contradictory dramatic mixture which von

Hofmannsthal had supplied him with in *The Knight of the Rose,* in *Ariadne at Naxos*, and in *Arabella.*

Alas for von Hofmannsthal, but here was another long-dead playwright who seemed nearly as gifted; and the musical opportunities were immense. There was, for instance, the fire which ended act two; what a gift for a composer to whom orchestration and counterpoint were as important as air and water! Or take the moment where Perpetua shoots the apple from the Duke's hand; in that one moment a single passing reference could add Rossini's marmoreal *William Tell* to the musical texture as nothing but an ironic footnote! And the Duke's great curtain speech, beginning:

> Shall I be sorry for myself? In Mortality's name,
> I'll be sorry for myself. Branches and boughs,
>   Brown hills, the valleys faint with brume,
>   A burnish on the lake . . .

There was a speech for a great tragic comedian, in the spirit of Falstaff; the final union of laughter and tears, punctuated by the sleepy comments of Reedbeck, to whose sonorous snore (trombones, no less than five of them, *con sordini?*) the opera would gently end . . .

What could be better? And yet he had come upon the play only by the unlikeliest series of accidents. At first he had planned to do a straight knockabout farce, in the idiom of *The Silent Woman*, just to warm himself up. Remembering that Zweig had adapted that libretto for him, in the old days, from a play by Ben Jonson, Strauss had begun to search out English plays of the period just after Jonson's, and had promptly run aground on an awful specimen called *Venice Preserv'd*, by one Thomas Otway. The Fry play had directly followed the Otway in the card catalogue, and he had looked at it out of curiosity; why should a twentieth-century playwright be punning on a title from the eighteenth?

After two pages of the Fry play, the minor puzzle of the pun disappeared entirely from his concern. His luck was running again; he had an opera.

Sindi worked miracles in arranging for the performance. The date of the premiere was set even before the score was finished, reminding Strauss pleasantly of those heady days when Fuerstner had been snatching the conclusion of *Elektra* off his work table a page at a time, before the ink was even dry, to rush it to the engraver before publication deadline. The situation now, however, was even more complicated, for some of the score had to be scribed, some of it taped, some of it engraved in the old way, to meet the new techniques of performance; there were moments when Sindi seemed to be turning quite grey.

But *Venus Observed* was, as usual, forthcoming complete from Strauss's pen in plenty of time. Writing the music in first draft had been hellishly hard work, much more like being reborn than had been that confused awakening in Barkun Kris's laboratory, with its overtones of being dead instead; but Strauss found that he still retained all of his old ability to score from the draft almost effortlessly, as undisturbed by Sindi's half-audible worrying in the room with him as he was by the terrifying supersonic bangs of the rockets that bulleted invisibly over the city.

When he was finished, he had two days still to spare before the beginning of rehearsals. With those, furthermore, he would have nothing to do. The techniques of performance in this age were so completely bound up with the electronic arts as to reduce his own experience – he, the master *Kapellmeister* of them all – to the hopelessly primitive.

He did not mind. The music, as written, would speak for itself. In the meantime he found it grateful to forget the months-long preoccupation with the stage for a while. He went back to the library and browsed lazily through old poems, vaguely seeking texts for a song or two. He knew better than to bother with recent poets; they could not speak to him, and he knew it. The Americans of his own age, he thought, might give him a clue to understanding this America of 2161; and if some such poem gave birth to a song, so much the better.

The search was relaxing and he gave himself up to enjoying it. Finally he struck a tape that he liked: a tape read in a cracked old voice that twanged of Idaho as that voice had twanged in 1910, in Strauss's own ancient youth. The poet's name was Pound; he said, on the tape

> . . . the souls of all men great
> At times pass through us,
> And we are melted into them, and are not
> Save reflexions of their souls.
> Thus I am Dante for a space and am
> One François Villon, ballad-lord and thief
> Or am such holy ones I may not write,
> Lest Blasphemy be writ against my name;
> This for an instant and the flame is gone.
> 'Tis as in midmost us there glows a sphere
> Translucent, molten gold, that is the 'I'
> And into this some form projects itself:
> Christus, or John, or eke the Florentine;
> And as the clear space is not if a form's
> Imposed thereon,
> So cease we from all being for the time,
> And these, the Masters of the Soul, live on.

He smiled. That lesson had been written again and again, from Plato onward. Yet the poem was a history of his own case, a sort of theory for the metempsychosis he had undergone, and in its formal way it was moving. It would be fitting to make a little hymn of it, in honour of his own rebirth, and of the poet's insight.

A series of solemn, breathless chords framed themselves in his inner ear, against which the words might be intoned in a high, gently blending hush at the beginning . . . and then a dramatic passage in which the great names of Dante and Villon would enter ringing like challenges to Time . . . He wrote for a while in his notebook before he returned the spool to its shelf.

These, he thought, are good auspices.

And so the night of the premiere arrived, the audience pouring into the hall, the 3-V cameras riding on no visible supports through the air, and Sindi calculating his share of his client's earnings by a complicated game he played on his fingers, the basic law of which seemed to be that one plus one equals ten. The hall filled to the roof with people from every class, as though what was to come would be a circus rather than an opera.

There were, surprisingly, nearly fifty of the aloof and aristocratic mind sculptors, clad in formal clothes which were exaggerated black versions of their surgeon's gowns. They had bought a bloc of seats near the front of the auditorium, where the gigantic 3-V figures which would shortly fill the 'stage' before them (the real singers would perform on a small stage in the basement) could not but seem monstrously out of proportion; but Strauss supposed that they had taken this into account and dismissed it.

There was a tide of whispering in the audience as the sculptors began to trickle in, and with it an undercurrent of excitement the meaning of which was unknown to Strauss. He did not attempt to fathom it, however; he was coping with his own mounting tide of opening-night tension, which, despite all the years, he had never quite been able to shake.

The sourceless, gentle light in the auditorium dimmed, and Strauss mounted the podium. There was a score before him, but he doubted that he would need it. Directly before him, poking up from among the musicians, were the inevitable 3-V snouts, waiting to carry his image to the singers in the basement.

The audience was quiet now. This was the moment. His baton swept up and then decisively down, and the prelude came surging up out of the pit.

For a little while he was deeply immersed in the always tricky business of keeping the enormous orchestra together and sensitive to the flexing of the musical web beneath his hand. As his control firmed and became secure, however, the task became slightly less demanding, and he was able to pay more attention to what the whole sounded like.

There was something decidedly wrong with it. Of course there were the occasional surprises as some bit of orchestral colour emerged with a different *Klang* than he had expected;

that happened to every composer, even after a lifetime of experience. And there were moments when the singers, entering upon a phrase more difficult to handle than he had calculated, sounded like someone about to fall off a tight-rope (although none of them actually fluffed once; they were as fine a troupe of voices as he had ever had to work with).

But these were details. It was the over-all impression that was wrong. He was losing not only the excitement of the premiere – after all, that couldn't last at the same pitch all evening – but also his very interest in what was coming from the stage and the pit. He was gradually tiring; his baton arm becoming heavier; as the second act mounted to what should have been an impassioned outpouring of shining tone, he was so bored as to wish he could go back to his desk to work on that song.

Then the act was over; only one more to go. He scarcely heard the applause. The twenty minutes' rest in his dressing room was just barely enough to give him the necessary strength.

And suddenly, in the middle of the last act, he understood.

There was nothing new about the music. It was the old Strauss all over again – but weaker, more dilute than ever. Compared with the output of composers like Krafft, it doubtless sounded like a masterpiece to this audience. But he knew.

The resolutions, the determination to abandon the old clichés and mannerisms, the decision to say something new – they had all come to nothing against the force of habit. Being brought to life again meant bringing to life as well all those deeply graven reflexes of his style. He had only to pick up his pen and they overpowered him with easy auto-matism, no more under his control than the jerk of a finger away from a flame.

His eyes filled; his body was young, but he was an old man, an old man. Another thirty-five years of this? Never. He had said all this before, centuries before. Nearly a half century condemned to saying it all over again, in a weaker and still weaker voice, aware that even this debased century would come to recognize in him only the burnt husk of greatness? – no; never, never.

He was aware, dully, that the opera was over. The audience was screaming its joy. He knew the sound. They had screamed that way when *Day of Peace* had been premiered, but they had been cheering the man he had been, not the man that *Day of Peace* showed with cruel clarity he had become. Here the sound was even more meaningless: cheers of ignorance, and that was all.

He turned slowly. With surprise, and with a surprising sense of relief, he saw that the cheers were not, after all, for him.

They were for Dr Barkun Kris.

Kris was standing in the middle of the bloc of mind sculptors, bowing to the audience. The sculptors nearest him were shaking his hand one after the other. More grasped at it as he made his way to the aisle, and walked forward to the podium. When he mounted the rostrum and took the composer's limp hand, the cheering became delirious.

Kris lifted his arm. The cheering died instantly to an intent hush.

'Thank you,' he said clearly. 'Ladies and gentlemen, before we take leave of Dr Strauss, let us again tell him what a privilege it has been for us to hear this fresh example of his mastery. I am sure no farewell could be more fitting.'

The ovation lasted five minutes, and would have gone another five if Kris had not cut it off.

'Dr Strauss,' he said, 'in a moment, when I speak a certain formulation to you, you will realize that your name is Jerom Bosch, born in our century and with a life in it all your own. The superimposed memories which have made you assume the mask, the *persona*, of a great composer will be gone. I tell you this so that you may understand why these people here share your applause with me.'

A wave of assenting sound.

'The art of mind sculpture – the creation of artificial personalities for aesthetic enjoyment – may never reach such a pinnacle again. For you should understand that as Jerom Bosch you had no talent for music at all; indeed, we searched a long time to find a man who was utterly unable to carry even the simplest tune. Yet we were able to impose upon such unpromising material not only the personality, but the genius, of a great composer. That genius belongs entirely to you – to the *persona* that thinks of itself as Richard Strauss. None of the credit goes to the man who volunteered for the sculpture. That is your triumph, and we salute you for it.'

Now the ovation could no longer be contained. Strauss, with a crooked smile, watched Dr Kris bow. This mind sculpturing was a suitably sophisticated kind of cruelty for this age; but the impulse, of course, had always existed. It was the same impulse that had made Rembrandt and Leonardo turn cadavers into art works.

It deserved a suitably sophisticated payment under the *lex talionis*: an eye for an eye, a tooth for a tooth – and a failure for a failure.

No, he need not tell Dr Kris that the 'Strauss' he had created was as empty of genius as a hollow gourd. The joke would always be on the sculptor, who was incapable of hearing the hollowness of the music now preserved on the 3-V tapes.

But for an instant a surge of revolt poured through his blood stream. *I am I*, he thought. *I am Richard Strauss until I die, and will never be Jerom Bosch, who was utterly unable to carry even the simplest tune.* His hand, still holding the baton, came sharply up, though whether to deliver or to ward off a blow he could not tell.

He let it fall again, and instead, at last, bowed – not to the audience, but to Dr Kris. He was sorry for nothing, as Kris turned to him to say the word that would plunge him back into oblivion, except that he would now have no chance to set that poem to music.

Harrison Bergeron

Kurt Vonnegut Jr

The year was 2081, and everybody was finally equal. They weren't only equal before God and the law, they were equal every which way. Nobody was smarter than anybody else; nobody was better looking than anybody else; nobody was stronger or quicker than anybody else. All this equality was due to the 211th, 212th and 213th Amendments to the Constitution, and to the unceasing vigilance of agents of the United States Handicapper General.

Some things about living still weren't quite right, though. April, for instance, still drove people crazy by not being spring time. And it was in that clammy month that the H-G men took George and Hazel Bergeron's fourteen-year-old son, Harrison, away.

It was tragic, all right, but George and Hazel couldn't think about it very hard. Hazel had a perfectly average intelligence, which meant she couldn't think about anything except in short bursts. And George, while his intelligence was way above normal, had a little mental handicap radio in his ear – he was required by law to wear it at all times. It was tuned to a government transmitter, and every twenty seconds or so, the transmitter would send out some sharp noise to keep people like George from taking unfair advantage of their brains.

George and Hazel were watching television. There were tears on Hazel's cheeks, but she'd forgotten for the moment what they were about, as the ballerinas came to the end of a dance.

A buzzer sounded in George's head. His thoughts fled in panic, like bandits from a burglar alarm.

'That was a real pretty dance, that dance they just did,' said Hazel.

'Huh?' said George.

'That dance – it was nice,' said Hazel.

'Yup,' said George. He tried to think a little about the ballerinas. They weren't really very good – no better than anybody else would have been, anyway. They were burdened with sashweights and bags of birdshot, and their faces were masked, so that no one, seeing a free and graceful gesture or a pretty face, would feel like something the cat dragged in. George was toying with the vague notion that maybe dancers shouldn't be handicapped. But he didn't get very far with it before another noise in his ear radio scattered his thoughts.

George winced. So did two out of the eight ballerinas.

Hazel saw him wince. Having no mental handicap herself, she had to ask George what the latest sound had been.

'Sounded like somebody hitting a milk bottle with a ball-pen hammer,' said George.

'I'd think it would be real interesting, hearing all the different sounds,' said Hazel, a little envious. 'The things they think up.'

'Um,' said George.

'Only, if I was Handicapper General, you know what I would do?' said Hazel. Hazel, as a matter of fact, bore a strong resemblance to the Handicapper General, a woman named Diana Moon Glampers. 'If I was Diana Moon Glampers,' said Hazel, 'I'd have chimes on Sunday – just chimes. Kind of in honour of religion.'

'I could think if it was just chimes,' said George.

'Well – maybe make 'em real loud,' said Hazel. 'I think I'd make a good Handicapper General.'

'Good as anybody else,' said George.

'Who knows better'n I do what normal is?' said Hazel.

'Right,' said George. He began to think glimmeringly about his abnormal son who was now in jail, about Harrison, but a twenty-one gun salute in his head stopped that.

'Boy!' said Hazel, 'that was a doozy, wasn't it?'

It was such a doozy that George was white and trembling, and tears stood on the rims of his red eyes. Two of the eight ballerinas had collapsed to the studio floor, were holding their temples.

'All of a sudden you look so tired,' said Hazel. 'Why don't you stretch out on the sofa, so's you can rest your handicap bag on the pillows, honeybunch.' She was referring to the forty-seven pounds of birdshot in a canvas bag, which was padlocked around George's neck. 'Go on and rest the bag for a while,' she said. 'I don't care if you're not equal to me for a while.'

George weighed the bag with his hands. 'I don't mind it,' he said. 'I don't notice it any more. It's just part of me.'

'You have been so tired lately – kind of wore out,' said Hazel. 'If there was just some way we could make a little hole in the bottom of the bag, and just take out a few of them lead balls. Just a few.'

'Two years in prison and two-thousand dollars fine for every ball I took out,' said George. 'I don't call that a bargain.'

'If you could just take a few out when you came home from work,' said Hazel. 'I mean – you don't compete with anybody around here. You just set around.'

'If I tried to get away with it,' said George, 'then other people'd get away with it – and pretty soon we'd be right back to the dark ages again, with everybody competing against everybody else. You wouldn't like that, would you?'

'I'd hate it,' said Hazel.

'There you are,' said George. 'The minute people start cheating on laws, what do you think happens to society?'

If Hazel hadn't been able to come up with an answer to this question, George couldn't have supplied one. A siren was going off in his head.

'Reckon it'd fall all apart,' said Hazel.

'What would?' said George blankly.

'Society,' said Hazel uncertainly. 'Wasn't that what you just said?'

'Who knows?' said George.

The television programme was suddenly interrupted for a news bulletin. It wasn't clear at first as to what the bulletin was about, since the announcer, like all announcers, had a serious speech impediment. For about half a minute, and in a state of high excitement, the announcer tried to say, 'Ladies and gentlemen – '

He finally gave up, handed the bulletin to a ballerina to read.

'That's all right,' Hazel said of the announcer, 'he tried. That's the big thing. He tried to do the best he could with what God gave him. He should get a nice raise for trying so hard.'

'Ladies and gentlemen – ' said the ballerina, reading the bulletin. She must have been extraordinarily beautiful, because the mask she wore was hideous. And it was easy to see that she was the strongest and most graceful of all the dancers, for her handicap bags were as big as those worn by two-hundred-pound men.

And she had to apologize at once for her voice, which was a very unfair voice for a woman to use. Her voice was a warm, luminous, timeless melody. 'Excuse me – ' she said, and she began again, making her voice absolutely uncompetitive.

'Harrison Bergeron, age fourteen,' she said in a grackle squawk, 'has just escaped from jail, where he was held on suspicion of plotting to overthrow the government. He is a genius and an athlete, is under-handicapped, and is extremely dangerous.'

A police photograph of Harrison Bergeron was flashed on the screen – upside down, then sideways, upside down again, then right-side up. The picture showed the full length of Harrison against a background calibrated in feet and inches. He was exactly seven feet tall.

The rest of Harrison's appearance was Halloween and hardware. Nobody had ever borne heavier handicaps. He had outgrown hindrances faster than the H-G men could think them up. Instead of a little ear radio for a mental handicap, he wore a tremendous pair of earphones, and spectacles with thick, wavy lenses besides. The spectacles were intended not only to make him half blind, but to give him whanging headaches besides.

Scrap metal was hung all over him. Ordinarily, there was a certain symmetry, a military neatness to the handicaps issued to strong people, but Harrison looked like a walking junkyard. In the race of life, Harrison carried three hundred pounds.

And to offset his good looks, the H-G men required that he wear at all times a red rubber ball for a nose, keep his eyebrows shaved off, and cover his even white teeth with black caps at snaggle-tooth random.

'If you see this boy,' said the ballerina, 'do not – I repeat, do not – try to reason with him.'

There was the shriek of a door being torn from its hinges.

Screams and barking cries of consternation came from the television set. The photograph of Harrison Bergeron on the screen jumped again and again, as though dancing to the tune of an earthquake.

George Bergeron correctly identified the earthquake, and well he might have – for many was the time his own home had danced to the same crashing tune. 'My God!' said George. 'That must be Harrison!'

The realization was blasted from his mind instantly by the sound of an automobile collision in his head.

When George could open his eyes again, the photograph of Harrison was gone. A living, breathing Harrison filled the screen.

Clanking, clownish, and huge, Harrison stood in the centre of the studio. The knob of the uprooted studio door was still in his hand. Ballerinas, technicians, musicians and announcers cowered on their knees before him, expecting to die.

'I am the Emperor!' cried Harrison. 'Do you hear? I am the Emperor! Everybody must do what I say at once!' He stamped his foot and the studio shook.

'Even as I stand here,' he bellowed, 'crippled, hobbled, sickened – I am a greater ruler than any man who ever lived! Now watch me become what I *can* become!'

Harrison tore the straps of his handicap harness like wet

tissue paper, tore straps guaranteed to support five thousand pounds.

Harrison's scrap-iron handicaps crashed to the floor.

Harrison thrust his thumbs under the bar of the padlock that secured his head harness. The bar snapped like celery. Harrison smashed his headphones and spectacles against the wall.

He flung away his rubber-ball nose, revealed a man that would have awed Thor, the god of thunder.

'I shall now select my Empress!' he said, looking down on the cowering people. 'Let the first woman who dares rise to her feet claim her mate and her throne!'

A moment passed, and then a ballerina arose, swaying like a willow.

Harrison plucked the mental handicap from her ear, snapped off her physical handicaps with marvellous delicacy. Last of all, he removed her mask.

She was blindingly beautiful.

'Now – ' said Harrison, taking her hand. 'Shall we show the people the meaning of the word dance? Music!' he commanded.

The musicians scrambled back into their chairs, and Harrison stripped them of their handicaps, too. 'Play your best,' he told them, 'and I'll make you barons and dukes and earls.'

The music began. It was normal at first – cheap, silly, false. But Harrison snatched two musicians from their chairs, waved them like batons as he sang the music as he wanted it played. He slammed them back into their chairs.

The music began again, and was much improved.

Harrison and his Empress merely listened to the music for a while – listened gravely, as though synchronizing their heart beats with it.

They shifted their weight to their toes.

Harrison placed his big hands on the girl's tiny waist, letting her sense the weightlessness that would soon be hers.

And then, in an explosion of joy and grace, into the air they sprang!

Not only were the laws of the land abandoned, but the law of gravity and the laws of motion as well.

They reeled, whirled, swivelled, flounced, capered, gambolled and spun.

They leaped like deer on the moon.

The studio ceiling was thirty feet high, but each leap brought the dancers nearer to it.

It became their obvious intention to kiss the ceiling.

They kissed it.

And then, neutralizing gravity with love and pure will, they remained suspended in air inches below the ceiling, and they kissed each other for a long, long time.

It was then that Diana Moon Glampers, the Handicapper General, came into the studio with a double-barrelled ten-gauge shot-gun. She fired twice, and the Emperor and the Empress were dead before they hit the floor.

Diana Moon Glampers loaded the gun again. She aimed it at the musicians and told them they had ten seconds to get their handicaps back on.

It was then that the Bergerons' television tube burned out.

Hazel turned to comment about the blackout to George. But George had gone out into the kitchen for a can of beer.

George came back in with the beer, paused while a handicap signal shook him up. And then he sat down again. 'You been crying?' he said to Hazel, watching her wipe her tears.

'Yup,' she said.

'What about?' he said.

'I forget,' she said. 'Something real sad on television.'

'What was it?' he said.

'It's kind of mixed up in my mind,' said Hazel.

'Forget sad things,' said George.

'I always do,' said Hazel.

'That's my girl,' said George. He winced. There was the sound of a riveting gun in his head.

'Gee – I could tell that one was a doozy,' said Hazel.

'You can say that again,' said George.

'Gee – ' said Hazel – 'I could tell that one was a doozy.'

The Voices of Time

J. G. Ballard

1

Later Powers often thought of Whitby, and the strange grooves the biologist had cut, apparently at random, all over the floor of the empty swimming pool. An inch deep and twenty feet long, interlocking to form an elaborate ideogram like a Chinese character, they had taken him all summer to complete, and he had obviously thought about little else, working away tirelessly through the long desert afternoons. Powers had watched him from his office window at the far end of the neurology wing, carefully marking out his pegs and string, carrying away the cement chips in a small canvas bucket. After Whitby's suicide no one had bothered about the grooves, but Powers often borrowed the supervisor's key and let himself into the disused pool, and would look down at the labyrinth of mouldering gulleys, half-filled with water leaking in from the chlorinator, an enigma now past any solution.

Initially, however, Powers was too preoccupied with completing his work at the clinic and planning his own final withdrawal. After the first frantic weeks of panic he had managed to accept an uneasy compromise which allowed him to view his predicament with the detached fatalism he had previously reserved for his patients. Fortunately he was moving down the physical and mental gradients simultaneously – lethargy and inertia blunted his anxieties, a slackening metabolism made it necessary to concentrate to produce a connected thought-train. In fact, the lengthening intervals of dreamless sleep were almost restful. He found himself beginning to look forward to them, made no effort to wake earlier than was essential.

At first he had kept an alarm clock by his bed, tried to compress as much activity as he could into the narrowing hours of consciousness, sorting out his library, driving over to Whitby's laboratory every morning to examine the latest batch of X-ray plates, every minute and hour rationed like the last drops of water in a canteen.

Anderson, fortunately, had unwittingly made him realize the pointlessness of this course.

After Powers had resigned from the clinic he still continued to drive in once a week for his check-up, now little more than a formality. On what turned out to be the last occasion Anderson had perfunctorily taken his blood count, noting Powers' slacker facial muscles, fading pupil reflexes, the unshaven cheeks.

He smiled sympathetically at Powers across the desk, wondering what to say to him. Once he had put on a show of encouragement with the more intelligent patients, even tried to provide some sort of explanation. But Powers was too difficult to reach – neurosurgeon extraordinary, a man always out on the periphery, only at ease working with unfamiliar materials. To himself, he thought: *I'm sorry, Robert. What can I say – 'Even the sun is growing cooler?'* He watched Powers drum his fingers restlessly on the enamel desk top, his eyes glancing at the spinal level charts hung around the office. Despite his unkempt appearance – he had been wearing the same unironed shirt and dirty white plimsolls a week ago – Powers looked composed and self-possessed, like a Conrad beachcomber more or less reconciled to his own weaknesses.

'What are you doing with yourself, Robert?' he asked. 'Are you still going over to Whitby's lab?'

'As much as I can. It takes me half an hour to cross the lake, and I keep on sleeping through the alarm clock. I may leave my place and move in there permanently.'

Anderson frowned. 'Is there much point? As far as I could make out, Whitby's work was pretty speculative – ' He broke off, realizing the implied criticism of Powers' own disastrous work at the clinic, but Powers seemed to ignore this, was examining the pattern of shadows on the ceiling. 'Anyway, wouldn't it be better to stay where you are, among your own things, read through Toynbee and Spengler again?'

Powers laughed shortly. 'That's the last thing I want to do. I want to *forget* Toynbee and Spengler, not try to remember them. In fact, Paul, I'd like to forget everything. I don't know whether I've got enough time, though. How much can you forget in three months?'

'Everything, I suppose, if you want to. But don't try to race the clock.'

Powers nodded quietly, repeating this last remark to himself. Racing the clock was exactly what he had been doing. As he stood up and said goodbye to Anderson he suddenly decided to throw away his alarm clock, escape from his futile obsession with time. To remind himself he unfastened his wristwatch and scrambled the setting, then slipped it into his pocket. Making his way out to the car park he reflected on the freedom this simple act gave him. He would explore the lateral byways now, the side doors, as it were, in the corridors of time. Three months could be an eternity.

He picked his car out of the line and strolled over to it, shielding his eyes from the heavy sunlight beating down across the parabolic sweep of the lecture theatre roof. He was about to climb in when saw that someone had traced with a finger across the dust caked over the windshield:

$$96,688,365,498,721$$

Looking over his shoulder, he recognized the white Packard parked next to him, peered inside and saw a lean-faced young man with blond sun-bleached hair and a high cerebrotonic forehead watching him behind dark glasses. Sitting beside him at the wheel was a raven-haired girl whom he had often seen around the psychology department. She had intelligent but somehow rather oblique eyes, and Powers remembered that the younger doctors called her 'the girl from Mars'.

'Hello, Kaldren,' Powers said to the young man. 'Still following me around?'

Kaldren nodded. 'Most of the time, Doctor.' He sized Powers up shrewdly. 'We haven't seen very much of you recently, as a matter of fact. Anderson said you'd resigned, and we noticed your laboratory was closed.'

Powers shrugged. 'I felt I needed a rest. As you'll understand, there's a good deal that needs rethinking.'

Kaldren frowned half-mockingly. 'Sorry to hear that, Doctor. But don't let these temporary setbacks depress you.' He noticed the girl watching Powers with interest. 'Coma's a fan of yours. I gave her your papers from *American Journal of Psychiatry*, and she's read through the whole file.'

The girl smiled pleasantly at Powers, for a moment dispelling the hostility between the two men. When Powers nodded to her she leaned across Kaldren and said, 'Actually I've just finished Noguchi's autobiography – the great Japanese doctor who discovered the spirochete. Somehow you remind me of him – there's so much of yourself in all the patients you worked on.'

Powers smiled wanly at her, then his eyes turned and locked involuntarily on Kaldren's. They stared at each other sombrely for a moment, and a small tic in Kaldren's right cheek began to flicker irritatingly. He flexed his facial muscles, after a few seconds mastered it with an effort, obviously annoyed that Powers should have witnessed this brief embarrassment.

'How did the clinic go today?' Powers asked. 'Have you had any more . . . headaches?'

Kaldren's mouth snapped shut; he looked suddenly irritable. 'Whose care am I in, Doctor? Yours or Anderson's? Is that the sort of question you should be asking now?'

Powers gestured deprecatingly. 'Perhaps not.' He cleared his throat; the heat was ebbing the blood from his head and he felt tired and eager to get away from them. He turned towards his car, then realized that Kaldren would probably follow, either try to crowd him into the ditch or block the road and make Powers sit in his dust all the way back to the lake. Kaldren was capable of any madness.

'Well, I've got to go and collect something,' he said, adding in a firmer voice, 'Get in touch with me, though, if you can't reach Anderson.'

He waved and walked off behind the line of cars. Reflected in the windows he could see Kaldren looking back and watching him closely.

He entered the neurology wing, paused thankfully in the cool foyer, nodding to the two nurses and the armed guard at the reception desk. For some reason the terminals sleeping in the adjacent dormitory block attracted hordes of would-be sightseers, most of them cranks with some magical antinarcoma remedy, or merely the idly curious, but a good number of quite normal people many of whom had travelled thousands of miles, impelled towards the clinic by some strange instinct, like animals migrating to a preview of their racial graveyards.

He walked along the corridor to the supervisor's office overlooking the recreation deck, borrowed the key and made his way out through the tennis courts and calisthenics rigs to the enclosed swimming pool at the far end. It had been disused for months, and only Powers' visits kept the lock free. Stepping through, he closed it behind him and walked past the peeling wooden stands to the deep end.

Putting a foot up on the diving board, he looked down at Whitby's ideogram. Damp leaves and bits of paper obscured it, but the outlines were just distinguishable. It covered almost the entire floor of the pool and at first glance appeared to represent a huge solar disc, with four radiating diamond-shaped arms, a crude Jungian mandala.

Wondering what had prompted Whitby to carve the device before his death, Powers noticed something moving through the debris in the centre of the disc. A black, horny-shelled animal about a foot long was nosing about in the slush, heaving itself on tired legs. Its shell was articulated, and vaguely resembled an armadillo's. Reaching the edge of the disc, it stopped and hesitated, then slowly backed away into the centre again, apparently unwilling or unable to cross the narrow groove.

Powers looked around, then stepped into one of the

changing stalls and pulled a small wooden clothes locker off its rusty wall bracket. Carrying it under one arm, he climbed down the chromium ladder into the pool and walked carefully across the slithery floor towards the animal. As he approached it sidled away from him, but he trapped it easily, using the lid to lever it into the box.

The animal was heavy, at least the weight of a brick. Powers tapped its massive olive-black carapace with his knuckle, noting the triangular warty head jutting out below its rim like a turtle's, the thickened pads beneath the first digits of the pentadactyl forelimbs.

He watched the three-lidded eyes blinking at him anxiously from the bottom of the box.

'Expecting some really hot weather?' he murmured. 'That lead umbrella you're carrying around should keep you cool.'

He closed the lid, climbed out of the pool and made his way back to the supervisor's office, then carried the box out to his car.

. . . *Kaldren continues to reproach me* [Powers wrote in his diary]. *For some reason he seems unwilling to accept his isolation, is elaborating a series of private rituals to replace the missing hours of sleep. Perhaps I should tell him of my own approaching zero, but he'd probably regard this as the final unbearable insult, that I should have in excess what he so desperately yearns for. God knows what might happen. Fortunately the nightmarish visions appear to have receded for the time being . . .*

Pushing the diary away, Powers leaned forward across the desk and stared out through the window at the white floor of the lake bed stretching towards the hills along the horizon. Three miles away, on the far shore, he could see the circular bowl of the radiotelescope revolving slowly in the clear afternoon air, as Kaldren tirelessly trapped the sky, sluicing in millions of cubic parsecs of sterile ether, like the nomads who trapped the sea along the shores of the Persian Gulf.

Behind him the air conditioner murmured quietly, cooling the pale blue walls half-hidden in the dim light. Outside the air was bright and oppressive, the heat waves rippling up from the clumps of gold-tinted cacti below the clinic, blurring the sharp terraces of the twenty-storey neurology block. There, in the silent dormitories behind the sealed shutters, the terminals slept their long dreamless sleep. There were now over five hundred of them in the clinic, the vanguard of a vast somnambulist army massing for its last march. Only five years had elapsed since the first narcoma syndrome had been recognized, but already huge government hospitals in the east were being readied for intakes in the thousands, as more and more cases came to light.

Powers felt suddenly tired, and glanced at his wrist, wondering how long he had to eight o'clock, his bedtime for the next week or so. Already he missed the dusk, soon would wake to his last dawn.

His watch was in his hip pocket. He remembered his decision not to use his time pieces, and sat back and stared at the bookshelves beside the desk. There were rows of green-covered AEC publications he had removed from Whitby's library, papers in which the biologist described his work out in the Pacific after the H-tests. Many of them Powers knew almost by heart, read a hundred times in an effort to grasp Whitby's last conclusions. Toynbee would certainly be easier to forget.

His eyes dimmed momentarily as the tall black wall in the rear of his mind cast its great shadow over his brain. He reached for the diary thinking of the girl in Kaldren's car – Coma he had called her, another of his insane jokes – and her reference to Noguchi. Actually the comparison should have been made with Whitby, not himself; the monsters in the lab were nothing more than fragmented mirrors of Whitby's mind, like the grotesque radio-shielded frog he had found that morning in the swimming pool.

Thinking of the girl Coma, and the heartening smile she had given him, he wrote:

Woke 6.33 a.m. Last session with Anderson. He made it plain he's seen enough of me, and from now on I'm better alone. To sleep 8.00? (These count-downs terrify me.)

He paused, then added:

Goodbye, Eniwetok.

2

He saw the girl again the next day at Whitby's laboratory. He had driven over after breakfast with the new specimen, eager to get it into a vivarium before it died. The only previous armoured mutant he had come across had nearly broken his neck. Speeding along the lake road a month or so earlier he had struck it with the off-side front wheel, expecting the small creature to flatten instantly. Instead its hard lead-packed shell had remained rigid, even though the organism within it had been pulped, had flung the car heavily into the ditch. He had gone back for the shell, later weighed it at the laboratory, found it contained over six hundred grammes of lead.

Quite a number of plants and animals were building up heavy metals as radiological shields. In the hills behind the beach house a couple of old-time prospectors were renovating the derelict gold-panning equipment abandoned over eighty years ago. They had noticed the bright yellow tints of the cacti, run an analysis and found that the plants were assimilating gold in extractable quantities, although the soil concentrations were unworkable. Oak Ridge was at last paying a dividend!

Waking that morning just before 6.45 – ten minutes later than the previous day (he had switched on the radio, heard one of the regular morning programmes as he climbed out of bed) – he had eaten a light unwanted breakfast, then spent an hour packing away some of the books in his library, crating them up and taping on address labels to his brother.

He reached Whitby's laboratory half an hour later. This was housed in a 100-foot wide geodesic dome built beside his chalet on the west shore of the lake about a mile from Kaldren's summer house. The chalet had been closed after Whitby's suicide, and many of the experimental plants and animals had died before Powers managed to receive permission to use the laboratory.

As he turned into the driveway he saw the girl standing on the apex of the yellow-ribbed dome, her slim figure silhouetted against the sky. She waved to him, then began to step down across the glass polyhedrons and jumped nimbly into the driveway beside the car.

'Hello,' she said, giving him a welcoming smile. 'I came over to see your zoo. Kaldren said you wouldn't let me in if he came so I made him stay behind.'

She waited for Powers to say something while he searched for his keys, then volunteered, 'If you like, I can wash your shirt.'

Powers grinned at her, peered down ruefully at his dust-stained sleeves. 'Not a bad idea. I thought I was beginning to look a little uncared for.' He unlocked the door, took Coma's arm. 'I don't know why Kaldren told you that – he's welcome here any time he likes.'

'What have you got in there?' Coma asked, pointing at the wooden box he was carrying as they walked between the gear-laden benches.

'A distant cousin of ours I found. Interesting little chap. I'll introduce you in a moment.'

Sliding partitions divided the dome into four chambers. Two of them were storerooms, filled with spare tanks, apparatus, cartons of animal food and test rigs. They crossed the third section, almost filled by a powerful X-ray projector, a giant 250 mega-amp GE Maxitron, angled on to a revolving table, concrete shielding blocks lying around ready for use like huge building bricks.

The fourth chamber contained Powers' zoo, the vivaria jammed together along the benches and in the sinks, big coloured cardboard charts and memos pinned onto the draught hoods above them, a tangle of rubber tubing and power leads trailing across the floor. As they walked past the lines of tanks dim forms shifted behind the frosted glass, and at the far end of the aisle there was a sudden scurrying in a large-scale cage by Powers' desk.

Putting the box down on his chair, he picked a packet of

peanuts off the desk and went over to the cage. A small black-haired chimpanzee wearing a dented jet pilot's helmet swarmed deftly up the bars to him, chirped happily and then jumped down to a miniature control panel against the rear wall of the cage. Rapidly it flicked a series of buttons and toggles, and a succession of coloured lights lit up like a jukebox and jangled out a two-second blast of music.

'Good boy,' Powers said encouragingly, patting the chimp's back and shovelling the peanuts into its hands. 'You're getting much too clever for that one, aren't you?'

The chimp tossed the peanuts into the back of its throat with the smooth easy motions of a conjurer, jabbering at Powers in a sing-song voice.

Coma laughed and took some of the nuts from Powers. 'He's sweet. I think he's talking to you.'

Powers nodded. 'Quite right, he is. Actually he's got a two-hundred word vocabulary, but his voice box scrambles it all up.' He opened a small refrigerator by the desk, took out half a packet of sliced bread and passed a couple of pieces to the chimp. It picked an electric toaster off the floor and placed it in the middle of a low wobbling table in the centre of the cage, whipped the pieces into the slots. Powers pressed a tab on the switchboard beside the cage and the toaster began to crackle softly.

'He's one of the brightest we've had here, about as intelligent as a five-year-old child, though much more self-sufficient in a lot of ways.' The two pieces of toast jumped out of their slots and the chimp caught them neatly, nonchalantly patting its helmet each time, then ambled off into a small ramshackle kennel and relaxed back with one arm out of a window, sliding the toast into its mouth.

'He built that house himself,' Powers went on, switching off the toaster. 'Not a bad effort, really.' He pointed to a yellow polythene bucket by the front door of the kennel, from which a battered-looking geranium protruded. 'Tends that plant, cleans up the cage, pours out an endless stream of wisecracks. Pleasant fellow all round.'

Coma was smiling broadly to herself. 'Why the space helmet, though?'

Powers hesitated. 'Oh, it – er – it's for his own protection. Sometimes he gets rather bad headaches. His predecessors all – ' He broke off and turned away. 'Let's have a look at some of the other inmates.'

He moved down the line of tanks, beckoning Coma with him. 'We'll start at the beginning.' He lifted the glass lid off one of the tanks, and Coma peered down into a shallow bath of water, where a small round organism with slender tendrils was nestling in a rockery of shells and pebbles.

'Sea anemone. Or was. Simple coelenterate with an open-ended body cavity.' He pointed down to a thickened ridge of tissue around the base. 'It's sealed up the cavity, converted the channel into a rudimentary notochord, first plant ever to develop a nervous system. Later the tendrils will knot themselves into a ganglion, but already they're sensitive to colour. Look.' He borrowed the violet handkerchief in Coma's breast pocket, spread it across the tank. The tendrils flexed and stiffened, began to weave slowly, as if they were trying to focus.

'The strange thing is that they're completely insensitive to white light. Normally the tendrils register shifting pressure gradients, like the tympanic diaphragms in your ears. Now it's almost as if they can *hear* primary colours, suggests it's readapting itself for a non-aquatic existence in a static world of violent colour contrasts.'

Coma shook her head, puzzled. 'Why, though?'

'Hold on a moment. Let me put you in the picture first.' They moved along the bench to a series of drum-shaped cages made of wire mosquito netting. Above the first was a large white cardboard screen bearing a blown-up microphoto of a tall pagoda-like chain, topped by the legend, DROSOPHILA: 15 ROENTGENS/MIN.

Powers tapped a small Perspex window in the drum. 'Fruitfly. Its huge chromosomes make it a useful test vehicle.' He bent down, pointed to a grey V-shaped honeycomb suspended from the roof. A few flies emerged from entrances, moving about busily. 'Usually it's solitary, a nomadic scavenger. Now it forms itself into well-knit social groups, has begun to secrete a thin sweet lymph something like honey.'

'What's this?' Coma asked, touching the screen.

'Diagram of a key gene in the operation.' He traced a spray of arrows leading from a link in the chain. The arrows were labelled, 'Lymph gland' and subdivided 'sphincter muscles, epithelium, templates'.

'It's rather like the perforated sheet music of a player piano,' Powers commented, 'or a computer punch tape. Knock out one link with an X-ray beam, lose a characteristic, change the score.'

Coma was peering through the window of the next cage and pulling an unpleasant face. Over her shoulder Powers saw she was watching an enormous spiderlike insect, as big as a hand, its dark hairy legs as thick as fingers. The compound eyes had been built up so that they resembled giant rubies.

'He looks unfriendly,' she said. 'What's that sort of rope ladder he's spinning?' As she moved a finger to her mouth the spider came to life, retreated into the cage and began spewing out a complex skein of interlinked grey thread which it slung in long loops from the roof of the cage.

'A web,' Powers told her. 'Except that it consists of nervous tissue. The ladders form an external neural plexus, an inflatable brain as it were, that he can pump up to whatever size the situation calls for. A sensible arrangement really, far better than our own.'

Coma backed away. 'Gruesome. I wouldn't like to go into his parlour.'

'Oh, he's not as frightening as he looks. Those huge eyes staring at you are blind. Or, rather, their optical sensitivity has shifted down the band, the retinas will only register gamma radiation. Your wristwatch has luminous hands. When you moved it across the window he started thinking. World War IV should really bring him into his element.'

They strolled back to Powers' desk. He put a coffee pan over a bunsen and pushed a chair across to Coma. Then he opened the box, lifted out the armoured frog and put it down on a sheet of blotting paper.

'Recognize him? Your old childhood friend, the common frog. He's built himself quite a solid little air-raid shelter.' He carried the animal across to a sink, turned on the tap and let the water play softly over its shell. Wiping his hands on his shirt, he came back to the desk.

Coma brushed her long hair off her forehead, watched him curiously.

'Well, what's the secret?'

Powers lit a cigarette. 'There's no secret. Teratologists have been breeding monsters for years. Have you ever heard of the "silent pair"?'

She shook her head.

Powers stared moodily at the cigarette for a moment, riding the kick the first one of the day always gave him. 'The so-called "silent pair" is one of modern genetics' oldest problems, the apparently baffling mystery of the two inactive genes that occur in a small percentage of all living organisms, and appear to have no intelligible role in their structure of development. For a long while now biologists have been trying to activate them, but the difficulty is partly in identifying the silent genes in the fertilized germ cells of parents known to contain them, and partly in focusing a narrow enough X-ray beam which will do no damage to the remainder of the chromosomes. However, after about ten years' work Dr Whitby successfully developed a whole-body irradiation technique based on his observation of radiobiological damage at Eniwetok.'

Powers paused for a moment. 'He had noticed that there appeared to be more biological damage after the tests – that is, a greater transport of energy – than could be accounted for by direct radiation. What was happening was that the protein latices in the genes were building up energy in the way that any vibrating membrane accumulates energy when it resonates – you remember the analogy of the bridge collapsing under the soldiers marching in step – and it occurred to him that if he could first identify the critical resonance frequency of the latices in any particular silent gene he could then radiate the entire living organism, and not simply its germ cells, with a low field that would act selectively on the silent gene and cause no damage to the remainder of the chromosomes, whose latices would resonate critically only at other specific frequencies.'

Powers gestured around the laboratory with his cigarette. 'You see some of the fruits of this "resonance transfer" technique around you.'

Coma nodded. 'They've had their silent genes activated?'

'Yes, all of them. These are only a few of the thousands of specimens who have passed through here, and as you've seen, the results are pretty dramatic.'

He reached up and pulled across a section of the sun curtain. They were sitting just under the lip of the dome, and the mounting sunlight had begun to irritate him.

In the comparative darkness Coma noticed a stroboscope winking slowly in one of the tanks at the end of the bench behind her. She stood up and went over to it, examining a tall sunflower with a thickened stem and greatly enlarged receptacle. Packed around the flower, so that only its head protruded, was a chimney of grey-white stones, neatly cemented together and labelled CRETACEOUS CHALK: 60,000,000 YEARS.

Beside it on the bench were three other chimneys, these labelled DEVONIAN SANDSTONE 290,000,000 YEARS; ASPHALT: 20 YEARS; POLYVINYLCHLORIDE: 6 MONTHS.

'Can you see those moist white discs on the sepals?' Powers pointed out. 'In some way they regulate the plant's metabolism. It literally *sees* time. The older the surrounding environment, the more sluggish its metabolism. With the asphalt chimney it will complete its annual cycle in a week, with the PVC one in a couple of hours.'

'Sees time,' Coma repeated, wonderingly. She looked up at Powers, chewing her lower lip reflectively. 'It's fantastic. Are these the creatures of the future, Doctor?'

'I don't know,' Powers admitted. 'But if they are, their world must be a monstrously surrealist one.'

3

He went back to the desk, pulled two cups from a drawer and poured out the coffee, switching off the bunsen. 'Some people have speculated that organisms possessing the silent pair of genes are the forerunners of a massive move up the evolutionary slope, that the silent genes are a sort of code, a divine message that we inferior organisms are carrying for our more highly developed descendants. It may well be true – perhaps we've broken the code too soon.'

'Why do you say that?'

'Well, as Whitby's death indicates, the experiments in this laboratory have all come to a rather unhappy conclusion. Without exception the organisms we've irradiated have entered a final phase of totally disorganized growth, producing dozens of specialized sensory organs whose function we can't even guess. The results are catastrophic – the anemone will literally explode, the Drosophila cannibalize themselves, and so on. Whether the future implicit in these plants and animals is ever intended to take place, or whether we're merely extrapolating – I don't know. Sometimes I think, though, that the new sensory organs developed are parodies of their real intentions. The specimens you've seen today are all in an early stage of their secondary growth cycles. Later on they begin to look distinctly bizarre.'

Coma nodded. 'A zoo isn't complete without its keeper,' she commented. 'What about man?'

Powers shrugged. 'About one in every 100,000 – the usual average – contain the silent pair. You might have them – or I. No one has volunteered yet to undergo whole-body irradiation. Apart from the fact that it would be classified as suicide, if the experiments here are any guide the experience would be savage and violent.'

He sipped at the thin coffee, feeling tired and somehow bored. Recapitulating the laboratory's work had exhausted him.

The girl leaned forward. 'You look awfully pale,' she said solicitously. 'Don't you sleep well?'

Powers managed a brief smile. 'Too well,' he admitted. 'It's no longer a problem with me.'

'I wish I could say that about Kaldren. I don't think he sleeps anywhere near enough. I hear him pacing around all night.' She added, 'Still, I suppose it's better than being a terminal. Tell me, Doctor, wouldn't it be worth trying this radiation technique on the sleepers at the clinic? It might wake them up before the end. A few of them must possess the silent genes.'

'They *all* do,' Powers told her. 'The two phenomena are very closely linked, as a matter of fact.' He stopped, fatigue dulling his brain, and wondered whether to ask the girl to leave. Then he climbed off the desk and reached behind it, picked up a tape-recorder.

Switching it on, he zeroed the tape and adjusted the speaker volume.

'Whitby and I often talked this over. Towards the end I took it all down. He was a great biologist, so let's hear it in his own words. It's absolutely the heart of the matter.'

He flipped the tape on, adding, 'I've played it over to myself a thousand times, so I'm afraid the quality is poor.'

An older man's voice, sharp and slightly irritable, sounded out above a low buzz of distortion, but Coma could hear it clearly.

Whitby: . . . for heaven's sake, Robert, look at those FAO statistics. Despite an annual increase of five per cent in acreage sown over the past fifteen years, world wheat crops have continued to decline by a factor of about two per cent. The same story repeats itself ad nauseam. Cereals and root crops, dairy yields, ruminant fertility – are all down. Couple these with a mass of parallel symptoms, anything you care to pick from altered migratory routes to longer hibernation periods, and the overall pattern is incontrovertible.

Powers: Population figures for Europe and North America show no decline, though.

Whitby: Of course not, as I keep pointing out. It will take a century for such a fractional drop in fertility to have any effect in areas where extensive birth control provides an artificial reservoir. One must look at the countries of the Far East, and particularly

at those where infant mortality has remained at a steady level.
The population of Sumatra, for example, has declined by over
fifteen per cent in the last twenty years. A fabulous decline! Do
you realize that only two or three decades ago the Neo-Malthu-
sians were talking about a 'world population explosion'? In fact,
it's an implosion. Another factor is –

Here the tape had been cut and edited, and Whitby's
voice, less querulous this time, picked up again.

. . . just as a matter of interest, tell me something: how long do
you sleep each night?
Powers: I don't know exactly; about eight hours, I suppose.
Whitby: The proverbial eight hours. Ask anyone and they say
automatically 'eight hours'. As a matter of fact you sleep about
ten and a half hours, like the majority of people. I've timed you
on a number of occasions. I myself sleep eleven. Yet thirty years
ago people did indeed sleep eight hours, and a century before that
they slept six or seven. In Vasari's *Lives* one reads of Michelangelo
sleeping for only four or five hours, painting all day at the age of
eighty and then working through the night over his anatomy table
with a candle strapped to his forehead. Now he's regarded as a
prodigy, but it was unremarkable then. How do you think the
ancients, from Plato to Shakespeare, Aristotle to Aquinas, were
able to cram so much work into their lives? Simply because they
had an extra six or seven hours every day. Of course, a second
disadvantage under which we labour is a lowered basal metabolic
rate – another factor no one will explain.
Powers: I suppose you could take the view that the lengthened
sleep interval is a compensation device, a sort of mass neurotic
attempt to escape from the terrifying pressures of urban life in the
late twentieth century.
Whitby: You could, but you'd be wrong. It's simply a matter of
biochemistry. The ribonucleic acid templates which unravel the
protein chains in all living organisms are wearing out, the dies
enscribing the protoplasmic signature have become blunted. After
all, they've been running now for over a thousand million years.
It's time to retool. Just as an individual organism's life span is
finite, or the life of a yeast colony or a given species, so the life
of an entire biological kingdom is of fixed duration. It's always
been assumed that the evolutionary slope reaches for ever upwards, but in fact the peak has already been reached, and the
pathway now leads downwards to the common biological grave.

It's a despairing and at present unacceptable vision of the future, but it's the only one. Five thousand centuries from now our descendants, instead of being multibrained star-men, will probably be naked prognathous idiots with hair on their foreheads, grunting their way through the remains of this clinic like Neolithic men caught in a macabre inversion of time. Believe me, I pity them, as I pity myself. My total failure, my absolute lack of any moral or biological right to existence, is implicit in every cell of my body . . .

The tape ended; the spool ran free and stopped. Powers closed the machine, then massaged his face. Coma sat quietly, watching him and listening to the chimp playing with a box of puzzle dice.

'As far as Whitby could tell,' Powers said, 'the silent genes represent a last desperate effort of the biological kingdom to keep its head above the rising waters. Its total life period is determined by the amount of radiation emitted by the sun, and once this reaches a certain point the sure-death line has been passed and extinction is inevitable. To compensate for this, alarms have been built in which alter the form of the organism and adapt it to living in a hotter radiological climate. Soft-skinned organisms develop hard shells, these contain heavy metals as radiation screens. New organs of perception are developed too. According to Whitby, though, it's all wasted effort in the long run – but sometimes I wonder.'

He smiled at Coma and shrugged. 'Well, let's talk about something else. How long have you known Kaldren?'

'About three weeks. Feels like ten thousand years.'

'How do you find him now? We've been rather out of touch lately.'

Coma grinned. 'I don't seem to see very much of him either. He makes me sleep all the time. Kaldren has many strange talents, but he lives just for himself. You mean a lot to him, Doctor. In fact, you're my one serious rival.'

'I thought he couldn't stand the sight of me.'

'Oh, that's just a sort of surface symptom. He really thinks of you continuously. That's why we spend all our time following you around.' She eyed Powers shrewdly. 'I think he feels guilty about something.'

'Guilty?' Powers exclaimed. '*He* does? I thought I was supposed to be the guilty one.'

'Why?' she pressed. She hesitated, then said, 'You carried out some experimental surgical technique on him, didn't you?'

'Yes,' Powers admitted. 'It wasn't altogether a success, like so much of what I seem to be involved with. If Kaldren feels guilty, I suppose it's because he feels he must take some of the responsibility.'

He looked down at the girl, her intelligent eyes watching him closely. 'For one or two reasons it may be necessary for you to know. You said Kaldren paced around all night and didn't get enough sleep. Actually he doesn't get any sleep at all.'

The girl nodded. 'You . . . ' She made a snapping gesture with her fingers.

' . . . narcotomized him,' Powers completed. 'Surgically speaking, it was a great success, one might well share a Nobel for it. Normally the hypothalamus regulates the period of sleep, raising the threshold of consciousness in order to relax the venous capillaries in the brain and drain them of accumulating toxins. However, by sealing off some of the control loops the subject is unable to receive the sleep cue, and the capillaries drain while he remains conscious. All he feels is a temporary lethargy, but this passes within three or four hours. Physically speaking, Kaldren has had another twenty years added to his life. But the psyche seems to need sleep for its own private reasons, and consequently Kaldren has periodic storms that tear him apart. The whole thing was a tragic blunder.'

Coma frowned pensively. 'I guessed as much. Your papers in the neurosurgery journals referred to the patient as K. A touch of pure Kafka that came all too true.'

'I may leave here for good, Coma,' Powers said. 'Make sure that Kaldren goes to his clinics. Some of the deep scar tissue will need to be cleaned away.'

'I'll try. Sometimes I feel I'm just another of his insane terminal documents.'

'What are those?'

'Haven't you heard? Kaldren's collection of final statements about homo sapiens. The complete works of Freud, Beethoven's deaf quartets, transcripts of the Nuremberg trials, an automatic novel, and so on.' She broke off. 'What's that you're drawing?'

'Where?'

She pointed to the desk blotter, and Powers looked down and realized he had been unconsciously sketching an elaborate doodle, Whitby's four-armed sun. 'It's nothing,' he said. Somehow, though, it had a strangely compelling force.

Coma stood up to leave. 'You must come and see us, Doctor. Kaldren has so much he wants to show you. He's just got hold of an old copy of the last signals sent back by the Mercury Seven, twenty years ago when they reached the moon, and can't think about anything else. You remember the strange messages they recorded before they died, full of poetic ramblings about the white gardens. Now that I think about it they behaved rather like the plants in your zoo here.'

She put her hands in her pockets, then pulled something out. 'By the way, Kaldren asked me to give you this.'

It was an old index card from the observatory library. In the centre had been typed the number:

$$96,688,365,498,720$$

'It's going to take a long time to reach zero at this rate,' Powers remarked drily. 'I'll have quite a collection when we're finished.'

After she had left he chucked the card into the waste bin and sat down at the desk, staring for an hour at the ideogram on the blotter.

Halfway back to his beach house the lake road forked to the left through a narrow saddle that ran between the hills to an abandoned Air Force weapons range on one of the remoter salt lakes. At the nearer end were a number of small bunkers and camera towers, one or two metal shacks and a low-roofed storage hangar. The white hills encircled the whole area, shutting it off from the world outside, and Powers liked to wander on foot down the gunnery aisles that had been marked down the two-mile length of the lake towards the concrete sight-screens at the far end. The abstract patterns made him feel like an ant on a bone-white chessboard, the rectangular screens at one end and the towers and bunkers at the other like opposing pieces.

His session with Coma had made Powers feel suddenly dissatisfied with the way he was spending his last months. *Goodbye, Eniwetok*, he had written, but in fact systematically forgetting everything was exactly the same as remembering it, a cataloguing in reverse, sorting out all the books in the mental library and putting them back in their right places upside down.

Powers climbed one of the camera towers, leaned on the rail and looked out along the aisles towards the sight-screens. Ricocheting shells and rockets had chipped away large pieces of the circular concrete bands that ringed the target bulls, but the outlines of the huge 100-yard-wide discs, alternately painted blue and red, were still visible.

For half an hour he stared quietly at them, formless ideas shifting through his mind. Then without thinking, he abruptly left the rail and climbed down the companionway. The storage hangar was fifty yards away. He walked quickly across to it, stepped into the cool shadows and peered around the rusting electric trolleys and empty flare drums. At the far end, behind a pile of lumber and bales of wire, were a stack of unopened cement bags, a mound of dirty sand and an old mixer.

Half an hour later he had backed the Buick into the hangar and hooked the cement mixer, charged with sand, cement and water scavenged from the drums lying around outside, onto the rear bumper, then loaded a dozen more bags into the car's trunk and rear seat. Finally he selected a few straight lengths of timber, jammed them through the window and set off across the lake towards the central target bull.

For the next two hours he worked away steadily in the centre of the great blue disc, mixing up the cement by hand, carrying it across to the crude wooden forms he had lashed together from the timber, smoothing it down so that it formed a six-inch-high wall around the perimeter of the bull. He worked without pause, stirring the cement with a tyre lever, scooping it out with a hub cap prised off one of the wheels.

By the time he finished and drove off, leaving his equipment where it stood, he had completed a thirty-foot-long section of wall.

4

June 7th: Conscious, for the first time, of the brevity of each day. As long as I was awake for over twelve hours I still orientated my time around the meridian; morning and afternoon set their old rhythms. Now, with just over eleven hours of consciousness left, they form a continuous interval, like a length of tape measure. I can see exactly how much is left on the spool and can do little to affect the rate at which it unwinds. Spend the time slowly packing away the library; the crates are too heavy to move and lie where they are filled.

Cell count down to 400,000.

Woke 8.10. To sleep 7.15. (Appear to have lost my watch without realizing it, had to drive into town to buy another.)

June 14th: 9½ hours. Time races, flashing past like an expressway. However, the last week of a holiday always goes faster than the first. At the present rate there should be about 4–5 weeks left. This morning I tried to visualize what the last week or so – the final 3, 2, 1, out – would be like, had a sudden chilling attack of pure fear, unlike anything I've ever felt before. Took me half an hour to steady myself enough for an intravenous. Kaldren pursues me like my luminescent shadow, chalked up on the gateway '96,688,365,498,702'.

Should confuse the mail man.

Woke 9.05. To sleep 6.36.

June 19th: 8¾ hours. Anderson rang up this morning. I nearly put the phone down on him, but managed to go through the pretence of making the final arrangements. He congratulated me on my stoicism, even used the word 'heroic'. Don't feel it. Despair erodes everything – courage, hope, self-discipline, all the better qualities. It's so damned difficult to sustain that impersonal attitude of passive acceptance implicit in the scientific tradition. I try to think of Galileo before the Inquisition, Freud surmounting the endless pain of his jaw cancer surgery.

Met Kaldren down town, had a long discussion about the Mercury Seven. He's convinced that they refused to leave the moon deliberately, after the 'reception party' waiting for them had put them in the cosmic picture. They were told by the mysterious emissaries from Orion that the exploration of deep space was pointless, that they were too late as the life of the universe is now virtually over!!! According to K. there are Air Force generals who take this nonsense seriously, but I suspect it's simply an obscure attempt on K.'s part to console me.

Must have the phone disconnected. Some contractor keeps calling me up about payment for 50 bags of cement he claims I collected ten days ago. Says he helped me load them onto a truck himself. I did drive Whitby's pick-up into town but only to get some lead screening. What does he think I'd do with all that cement? Just the sort of irritating thing you don't expect to hang over your final exit. (Moral: don't try too hard to forget Eniwetok.)

Woke 9.40. To sleep 4.15.

June 25th: 7½ hours. Kaldren was snooping around the lab again today. Phoned me there, when I answered a recorded voice he'd rigged up rambled out a long string of numbers, like an insane super-Tim. These practical jokes of his get rather wearing. Fairly soon I'll have to go over and come to terms with him, much as I hate the prospect. Anyway, Miss Mars is a pleasure to look at.

One meal is enough now, topped up with a glucose shot. Sleep is still 'black', completely unrefreshing. Last night I took a 16-mm film of the first three hours, screened it this morning at the lab. The first true horror movie; I looked like a half-animated corpse.

Woke 10.25: To sleep 3.45.

July 3rd: 5¾ hours. Little done today. Deepening lethargy, dragged myself over to the lab, nearly left the road twice. Concentrated enough to feed the zoo and get the log up to date. Read through the operating manuals Whitby left for the last time, decided on a delivery rate of 40 roentgens/min. target distance of 350 cm. Everything is ready now.

Woke 11.05. To sleep 3.15.

Powers stretched, shifted his head slowly across the pillow, focusing on the shadows cast onto the ceiling by the blind. Then he looked down at his feet, saw Kaldren sitting on the end of the bed, watching him quietly.

'Hello, Doctor,' he said, putting out his cigarette. 'Late night? You look tired.'

Powers heaved himself onto one elbow, glanced at his watch. It was just after eleven. For a moment his brain blurred, and he swung his legs around and sat on the edge of the bed, elbows on his knees, massaging some life into his face.

He noticed that the room was full of smoke. 'What are you doing here?' he asked Kaldren.

'I came over to invite you to lunch.' He indicated the bedside phone. 'Your line was dead so I drove round. Hope you don't mind me climbing in. Rang the bell for about half an hour. I'm surprised you didn't hear it.'

Powers nodded, then stood up and tried to smooth the creases out of his cotton slacks. He had gone to sleep without changing for over a week, and they were damp and stale.

As he started for the bathroom door Kaldren pointed to the camera tripod on the other side of the bed. 'What's this? Going into the blue movie business, Doctor?'

Powers surveyed him dimly for a moment, glanced at the tripod without replying and then noticed his open diary on the bedside table. Wondering whether Kaldren had read the last entries, he went back and picked it up, then stepped into the bathroom and closed the door behind him.

From the mirror cabinet he took out a syringe and an

ampoule, after the shot leaned against the door waiting for the stimulant to pick up.

Kaldren was in the lounge when he returned to him, reading the labels on the crates lying about in the centre of the floor.

'Okay, then,' Powers told him, 'I'll join you for lunch.' He examined Kaldren carefully. He looked more subdued than usual, there was an air almost of deference about him.

'Good,' Kaldren said. 'By the way, are you leaving?'

'Does it matter?' Powers asked curtly. 'I thought you were in Anderson's care?'

Kaldren shrugged. 'Please yourself. Come round at about twelve,' he suggested, adding pointedly, 'That'll give you time to clean up and change. What's that all over your shirt? Looks like lime.'

Powers peered down, brushed at the white streaks. After Kaldren had left he threw the clothes away, took a shower and unpacked a clean suit from one of the trunks.

Until this liaison with Coma, Kaldren lived alone in the old abstract summer house on the north shore of the lake. This was a seven-storey folly originally built by an eccentric millionaire mathematician in the form of a spiralling concrete ribbon that wound around itself like an insane serpent, serving walls, floors, and ceilings. Only Kaldren had solved the building, a geometric model of $\sqrt{-1}$, and consequently he had been able to take it off the agents' hands at a comparatively low rent. In the evenings Powers had often watched him from the laboratory, striding restlessly from one level to the next, swinging through the labyrinth of inclines and terraces to the rooftop, where his lean angular figure stood out like a gallows against the sky, his lonely eyes sifting out radio lanes for the next day's trapping.

Powers noticed him there when he drove up at noon, poised on a ledge 150 feet above, head raised theatrically to the sky.

'Kaldren!' he shouted up suddenly into the silent air, half-hoping he might be jolted into losing his footing.

Kaldren broke out of his reverie and glanced down into

the court. Grinning obliquely, he waved his right arm in a slow semicircle.

'Come up,' he called, then turned back to the sky.

Powers leaned against the car. Once, a few months previously, he had accepted the same invitation, stepped through the entrance and within three minutes lost himself helplessly in a second-floor cul-de-sac. Kaldren had taken half an hour to find him.

Powers waited while Kaldren swung down from his eyrie, vaulting through the wells and stairways, then rode up in the elevator with him to the penthouse suite.

They carried their cocktails through into a wide glass-roofed studio, the huge white ribbon of concrete uncoiling around them like toothpaste squeezed from an enormous tube. On the staged levels running parallel and across them rested pieces of grey abstract furniture, giant photographs on angled screens, carefully labelled exhibits laid out on low tables, all dominated by twenty-foot-high black letters on the rear wall which spelled out the single vast word:

YOU

Kaldren pointed to it. 'What you might call the supra-liminal approach.' He gestured Powers in conspiratorially, finishing his drink in a gulp. 'This is *my* laboratory, Doctor,' he said with a note of pride. 'Much more significant than yours, believe me.'

Powers smiled wryly to himself and examined the first exhibit, an old EEG tape traversed by a series of faded inky wriggles. It was labelled EINSTEIN, A ALPHA WAVES, 1922.

He followed Kaldren around, sipping slowly at his drink, enjoying the brief feeling of alertness the amphetamine provided. Within two hours it would fade, leaving his brain feeling like a block of blotting paper.

Kaldren chattered away, explaining the significance of the so-called Terminal Documents. 'They're end-prints,

Powers, final statements, the products of total fragmentation. When I've got enough together I'll build a new world for myself out of them.' He picked a thick paperbound volume off one of the tables, riffled through its pages. 'Association tests of the Nuremberg Twelve. I have to include these . . . '

Powers strolled on absently without listening. Over in the corner were what appeared to be three ticker-tape machines, lengths of tape hanging from their mouths. He wondered whether Kaldren was misguided enough to be playing the stock market, which had been declining slowly for twenty years.

'Powers,' he heard Kaldren say. 'I was telling you about the Mercury Seven.' He pointed to a collection of type-written sheets tacked to a screen. 'These are transcripts of their final signals radioed back from the recording monitors.'

Powers examined the sheets cursorily, read a line at random.

' . . . BLUE . . . PEOPLE . . . RE-CYCLE . . . OR-ION . . . TELEMETERS . . . '

Powers nodded non-committally. 'Interesting. What are the ticker tapes for over there?'

Kaldren grinned. 'I've been waiting for months for you to ask me that. Have a look.'

Powers went over and picked up one of the tapes. The machine was labelled AURIGA 225-G. INTERVAL: 69 HOURS.

The tape read:

$$96,688,365,498,695$$
$$96,688,365,498,694$$
$$96,688,365,498,693$$
$$96,688,365,498,692$$

Powers dropped the tape. 'Looks rather familiar. What does the sequence represent?'

Kaldren shrugged. 'No one knows.'

'What do you mean? It must replicate something.'

'Yes, it does. A diminishing mathematical progression. A countdown, if you like.'

Powers picked up the tape on the right, tabbed ARIES 44R951. INTERVAL: 49 DAYS.

Here the sequence ran:

876,567,988,347,779,877,654,434
876,567,988,347,779,877,654,433
876,567,988,347,779,877,654,432

Powers looked round. 'How long does it take each signal to come through?'

'Only a few seconds. They're tremendously compressed laterally, of course. A computer at the observatory breaks them down. They were first picked up at Jodrell Bank about twenty years ago. Nobody bothers to listen to them now.'

Powers returned to the last tape.

6,554
6,553
6,552
6,551

'Nearing the end of its run,' he commented. He glanced at the label on the hood, which read UNIDENTIFIED RADIO SOURCE, CANES VENATICI. INTERVAL: 97 WEEKS.

He showed the tape to Kaldren. 'Soon be over.'

Kaldren shook his head. He lifted a heavy directory-sized volume off a table, cradled it in his hands. His face had suddenly become sombre and haunted. 'I doubt it,' he said. 'Those are only the last four digits. The whole number contains over fifty million.'

He handed the volume to Powers, who turned to the title page. 'Master Sequence of Serial Signal received by Jodrell Bank Radio-Observatory, University of Manchester, England, 0012–59 hours, 21–5–72. Source: NGC9743, Canes Venatici.' He thumbed the thick stack of closely printed pages, millions of numerals, as Kaldren had said, running up and down across a thousand consecutive pages.

Powers shook his head, picked up the tape again and stared at it thoughtfully.

'The computer only breaks down the last four digits,' Kaldren explained. 'The whole series comes over in each

15-second-long package, but it took IBM more than two years to unscramble one of them.'

'Amazing,' Powers commented. 'But what is it?'

'A countdown, as you can see. NGC9743, somewhere in Canes Venatici. The big spirals there are breaking up, and they're saying goodbye. God knows who they think we are but they're letting us know all the same, beaming it out on the hydrogen line for everyone in the universe to hear.' He paused. 'Some people have put other interpretations on them, but there's one piece of evidence that rules out everything else.'

'Which is?'

Kaldren pointed to the last tape from Canes Venatici. 'Simply that it's been estimated that by the time this series reaches zero the universe will have just ended.'

Powers fingered the tape reflectively. 'Thoughtful of them to let us know what the real time is,' he remarked.

'I agree it is,' Kaldren said quietly. 'Applying the inverse square law that signal source is broadcasting at a strength of about three million megawatts raised to the hundredth power. About the size of the entire Local Group. Thoughtful is the word.'

Suddenly he gripped Powers' arm, held it tightly and peered into his eyes closely, his throat working with emotion.

'You're not alone, Powers, don't think you are. These are the voices of time, and they're all saying goodbye to you. Think of yourself in a wider context. Every particle in your body, every grain of sand, every galaxy carries the same signature. As you've just said, you know what the time is now, so what does the rest matter? There's no need to go on looking at the clock.'

Powers took his hand, squeezed it firmly. 'Thanks, Kaldren. I'm glad you understand.' He walked over to the window, looked down across the white lake. The tension between himself and Kaldren had dissipated, he felt that all his obligations to him had at last been met. Now he wanted to leave as quickly as possible, forget him as he had forgotten the faces of the countless other patients whose exposed brains had passed between his fingers.

He went back to the ticker machines, tore the tapes from their slots and stuffed them into his pockets. 'I'll take these along to remind myself. Say goodbye to Coma for me, will you.'

He moved towards the door, when he reached it looked back to see Kaldren standing in the shadow of the three giant letters on the far wall, his eyes staring listlessly at his feet.

As Powers drove away he noticed that Kaldren had gone up onto the roof, watched him in the driving mirror waving slowly until the car disappeared around a bend.

5

The outer circle was now almost complete. A narrow segment, an arc about ten feet long, was missing, but otherwise the low perimeter wall ran continuously six inches off the concrete floor around the outer lane of the target bull, enclosing the huge rebus within it. Three concentric circles, the largest a hundred yards in diameter, separated from each other by ten-foot intervals, formed the rim of the device, divided into four segments by the arms of an enormous cross radiating from its centre, where a small round platform had been built a foot above the ground.

Powers worked swiftly, pouring sand and cement into the mixer, tipping in water until a rough paste formed, then carried it across to the wooden forms and tamped the mixture down into the narrow channel.

Within ten minutes he had finished, quickly dismantled the forms before the cement had set and slung the timbers into the back seat of the car. Dusting his hands on his trousers, he went over to the mixer and pushed it fifty yards away into the long shadow of the surrounding hills.

Without pausing to survey the gigantic cipher on which he had laboured patiently for so many afternoons, he climbed into the car and drove off on a wake of bone-white dust, splitting the pools of indigo shadow.

He reached the laboratory at three o'clock, jumped from the car as it lurched back on its brakes. Inside the entrance he first switched on the lights, then hurried around, pulling the sun curtains down and shackling them to the floor slots, effectively turning the dome into a steel tent.

In their tanks behind him the plants and animals stirred quietly, responding to the sudden flood of cold fluorescent light. Only the chimpanzee ignored him. It sat on the floor of its cage, neurotically jamming the puzzle dice into the polythene bucket, exploding in bursts of sudden rage when the pieces refused to fit.

Powers went over to it, noticing the shattered glass fibre reinforcing panels bursting from the dented helmet. Already the chimp's face and forehead were bleeding from self-inflicted blows. Powers picked up the remains of the geranium that had been hurled through the bars, attracted the chimp's attention with it, then tossed a black pellet he had taken from a capsule in the desk drawer. The chimp caught it with a quick flick of the wrist, for a few seconds juggled the pellet with a couple of dice as it concentrated on the puzzle, then pulled it out of the air and swallowed it in a gulp.

Without waiting, Powers slipped off his jacket and stepped towards the X-ray theatre. He pulled back the high sliding doors to reveal the long glassy metallic snout of the Maxitron, then started to stack the lead screening shields against the rear wall.

A few minutes later the generator hummed into life.

The anemone stirred. Basking in the warm subliminal sea of radiation rising around it, prompted by countless pelagic memories, it reached tentatively across the tank, groping blindly towards the dim uterine sun. Its tendrils flexed, the thousands of dormant neural cells in their tips regrouping and multiplying, each harnessing the unlocked energies of its nucleus. Chains forged themselves, latices tiered upwards into multi-faceted lenses, focused slowly on the vivid spectral outlines of the sounds dancing like phosphorescent waves around the darkened chamber of the dome.

Gradually an image formed, revealing an enormous black fountain that poured an endless stream of brilliant light over the circle of benches and tanks. Beside it a figure moved, adjusting the flow through its mouth. As it stepped across the floor its feet threw off vivid bursts of colour, its hands racing along the benches conjured up a dazzling chiaroscuro, balls of blue and violet light that exploded fleetingly in the darkness like miniature starshells.

Photons murmured. Steadily, as it watched the glimmering screen of sounds around it, the anemone continued to expand. Its ganglia linked, heeding a new source of stimuli from the delicate diaphragms in the crown of its notochord. The silent outlines of the laboratory began to echo softly, waves of muted sound fell from the arc lights and echoed off the benches and furniture below. Etched in sound, their angular forms resonated with sharp persistent overtones. The plastic-ribbed chairs were a buzz of staccato discords, the square-sided desk a continuous double-featured tone.

Ignoring these sounds once they had been perceived, the anemone turned to the ceiling, which reverberated like a shield in the sounds pouring steadily from the fluorescent tubes. Streaming through a narrow skylight, its voice clear and strong, interweaved by numberless overtones, the sun sang . . .

It was a few minutes before dawn when Powers left the laboratory and stepped into his car. Behind him the great dome lay silently in the darkness, the thin shadows of the white moonlit hills falling across its surface. Powers freewheeled the car down the long curving drive to the lake road below, listening to the tyres cutting across the blue gravel, then let out the clutch and accelerated the engine.

As he drove along, the limestone hills half hidden in the darkness on his left, he gradually became aware that, although no longer looking at the hills, he was still in some oblique way conscious of their forms and outlines in the back of his mind. The sensation was undefined but none the less certain, a strange almost visual impression that emanated most strongly from the deep clefts and ravines dividing one cliff face from the next. For a few minutes Powers let it play upon him, without trying to identify it, a dozen strange images moving across his brain.

The road swung up around a group of chalets built onto the lake shore, taking the car right under the lee of the hills, and Powers suddenly felt the massive weight of the escarpment rising up into the dark sky like a cliff of luminous chalk, and realized the identity of the impression now registering powerfully within his mind. Not only could he see the escarpment, but he was aware of its enormous age, felt distinctly the countless millions of years since it had first reared out of the magna of the earth's crust. The ragged crests three hundred feet above him, the dark gulleys and fissures, the smooth boulders by the roadside at the foot of the cliff, all carried a distinct image of themselves across to him, a thousand voices that together told of the total time that had elapsed in the life of the escarpment, a psychic picture as defined and clear as the visual image brought to him by his eyes.

Involuntarily, Powers had slowed the car, and turning his eyes away from the hill face he felt a second wave of time sweep across the first. The image was broader but of shorter perspectives, radiating from the wide disc of the salt lake, breaking over the ancient limestone cliffs like shallow rollers dashing against a towering headland.

Closing his eyes, Powers lay back and steered the car along the interval between the two time fronts, feeling the images deepen and strengthen within his mind. The vast age of the landscape, the inaudible chorus of voices resonating from the lake and from the white hills, seemed to carry him back through time, down endless corridors to the first thresholds of the world.

He turned the car off the road along the track leading towards the target range. On either side of the culvert the cliff faces boomed and echoed with vast impenetrable time fields, like enormous opposed magnets. As he finally emerged between them onto the flat surface of the lake it seemed to Powers that he could feel the separate identity of each sand grain and salt crystal calling to him from the surrounding ring of hills.

He parked the car beside the mandala and walked slowly towards the outer concrete rim curving away into the shadows. Above him he could hear the stars, a million cosmic voices that crowded the sky from one horizon to the next, a true canopy of time. Like jostling radio beacons, their long aisles interlocking at countless angles, they plunged into the sky from the narrowest recesses of space. He saw the dim red disc of Sirius, heard its ancient voice, untold millions of years old, dwarfed by the huge spiral nebulae in Andromeda, a gigantic carousel of vanished universes, their voices almost as old as the cosmos itself. To Powers the sky seemed an endless babel, the time-song of a thousand galaxies overlaying each other in his mind. As he moved slowly towards the centre of the mandala he craned up at the glittering traverse of the Milky Way, searching the confusion of clamouring nebulae and constellations.

Stepping into the inner circle of the mandala, a few yards from the platform at its centre, he realized that the tumult was beginning to fade, and that a single stronger voice had emerged and was dominating the others. He climbed onto the platform, raised his eyes to the darkened sky, moving through the constellations to the island galaxies beyond them, hearing the thin archaic voices reaching to him across the millennia. In his pockets he felt the paper tapes, and turned to find the distant diadem of Canes Venatici, heard its great voice mounting in his mind.

Like an endless river, so broad that its banks were below the horizon, it flowed steadily towards him, a vast course of time that spread outwards to fill the sky and the universe, enveloping everything within them. Moving slowly, the forward direction of its majestic current almost imperceptible, Powers knew that its source was the source of the cosmos itself. As it passed him, he felt its massive magnetic pull, let himself be drawn into it, borne gently on its powerful back. Quietly it carried him away, and he rotated slowly, facing the direction of the tide. Around him the outlines of the hills and the lake had faded, but the image of the mandala, like a cosmic clock, remained fixed before his eyes, illuminating the broad surface of the stream. Watching it constantly, he felt his body gradually dissolving, its physical dimensions melting into the vast continuum of the current, which bore him out into the centre of the great channel sweeping him onwards, beyond hope but at last at rest, down the broadening reaches of the river of eternity.

As the shadows faded, retreating into the hill slopes, Kaldren stepped out of his car, walked hesitantly towards the concrete rim of the outer circle. Fifty yards away, at the centre, Coma knelt beside Powers' body, her small hands pressed to his dead face. A gust of wind stirred the sand, dislodging a strip of tape that drifted towards Kaldren's feet. He bent down and picked it up, then rolled it carefully in his hands and slipped it into his pocket. The dawn air was cold, and he turned up the collar of his jacket, watching Coma impassively.

'It's six o'clock,' he told her after a few minutes. 'I'll go and get the police. You stay with him.' He paused and then added, 'Don't let them break the clock.'

Coma turned and looked at him. 'Aren't you coming back?'

'I don't know.' Nodding to her, Kaldren swung on his heel and went over to the car.

He reached the lake road, five minutes later parked the car in the drive outside Whitby's laboratory.

The dome was in darkness, all its windows shuttered, but the generator still hummed in the X-ray theatre. Kaldren stepped through the entrance and switched on the lights. In the theatre he touched the grills of the generator, felt the warm cylinder of the beryllium end-window. The circular target table was revolving slowly, its setting at 1 rpm, a steel restraining chair shackled to it hastily. Grouped in a semicircle a few feet away were most of the tanks and cages, piled on top of each other haphazardly. In one of them an enormous squidlike plant had almost managed to climb from its vivarium. Its long translucent tendrils clung to the edges of the tank, but its body had burst into a jellified pool of globular mucilage. In another an enormous spider had trapped itself in its own web, hung helplessly in the centre of a huge three-dimensional maze of phosphorescing thread, twitching spasmodically.

All the experimental plants and animals had died. The chimp lay on its back among the remains of the hutch, the helmet forward over its eyes. Kaldren watched it for a moment, then sat down on the desk and picked up the phone.

While he dialled the number he noticed a film reel lying on the blotter. For a moment he stared at the label, then slid the reel into his pocket beside the tape.

After he had spoken to the police he turned off the lights and went out to the car, drove off slowly down the drive.

When he reached the summer house the early sunlight was breaking across the ribbonlike balconies and terraces. He took the lift to the penthouse, made his way through into the museum. One by one he opened the shutters and let the sunlight play over the exhibits. Then he pulled a chair over to a side window, sat back and stared up at the light pouring through into the room.

Two or three hours later he heard Coma outside, calling up to him. After half an hour she went away, but a little later a second voice shouted up at Kaldren. He left his chair and closed all the shutters overlooking the front courtyard, and eventually he was left undisturbed.

Kaldren returned to his seat and lay back quietly, his eyes gazing across the lines of exhibits. Half asleep, periodically he leaned up and adjusted the flow of light through the shutter, thinking to himself as he would do through the coming months, of Powers and his strange mandala, and of the seven and their journey to the white gardens of the moon, and the blue people who had come from Orion and spoken in poetry to them of ancient beautiful worlds beneath golden suns in the island galaxies, vanished for ever now in the myriad deaths of the cosmos.

Specialist

Robert Sheckley

The photon storm struck without warning, pouncing upon the Ship from behind a bank of giant red stars. Eye barely had time to flash a last-second warning through Talker before it was upon them.

It was Talker's third journey into deep space, and his first light-pressure storm. He felt a sudden pang of fear as the Ship yawed violently, caught the force of the wave-front and careened end for end. Then the fear was gone, replaced by a strong pulse of excitement.

Why should he be afraid, he asked himself – hadn't he been trained for just this sort of emergency?

He had been talking to Feeder when the storm hit, but he cut off the conversation abruptly. He hoped Feeder would be all right. It was the youngster's first deep-space trip.

The wire-like filaments that made up most of Talker's body were extended throughout the Ship. Quickly he withdrew all except the ones linking him to Eye, Engine, and the Walls. This was strictly their job now. The rest of the Crew would have to shift for themselves until the storm was over.

Eye had flattened his disc-like body against a Wall, and had one seeing organ extended outside the Ship. For greater concentration, the rest of his seeing organs were collapsed, clustered against his body.

Through Eye's seeing organ, Talker watched the storm. He translated Eye's purely visual image into a direction for

Engine, who shoved the Ship around to meet the waves. At appreciably the same time, Talker translated direction into velocity for the Walls who stiffened to meet the shocks.

The coordination was swift and sure – Eye measuring the waves, Talker relaying the messages to Engine and Walls, Engine driving the Ship nose-first into the waves, and Walls bracing to meet the shock.

Talker forgot any fear he might have had in the swiftly functioning teamwork. He had no time to think. As the Ship's communication system, he had to translate and flash his messages at top speed, coordinating information and directing action.

In a matter of minutes, the storm was over.

'All right,' Talker said. 'Let's see if there was any damage!' His filaments had become tangled during the storm, but he untwisted and extended them through the Ship, plugging everyone into circuit. 'Engine?'

'I'm fine,' Engine said. The tremendous old fellow had dampened his plates during the storm, easing down the atomic explosions in his stomach. No storm could catch an experienced spacer like Engine unaware.

'Walls?'

The Walls reported one by one, and this took a long time. There were almost a thousand of them, thin, rectangular fellows making up the entire skin of the Ship. Naturally, they had reinforced their edges during the storm, giving the whole Ship resiliency. But one or two were dented badly.

Doctor announced that he was all right. He removed Talker's filament from his head, taking himself out of circuit, and went to work on the dented Walls. Made mostly of hands, Doctor had clung to an Accumulator during the storm.

'Let's go a little faster now!' Talker said, remembering that there still was the problem of determining where they were. He opened the circuit to the four Accumulators. 'How are you?' he asked.

There was no answer. The Accumulators were asleep. They had had their receptors open during the storm and were bloated on energy. Talker twitched his filaments around them, but they didn't stir.

'Let me!' Feeder said. Feeder had taken quite a beating before planting his suction cups to a Wall, but his cockiness was intact. He was the only member of the Crew who never needed Doctor's attention; his body was quite capable of repairing itself.

He scuttled across the floor on a dozen or so tentacles, and booted the nearest Accumulator. The big, conical storage unit opened one eye, then closed it again. Feeder kicked him again, getting no response. He reached for the Accumulator's safety valve and drained off some energy.

'Stop that!' the Accumulator said.

'Then wake up and report!' Talker told him.

The Accumulators said testily that they were all right, as any fool could see. They had been anchored to the floor during the storm.

The rest of the inspection went quickly. Thinker was fine, and Eye was ecstatic over the beauty of the storm. There was only one casualty.

Pusher was dead. Bipedal, he didn't have the stability of the rest of the Crew. The storm had caught him in the middle of a floor, thrown him against a stiffened Wall, and broken several of his important bones. He was beyond Doctor's skill to repair.

They were silent for a while. It was always serious when a part of the Ship died. The Ship was a cooperative unit, composed entirely of the Crew. The loss of any member was a blow to all the rest.

It was especially serious now. They had just delivered a cargo to a port several thousand light years from Galactic Centre. There was no telling where they might be.

Eye crawled to a Wall and extended a seeing organ outside. The Walls let it through, then sealed around it. Eye's organ pushed out, far enough from the Ship so he could view the entire sphere of stars. The picture travelled through Talker, who gave it to Thinker.

Thinker lay in one corner of the room, a great shapeless blob of protoplasm. Within him were all the memories of his space-going ancestors. He considered the picture, compared it rapidly with others stored in his cells, and said, 'No galactic planets within reach.'

Talker automatically translated for everyone. It was what they had feared.

Eye, with Thinker's help, calculated that they were several hundred light years off their course, on the galactic periphery.

Every Crew member knew what that meant. Without a Pusher to boost the Ship to a multiple of the speed of light, they would never get home. The trip back, without a Pusher, would take longer than most of their lifetimes.

'What would you suggest?' Talker asked Thinker.

This was too vague a question for the literal-minded Thinker. He asked to have it rephrased.

'What would be our best line of action,' Talker asked, 'to get back to a galactic planet?'

Thinker needed several minutes to go through all the possibilities stored in his cells. In the meantime, Doctor had patched the Walls and was asking to be given something to eat.

'In a little while we'll all eat,' Talker said, twitching his tendrils nervously. Even though he was the second youngest Crew member – only Feeder was younger – the responsibility was largely on him. This was still an emergency; he had to coordinate information and direct action.

One of the Walls suggested that they get good and drunk. This unrealistic solution was vetoed at once. It was typical of the Walls' attitude, however. They were fine workers and good shipmates, but happy-go-lucky fellows at best. When they returned to their home planets, they would probably blow all their wages on a spree.

'Loss of the Ship's Pusher cripples the Ship for sustained faster-than-light speeds,' Thinker began without preamble. 'The nearest galactic planet is four hundred and five light years off.'

Talker translated all this instantly along his wave-packet body.

'Two courses of action are open. First, the Ship can proceed to the nearest galactic planet under atomic power from Engine. This will take approximately two hundred years. Engine might still be alive at this time, although no one else will.

'Second, locate a primitive planet in this region, upon which are latent Pushers. Find one and train him. Have him push the Ship back to galactic territory.'

Thinker was silent, having given all the possibilities he could find in the memories of his ancestors.

They held a quick vote and decided upon Thinker's second alternative. There was no choice, really. It was the only one which offered them any hope of getting back to their homes.

'All right,' Talker said. 'Let's eat! I think we all deserve it.'

The body of the dead Pusher was shoved into the mouth of Engine, who consumed it at once, breaking down the atoms to energy. Engine was the only member of the Crew who lived on atomic energy.

For the rest, Feeder dashed up and loaded himself from the nearest Accumulator. Then he transformed the food within him into the substances each member ate. His body chemistry changed, altered, adapted, making the different foods for the Crew.

Eye lived entirely on a complex chlorophyll chain. Feeder reproduced this for him, then went over to give Talker his hydrocarbons, and the Walls their chlorine compound. For Doctor he made a fascimile of a silicate fruit that grew on Doctor's native planet.

Finally, feeding was over and the Ship back in order. The Accumulators were stacked in a corner, blissfully sleeping again. Eye was extending his vision as far as he could, shaping his main seeing organ for high-powered telescopic reception. Even in this emergency, Eye couldn't resist making verses. He announced that he was at work on a new narrative poem, called *Peripheral Glow*. No one wanted to hear it, so Eye fed it to Thinker, who stored everything, good or bad, right or wrong.

Engine never slept. Filled to the brim on Pusher, he shoved the Ship along at several times the speed of light.

The Walls were arguing among themselves about who had been the drunkest during their last leave.

Talker decided to make himself comfortable. He released his hold on the Walls and swung in the air, his small round body suspended by his criss-crossed network of filaments.

He thought briefly about Pusher. It was strange. Pusher had been everyone's friend and now he was forgotten. That wasn't because of indifference; it was because the Ship was a unit. The loss of a member was regretted, but the important thing was for the unit to go on.

The Ship raced through the suns of the periphery.

Thinker laid out a search spiral, calculating their odds on finding a Pusher planet at roughly four to one. In a week they found a planet of primitive Walls. Dropping low, they could see the leathery, rectangular fellows basking in the sun, crawling over rocks, stretching themselves thin in order to float in the breeze.

All the Ship's Walls heaved a sigh of nostalgia. It was just like home.

These Walls on the planet hadn't been contacted by a galactic team yet, and were still unaware of their great destiny – to join in the vast Cooperation of the Galaxy.

There were plenty of dead worlds in the spiral, and worlds too young to bear life. They found a planet of Talkers. The Talkers had extended their spidery communication lines across half a continent.

Talker looked at them eagerly, through Eye. A wave of self-pity washed over him. He remembered home, his family, his friends. He thought of the tree he was going to buy when he got back.

For a moment, Talker wondered what he was doing here, part of a Ship in a far corner of the Galaxy.

He shrugged off the mood. They were bound to find a Pusher planet, if they looked long enough.

At least, he hoped so.

There was a long stretch of arid worlds as the Ship sped

through the unexplored periphery. Then a planetful of primeval Engines, swimming in a radioactive ocean.

'This is rich territory,' Feeder said to Talker. 'Galactic should send a Contact party here.'

'They probably will, after we get back,' Talker said.

They were good friends, above and beyond the all-enveloping friendship of the Crew. It wasn't only because they were the youngest Crew members, although that had something to do with it. They both had the same kind of functions and that made for a certain rapport. Talker translated languages; Feeder transformed foods. Also, they looked somewhat alike. Talker was a central core with radiating filaments; Feeder was a central core with radiating tentacles.

Talker thought that Feeder was the next most aware being on the Ship. He was never really able to understand how some of the others carried on the processes of consciousness.

More suns, more planets! Engine started to overheat. Usually, Engine was used only for taking off and landing, and for fine manoeuvring in a planetary group. Now he had been running continuously for weeks, both over and under the speed of light. The strain was telling on him.

Feeder, with Doctor's help, rigged a cooling system for him. It was crude, but it had to suffice. Feeder rearranged nitrogen, oxygen and hydrogen atoms to make a coolant for the system. Doctor diagnosed a long rest for Engine. He said that the gallant old fellow couldn't stand the strain for more than a week.

The search continued, with the Crew's spirits gradually dropping. They all realized that Pushers were rather rare in the Galaxy, as compared to the fertile Walls and Engines.

The Walls were getting pock-marked from interstellar dust. They complained that they would need a full beauty treatment when they got home. Talker assured them that the company would pay for it.

Even Eye was getting bloodshot from staring into space so continuously.

They dipped over another planet. Its characteristics were flashed to Thinker, who mulled over them.

Closer, and they could make out the forms.

Pushers! Primitive Pushers!

They zoomed back into space to make plans. Feeder produced twenty-three different kinds of intoxicants for a celebration.

The Ship wasn't fit to function for three days.

'Everyone ready now?' Talker asked, a bit fuzzily. He had a hangover that burned all along his nerve ends. What a drunk he had thrown! He had a vague recollection of embracing Engine, and inviting him to share his tree when they got home.

He shuddered at the idea.

The rest of the Crew were pretty shaky, too. The Walls were letting air leak into space; they were just too wobbly to seal their edges properly. Doctor had passed out.

But the worst off was Feeder. Since his system could adapt to any type of fuel except atomic, he had been sampling every batch he made, whether it was an unbalanced iodine, pure oxygen or a supercharged ester. He was really miserable. His tentacles, usually a healthy aqua, were shot through with orange streaks. His system was working furiously, purging itself of everything, and Feeder was suffering the effects of the purge.

The only sober ones were Thinker and Engine. Thinker didn't drink, which was unusual for a spacer, though typical of Thinker, and Engine couldn't.

They listened while Thinker reeled off some astounding facts. From Eye's pictures of the planet's surface, Thinker had detected the presence of metallic construction. He put forth the alarming suggestion that these Pushers had constructed a mechanical civilization.

'That's impossible,' three of the Walls said flatly, and most of the Crew were inclined to agree with them. All the metal they had ever seen had been buried in the ground or lying around in worthless oxidized chunks.

'Do you mean that they make things out of metal?' Talker demanded. 'Out of just plain dead metal? What could they make?'

'They couldn't make anything,' Feeder said positively. 'It

would break down constantly. I mean metal doesn't *know* when it's weakening.'

But it seemed to be true. Eye magnified his pictures, and everyone could see that the Pushers had made vast shelters, vehicles, and other articles from inanimate material.

The reason for this was not readily apparent, but it wasn't a good sign. However, the really hard part was over. The Pusher planet had been found. All that remained was the relatively easy job of convincing a native Pusher.

That shouldn't be too difficult. Talker knew that co-operation was the keystone of the Galaxy, even among primitive peoples.

The Crew decided not to land in a populated region. Of course, there was no reason not to expect a friendly greeting, but it was the job of a Contact Team to get in touch with them as a race. All they wanted was an individual.

Accordingly, they picked out a sparsely populated land-mass, drifting in while that side of the planet was dark.

They were able to locate a solitary Pusher almost at once.

Eye adapted his vision to see in the dark, and they followed the Pusher's movements. He lay down, after a while, beside a small fire. Thinker told them that this was a well-known resting habit of Pushers.

Just before dawn, the Walls opened, and Feeder, Talker and Doctor came out.

Feeder dashed forward and tapped the creature on the shoulder. Talker followed with a communication tendril.

The Pusher opened his seeing organs, blinked them, and made a movement with his eating organ. Then he leaped to his feet and started to run.

The three Crew members were amazed. The Pusher hadn't even waited to find out what the three of them wanted!

Talker extended a filament rapidly, and caught the Pusher, fifty feet away, by a limb. The Pusher fell.

'Treat him gently!' Feeder said. 'He might be startled by our appearance.' He twitched his tendrils at the idea of a Pusher – one of the strangest sights in the Galaxy, with his multiple organs – being startled at someone else's appearance.

Feeder and Doctor scurried to the fallen Pusher, picked him up and carried him back to the Ship.

The Walls sealed again. They released the Pusher and prepared to talk.

As soon as he was free, the Pusher sprang to his limbs and ran at the place where the Walls had sealed. He pounded against them frantically, his eating organ open and vibrating.

'Stop that!' the Wall said. He bulged, and the Pusher tumbled to the floor. Instantly, he jumped up and started to run forward.

'Stop him!' Talker said. 'He might hurt himself.'

One of the Accumulators woke up enough to roll into the Pusher's path. The Pusher fell, got up again, and ran on.

Talker had his filaments in the front of the Ship also, and he caught the Pusher in the bow. The Pusher started to tear at his tendrils, and Talker let go hastily.

'Plug him into the communication system!' Feeder shouted. 'Maybe we can reason with him.'

Talker advanced a filament towards the Pusher's head, waving it in the universal sign of communication. But the Pusher continued his amazing behaviour, jumping out of the way. He had a piece of metal in his hand and he was waving it frantically.

'What do you think he's going to do with that?' Feeder asked. The Pusher started to attack the side of the Ship, pounding at one of the Walls. The Wall stiffened instinctively and the metal snapped.

'Leave him alone,' Talker said. 'Give him a chance to calm down.'

Talker consulted with Thinker, but they couldn't decide what to do about the Pusher. He wouldn't accept communication. Every time Talker extended a filament, the Pusher showed all the signs of violent panic. Temporarily, it was an impasse.

Thinker vetoed the plan of finding another Pusher on the planet. He considered this Pusher's behaviour typical;

nothing would be gained by approaching another. Also, a planet was supposed to be contacted only by a Contact Team.

If they couldn't communicate with this Pusher, they never would with another on the planet.

'I think I know what the trouble is,' Eye said. He crawled up on an Accumulator. 'These Pushers have evolved a mechanical civilization. Consider for a minute how they went about it. They developed the use of their fingers, like Doctor, to shape metal. They utilized their seeing organs, like myself. And probably countless other organs.' He paused for effect.

'These Pushers have become unspecialized.'

'They argued over it for several hours. The Walls maintained that no intelligent creature could be unspecialized. It was unknown in the Galaxy. But the evidence was before them – the Pusher cities, their vehicles. This Pusher, exemplifying the rest, seemed capable of a multitude of things.

He was able to do everything except Push.

Thinker supplied a partial explanation. 'This is not a primitive planet. It is relatively old and should have been in the Cooperation thousands of years ago. Since it was not, the Pushers upon it were robbed of their birthright. Their ability, their speciality was to Push, but there was nothing *to* Push. Naturally, they have developed a deviant culture.

'Exactly what this culture is, we can only guess. But on the basis of the evidence, there is reason to believe that these Pushers are – uncooperative.'

Thinker had a habit of uttering the most shattering statement in the quietest possible way.

'It is entirely possible,' Thinker went on inexorably, 'that these Pushers will have nothing to do with us. In which case, our chances are approximately two hundred and eighty-three to one against finding another Pusher planet.'

'We can't be sure he won't cooperate,' Talker said, 'until we get him into communication.' He found it almost impossible to believe that any intelligent creature would refuse to cooperate willingly.

'But how?' Feeder asked. They decided upon a course of

action. Doctor walked slowly up to the Pusher, who backed away from him. In the meantime, Talker extended a filament outside the Ship, around, and in again, behind the Pusher.

The Pusher backed against a Wall – and Talker shoved the filament through the Pusher's head, into the communication socket in the centre of his brain.

The Pusher collapsed.

When he came to, Feeder and Doctor had to hold the Pusher's limbs, or he would have ripped out the communication line. Talker exercised his skill in learning the Pusher's language.

It wasn't too hard. All Pusher languages were of the same family, and this was no exception. Talker was able to catch enough surface thoughts to form a pattern.

He tried to communicate with the Pusher.

The Pusher was silent.

'I think he needs food,' Feeder said. They remembered that it had been almost two days since they had taken the Pusher on board. Feeder worked up some standard Pusher food and offered it.

'My God! A steak!' the Pusher said.

The Crew cheered along Talker's communication circuits. The Pusher had said his first words.

Talker examined the words and searched his memory. He knew about two hundred Pusher languages and many more simple variations. He found that this Pusher was speaking a cross between two Pusher tongues.

After the Pusher had eaten, he looked around. Talker caught his thoughts and broadcast them to the Crew.

The Pusher had a queer way of looking at the Ship. He saw it as a riot of colours. The walls undulated. In front of him was something resembling a gigantic spider, coloured black and green, with his web running all over the Ship and into the heads of all the creatures. He saw Eye as a strange, naked little animal, something between a skinned rabbit and an egg yolk – whatever those things were.

Talker was fascinated by the new perspective the Pusher's

mind gave him. He had never seen things that way before. But now that the Pusher was pointing it out, Eye *was* a pretty funny-looking creature.

They settled down to communication.

'What in hell *are* you things?' the Pusher asked, much calmer now than he had been during the two days. 'Why did you grab me? Have I gone nuts?'

'No,' Talker said, 'you are not psychotic. We are a galactic trading ship. We were blown off our course by a storm and our Pusher was killed.'

'Well, what does that have to do with me?'

'We would like you to join our crew,' Talker said, 'to be our new Pusher.'

The Pusher thought it over after the situation was explained to him. Talker could catch the feeling of conflict in the Pusher's thoughts. He hadn't decided whether to accept this as a real situation or not. Finally, the Pusher decided that he wasn't crazy.

'Look, boys,' he said, 'I don't know what you are or how this makes sense. I have to get out of here. I'm on a furlough, and if I don't get back soon, the US Army's going to be very interested.'

Talker asked the Pusher to give him more information about 'army', and he fed it to Thinker.

'These Pushers engage in personal combat,' was Thinker's conclusion.

'But *why*?' Talker asked. Sadly he admitted to himself that Thinker might have been right; the Pusher didn't show many signs of willingness to cooperate.

'I'd like to help you lads out,' Pusher said, 'but I don't know where you get the idea that I could push anything this size. You'd need a whole division of tanks just to budge it.'

'Do you approve of these wars?' Talker asked, getting a suggestion from Thinker.

'Nobody likes war – not those who have to do the dying at least.'

'Then why do you fight them?'

The Pusher made a gesture with his eating organ, which

Eye picked up and sent to Thinker. 'It's kill or be killed. You guys know what war is, don't you?'

'We don't have any wars,' Talker said.

'You're lucky,' the Pusher said bitterly. 'We do. Plenty of them.'

'Of course,' Talker said. He had the full explanation from Thinker now. 'Would you like to end them?'

'Of course I would.'

'Then come with us! Be our Pusher!'

The Pusher stood up and walked up to an Accumulator. He sat down on it and doubled the ends of his upper limbs.

'How the hell can I stop all wars?' the Pusher demanded. 'Even if I went to the big shots and told them – '

'You won't have to,' Talker said. 'All you have to do is come with us. Push us to our base. Galactic will send a Contact Team to your planet. That will end your wars.'

'The hell you say,' the Pusher replied. 'You boys are stranded here, huh? Good enough! No monsters are going to take over Earth.'

Bewildered, Talker tried to understand the reasoning. Had he said something wrong? Was it possible that the Pusher didn't understand him?

'I thought you wanted to end wars,' Talker said.

'Sure I do. But I don't want anyone *making* us stop. I'm no traitor. I'd rather fight.'

'No one will make you stop. You will just stop because there will be no further need for fighting.'

'Do you know why we're fighting?'

'It's obvious.'

'Yeah? What's your explanation?'

'You Pushers have been separated from the main stream of the Galaxy,' Talker explained. 'You have your speciality – pushing – but nothing to push. Accordingly, you have no real jobs. You play with things – metal, inanimate objects – but find no real satisfaction. Robbed of your true vocation, you fight from sheer frustration.

'Once you find your place in the galactic Cooperation – and I assure you that it is an important place – your fighting will stop. Why should you fight, which is an unnatural occupation, when you can push? Also, your mechanical civilization will end, since there will be no need for it.'

The Pusher shook his head in what Talker guessed was a gesture of confusion. 'What is this pushing?'

Talker told him as best he could. Since the job was out of his scope, he had only a general idea of what a Pusher did.

'You mean to say that *that* is what every Earthman should be doing?'

'Of course,' Talker said. 'It is your great speciality.'

The Pusher thought about it for several minutes. 'I think you want a physicist or a mentalist or something. I could never do anything like that. I'm a junior architect. And besides – well, it's difficult to explain.'

But Talker had already caught Pusher's objection. He saw a Pusher female in his thoughts. No, two, three. And he caught a feeling of loneliness, strangeness. The Pusher was filled with doubts. He was afraid.

'When we reach Galactic,' Talker said, hoping it was the right thing, 'you can meet other Pushers. Pusher females, too. All you Pushers look alike, so you should become friends with them. As far as loneliness in the Ship goes – it just doesn't exist. You don't understand the Cooperation yet. No one is lonely in the Cooperation.'

The Pusher was still considering the idea of there being other Pushers. Talker couldn't understand why he was so startled at that. The Galaxy was filled with Pushers, Feeders, Talkers, and many other species, endlessly duplicated.

'I can't believe that anybody could end all war,' Pusher said. 'How do I know you're not lying?'

Talker felt as if he had been struck in the core. Thinker must have been right when he said these Pushers would be uncooperative. Was this going to be the end of Talker's career? Were he and the rest of the Crew going to spend the rest of their lives in space, because of the stupidity of a bunch of Pushers?

Even thinking this, Talker was able to feel sorry for the Pusher. It must be terrible, he thought. Doubting, uncertain, never trusting anyone. If these Pushers didn't find their place in the Galaxy, they would exterminate themselves. Their place in the Cooperation was long overdue.

'What can I do to convince you?' Talker asked.

In despair, he opened all the circuits to the Pusher. He let the Pusher see Engine's good-natured gruffness, the devil-may-care humour of the Walls; he showed him Eye's poetic attempts, and Feeder's cocky good nature. He opened his own mind and showed the Pusher a picture of his home planet, his family, the tree he was planning to buy when he got home.

The pictures told the story of all of them, from different planets, representing different ethics, united by a common bond – the galactic Cooperation.

The Pusher watched it all in silence.

After a while, he shook his head. The thought accompanying the gesture was uncertain, weak – but negative.

Talker told the Walls to open. They did, and the Pusher stared in amazement.

'You may leave,' Talker said. 'Just remove the communication line and go.'

'What will you do?'

'We will look for another Pusher planet.'

'Where? Mars? Venus?'

'We don't know. All we can do is hope there is another in this region.'

The Pusher looked at the opening, then back at the Crew. He hesitated and his face screwed up in a grimace of indecision.

'All that you showed me was true?'

No answer was necessary.

'All right,' the Pusher said suddenly. 'I'll go. I'm a damned fool, but I'll go. If this means what you say – it *must* mean what you say!'

Talker saw that the agony of the Pusher's decision had forced him out of contact with reality. He believed that he was in a dream, where decisions are easy and unimportant.

'There's just one little trouble,' Pusher said with the lightness of hysteria. 'Boys, I'll be damned if I know how to push. You said something about faster-than-light? I can't even run the mile in an hour.'

'Of course you can push,' Talker assured him, hoping he was right. He knew what a Pusher's abilities were; but this one –

'Just try it.'

'Sure,' Pusher agreed. 'I'll probably wake up out of this, anyhow.'

They sealed the ship for take-off while Pusher talked to himself.

'Funny,' Pusher said. 'I thought a camping trip would be a nice way to spend a furlough and all I do is get nightmares!'

Engine boosted the Ship into the air. The Walls were sealed and Eye was guiding them away from the planet.

'We're in open space now,' Talker said. Listening to Pusher, he hoped his mind hadn't cracked. 'Eye and Thinker will give a direction, I'll transmit it to you, and you push along it.'

'You're crazy,' Pusher mumbled. 'You must have the wrong planet. I wish you nightmares would go away.'

'You're in the Cooperation now,' Talker said desperately. 'There's the direction. Push!'

The Pusher didn't do anything for a moment. He was slowly emerging from his fantasy, realizing that he wasn't in a dream, after all. He felt the Cooperation. Eye to Thinker, Thinker to Talker, Talker to Pusher, all inter-coordinated with Walls, and with each other.

'What is this?' Pusher asked. He felt the oneness of the Ship, the great warmth, the closeness achieved only in the Cooperation.

He pushed.

Nothing happened.

'Try again,' Talker begged.

Pusher searched his mind. He found a deep well of doubt and fear. Staring into it, he saw his own tortured face.

Thinker illuminated it for him.

Pushers had lived with this doubt and fear for centuries. Pushers had fought through fear, killed through doubt.

That was where the Pusher organ was!

Human – specialist – Pusher – he entered fully into the Crew, merged with them, threw mental arms around the shoulders of Thinker and Talker.

Suddenly, the Ship shot forward at eight times the speed of light. It continued to accelerate.

He Walked around the Horses

H. Beam Piper

In November 1809, an Englishman named Benjamin Bathurst vanished, inexplicably and utterly.

He was en route to Hamburg from Vienna, where he had been serving as his Government's envoy to the court of what Napoleon had left of the Austrian Empire. At an inn in Perleburg, in Prussia, while examining a change of horses for his coach, he casually stepped out of sight of his secretary and his valet. He was not seen to leave the inn yard. He was not seen again, ever.

At least, not in this continuum . . .

1

(From Baron Eugen von Krutz, Minister of Police, to His Excellency the Count von Berchtenwald, Chancellor to His Majesty Friedrich Wilhelm III of Prussia)

25 November 1809

Your Excellency:

A circumstance has come to the notice of this Ministry, the significance of which I am at a loss to define, but, since it appears to involve matters of state, both here and abroad, I am convinced that it is of sufficient importance to be brought to the personal attention of your Excellency. Frankly, I am unwilling to take any further action in the matter without your Excellency's advice.

Briefly, the situation is this: We are holding, here at the Ministry of Police, a person giving his name as Benjamin

Bathurst, who claims to be a British diplomat. This person was taken into custody by the police at Perleburg yesterday, as a result of a disturbance at an inn there; he is being detained on technical charges of causing disorder in a public place, and of being a suspicious person. When arrested, he had in his possession a dispatch case, containing a number of papers; these are of such an extraordinary nature that the local authorities declined to assume any responsibility beyond having the man sent here to Berlin.

After interviewing this person and examining his papers, I am, I must confess, in much the same position. This is not, I am convinced, any ordinary police matter; there is something very strange and disturbing here. The man's statements, taken alone, are so incredible as to justify the assumption that he is mad. I cannot, however, adopt this theory, in view of his demeanour, which is that of a man of perfect rationality, and because of the existence of these papers. The whole thing is mad; incomprehensible!

The papers in question accompany, along with copies of the various statements taken in Perleburg, and a personal letter to me from my nephew, Lieutenant Rudolph von Tarlburg. This last is deserving of your Excellency's particular attention; Lieutenant von Tarlburg is a very level-headed young officer, not at all inclined to be fanciful or imaginative. It would take a great deal to affect him as he describes.

The man calling himself Benjamin Bathurst is now lodged in an apartment here at the Ministry; he is being treated with every consideration, and, except for freedom of movement, accorded every privilege.

I am, most anxiously awaiting your Excellency's advice, etc., etc.,

KRUTZ.

2

(Report of Traugott Zeller, *Oberwachtmeister*, *Staatspolizei*, made at Perleburg, 25 November 1809)

At about ten minutes past two of the afternoon of Saturday, 25 November, while I was at the police station, there entered a man known to me as Franz Bauer, an inn servant employed by Christian Hauck, at the sign of the Sword and Sceptre, here in Perleburg. This man Franz Bauer made complaint to Staatspolizeikapitän Ernst Hartenstein, saying that there was a madman making trouble at the inn where he, Franz Bauer, worked. I was therefore directed by Staatspolizeikapitän Hartenstein to go to the Sword and Sceptre Inn, there to act at discretion to maintain the peace.

Arriving at the inn in company with the said Franz Bauer, I found a considerable crowd of people in the common-room, and, in the midst of them, the innkeeper, Christian Hauck, in altercation with a stranger. This stranger was a gentlemanly-appearing person, dressed in travelling clothes, who had under his arm a small leather dispatch case. As I entered, I could hear him, speaking in German with a strong English accent, abusing the innkeeper, the said Christian Hauck, and accusing him of having drugged his, the stranger's, wine, and of having stolen his, the stranger's, coach and four, and of having abducted his, the stranger's, secretary and servants. This the said Christian Hauck was loudly denying, and the other people in the inn were taking the innkeeper's part, and mocking the stranger for a madman.

On entering, I commanded everyone to be silent, in the King's name, and then, as he appeared to be the complaining party of the dispute, I required the foreign gentleman to state to me what was the trouble. He then repeated his accusations against the innkeeper, Hauck, saying that Hauck, or, rather, another man who resembled Hauck and who had claimed to be the innkeeper, had drugged his wine and stolen his coach and made off with his secretary and his servants. At this point, the innkeeper and the bystanders all began shouting denials and contradictions, so that I had to pound on a table with my truncheon to command silence.

I then required the innkeeper, Christian Hauck, to answer the charges which the stranger had made; this he did with a complete denial of all of them, saying that the stranger had had no wine in his inn, and that he had not been inside the inn until a few minutes before, when he had burst in shouting accusations, and that there had been no secretary, and no valet, and no coachman, and no coach and four, at the inn, and that the gentleman was raving mad. To all this, he called the people who were in the commonroom to witness.

I then required the stranger to account for himself. He said that his name was Benjamin Bathurst, and that he was a British diplomat, returning to England from Vienna. To prove this, he produced from his dispatch case sundry papers. One of these was a letter of safe conduct, issued by the Prussian Chancellery, in which he was named and described as Benjamin Bathurst. The other papers were English, all bearing seals, and appearing to be official documents.

Accordingly, I requested him to accompany me to the police station, and also the innkeeper, and three men whom the innkeeper wanted to bring as witnesses.

TRAUGOTT ZELLER
Oberwachtmeister

Report approved,

ERNST HARTENSTEIN
Staatspolizeikapitän

3

(Statement of the self-so-called Benjamin Bathurst, taken at the police station at Perleburg, 25 November 1809)

My name is Benjamin Bathurst, and I am Envoy Extraordinary and Minister Plenipotentiary of the Government of His Britannic Majesty to the court of His Majesty Franz I, Emperor of Austria, or at least I was until the events following the Austrian surrender made necessary my return to London. I left Vienna on the morning of Monday, the 20th, to go to Hamburg to take ship home; I was travelling in my own coach and four, with my secretary, Mr Bertram Jardine, and my valet, William Small, both British subjects, and a coachman, Josef Bidek, an Austrian subject, whom I had hired for the trip. Because of the presence of French troops, whom I was anxious to avoid, I was forced to make a detour west as far as Salzburg before turning north toward Magdeburg, where I crossed the Elbe. I was unable to get a change of horses for my coach after leaving Gera, until I reached Perleburg, where I stopped at the Sword and Sceptre Inn.

Arriving there, I left my coach in the inn yard, and I and my secretary, Mr Jardine, went into the inn. A man, not this fellow here, but another rogue, with more beard and less paunch, and more shabbily dressed, but as like him as though he were his brother, represented himself as the innkeeper, and I dealt with him for a change of horses, and ordered a bottle of wine for myself and my secretary, and also a pot of beer apiece for my valet and the coachman, to be taken outside to them. Then Jardine and I sat down to our wine, at a table in the commonroom, until the man who claimed to be the innkeeper came back and told us that the fresh horses were harnessed to the coach and ready to go. Then we went outside again.

I looked at the two horses on the off-side, and then walked around in front of the team to look at the two nigh-side horses, and as I did, I felt giddy, as though I were about to fall, and everything went black before my eyes. I thought I was having a fainting spell, something I am not at all subject to, and I put out my hand to grasp the hitching bar, but could not find it. I am sure, now, that I was unconscious for some time, because when my head cleared, the coach and horses were gone, and in their place was a big farm wagon, jacked up in front, with the right wheel off, and two peasants were greasing the detached wheel.

I looked at them for a moment, unable to credit my eyes, and then I spoke to them in German, saying, 'Where the devil's my coach and four?'

They both straightened, startled; the one who was holding the wheel almost dropped it.

'Pardon, Excellency,' he said. 'There's been no coach and four here, all the time we've been here.'

'Yes,' said his mate, 'and we've been here since just after noon.'

I did not attempt to argue with them. It occurred to me – and it is still my opinion – that I was the victim of some plot; that my wine had been drugged, that I had been unconscious for some time during which my coach had been removed and this wagon substituted for it, and that these peasants had been put to work on it and instructed what to say if questioned. If my arrival at the inn had been anticipated, and everything put in readiness, the whole business would not have taken ten minutes.

I therefore entered the inn, determined to have it out with this rascally innkeeper, but when I returned to the commonroom, he was nowhere to be seen, and this other fellow, who has also given his name as Christian Hauck, claimed to be the innkeeper and denied knowledge of any of the things I have just stated. Furthermore, there were four cavalrymen, Uhlans, drinking beer and playing cards at the table where Jardine and I had had our wine, and they claimed to have been there for several hours.

I have no idea why such an elaborate prank, involving the participation of many people, should be played on me, except at the instigation of the French. In that case, I cannot understand why Prussian soldiers should lend themselves to it.

BENJAMIN BATHURST

4

(Statement of Christian Hauck, innkeeper, taken at the police station at Perleburg, 25 November 1809)

May it please your Honour, my name is Christian Hauck, and I keep an inn at the sign of the Sword and Sceptre, and have these past fifteen years, and my father, and his father before him, for the past fifty years, and never has there been a complaint like this against my inn. Your Honour, it is a hard thing for a man who keeps a decent house, and pays his taxes, and obeys the laws, to be accused of crimes of this sort.

I know nothing of this gentleman, nor of his coach nor his secretary nor his servants; I never set eyes on him before he came bursting into the inn from the yard, shouting and raving like a madman, and crying out, 'Where the devil's that rogue of an innkeeper?'

I said to him, 'I am the innkeeper; what cause have you to call me a rogue, sir?'

The stranger replied: 'You're not the innkeeper I did business with a few minutes ago, and he's the rascal I have a row to pick with. I want to know what the devil's been done with my coach, and what's happened to my secretary and my servants.'

I tried to tell him that I knew nothing of what he was talking about, but he would not listen, and gave me the lie, saying that he had been drugged and robbed, and his people kidnapped. He even had the impudence to claim that he and his secretary had been sitting at a table in that room, drinking wine, not fifteen minutes before, when there had been four non-commissioned officers of the Third Uhlans at that table since noon. Everybody in the room spoke up for me, but he would not listen, and was shouting that we were all robbers, and kidnappers, and French spies, and I don't know what all, when the police came.

Your Honour, the man is mad. What I have told you about this is the truth, and all that I know about this business, so help me God.

CHRISTIAN HAUCK

5

(Statement of Franz Bauer, inn servant, taken at the police station at Perleburg, 25 November 1809)

May it please your Honour, my name is Franz Bauer, and I am a servant at the Sword and Sceptre Inn, kept by Christian Hauck.

This afternoon, when I went into the inn yard to empty a bucket of slops on the dung heap by the stables, I heard voices and turned around, to see this gentleman speaking to Wilhelm Beick and Fritz Herzer, who were greasing their wagon in the yard. He had not been in the yard when I had turned around to empty the bucket, and I thought that he must have come in from the street. This gentleman was asking Beick and Herzer where was his coach, and when they told him they didn't know, he turned and ran into the inn.

Of my own knowledge, the man had not been inside the inn before then, nor had there been any coach, or any of the people he spoke of, at the inn, and none of the things he spoke of happened there, for otherwise I would know, since I was at the inn all day.

When I went back inside, I found him in the common-room, shouting at my master, and claiming that he had been drugged and robbed. I saw that he was mad, and was afraid that he would do some mischief, so I went for the police.

FRANZ BAUER
his (X) mark

6

(Statements of Wilhelm Beick and Fritz Herzer, peasants, taken at the police station at Perleburg, 25 November 1809)

May it please your Honour, my name is Wilhelm Beick, and I am a tenant on the estate of the Baron von Hentig. On this day, I and Fritz Herzer were sent into Perleburg with a load of potatoes and cabbages which the innkeeper at the Sword and Sceptre had bought from the estate super-intendent. After we had unloaded them, we decided to grease our wagon, which was very dry, before going back, so we unhitched and began working on it. We took about two hours, starting just after we had eaten lunch, and in all that time there was no coach and four in the inn yard. We were just finishing when this gentleman spoke to us, de-manding to know where his coach was. We told him that there had been no coach in the yard all the time we had been there, so he turned around and ran into the inn. At the time, I thought that he had come out of the inn before speaking to us, for I know that he could not have come in from the street. Now I do not know where he came from, but I know that I never saw him before that moment.

WILHELM BEICK
his (X) mark

I have heard the above testimony, and it is true to my own knowledge, and I have nothing to add to it.

FRITZ HERZER
his (X) mark

7

(From Staatspolizeikapitän Ernst Hartenstein, to His Excellency, the Baron von Krutz, Minister of Police)

25 November 1809

Your Excellency:

The accompanying copies of statements taken this day will explain how the prisoner, the sclf-so-called Benjamin Bathurst, came into my custody. I have charged him with causing disorder and being a suspicious person, to hold him until more can be learned about him. However, as he represents himself to be a British diplomat, I am unwilling to assume any further responsibility, and am having him sent to your Excellency, in Berlin.

In the first place, your Excellency, I have the strongest doubts of the man's story. The statement which he made before me, and signed, is bad enough, with a coach and four turning into a farm wagon, like Cinderella's coach into a pumpkin, and three people vanishing as though swallowed by the earth. Your Excellency will permit me to doubt that there ever was any such coach, or any such people. But all this is perfectly reasonable and credible, beside the things he said to me, of which no record was made.

Your Excellency will have noticed, in his statement, certain allusions to the Austrian surrender, and to French troops in Austria. After his statement had been taken down, I noticed these allusions, and I inquired, what surrender, and what were French troops doing in Austria. The man looked at me in a pitying manner, and said:

'News seems to travel slowly, hereabouts; peace was concluded at Vienna on the 14th of last month. And as for what French troops are doing in Austria, they're doing the same things Bonaparte's brigands are doing everywhere in Europe.'

'And who is Bonaparte?' I asked.

He stared at me as though I had asked him, 'Who is the Lord Jehovah?' Then, after a moment, a look of comprehension came into his face.

'So; you Prussians conceded him the title of Emperor, and refer to him as Napoleon,' he said. 'Well, I can assure you that His Britannic Majesty's Government haven't done so, and never will; not so long as one Englishman has a finger left to pull a trigger. General Bonaparte is a usurper; His Britannic Majesty's Government do not recognize any sovereignty in France except the House of Bourbon.' This he said very sternly, as though rebuking me.

It took me a moment or so to digest that, and to appreciate all its implications. Why, this fellow evidently believed, as a matter of fact, that the French Monarchy had been overthrown by some military adventurer called Bonaparte, who was calling himself the Emperor Napoleon, and who had made war on Austria and forced a surrender. I made no attempt to argue with him – one wastes time arguing with madmen – but if this man could believe that, the transformation of a coach and four into a cabbage wagon was a small matter indeed. So, to humour him, I asked him if he thought General Bonaparte's agents were responsible for his trouble at the inn.

'Certainly,' he replied. 'The chances are they didn't know me to see me, and took Jardine for the Minister, and me for the secretary, so they made off with poor Jardine. I wonder, though, that they left me my dispatch case. And that reminds me: I'll want that back. Diplomatic papers, you know.'

I told him, very seriously, that we would have to check his credentials. I promised him I would make every effort to locate his secretary and his servants and his coach, took a complete description of all of them, and persuaded him to go into an upstairs room, where I kept him under guard. I did start inquiries, calling in all my informers and spies, but, as I expected, I could learn nothing. I could not find anybody, even, who had seen him anywhere in Perleburg before he appeared at the Sword and Sceptre, and that rather surprised me, as somebody should have seen him enter the town, or walk along the street.

In this connection, let me remind your Excellency of the discrepancy in the statements of the servant, Franz Bauer, and of the two peasants. The former is certain the man entered the inn yard from the street; the latter are just as positive that he did not. Your Excellency, I do not like such puzzles, for I am sure that all three were telling the truth to the best of their knowledge. They are ignorant common folk, I admit, but they should know what they did or did not see.

After I got the prisoner into safe keeping, I fell to examining his papers, and I can assure your Excellency that they gave me a shock. I had paid little heed to his ravings about the King of France being dethroned, or about this General Bonaparte who called himself the Emperor Napoleon, but I found all these things mentioned in his papers and dispatches, which had every appearance of being official documents. There was repeated mention of the taking, by the French, of Vienna, last May, and of the capitulation of the Austrian Emperor to this General Bonaparte, and of battles being fought all over Europe, and I don't know what other fantastic things. Your Excellency, I have heard of all sorts of madmen – one believing himself to be the Archangel Gabriel, or Mohammed, or a werewolf, and another convinced that his bones are made of glass, or that he is pursued and tormented by devils – but, so help me God, this is the first time I have heard of a madman who had documentary proof for his delusions! Does your Excellency wonder, then, that I want no part of this business?

But the matter of his credentials was even worse. He had papers, sealed with the seal of the British Foreign Office, and to every appearance genuine – but they were signed, as Foreign Minister, by one George Canning, and all the world knows that Lord Castlereagh has been Foreign Minister these last five years. And to cap it all, he had a safe conduct sealed with the seal of the Prussian Chancellery – the very seal, for I compared it, under a strong magnifying glass, with one that I knew to be genuine, and they were identical! – and yet, this letter was signed, as Chancellor, not by Count von Berchtenwald, but by Baron vom und zum Stein, the Minister of Agriculture, and the signature, as far as I could see, appeared to be genuine! This is too much for me, your Excellency; I must ask to be excused from dealing with this matter, before I become as mad as my prisoner!

I made arrangements, accordingly, with Colonel Keitel, of the Third Uhlans, to furnish an officer to escort this man into Berlin. The coach in which they come belongs to this police station, and the driver is one of my men. He should be furnished expense money to get back to Perleburg. The guard is a corporal of Uhlans, the orderly of the officer. He will stay with the *Herr Oberleutnant*, and both of them will return here at their own convenience and expense.

I have the honour, your Excellency, to be, etc., etc.,

ERNST HARTENSTEIN
Staatspolizeikapitän

8

(From Oberleutnant Rudolf von Tarlburg, to Baron Eugen von Krutz)

26 November 1809

Dear Uncle Eugen:

This is in no sense a formal report; I made that at the Ministry, when I turned the Englishman and his papers over to one of your officers – a fellow with red hair and a face like a bulldog. But there are a few things which you should be told, which wouldn't look well in an official report, to let you know just what sort of a rare fish has gotten into your net.

I had just come in from drilling my platoon, yesterday, when Colonel Keitel's orderly told me that the colonel wanted to see me in his quarters. I found the old fellow in undress in his sitting room, smoking his big pipe.

'Come in, Lieutenant; come in and sit down, my boy!' he greeted me, in that bluff, hearty manner which he always adopts with his junior officers when he has some particularly nasty job to be done. 'How would you like to take a little trip into Berlin! I have an errand, which won't take half an hour, and you can stay as long as you like, just so you're back by Thursday, when your turn comes up for road patrol.'

Well, I thought, this is the bait. I waited to see what the hook would look like, saying that it was entirely agreeable with me, and asking what his errand was.

'Well, it isn't for myself, Tarlburg,' he said. 'It's for this fellow Hartenstein, the *Staatspolizeikapitän* here. He has something he wants done at the Ministry of Police, and I thought of you because I've heard you're related to the Baron von Krutz. You are, aren't you?' he asked, just as though he didn't know all about who all his officers are related to.

'That's right, Colonel; the Baron is my uncle,' I said. 'What does Hartenstein want done?'

'Why, he has a prisoner whom he wants taken to Berlin and turned over at the Ministry. All you have to do is to take him in, in a coach, and see he doesn't escape on the way, and get a receipt for him, and for some papers. This is a very important prisoner; I don't think Hartenstein has anybody he can trust to handle him. A state prisoner. He claims to be some sort of a British diplomat, and for all Hartenstein knows, maybe he is. Also, he is a madman.'

'A madman?' I echoed.

'Yes, just so. At least, that's what Hartenstein told me. I wanted to know what sort of a madman – there are various kinds of madmen, all of whom must be handled differently – but all Hartenstein would tell me was that he had unrealistic beliefs about the state of affairs in Europe.'

'Ha! What diplomat hasn't?' I asked.

Old Keitel gave a laugh, somewhere between the bark of a dog and the croaking of a raven.

'Yes, naturally! The unrealistic beliefs of diplomats are what soldiers die of,' he said. 'I said as much to Hartenstein, but he wouldn't tell me anything more. He seemed to regret having said even that much. He looked like a man who's seen a particularly terrifying ghost.' The old man puffed hard at his famous pipe for a while, blowing smoke up through his moustache. 'Rudi, Hartenstein has pulled a hot potato out of the ashes, this time, and he wants to toss it to your uncle, before he burns his fingers. I think that's one reason why he got me to furnish an escort for his Englishman. Now, look; you must take this unrealistic diplomat, or this undiplomatic madman, or whatever in blazes he is, into Berlin. And understand this.' He pointed his pipe at me as though it were a pistol. 'Your orders are to take him there and turn him over at the Ministry of Police. Nothing has been said about whether you turn him over alive or dead, or half one and half the other. I know nothing about this business, and want to know nothing; if Hartenstein wants us to play gaol warders for him, then, *bei Gott*, he must be satisfied with our way of doing it!'

Well, to cut short the story, I looked at the coach Hartenstein had placed at my disposal, and I decided to chain the left door shut on the outside so that it couldn't be opened from within. Then, I would put my prisoner on my left, so that the only way out would be past me. I decided not to carry any weapons which he might be able to snatch from me, so I took off my sabre and locked it in the seat box, along with the dispatch case containing the Englishman's papers. It was cold enough to wear a greatcoat in comfort, so I wore mine, and in the right side pocket, where my prisoner couldn't reach, I put a little leaded bludgeon, and also a brace of pocket pistols. Hartenstein was going to furnish me a guard as well as a driver, but I said that I would take a servant who could act as guard. The servant, of course, was my orderly, old Johann; I gave him my double hunting gun to carry, with a big charge of boar-shot in one barrel and an ounce ball in the other.

In addition, I armed myself with a big bottle of cognac.

I thought that if I could shoot my prisoner often enough with that, he would give me no trouble.

As it happened, he didn't, and none of my precautions – except the cognac – were needed. The man didn't look like a lunatic to me. He was a rather stout gentleman, of past middle age, with a ruddy complexion and an intelligent face. The only unusual thing about him was his hat, which was a peculiar contraption, looking like the pot out of a close stool. I put him in the carriage, and then offered him a drink out of my bottle, taking one about half as big myself. He smacked his lips over it and said, 'Well, that's real brandy; whatever we think of their detestable politics, we can't criticize the French for their liquor.' Then, he said, 'I'm glad they're sending me in the custody of a military gentleman, instead of a confounded gendarme. Tell me the truth, Lieutenant: am I under arrest for anything?'

'Why,' I said, 'Captain Hartenstein should have told you about that. All I know is that I have orders to take you to the Ministry of Police, in Berlin, and not to let you escape on the way. These orders I will carry out; I hope you don't hold that against me.'

He assured me that he did not, and we had another drink on it – I made sure, again, that he got twice as much as I did – and then the coachman cracked his whip and we were off for Berlin.

Now, I thought, I am going to see just what sort of a madman this is, and why Hartenstein is making a state affair out of a squabble at an inn. So I decided to explore his unrealistic beliefs about the state of affairs in Europe.

After guiding the conversation to where I wanted it, I asked him: 'What, Herr Bathurst, in your belief, is the real, underlying cause of the present tragic situation in Europe?'

That, I thought, was safe enough. Name me one year, since the days of Julius Caesar, when the situation in Europe hasn't been tragic! And it worked, to perfection.

'In my belief,' says this Englishman, 'the whole damnable mess is the result of the victory of the rebellious colonists in North America, and their blasted republic.'

Well, you can imagine, that gave me a start. All the world

knows that the American Patriots lost their war for independence from England; that their army was shattered, that their leaders were either killed or driven into exile. How many times, when I was a little boy, did I not sit up long past my bedtime, when old Baron von Steuben was a guest at Tarlburg-Schloss, listening open-mouthed and wide-eyed to his stories of that gallant lost struggle! How I used to shiver at his tales of the terrible Winter camp, or thrill at the battles, or weep as he told how he held the dying Washington in his arms, and listened to his noble last words, at the Battle of Doylestown. And here, this man was telling me that the Patriots had really won, and set up the republic for which they had fought! I had been prepared for some of what Hartenstein had called unrealistic beliefs, but nothing as fantastic as this.

'I can cut it even finer than that,' Bathurst continued. 'It was the defeat of Burgoyne at Saratoga. We made a good bargain when we got Benedict Arnold to turn his coat, but we didn't do it soon enough. If he hadn't been on the field that day, Burgoyne would have gone through Gates' army like a hot knife through butter.'

But Arnold hadn't been at Saratoga. I know; I have read much of the American War. Arnold was shot dead on New Year's Day of 1776, during the attempted storming of Quebec. And Burgoyne had done just as Bathurst had said: he had gone through Gates like a knife, and down the Hudson to join Howe.

'But, Herr Bathurst,' I asked, 'how could that affect the situation in Europe? America is thousands of miles away, across the ocean.'

'Ideas can cross oceans quicker than armies. When Louis XVI decided to come to the aid of the Americans, he doomed himself and his regime. A successful resistance to royal authority in America was all the French Republicans needed to inspire them. Of course, we have Louis' own weakness to blame, too. If he'd given those rascals a whiff of grapeshot when the mob tried to storm Versailles in 1790 there'd have been no French Revolution.'

But he had. When Louis XVI ordered the howitzers

turned on the mob at Versailles, and then sent the dragoons to ride down the survivors, the Republican movement had been broken. That had been when Cardinal Talleyrand, who had then been merely Bishop of Autun, had come to the fore and became the power that he is today in France; the greatest King's Minister since Richelieu.

'And, after that, Louis' death followed as surely as night after day,' Bathurst was saying. 'And because the French had no experience in self-government, their republic was foredoomed. If Bonaparte hadn't seized power, somebody else would have; when the French murdered their king, they delivered themselves to dictatorship. And a dictator, unsupported by the prestige of royalty, has no choice but to lead his people into foreign war, to keep them from turning upon him.'

It was like that all the way to Berlin. All these things seem foolish, by daylight, but as I sat in the darkness of that swaying coach, I was almost convinced of the reality of what he told me. I tell you, Uncle Eugen, it was frightening, as though he were giving me a view of Hell. *Gott im Himmel*, the things that man talked of! Armies swarming over Europe; sack and massacre, and cities burning; blockades, and starvation; kings deposed, and thrones tumbling like tenpins! Battles in which the soldiers of every nation fought, and in which tens of thousands were mowed down like ripe grain; and, over all, the Satanic figure of a little man in a grey coat, who dictated peace to the Austrian Emperor in Schoenbrunn, and carried the Pope away a prisoner to Savona.

Madman, eh? Unrealistic beliefs, says Hartenstein? Well, give me madmen who drool spittle, and foam at the mouth, and shriek obscene blasphemies. But not this pleasant-seeming gentleman who sat beside me and talked of horrors in a quiet, cultured voice, while he drank my cognac.

But not all my cognac! If your man at the Ministry – the one with red hair and the bulldog face – tells you that I was drunk when I brought in that Englishman, you had better believe him!

RUDI

9

(From Count von Berchtenwald, to the British Minister)

28 November 1809

Honoured Sir:

The accompanying *dossier* will acquaint you with the problem confronting this Chancellery, without needless repetition on my part. Please to understand that it is not, and never was, any part of the intentions of the Government of His Majesty Friedrich Wilhelm III to offer any injury or indignity to the Government of His Britannic Majesty George III. We would never contemplate holding in arrest the person, or tampering with the papers, of an accredited envoy of your Government. However, we have the gravest doubt, to make a considerable understatement, that this person who calls himself Benjamin Bathurst is any such envoy, and we do not think that it would be any service to the Government of His Britannic Majesty to allow an impostor to travel about Europe in the guise of a British diplomatic representative. We certainly should not thank the Government of His Britannic Majesty for failing to take steps to deal with some person who, in England, might falsely represent himself to be a Prussian diplomat.

This affair touches us almost as closely as it does your own Government; this man had in his possession a letter of safe conduct, which you will find in the accompanying dispatch case. It is of the regular form, as issued by this Chancellery, and is sealed with the Chancellery seal, or with a very exact counterfeit of it. However, it has been signed, as Chancellor of Prussia, with a signature indistinguishable from that of the Baron vom und zum Stein, who is the present Minister of Agriculture. Baron Stein was shown the signature, with the rest of the letter covered, and without hesitation acknowledged it for his own writing. However, when the letter was uncovered and shown him, his surprise and horror were such as would require the pen of a Goethe or a Schiller to describe, and he denied categorically ever having seen the document before.

I have no choice but to believe him. It is impossible to think that a man of Baron Stein's honourable and serious character would be party to the fabrication of a paper of this sort. Even aside from this, I am in the thing as deeply as he; if it is signed with his signature, it is also sealed with my seal, which has not been out of my personal keeping in the ten years that I have been Chancellor here. In fact, the word 'impossible' can be used to describe the entire business. It was impossible for the man Benjamin Bathurst to have entered the inn yard – yet he did. It was impossible that he should carry papers of the sort found in his dispatch case, or that such papers should exist – yet I am sending them to you with this letter. It is impossible that Baron von und zum Stein should sign a paper of the sort he did, or that it should be sealed by the Chancellery – yet it bears both Stein's signature and my seal.

You will also find in the dispatch case other credentials ostensibly originating with the British Foreign Office of the same character, being signed by persons having no connection with the Foreign Office, or even with the Government, but being sealed with apparently authentic seals. If you send these papers to London, I fancy you will find that they will there create the same situation as that caused here by this letter of safe-conduct.

I am also sending you a charcoal sketch of the person who calls himself Benjamin Bathurst. This portrait was taken without its subject's knowledge. Baron von Krutz's nephew, Lieutenant von Tarlburg, who is the son of our mutual friend Count von Tarlburg, has a *little friend*, a very clever young lady who is, as you will see, an expert at this sort of work; she was introduced into a room at the Ministry of Police and placed behind a screen, where she could sketch our prisoner's face. If you should send this picture to London, I think that there is a good chance that it might be recognized. I can vouch that it is an excellent likeness.

To tell the truth, we are at our wits' end about this affair. I cannot understand how such excellent imitations of these various seals could be made, and the signature of the Baron vom und zum Stein is the most expert forgery that I have ever seen, in thirty years' experience as a statesman. This would indicate careful and painstaking work on the part of somebody; how, then, do we reconcile this with such clumsy mistakes, recognizable as such by any schoolboy, as signing the name of Baron Stein as Prussian Chancellor, or Mr George Canning, who is a member of the opposition party and not connected with your Government, as British Foreign Secretary?

These are mistakes which only a madman would make. There are those who think our prisoner is a madman, because of his apparent delusions about the great conqueror, General Bonaparte, *alias* the Emperor Napoleon. Madmen have been known to fabricate evidence to support their delusions, it is true, but I shudder to think of a madman having at his disposal the resources to manufacture the papers you will find in this dispatch case. Moreover, some of our foremost medical men, who have specialized in the disorders of the mind, have interviewed this man Bathurst and say that, save for his fixed belief in a non-existent situation, he is perfectly rational.

Personally, I believe that the whole thing is a gigantic hoax, perpetrated for some hidden and sinister purpose, possibly to create confusion, and undermine the confidence existing between your Government and mine, and to set against one another various persons connected with both Governments, or else as a mask for some other conspiratorial activity. Without specifying any Sovereigns or Governments who might wish to do this, I can think of two groups, namely, the Jesuits, and the outlawed French Republicans, either of whom might conceive such a situation to be to their advantage. Only a few months ago, you will recall, there was a Jacobin plot unmasked at Köln.

But, whatever this business may portend, I do not like it. I want to get to the bottom of it as soon as possible, and I will thank you, my dear Sir, and your Government, for any assistance you may find possible.

I have the honour, Sir, to be, etc., etc., etc.,

BERCHTENWALD

10

28 November 1809

Count von Berchtenwald:

Within the past half-hour, that is, at about eleven o'clock tonight, the man calling himself Benjamin Bathurst was shot and killed by a sentry at the Ministry of Police, while attempting to escape from custody.

A sentry on duty in the rear courtyard of the Ministry observed a man attempting to leave the building in a suspicious and furtive manner. This sentry, who was under the strictest orders to allow no one to enter or leave without written authorization, challenged him; when he attempted to run, the sentry fired his musket at him, bringing him down. At the shot, the Sergeant of the Guard rushed into the courtyard with his detail, and the man whom the sentry had shot was found to be the Englishman, Benjamin Bathurst. He had been hit in the chest with an ounce ball, and died before the doctor could arrive, and without recovering consciousness.

An investigation revealed that the prisoner, who was confined on the third floor of the building, had fashioned a rope from his bedding, his bed cord, and the leather strap of his bell pull; this rope was only long enough to reach to the window of the office on the second floor, directly below, but he managed to enter this by kicking the glass out of the window. I am trying to find out how he could do this without being heard; I can assure your Excellency that somebody is going to smart for this night's work. As for the sentry, he acted within his orders; I have commended him for doing his duty, and for good shooting, and I assume full responsibility for the death of the prisoner at his hands.

I have no idea why the self-so-called Benjamin Bathurst,

who, until now, was well-behaved and seemed to take his confinement philosophically, should suddenly make this rash and fatal attempt, unless it was because of those infernal dunderheads of madhouse doctors who have been bothering him. Only this afternoon, your Excellency, they deliberately handed him a bundle of newspapers – Prussian, Austrian, French, and English – all dated within the last month. They wanted, they said, to see how he would react. Well, God pardon them, they've found out!

What does your Excellency think should be done about giving the body burial?

KRUTZ

(From the British Minister to the Count von Berchtenwald)

20 December 1809

My Dear Count von Berchtenwald:
Reply from London to my letter of the 28th *ult.*, which accompanied the dispatch case and the other papers, has finally come to hand. The papers which you wanted returned – the copies of the statements taken at Perleburg, the letter to the Baron von Krutz from the police captain, Hartenstein, and the personal letter of Krutz's nephew, Lieutenant von Tarlburg, and the letter of safe-conduct found in the dispatch case – accompany herewith. I don't know what the people at Whitehall did with the other papers; tossed them into the nearest fire, for my guess. Were I in your Excellency's place, that's where the papers I am returning would go.

I have heard nothing, yet, from my dispatch of the 29th *ult.* concerning the death of the man who called himself Benjamin Bathurst, but I doubt very much if any official notice will ever be taken of it. Your Government had a perfect right to detain the fellow, and, that being the case, he attempted to escape at his own risk. After all, sentries are not required to carry loaded muskets in order to discourage them from putting their hands in their pockets.

To hazard a purely unofficial opinion, I should not imagine that London is very much dissatisfied with this *dénouement*. His Majesty's Government are a hard-headed and matter-of-fact set of gentry who do not relish mysteries, least of all mysteries whose solution may be more disturbing than the original problem.

This is entirely confidential, your Excellency, but those papers which were in that dispatch case kicked up the devil's own row in London, with half the Government bigwigs protesting their innocence to high Heaven, and the rest accusing one another of complicity in the hoax. If that was somebody's intention, it was literally a howling success. For a while, it was even feared that there would be questions in Parliament, but eventually the whole vexatious business was hushed.

You may tell Count Tarlburg's son that his little friend is a most talented young lady; her sketch was highly com-mended by no less an authority than Sir Thomas Lawrence, and here, your Excellency, comes the most bedevilling part of a thoroughly bedevilled business. The picture was in-stantly recognized. It is a very fair likeness of Benjamin Bathurst, or, I should say, Sir Benjamin Bathurst, who is King's Lieutenant-Governor for the Crown Colony of Geor-gia. As Sir Thomas Lawrence did his portrait a few years back, he is in an excellent position to criticize the work of Lieutenant von Tarlburg's young lady. However, Sir Ben-jamin Bathurst was known to have been in Savannah, at-tending to the duties of his office, and in the public eye, all the while that his double was in Prussia. Sir Benjamin does not have a twin brother. It has been suggested that this fellow might be a half-brother, born on the wrong side of the blanket, but, as far as I know, there is no justification for this theory.

The General Bonaparte, alias the Emperor Napoleon, who is given so much mention in the dispatches, seems also to have a counterpart in actual life; there is, in the French army, a Colonel of Artillery by that name, a Corsican who Gallicized his original name of Napolione Buonaparte. He is a most brilliant military theoretician; I am sure some of your own officers, like General Scharnhorst, could tell you about him. His loyalty to the French Monarchy has never been questioned.

This same correspondence to fact seems to crop up everywhere in that amazing collection of pseudo-dispatches and psuedo-statepapers. The United States of America, you will recall, was the style by which the rebellious colonies referred to themselves, in the Declaration of Philadelphia. The James Madison who is mentioned as the current President of the United States is now living, in exile, in Switzerland. His alleged predecessor in office, Thomas Jefferson, was the author of the rebel Declaration; after the defeat of the rebels, he escaped to Havana, and died, several years ago, in the Principality of Lichtenstein.

I was quite amused to find our old friend Cardinal Talleyrand – without the ecclesiastical title – cast in the role of chief advisor to the usurper, Bonaparte. His Eminence, I have always thought, is the sort of fellow who would land on his feet on top of any heap, and who would as little scruple to be Prime Minister to His Satanic Majesty as to His Most Christian Majesty.

I was baffled, however, by one name, frequently mentioned in those fantastic papers. This was the English General, Wellington. I haven't the least idea who this person might be.

I have the honour, your Excellency, etc., etc., etc.,

ARTHUR WELLESLEY

The Game of Rat and Dragon

Cordwainer Smith

The Table

Pinlighting is a hell of a way to earn a living. Underhill was furious as he closed the door behind himself. It didn't make much sense to wear a uniform and look like a soldier if people didn't appreciate what you did.

He sat down in his chair, laid his head back in the headrest and pulled the helmet down over his forehead.

As he waited for the pin-set to warm up, he remembered the girl in the outer corridor. She had looked at it, then looked at him scornfully.

'Meow.' That was all she had said. Yet it had cut him like a knife.

What did she think he was – a fool, a loafer, a uniformed nonentity? Didn't she know that for every half hour of pinlighting, he got a minimum of two months' recuperation in the hospital?

By now the set was warm. He felt the squares of space around him, sensed himself at the middle of an immense grid, a cubic grid, full of nothing. Out in that nothingness, he could sense the hollow aching horror of space itself and could feel the terrible anxiety which his mind encountered whenever it met the faintest trace of inert dust.

As he relaxed, the comforting solidity of the Sun, the clockwork of the familiar planets and the Moon rang in on him. Our own solar system was as charming and as simple as an ancient cuckoo clock filled with familiar ticking and with reassuring noises. The odd little moons of Mars swung around their planet like frantic mice, yet their regularity was itself an assurance that all was well. Far above the plane of the ecliptic, he could feel half a ton of dust more or less drifting outside the lanes of human travel.

Here there was nothing to fight, nothing to challenge the mind, to tear the living soul out of a body with its roots dripping in effluvium as tangible as blood.

Nothing ever moved in on the Solar System. He could wear the pin-set forever and be nothing more than a sort of telepathic astronomer, a man who could feel the hot, warm protection of the Sun throbbing and burning against his living mind.

Woodley came in.

'Same old ticking world,' said Underhill. 'Nothing to report. No wonder they didn't develop the pin-set until they began to planoform. Down here with the hot Sun around us, it feels so good and so quiet. You can feel everything spinning and turning. It's nice and sharp and compact. It's sort of like sitting around home.'

Woodley grunted. He was not much given to flights of fantasy.

Undeterred, Underhill went on, 'It must have been pretty good to have been an Ancient Man. I wonder why they burned up their world with war. They didn't have to planoform. They didn't have to go out to earn their living among the stars. They didn't have to dodge the Rats or play the Game. They couldn't have invented pinlighting because they didn't have any need of it, did they, Woodley?'

Woodley grunted, 'Uh-huh.' Woodley was twenty-six years old and due to retire in one more year. He already had a farm picked out. He had gotten through ten years of hard work pinlighting with the best of them. He had kept his sanity by not thinking very much about his job, meeting the strains of the task whenever he had to meet them and thinking nothing more about his duties until the next emergency arose.

Woodley never made a point of getting popular among the Partners. None of the Partners liked him very much. Some of them even resented him. He was suspected of thinking ugly thoughts of the Partners on occasion, but since none of the Partners ever thought a complaint in articulate form, the other pinlighters and the Chiefs of the Instrumentality left him alone.

Underhill was still full of the wonder of their job. Happily he babbled on, 'What does happen to us when we planoform? Do you think it's sort of like dying? Did you ever see anybody who had his soul pulled out?'

'Pulling souls is just a way of talking about it,' said Woodley. 'After all these years, nobody knows whether we have souls or not.'

'But I saw one once. I saw what Dogwood looked like when he came apart. There was something funny. It looked wet and sort of sticky as if it were bleeding and it went out of him – and you know what they did to Dogwood? They took him away, up in that part of the hospital where you and I never go – way up at the top part where the others are, where the others always have to go if they are alive after the Rats of the Up-and-Out have gotten them.'

Woodley sat down and lit an ancient pipe. He was burning something called tobacco in it. It was a dirty sort of habit, but it made him look very dashing and adventurous.

'Look here, youngster. You don't have to worry about that stuff. Pinlighting is getting better all the time. The Partners are getting better. I've seen them pinlight two Rats forty-six million miles apart in one and a half milliseconds. As long as people had to try to work the pin-sets themselves, there was always the chance that with a minimum of four hundred milliseconds for the human mind to set a pinlight, we wouldn't light the Rats up fast enough to protect our planoforming ships. The Partners have changed all that. Once they get going, they're faster than the Rats. And they always will be. I know it's not easy, letting a Partner share your mind – '

'It's not easy for them, either,' said Underhill.

'Don't worry about them. They're not human. Let them take care of themselves. I've seen more pinlighters go crazy from monkeying around with Partners than I have ever seen caught by the Rats. How many do you actually know of them that got grabbed by Rats?'

Underhill looked down at his fingers, which shone green and purple in the vivid light thrown by the tuned-in pin-set, and counted ships. The thumb for the *Andromeda*, lost with crew and passengers, the index finger and the middle finger for *Release Ships* 43 and 56, found with their pin-sets burned out and every man, woman, and child on board dead or insane. The ring finger, the little finger, and the thumb of the other hand were the first three battleships to be lost to the Rats – lost as people realized that there was something out there *underneath space itself* which was alive, capricious and malevolent.

Planoforming was sort of funny. It felt like –

Like nothing much.

Like the twinge of a mild electric shock.

Like the ache of a sore tooth bitten on for the first time.

Like a slightly painful flash of light against the eyes.

Yet in that time, a forty-thousand-ton ship lifting free above Earth disappeared somehow or other into two dimensions and appeared half a light year or fifty light years off.

At one moment, he would be sitting in the Fighting Room, the pin-set ready and the familiar Solar System ticking around inside his head. For a second or a year (he could never tell how long it really was, subjectively), the funny little flash went through him and then he was loose in the Up-and-Out, the terrible open spaces between the stars, where the stars themselves felt like pimples on his telepathic mind and the planets were too far away to be sensed or read.

Somewhere in this outer space, a gruesome death awaited, death and horror of a kind which Man had never encountered until he reached out for interstellar space itself. Apparently the light of the suns kept the dragons away.

Dragons. That was what people called them. To ordinary people, there was nothing, nothing except the shiver of planoforming and the hammer blow of sudden death or the dark spastic note of lunacy descending into their minds.

But to the telepaths, they were Dragons.

In the fraction of a second between the telepath's awareness of a hostile something out in the black, hollow nothingness of space and the impact of a ferocious, ruinous psychic blow against all living things within the ship, the telepaths had sensed entities something like the Dragons of ancient human lore, beasts more clever than beasts, demons more tangible than demons, hungry vortices of aliveness and hate compounded by unknown means out of the thin tenuous matter between the stars.

It took a surviving ship to bring back the news – a ship in which, by sheer chance, a telepath had a light beam ready, turning it out at the innocent dust so that, within the panorama of his mind, the Dragon dissolved into nothing at all and the other passengers, themselves non-telepathic, went about their way not realizing that their own immediate deaths had been averted.

From then on, it was easy – almost.

Planoforming ships always carried telepaths. Telepaths had their sensitiveness enlarged to an immense range by the pin-sets, which were telepathic amplifiers adapted to the mammal mind. The pin-sets in turn were electronically geared into small dirigible light-bombs. Light did it.

Light broke up the Dragons, allowed the ships to reform three-dimensionally, skip, skip, skip, as they moved from star to star.

The odds suddenly moved down from a hundred to one against mankind to sixty to forty in mankind's favour.

This was not enough. The telepaths were trained to become ultra-sensitive, trained to become aware of the Dragons in less than a millisecond.

But it was found that the Dragons could move a million miles in just under two milliseconds and that this was not enough for the human mind to activate the light beams.

Attempts had been made to sheath the ships in light at all times.

This defence wore out.

As mankind learned about the Dragons, so too, apparently the Dragons learned about mankind. Somehow they flattened their own bulk and came in on extremely flat trajectories very quickly.

Intense light was needed, light of sunlight intensity. This could be provided only by light-bombs. Pinlighting came into existence.

Pinlighting consisted of the detonation of ultra-vivid miniature photonuclear bombs, which converted a few ounces of a magnesium isotope into pure visible radiance.

The odds kept coming down in mankind's favour, yet ships were being lost.

It became so bad that people didn't even want to find the ships because the rescuers knew what they would see. It was sad to bring back to Earth three hundred bodies ready for burial and two hundred or three hundred lunatics, damaged beyond repair, to be wakened, and fed, and cleaned, and put to sleep, wakened and fed again until their lives were ended.

Telepaths tried to reach into the minds of the psychotics who had been damaged by the Dragons, but they found nothing there beyond vivid spouting columns of fiery terror bursting from the primordial id itself, the volcanic sources of life.

Then came the Partners.

Man and Partner could do together what Man could not do alone. Men had the intellect. Partners had the speed.

The Partners rode in their tiny craft, no larger than footballs, outside the spaceships. They planoformed with the ships. They rode beside them in their six-pound craft ready to attack.

The tiny ships of the Partners were swift. Each carried a dozen pinlights, bombs no bigger than thimbles.

The Pinlighters threw the Partners – quite literally threw – by means of mind-to-firing relays direct at the Dragons.

What seemed to be Dragons to the human mind appeared in the form of gigantic Rats in the minds of the Partners.

Out in the pitiless nothingness of space, the Partners' minds responded to an instinct as old as life. The Partners attacked, striking with a speed faster than Man's, going from attack to attack until the Rats or themselves were destroyed. Almost all the time it was the Partners who won.

With the safety of the interstellar skip, skip, skip of the

ships, commerce increased immensely, the population of all the colonies went up, and the demand for trained Partners increased.

Underhill and Woodley were a part of the third generation of pinlighters and yet, to them, it seemed as though their craft had endured forever.

Gearing space into minds by means of the pin-set, adding the Partners to those minds, keying up the mind for the tension of a fight on which all depended – this was more than human synapses could stand for long. Underhill needed his two months' rest after half an hour of fighting. Woodley needed his retirement after ten years of service. They were young. They were good. But they had limitations.

So much depended on the choice of Partners, so much on the sheer luck of who drew whom.

The Shuffle

Father Moontree and the little girl named West entered the room. They were the other two pinlighters. The human complement of the Fighting Room was now complete.

Father Moontree was a red-faced man of forty-five who had lived the peaceful life of a farmer until he reached his fortieth year. Only then, belatedly, did the authorities find he was telepathic and agree to let him late in life enter upon the career of pinlighter. He did well at it, but he was fantastically old for this kind of business.

Father Moontree looked at the glum Woodley and the musing Underhill. 'How're the youngsters today? Ready for a good fight?'

'Father always wants a fight,' giggled the little girl named West. She was such a little little girl. Her giggle was high and childish. She looked like the last person in the world one would expect to find in the rough, sharp duelling of pinlighting.

Underhill had been amused one time when he found one of the most sluggish of the Partners coming away happy from contact with the mind of the girl named West.

Usually the Partners didn't care much about the human

minds with which they were paired for the journey. The Partners seemed to take the attitude that human minds were complex and fouled up beyond belief, anyhow. No Partner ever questioned the superiority of the human mind, though very few of the Partners were much impressed by that superiority.

The Partners liked people. They were willing to fight with them. They were even willing to die for them. But when a Partner liked an individual the way, for example, that Captain Wow or the Lady May liked Underhill, the liking had nothing to do with intellect. It was a matter of temperament, of feel.

Underhill knew perfectly well that Captain Wow regarded his, Underhill's, brains as silly. What Captain Wow liked was Underhill's friendly emotional structure, the cheerfulness and glint of wicked amusement that shot through Underhill's unconscious thought patterns, and the gaiety with which Underhill faced danger. The words, the history books, the ideas, the science – Underhill could sense all that in his own mind, reflected back from Captain Wow's mind, as so much rubbish.

Miss West looked at Underhill. 'I bet you've put stickum on the stones.'

'I did not!'

Underhill felt his ears grow red with embarrassment. During his novitiate, he had tried to cheat in the lottery because he got particularly fond of a special Partner, a lovely young mother named Murr. It was so much easier to operate with Murr and she was so affectionate toward him that he forgot pinlighting was hard work and that he was not instructed to have a good time with his Partner. They were both designed and prepared to go into deadly battle together.

One cheating had been enough. They had found him out and he had been laughed at for years.

Father Moontree picked up the imitation leather cup and shook the stone dice which assigned them their Partners for the trip. By senior rights, he took first draw.

He grimaced. He had drawn a greedy old character, a tough old male whose mind was full of slobbering thoughts of food, veritable oceans full of half-spoiled fish. Father Moontree had once said that he burped cod liver oil for weeks after drawing that particular glutton, so strongly had the telepathic image of fish impressed itself upon his mind. Yet the glutton was a glutton for danger as well as for fish. He had killed sixty-three Dragons, more than any other Partner in the service, and was quite literally worth his weight in gold.

The little girl West came next. She drew Captain Wow. When she saw who it was, she smiled.

'I *like* him,' she said. 'He's such fun to fight with. He feels so nice and cuddly in my mind.'

'Cuddly, hell,' said Woodley. 'I've been in his mind, too. It's the most leering mind in this ship, bar none.'

'Nasty man,' said the little girl. She said it declaratively, without reproach.

Underhill, looking at her, shivered.

He didn't see how she could take Captain Wow so calmly. Captain Wow's mind *did* leer. When Captain Wow got excited in the middle of a battle, confused images of Dragons, deadly Rats, luscious beds, the smell of fish, and the shock of space all scrambled together in his mind as he and Captain Wow, their consciousnesses linked together through the pin-set, became a fantastic composite of human being and Persian cat.

That's the trouble with working with cats, thought Underhill. It's a pity that nothing else anywhere will serve as Partners. Cats were all right once you got in touch with them telepathically. They were smart enough to meet the needs of the fight, but their motives and desires were certainly different from those of humans.

They were companionable enough as long as you thought tangible images at them, but their minds just closed up and went to sleep when you recited Shakespeare or Colegrove, or if you tried to tell them what space was.

It was sort of funny realizing that the Partners who were so grim and mature out here in space were the same cute little animals that people had used as pets for thousands of years back on Earth. He had embarrassed himself more than once while on the ground saluting perfectly ordinary non-telepathic cats because he had forgotten for the moment that they were not Partners.

He picked up the cup and shook out his stone dice.

He was lucky – he drew the Lady May.

The Lady May was the most thoughtful Partner he had ever met. In her, the finely bred pedigree mind of a Persian cat had reached one of its highest peaks of development. She was more complex than any human woman, but the complexity was all one of emotions, memory, hope and discriminated experience – experience sorted through without benefit of words.

When he had first come into contact with her mind, he was astonished at its clarity. With her he remembered her kittenhood. He remembered every mating experience she had ever had. He saw in a half-recognizable gallery all the other pinlighters with whom she had been paired for the fight. And he saw himself radiant, cheerful and desirable.

He even thought he caught the edge of a longing –

A very flattering and yearning thought: *What a pity he is not a cat.*

Woodley picked up the last stone. He drew what he deserved – a sullen, scarred old tomcat with none of the verve of Captain Wow. Woodley's Partner was the most animal of all the cats on the ship, a low, brutish type with a dull mind. Even telepathy had not refined his character. His ears were half chewed off from the first fights in which he had engaged.

He was a serviceable fighter, nothing more.

Woodley grunted.

Underhill glanced at him oddly. Didn't Woodley ever do anything but grunt?

Father Moontree looked at the other three. 'You might as well get your Partners now. I'll let the Scanner know we're ready to go into the Up-and-Out.'

The Deal

Underhill spun the combination lock on the Lady May's cage. He woke her gently and took her into his arms. She humped her back luxuriously, stretched her claws, started to purr, thought better of it, and licked him on the wrist instead. He did not have the pin-set on, so their minds were closed to each other, but in the angle of her moustache and in the movement of her ears, he caught some sense of the gratification she experienced in finding him as her Partner.

He talked to her in human speech, even though speech meant nothing to a cat when the pin-set was not on.

'It's a damn shame, sending a sweet little thing like you whirling around in the coldness of nothing to hunt for Rats that are bigger and deadlier than all of us put together. You didn't ask for this kind of fight, did you?'

For answer, she licked his hand, purred, tickled his cheek with her long fluffy tail, turned around and faced him, golden eyes shining.

For a moment they stared at each other, man squatting, cat standing erect on her hind legs, front claws digging into his knee. Human eyes and cat eyes looked across an immensity which no words could meet, but which affection spanned in a single glance.

'Time to get in,' he said.

She walked docilely into her spheriod carrier. She climbed in. He saw to it that her miniature pin-set rested firmly and comfortably against the base of her brain. He made sure that her claws were padded so that she could not tear herself in the excitement of battle.

Softly he said to her, 'Ready?'

For answer, she preened her back as much as her harness would permit and purred softly within the confines of the frame that held her.

He slapped down the lid and watched the sealant ooze around the seam. For a few hours, she was welded into her projectile until a workman with a short cutting arc would remove her after she had done her duty.

He picked up the entire projectile and slipped it into the

ejection tube. He closed the door of the tube, spun the lock, seated himself in his chair, and put his own pin-set on.

Once again he flung the switch.

He sat in a small room, *small, small, warm, warm*, the bodies of the other three people moving close around him, the tangible lights in the ceiling bright and heavy against his closed eyelids.

As the pin-set warmed, the room fell away. The other people ceased to be people and became small glowing heaps of fire, embers, dark red fire, with the consciousness of life burning like old red coals in a country fireplace.

As the pin-set warmed a little more, he felt Earth just below him, felt the ship slipping away, felt the turning Moon as it swung on the far side of the world, felt the planets and the hot, clear goodness of the Sun which kept the Dragons so far from mankind's native ground.

Finally, he reached complete awareness.

He was telepathically alive to a range of millions of miles. He felt the dust which he had noticed earlier high above the ecliptic. With a thrill of warmth and tenderness, he felt the consciousness of the Lady May pouring over into his own. Her consciousness was as gentle and clear and yet sharp to the taste of his mind as if it were scented oil. It felt relaxing and reassuring. He could sense her welcome of him. It was scarcely a thought, just a raw emotion of greeting.

At last they were one again.

In a tiny remote corner of his mind, as tiny as the smallest toy he had ever seen in his childhood, he was still aware of the room and the ship, and of Father Moontree picking up a telephone and speaking to a Scanner captain in charge of the ship.

His telepathic mind caught the idea long before his ears could frame the words. The actual sound followed the idea the way that thunder on an ocean beach follows the lightning inward from far out over the seas.

'The Fighting Room is ready. Clear to planoform, sir.'

The Play

Underhill was always a little exasperated the way that the Lady May experienced things before he did.

He was braced for the quick vinegar thrill of planoforming, but he caught her report of it before his own nerves could register what happened.

Earth had fallen so far away that he groped for several milliseconds before he found the Sun in the upper rear right-hand corner of his telepathic mind.

That was a good jump, he thought. This way we'll get there in four or five skips.

A few hundred miles outside the ship, the Lady May thought back at him, 'O warm, O generous, O gigantic man! O brave, O friendly, O tender and huge Partner! O wonderful with you, with you so good, good, good, warm, warm, now to fight, now to go, good with you . . . '

He knew that she was not thinking words, that his mind took the clear amiable babble of her cat intellect and translated it into images which his own thinking could record and understand.

Neither one of them was absorbed in the game of mutual greetings. He reached out far beyond her range of perception to see if there was anything near the ship. It was funny how it was possible to do two things at once. He could scan space with his pin-set mind and yet at the same time catch a vagrant thought of hers, a lovely, affectionate thought about a son who had had a golden face and a chest covered with soft, incredibly downy white fur.

While he was still searching, he caught the warning from her.

We jump again!

And so they had. The ship had moved to a second planoform. The stars were different. The Sun was immeasurably far behind. Even the nearest stars were barely in contact. This was good Dragon country, this open, nasty, hollow kind of space. He reached farther, faster, sensing and looking for danger, ready to fling the Lady May at danger wherever he found it.

Terror blazed up in his mind, so sharp, so clear, that it came through as a physical wrench.

The little girl named West had found something – something immense, long, black, sharp, greedy, horrific. She flung Captain Wow at it.

Underhill tried to keep his own mind clear. 'Watch out!' he shouted telepathically at the others, trying to move the Lady May around.

At one corner of the battle, he felt the lustful rage of Captain Wow as the big Persian tomcat detonated lights while he approached the streak of dust which threatened the ship and the people within.

The lights scored near-misses.

The dust flattened itself, changing from the shape of a sting ray into the shape of a spear.

Not three milliseconds had elapsed.

Father Moontree was talking human words and was saying in a voice that moved like cold molasses out of a heavy jar, 'C–A–P–T–A–I–N.' Underhill knew that the sentence was going to be 'Captain, move fast!'

The battle would be fought and finished before Father Moontree got through talking.

Now, fractions of a millisecond later, the Lady May was directly in line.

Here was where the skill and speed of the Partners came in. She could react faster than he. She could see the threat as an immense Rat coming directly at her.

She could fire the light-bombs with a discrimination which he might miss.

He was connected with her mind, but he could not follow it.

His consciousness absorbed the tearing wound inflicted by the alien enemy. It was like no wound on Earth – raw, crazy pain which started like a burn at his navel. He began to writhe in his chair.

Actually he had not yet had time to move a muscle when the Lady May struck back at their enemy.

Five evenly spaced photonuclear bombs blazed out across a hundred thousand miles.

The pain in his mind and body vanished.

He felt a moment of fierce, terrible, feral elation running through the mind of the Lady May as she finished her kill. It was always disappointing to the cats to find out that their enemies whom they sensed as gigantic space Rats disappeared at the moment of destruction.

Then he felt her hurt, the pain and the fear that swept over both of them as the battle, quicker than the movement of an eyelid, had come and gone. In the same instant, there came the sharp and acid twinge of planoform.

Once more the ship went skip.

He could hear Woodley thinking at him. 'You don't have to bother much. This old son of a gun and I will take over for a while.'

Twice again the twinge, the skip.

He had no idea where he was until the lights of the Caledonia space board shone below.

With a weariness that lay almost beyond the limits of thought, he threw his mind back into rapport with the pinset, fixing the Lady May's projectile gently and neatly in its launching tube.

She was half dead with fatigue, but he could feel the beat of her heart, could listen to her panting, and he grasped the grateful edge of a thanks reaching from her mind to his.

The Score

They put him in the hospital at Caledonia.

The doctor was friendly but firm. 'You actually got touched by that Dragon. That's as close a shave as I've ever seen. It's all so quick that it'll be a long time before we know what happened scientifically, but I suppose you'd be ready for the insane asylum now if the contact had lasted several tenths of a millisecond longer. What kind of cat did you have out in front of you?'

Underhill felt the words coming out of him slowly. Words were such a lot of trouble compared with the speed and the joy of thinking, fast and sharp and clear, mind to mind! But words were all that could reach ordinary people like this doctor.

His mouth moved heavily as he articulated words, 'Don't call our Partners cats. The right thing to call them is Partners. They fight for us in a team. You ought to know we call them Partners, not cats. How is mine?'

'I don't know,' said the doctor contritely. 'We'll find out for you. Meanwhile, old man, you take it easy. There's nothing but rest that can help you. Can you make yourself sleep, or would you like us to give you some kind of sedative?'

'I can sleep,' said Underhill. 'I just want to know about the Lady May.'

The nurse joined in. She was a little antagonistic. 'Don't you want to know about the other people?'

'They're okay,' said Underhill. 'I knew that before I came in here.'

He stretched his arms and sighed and grinned at them. He could see they were relaxing and were beginning to treat him as a person instead of a patient.

'I'm all right,' he said. 'Just let me know when I can go see my Partner.'

A new thought struck him. He looked wildly at the doctor. 'They didn't send her off with the ship, did they?'

'I'll find out right away,' said the doctor. He gave Underhill a reassuring squeeze of the shoulder and left the room.

The nurse took a napkin off a goblet of chilled fruit juice.

Underhill tried to smile at her. There seemed to be something wrong with the girl. He wished she would go away. First she had started to be friendly and now she was distant again. It's a nuisance being telepathic, he thought. You keep trying to reach even when you are not making contact.

Suddenly she swung around on him.

'You pinlighters! You and your damn cats!'

Just as she stamped out, he burst into her mind. He saw himself a radiant hero, clad in his smooth suede uniform, the pin-set crown shining like ancient royal jewels around his head. He saw his own face, handsome and masculine, shining out of her mind. He saw himself very far away and he saw himself as she hated him.

She hated him in the secrecy of her own mind. She hated him because he was – she thought – proud, and strange, and rich, better and more beautiful than people like her.

He cut off the sight of her mind and, as he buried his face in the pillow, he caught an image of the Lady May.

'She *is* a cat,' he thought. 'That's all she is – a *cat!*'

But that was not how his mind saw her – quick beyond all dreams of speed, sharp, clever, unbelievably graceful, beautiful, wordless and undemanding.

Where would he ever find a woman who could compare with her?

The Nine Billion Names of God

Arthur C. Clarke

'This is a slightly unusual request,' said Dr Wagner, with what he hoped was commendable restraint. 'As far as I know, it's the first time anyone's been asked to supply a Tibetan monastery with an Automatic Sequence Computer. I don't wish to be inquisitive, but I should hardly have thought that your – ah – establishment had much use for such a machine. Could you explain just what you intend to do with it?'

'Gladly,' replied the Lama, readjusting his silk robe and carefully putting away the slide rule he had been using for currency conversions. 'Your Mark V Computer can carry out any routine mathematical operation involving up to ten digits. However, for our work we are interested in *letters*, not numbers. As we wish you to modify the output circuits, the machine will be printing words, not columns of figures.'

'I don't quite understand . . .'

'This is a project on which we have been working for the last three centuries – since the lamasery was founded, in fact. It is somewhat alien to your way of thought, so I hope you will listen with an open mind while I explain it.'

'Naturally.'

'It is really quite simple. We have been compiling a list which shall contain all the possible names of God.'

'I beg your pardon?'

'We have reason to believe,' continued the Lama imperturbably, 'that all such names can be written with not more than nine letters in an alphabet we have devised.'

'And you have been doing this for three centuries?'

'Yes: we expected it would take us about fifteen thousand years to complete the task.'

'Oh.' Dr Wagner looked a little dazed. 'Now I see why you wanted to hire one of our machines. But exactly what is the *purpose* of this project?'

The Lama hesitated for a fraction of a second and Wagner wondered if he had offended him. If so, there was no trace of annoyance in the reply.

'Call it ritual, if you like, but it's a fundamental part of our belief. All the many names of the Supreme Being – God, Jehovah, Allah, and so on – they are only man-made labels. There is a philosophical problem of some difficulty here, which I do not propose to discuss, but somewhere among all the possible combinations of letters which can occur are what one may call the *real* names of God. By systematic permutation of letters, we have been trying to list them all.'

'I see. You've been starting at AAAAAAAA . . . and working up to ZZZZZZZZ . . . '

'Exactly – though we use a special alphabet of our own. Modifying the electromatic typewriters to deal with this is, of course, trivial. A rather more interesting problem is that of devising suitable circuits to eliminate ridiculous combinations. For example, no letter must occur more than three times in succession.'

'Three? Surely you mean two.'

'Three is correct. I am afraid it would take too long to explain why, even if you understood our language.'

'I'm sure it would,' said Wagner hastily. 'Go on.'

'Luckily, it will be a simple matter to adapt your Automatic Sequence Computer for this work, since once it has been programmed properly it will permute each letter in turn and print the result. What would have taken us fifteen thousand years it will be able to do in a hundred days.'

Dr Wagner was scarcely conscious of the faint sounds from the Manhattan streets far below. He was in a different world, a world of natural, not man-made mountains. High up in their remote aeries these monks had been patiently at work, generation after generation, compiling their lists of meaningless words. Was there any limit to the follies of mankind? Still, he must give no hint of his inner thoughts. The customer was always right . . .

'There's no doubt,' replied the doctor, 'that we can modify the Mark V to print lists of this nature. I'm much more worried about the problem of installation and maintenance. Getting out to Tibet, in these days, is not going to be easy.'

'We can arrange that. The components are small enough to travel by air – that is one reason why we chose your machine. If you can get them to India, we will provide transport from there.'

'And you want to hire two of our engineers?'

'Yes, for the three months which the project should occupy.'

'I've no doubt that Personnel can manage that.' Dr Wagner scribbled a note on his desk pad. 'There are just two other points – '

Before he could finish the sentence the Lama had produced a small slip of paper.

'This is my certified credit balance at the Asiatic Bank.'

'Thank you. It appears to be – ah – adequate. The second matter is so trivial that I hesitate to mention it – but it's surprising how often the obvious gets overlooked. What source of electrical energy have you?'

'A diesel generator providing 50 kilowatts at 110 volts. It was installed about five years ago and is quite realiable. It's made life at the lamasery much more comfortable, but of course it was really installed to provide power for the motors driving the prayer wheels.'

'Of course,' echoed Dr Wagner. 'I should have thought of that.'

The view from the parapet was vertiginous, but in time one gets used to anything. After three months, George Hanley was not impressed by the two-thousand-foot swoop into the abyss or the remote chequerboard of fields in the valley below. He was leaning against the wind-smoothed stones and staring morosely at the distant mountains whose names he had never bothered to discover.

This, thought George, was the craziest thing that had ever happened to him. 'Project Shangri-La', some wit at the labs had christened it. For weeks now the Mark V had been churning out acres of sheets covered with gibberish. Patiently, inexorably, the computer had been rearranging letters in all their possible combinations, exhausting each class before going on to the next. As the sheets had emerged from the electromatic typewriters, the monks had carefully cut them up and pasted them into enormous books. In another week, heaven be praised, they would have finished. Just what obscure calculations had convinced the monks that they needn't bother to go on to words of ten, twenty, or a hundred letters, George didn't know. One of his recurring nightmares was that there would be some change of plan, and that the High Lama (whom they'd naturally called Sam Jaffe, though he didn't look a bit like him) would suddenly announce that the project would be extended to approximately 2060 AD. They were quite capable of it.

George heard the heavy wooden door slam in the wind as Chuck came out onto the parapet beside him. As usual, Chuck was smoking one of the cigars that made him so popular with the monks – who, it seemed, were quite willing to embrace all the minor and most of the major pleasures of life. That was one thing in their favour: they might be crazy, but they weren't bluenoses. Those frequent trips they took down to the village, for instance . . .

'Listen, George,' said Chuck urgently. 'I've learned something that means trouble.'

'What's wrong? Isn't the machine behaving?' That was the worst contingency George could imagine. It might delay his return, than which nothing could be more horrible. The way he felt now, even the sight of a TV commercial would seem like manna from heaven. At least it would be some link with home.

'No – it's nothing like that.' Chuck settled himself on the parapet, which was unusual because normally he was scared of the drop. 'I've just found what all this is about.'

'What d'ya mean – I thought we knew.'

'Sure – we know what the monks are trying to do. But we didn't know *why*. It's the craziest thing – '

'Tell me something new,' growled George.

' – but old Sam's just come clean with me. You know the way he drops in every afternoon to watch the sheets roll out. Well, this time he seemed rather excited, or at least as near as he'll ever get to it. When I told him that we were on the last cycle he asked me, in that cute English accent of his, if I'd ever wondered what they were trying to do. I said "Sure" – and he told me.'

'Go on: I'll buy it.'

'Well, they believe that when they have listed all His names – and they reckon that there are about nine billion of them – God's purpose will be achieved. The human race will have finished what it was created to do, and there won't be any point in carrying on. Indeed, the very idea is something like blasphemy.'

'Then what do they expect us to do? Commit suicide?'

'There's no need for that. When the list's completed, God steps in and simply winds things up . . . bingo!'

'Oh, I get it. When we finish our job, it will be the end of the world.'

Chuck gave a nervous little laugh.

'That's just what I said to Sam. And do you know what happened? He looked at me in a very queer way, like I'd been stupid in class, and said, "It's nothing as trivial as *that*." '

George thought this over for a moment.

'That's what I call taking the Wide View,' he said presently. 'But what d'ya suppose we should do about it? I don't see that it makes the slightest difference to us. After all, we already knew that they were crazy.'

'Yes – but don't you see what may happen? When the list's complete and the Last Trump doesn't blow – or whatever it is they expect – *we* may get the blame. It's our machine they've been using. I don't like the situation one little bit.'

'I see,' said George slowly. 'You've got a point there. But

this sort of thing's happened before, you know. When I was a kid down in Louisiana we had a crackpot preacher who said the world was going to end next Sunday. Hundreds of people believed him – even sold their homes. Yet when nothing happened, they didn't turn nasty as you'd expect. They just decided that he'd made a mistake in his calculations and went right on believing. I guess some of them still do.'

'Well, this isn't Louisiana, in case you hadn't noticed. There are just two of us and hundreds of these monks. I like them, and I'll be sorry for old Sam when his lifework backfires on him. But all the same, I wish I was somewhere else.'

'I've been wishing that for weeks. But there's nothing we can do until the contract's finished and the transport arrives to fly us out.'

'Of course,' said Chuck thoughtfully, 'we could always try a bit of sabotage.'

'Like hell we could! That would make things worse.'

'Not the way I meant. Look at it like this. The machine will finish its run four days from now, on the present twenty-hours-a-day basis. The transport calls in a week. Okay – then all we need do is to find something that wants replacing during one of the overhaul periods – something that will hold up the work for a couple of days. We'll fix it, of course, but not too quickly. If we time matters properly, we can be down at the airfield when the last name pops out of the register. They won't be able to catch us then.'

'I don't like it,' said George. 'It will be the first time I ever walked out on a job. Besides, it would make them suspicious. No. I'll sit tight and take what comes.'

'I *still* don't like it,' he said, seven days later, as the tough little mountain ponies carried them down the winding road. 'And don't you think I'm running away because I'm afraid. I'm just sorry for those poor old guys up there, and I don't want to be around when they find what suckers they've been. Wonder how Sam will take it?'

'It's funny,' replied Chuck, 'but when I said goodbye I got the idea he knew we were walking out on him – and that he didn't care because he knew the machine was running smoothly and that the job would soon be finished. After that – well, of course, for him there just isn't any After That . . . '

George turned in his saddle and stared back up the mountain road. This was the last place from which one could get a clear view of the lamasery. The squat, angular buildings were silhouetted against the afterglow of the sunset; here and there, lights gleamed like portholes in the sides of an ocean liner. Electric lights, of course, sharing the same circuit as the Mark V. How much longer would they share it, wondered George. Would the monks smash up the computer in their rage and disappointment? Or would they just sit down quietly and begin their calculations all over again?

He knew exactly what was happening up on the mountain at this very moment. The High Lama and his assistants would be sitting in their silk robes, inspecting the sheets as the junior monks carried them away from the typewriters and pasted them into the great volumes. No one would be saying anything. The only sound would be the incessant patter, the never-ending rainstorm, of the keys hitting the paper, for the Mark V itself was utterly silent as it flashed through its thousands of calculations a second. Three months of this, thought George, was enough to start anyone climbing up the wall.

'There she is!' called Chuck, pointing down into the valley. 'Ain't she beautiful!'

She certainly was, thought George. The battered old DC3 lay at the end of the runway like a tiny silver cross. In two hours she would be bearing them away to freedom and sanity. It was a thought worth savouring like a fine liqueur. George let it roll around his mind as the pony trudged patiently down the slope.

The swift night of the high Himalayas was now almost upon them. Fortunately the road was very good, as roads went in this region, and they were both carrying torches. There was not the slightest danger, only a certain discomfort from the bitter cold. The sky overhead was perfectly clear and ablaze with the familiar, friendly stars. At least there would be no risk, thought George, of the pilot's being unable to take off because of weather conditions. That had been his only remaining worry.

He began to sing, but gave it up after a while. This vast arena of mountains, gleaming like whitely hooded ghosts on every side, did not encourage such ebullience. Presently George glanced at his watch.

'Should be there in an hour,' he called back over his shoulder to Chuck. Then he added, in an afterthought, 'Wonder if the computer's finished its run? It was due about now.'

Chuck didn't reply, so George swung around in his saddle. He could just see Chuck's face, a white oval turned towards the sky.

'Look,' whispered Chuck, and George lifted his eyes to heaven. (There is always a last time for everything.)

Overhead, without any fuss, the stars were going out.

The Streets of Askelon

Harry Harrison

Somewhere above, hidden by the eternal clouds of Wesker's World, a thunder rumbled and grew. Trader John Garth stopped when he heard it, his boots sinking slowly into the muck, and cupped his good ear to catch the sound. It swelled and waned in the thick atmosphere, growing louder.

'That noise is the same as the noise of your sky-ship,' Itin said, with stolid Wesker logicality, slowly pulverizing the idea in his mind and turning over the bits one by one for closer examination. 'But your ship is still sitting where you landed it. It must be, even though we cannot see it, because you are the only one who can operate it. And even if anyone else could operate it we would have heard it rising into the sky. Since we did not, and if this sound is a sky-ship sound, then it must mean . . . '

'Yes, another ship,' Garth said, too absorbed in his own thoughts to wait for the laborious Weskerian chains of logic to clank their way through to the end. Of course it was another spacer, it had been only a matter of time before one appeared, and undoubtedly this one was homing on the SS radar reflector as he had done. His own ship would show up clearly on the newcomer's screen and they would probably set down as close to it as they could.

'You better go ahead, Itin,' he said. 'Use the water so you can get to the village quickly. Tell everyone to get back into the swamps, well clear of the hard ground. That ship is landing on instruments and anyone underneath at touch-down is going to be cooked.'

This immediate threat was clear enough to the little Wesker amphibian. Before Garth finished speaking Itin's ribbed ears had folded like a bat's wing and he slipped silently into the nearby canal. Garth squelched on through the mud, making as good time as he could over the clinging surface. He had just reached the fringes of the village clearing when the rumbling grew to a head-splitting roar and the spacer broke through the low-hanging layer of clouds above. Garth shielded his eyes from the down-reaching tongue of flame and examined the growing form of the grey-black ship with mixed feelings.

After almost a standard year on Wesker's World he had to fight down a longing for human companionship of any kind. While this buried fragment of herd-spirit chattered for the rest of the monkey tribe, his trader's mind was busily drawing a line under a column of figures and adding up the total. This could very well be another trader's ship, and if it were his monopoly of the Wesker trade was at an end. Then again, this might not be a trader at all, which was the reason he stayed in the shelter of the giant fern and loosened his gun in its holster.

The ship baked dry a hundred square metres of mud, the roaring blast died, and the landing feet crunched down through the crackling crust. Metal creaked and settled into place while the cloud of smoke and steam slowly drifted lower in the humid air.

'Garth – you native-cheating extortionist – where are you?' the ship's speaker boomed. The lines of the spacer had looked only slightly familiar, but there was no mistaking the rasping tones of that voice. Garth wore a smile when he stepped out into the open and whistled shrilly through two fingers. A directional microphone ground out of its casing on the ship's fin and turned in his direction.

'What are you doing here, Singh?' he shouted towards the mike. 'Too crooked to find a planet of your own and have to come here to steal an honest trader's profits?'

'Honest!' the amplified voice roared. 'This from the man who has been in more gaols than cathouses – and that a goodly number in itself, I do declare. Sorry, friend of my youth, but I cannot join you in exploiting this aboriginal pesthole. I am on course to a more fairly atmosphered world where a fortune is waiting to be made. I only stopped here since an opportunity presented to turn an honest credit by running a taxi service. I bring you friendship, the perfect companionship, a man in a different line of business who might help you in yours. I'd come out and say hello myself, except I would have to decon for biologicals. I'm cycling the passenger through the lock so I hope you won't mind helping with his luggage.'

At least there would be no other trader on the planet now, that worry was gone. But Garth still wondered what sort of passenger would be taking one-way passage to an uninhabited world. And what was behind that concealed hint of merriment in Singh's voice? He walked around to the far side of the spacer where the ramp had dropped, and looked up at the man in the cargo lock who was wrestling ineffectually with a large crate. The man turned towards him and Garth saw the clerical dog-collar and knew just what it was Singh had been chuckling about.

'What are you doing here?' Garth asked; in spite of his attempt at self-control he snapped the words. If the man noticed this he ignored it, because he was still smiling and putting out his hand as he came down the ramp.

'Father Mark,' he said. 'Of the Missionary Society of Brothers. I'm very pleased to . . .'

'I said what are you doing here.' Garth's voice was under control now, quiet and cold. He knew what had to be done, and it must be done quickly or not at all.

'That should be obvious,' Father Mark said, his good nature still unruffled. 'Our missionary society has raised funds to send spiritual emissaries to alien worlds for the first time. I was lucky enough . . .'

'Take your luggage and get back into the ship. You're not wanted here and have no permission to land. You'll be a liability and there is no one on Wesker to take care of you. Get back into the ship.'

'I don't know who you are, sir, or why you are lying to me,' the priest said. He was still calm but the smile was gone. 'But I have studied galactic law and the history of this planet very well. There are no diseases or beasts here that I should have any particular fear of. It is also an open planet, and until the Space Survey changes that status I have as much right to be here as you do.'

The man was of course right, but Garth couldn't let him know that. He had been bluffing, hoping the priest didn't know his rights. But he did. There was only one distasteful course left for him, and he had better do it while there was still time.

'Get back in that ship,' he shouted, not hiding his anger now. With a smooth motion his gun was out of the holster and the pitted black muzzle only inches from the priest's stomach. The man's face turned white, but he did not move.

'What the hell are you doing, Garth!' Singh's shocked voice grated from the speaker. 'The guy paid his fare and you have no right at all to throw him off the planet.'

'I have this right,' Garth said, raising his gun and sighting between the priest's eyes. 'I give him thirty seconds to get back aboard the ship or I pull the trigger.'

'Well I think you are either off your head or playing a joke,' Singh's exasperated voice rasped down at them. 'If a joke, it is in bad taste, and either way you're not getting away with it. Two can play at that game, only I can play it better.'

There was the rumble of heavy bearings and the remote-controlled four-gun turret on the ship's side rotated and pointed at Garth. 'Now – down gun and give Father Mark a hand with the luggage,' the speaker commanded, a trace of humour back in the voice now. 'As much as I would like to help, old friend, I cannot. I feel it is time you had a chance to talk to the father; after all, I have had the opportunity of speaking with him all the way from Earth.'

Garth jammed the gun back into the holster with an acute feeling of loss. Father Mark stepped forward, the winning smile back now and a bible taken from a pocket of his robe, in his raised hand. 'My son,' he said.

'I'm not your son,' was all Garth could choke out as defeat welled up in him. His fist drew back as the anger rose, and the best he could do was open the fist so he struck only with the flat of his hand. Still the blow sent the priest crashing to the ground and fluttered the pages of the book splattering into the thick mud.

Itin and the other Weskers had watched everything with seemingly emotionless interest, and Garth made no attempt to answer their unspoken questions. He started towards his house, but turned back when he saw they were still unmoving.

'A new man has come,' he told them. 'He will need help with the things he has brought. If he doesn't have any place for them, you can put them in the big warehouse until he has a place of his own.'

He watched them waddle across the clearing towards the ship, then went inside and gained a certain satisfaction from slamming the door hard enough to crack one of the panes. There was an equal amount of painful pleasure in breaking out one of the remaining bottles of Irish whiskey that he had been saving for a special occasion. Well this was special enough, though not really what he had had in mind. The whiskey was good and burned away some of the bad taste in his mouth, but not all of it. If his tactics had worked, success would have justified everything. But he had failed and in addition to the pain of failure there was the acute feeling that he had made a horse's ass out of himself. Singh had blasted off without any goodbyes. There was no telling what sense he had made of the whole matter, though he would surely carry some strange stories back to the traders' lodge. Well, that could be worried about the next time Garth signed in. Right now he had to go about setting things right with the missionary. Squinting out through the rain he saw the man struggling to erect a collapsible tent while the entire population of the village stood in ordered ranks and watched. Naturally none of them offered to help.

By the time the tent was up and the crates and boxes stowed inside it the rain had stopped. The level of fluid in the bottle was a good bit lower and Garth felt more like facing up to the unavoidable meeting. In truth, he was looking forward to talking to the man. This whole nasty business aside, after an entire solitary year any human companionship looked good. *Will you join me now for dinner. John Garth*, he wrote on the back of an old invoice. But maybe the guy was too frightened to come? Which was no way to start any kind of relationship. Rummaging under the bunk, he found a box that was big enough and put his pistol inside. Itin was of course waiting outside the door when he opened it, since this was his tour as Knowledge Collector. He handed him the note and box.

'Would you take these to the new man,' he said.

'Is the new man's name New Man?' Itin asked.

'No, it's not!' Garth snapped. 'His name is Mark. But I'm only asking you to deliver this, not get involved in conversation.'

As always when he lost his temper, the literal-minded Weskers won the round. 'You are not asking for conversation,' Itin said slowly, 'but Mark may ask for conversation. And others will ask me his name, if I do not know his na . . .' The voice cut off as Garth slammed the door. This didn't work in the long run either because next time he saw Itin – a day, a week, or even a month later – the monologue would be picked up on the very word it had ended and the thought rambled out to its last frayed end. Garth cursed under his breath and poured water over a pair of the tastier concentrates that he had left.

'Come in,' he said when there was a quiet knock on the door. The priest entered and held out the box with the gun.

'Thank you for the loan, Mr Garth, I appreciate the spirit that made you send it. I have no idea what caused the unhappy affair when I landed, but I think it would be best forgotten if we are going to be on this planet together for any length of time.'

'Drink?' Garth asked, taking the box and pointing to the bottle on the table. He poured two glasses full and handed one to the priest. 'That's about what I had in mind, but I still owe you an explanation of what happened out there.' He scowled into his glass for a second, then raised it to the other man. 'It's a big universe and I guess we have to make out as best we can. Here's to Sanity.'

'God be with you,' Father Mark said, and raised his glass as well.

'Not with me or with this planet,' Garth said firmly. 'And that's the crux of the matter.' He half-drained the glass and sighed.

'Do you say that to shock me?' the priest asked with a smile. 'I assure you it doesn't.'

'Not intended to shock. I meant it quite literally. I suppose I'm what you would call an atheist, so revealed religion is no concern of mine. While these natives, simple and unlettered stone-age types that they are, have managed to come this far with no superstitions or traces of deism whatsoever. I had hoped that they might continue that way.'

'What are you saying?' the priest frowned. 'Do you mean they have no gods, no belief in the hereafter? They must die . . . ?'

'Die they do, and to dust return like the rest of the animals. They have thunder, trees and water without having thunder-gods, tree spirits, or water nymphs. They have no ugly little gods, taboos, or spells to hag-ride and limit their lives. They are the only primitive people I have ever encountered who are completely free of superstition and appear to be much happier and saner because of it. I just wanted to keep them that way.'

'You wanted to keep them from God – from salvation?' The priest's eyes widened and he recoiled slightly.

'No,' Garth said. 'I wanted to keep them from superstition until they knew more and could think about it realistically without being absorbed and perhaps destroyed by it.'

'You're being insulting to the Church, sir, to equate it with superstition . . .'

'Please,' Garth said, raising his hand. 'No theological arguments. I don't think your society footed the bill for this trip just to attempt a conversion on me. Just accept the fact that my beliefs have been arrived at through careful thought over a period of years, and no amount of undergraduate metaphysics will change them. I'll promise not to try and convert you – if you will do the same for me.'

'Agreed, Mr Garth. As you have reminded me, my mission here is to save these souls, and that is what I must do. But why should my work disturb you so much that you try and keep me from landing? Even threaten me with your gun, and . . . ' The priest broke off and looked into his glass.

'And even slug you?' Garth asked, suddenly frowning. 'There was no excuse for that, and I would like to say that I'm sorry. Plain bad manners and an even worse temper. Live alone long enough and you find yourself doing that kind of thing.' He brooded down at his big hands where they lay on the table, reading memories into the scars and callouses patterned there. 'Let's just call it frustration, for lack of a better word. In your business you must have had a lot of chance to peep into the darker places in men's minds and you should know a bit about motives and happiness. I have had too busy a life ever to consider settling down and raising a family, and right up until recently I never missed it. Maybe leakage radiation is softening up my brain, but I had begun to think of these furry and fishy Weskers as being a little like my own children, that I was somehow responsible to them.'

'We are all His children,' Father Mark said quietly.

'Well, here are some of His children that can't even imagine His existence,' Garth said, suddenly angry at himself for allowing gentler emotions to show through. Yet he forgot himself at once, leaning forward with the intensity of his feelings. 'Can't you realize the importance of this? Live with these Weskers awhile and you will discover a simple and happy life that matches the state of grace you people are always talking about. They get *pleasure* from their lives – and cause no one pain. By circumstances they have evolved on an almost barren world, so have never had a chance to grow out of a physical stone-age culture. But mentally they are our match – or perhaps better. They have all learned my language so I can easily explain the many things they want to know. Knowledge and the gaining of knowledge gives them real satisfaction. They tend to be exasperating at times because every new fact must be related to the structure of all other things, but the more they learn the faster this process becomes. Some day they are going to be man's equal in every way, perhaps surpass us. If – would you do me a favour?'

'Whatever I can.'

'Leave them alone. Or teach them if you must – history and science, philosophy, law, anything that will help them face the realities of the greater universe they never even knew existed before. But don't confuse them with your hatreds and pain, guilt, sin, and punishment. Who knows the harm . . .'

'You are being insulting, sir!' the priest said, jumping to his feet. The top of his grey head barely came to the massive spaceman's chin, yet he showed no fear in defending what he believed. Garth, standing now himself, was no longer the penitent. They faced each other in anger, as men have always stood, unbending in the defence of that which they think right.

'Yours is the insult,' Garth shouted. 'The incredible egotism to feel that your derivative little mythology, differing only slightly from the thousands of others that still burden men, can do anything but confuse their still fresh minds! Don't you realize that they believe in truth – and have never heard of such a thing as a lie. They have not been trained yet to understand that other kinds of minds can think differently from theirs. Will you spare them this . . . ?'

'I will do my duty which is His will, Mr Garth. These are God's creatures here, and they have souls. I cannot shirk my duty, which is to bring them His word, so that they may be saved and enter into the kingdom of heaven.'

When the priest opened the door the wind caught it and blew it wide. He vanished into the stormswept darkness and the door swung back and forth and a splatter of raindrops blew in. Garth's boots left muddy footprints when he closed the door, shutting out the sight of Itin sitting patiently and uncomplaining in the storm, hoping only that Garth might stop for a moment and leave with him some of the wonderful knowledge of which he had so much.

By unspoken consent that first night was never mentioned again. After a few days of loneliness, made worse because each knew of the other's proximity, they found themselves talking on carefully neutral ground. Garth slowly packed and stowed away his stock and never admitted that his work was finished and he could leave at any time. He had a fair amount of interesting drugs and botanicals that would fetch a good price. And the Wesker Artefacts were sure to create a sensation in the sophisticated galactic market. Crafts on the planet here had been limited before his arrival, mostly pieces of carving painfully chipped into the hard wood with fragments of stone. He had supplied tools and a stock of raw metal from his own supplies, nothing more than that. In a few months the Weskers had not only learned to work with the new materials, but had translated their own designs and forms into the most alien – but most beautiful – artefacts that he had ever seen. All he had to do was release these on the market to create a primary demand, then return for a new supply. The Weskers wanted only books and tools and knowledge in return, and through their own efforts he knew they would pull themselves into the galactic union.

This is what Garth had hoped. But a wind of change was blowing through the settlement that had grown up around his ship. No longer was he the centre of attention and focal point of the village life. He had to grin when he thought of his fall from power; yet there was very little humour in the smile. Serious and attentive Weskers still took turns of duty as Knowledge Collectors, but their recording of dry facts was in sharp contrast to the intellectual hurricane that surrounded the priest.

Where Garth had made them work for each book and machine, the priest gave freely. Garth had tried to be progressive in his supply of knowledge, treating them as bright but unlettered children. He had wanted them to walk before they could run, to master one step before going on to the next.

Father Mark simply brought them the benefits of Christianity. The only physical work he required was the construction of a church, a place of worship and learning. More

Weskers had appeared out of the limitless planetary swamps and within days the roof was up, supported on a framework of poles. Each morning the congregation worked a little while on the walls, then hurried inside to learn the all-promising, all-encompassing, all-important facts about the universe.

Garth never told the Weskers what he thought about their new interest, and this was mainly because they had never asked him. Pride or honour stood in the way of his grabbing a willing listener and pouring out his grievances. Perhaps it would have been different if Itin was on Collecting duty; he was the brightest of the lot; but Itin had been rotated the day after the priest had arrived and Garth had not talked to him since.

It was a surprise then when after seventeen of the trebly-long Wesker days, he found a delegation at his doorstep when he emerged after breakfast. Itin was their spokesman, and his mouth was open slightly. Many of the other Weskers had their mouths open as well, one even appearing to be yawning, clearly revealing the double row of sharp teeth and the purple-black throat. The mouths impressed Garth as to the seriousness of the meeting: this was the one Wesker expression he had learned to recognize. An open mouth indicated some strong emotion; happiness, sadness, anger, he could never be really sure which. The Weskers were normally placid and he had never seen enough open mouths to tell what was causing them. But he was surrounded by them now.

'Will you help us, John Garth,' Itin said. 'We have a question.'

'I'll answer any question you ask,' Garth said, with more than a hint of misgiving. 'What is it?'

'Is there a God?'

'What do you mean by "God"?' Garth asked in turn. What should he tell them?

'God is our Father in Heaven, who made us all and protects us. Whom we pray to for aid, and if we are Saved will find a place . . . '

'That's enough,' Garth said. 'There is no God.'

All of them had their mouths open now, even Itin, as they looked at Garth and thought about his answer. The rows of pink teeth would have been frightening if he hadn't known these creatures so well. For one instant he wondered if perhaps they had been already indoctrinated and looked upon him as a heretic, but he brushed the thought away.

'Thank you,' Itin said, and they turned and left.

Though the morning was still cool, Garth noticed that he was sweating and wondered why.

The reaction was not long in coming. Itin returned that same afternoon. 'Will you come to the church?' he asked. 'Many of the things that we study are difficult to learn, but none as difficult as this. We need your help because we must hear you and Father Mark talk together. This is because he says one thing is true and you say another is true and both cannot be true at the same time. We must find out what is true.'

'I'll come, of course,' Garth said, trying to hide the sudden feeling of elation. He had done nothing, but the Weskers had come to him anyway. There could still be grounds for hope that they might yet be free.

It was hot inside the church, and Garth was surprised at the number of Weskers who were there, more than he had seen gathered at any one time before. There were many open mouths. Father Mark sat at a table covered with books. He looked unhappy but didn't say anything when Garth came in. Garth spoke first.

'I hope you realize this is their idea – that they came to me of their own free will and asked me to come here?'

'I know that,' the priest said resignedly. 'At times they can be very difficult. But they are learning and want to believe, and that is what is important.'

'Father Mark, Trader Garth, we need your help,' Itin said. 'You both know many things that we do not know. You must help us come to religion which is not an easy thing to do.' Garth started to say something, then changed his mind. Itin went on, 'We have read the bibles and all the books that Father Mark gave us, and one thing is clear. We have discussed this and we are all agreed. These books are very different from the ones that Trader Garth gave us. In Trader Garth's books there is the universe which we have not seen, and it goes on without God, for he is mentioned nowhere; we have searched very carefully. In Father Mark's books He is everywhere and nothing can go without Him. One of these must be right and the other must be wrong. We do not know how this can be, but after we find out which is right then perhaps we will know. If God does not exist . . . '

'Of course He exists, my children,' Father Mark said in a voice of heartfelt intensity. 'He is our Father in Heaven who has created us all . . .'

'Who created God?' Itin asked and the murmur ceased and every one of the Weskers watched Father Mark intensely. He recoiled a bit under the impact of their eyes, then smiled.

'Nothing created God, since He is the Creator. He always was . . .'

'If He always was in existence – why cannot the universe have always been in existence? Without having had a creator?' Itin broke in with a rush of words. The importance of the question was obvious. The priest answered slowly, with infinite patience.

'Would that the answers were that simple, my children. But even the scientists do not agree about the creation of the universe. While they doubt – we who have seen the light *know*. We can see the miracle of creation all about us. And how can there be a creation without a Creator? That is He, our Father, our God in Heaven. I know you have doubts; that is because you have souls and free will. Still, the answer is so simple. Have faith, that is all you need. Just believe.'

'How can we believe without proof?'

'If you cannot see that this world itself is proof of His existence, then I say to you that belief needs no proof – if you have faith!'

A babble of voices arose in the room and more of the Wesker mouths were open now as they tried to force their thoughts through the tangled skein of words and separate the thread of truth.

'Can you tell us, Garth?' Itin asked, and the sound of his voice quieted the hubbub.

'I can tell you to use the scientific method which can examine all things – including itself – and give you answers that can prove the truth or falsity of any statement.'

'That is what we must do,' Itin said, 'we had reached the same conclusion.' He held a thick book before him and a ripple of nods ran across the watchers. 'We have been studying the bible as Father Mark told us to do, and we have found the answer. God will make a miracle for us, thereby proving that He is watching us. And by this sign we will know Him and go to Him.'

'That is the sin of false pride,' Father Mark said. 'God needs no miracles to prove His existence.'

'Be *we* need a miracle!' Itin shouted, and though he wasn't human there was need in his voice. 'We have read here of many smaller miracles, loaves, fishes, wine, snakes – many of them, for much smaller reasons. Now all He need do is make a miracle and He will bring us all to Him – the wonder of an entire new world worshipping at His throne, as you have told us, Father Mark. And you have told us how important this is. We have discussed this and find that there is only one miracle that is best for this kind of thing.'

His boredom at the theological wrangling drained from Garth in an instant. He had not been really thinking or he would have realized where all this was leading. He could see the illustration in the bible where Itin held it open, and knew in advance what picture it was. He rose slowly from his chair, as if stretching, and turned to the priest behind him.

'Get ready!' he whispered. 'Get out the back and get to the ship; I'll keep them busy here. I don't think they'll harm me.'

'What do you mean . . . ?' Father Mark asked, blinking in surprise.

'Get out, you fool!' Garth hissed. 'What miracle do you think they mean? What miracle is supposed to have converted the world to Christianity?'

'No!' Father Mark said. 'It cannot be. It just cannot be . . . !'

'*Get moving!*' Garth shouted, dragging the priest from the chair and hurling him towards the rear wall. Father Mark stumbled to a halt, turned back. Garth leaped for him, but it was already too late. The amphibians were small, but there were so many of them. Garth lashed out and his fist struck Itin, hurling him back into the crowd. The others came on as he fought his way towards the priest. He beat at them but it was like struggling against waves. The furry, musky bodies washed over and engulfed him. He fought until they tied him, and he still struggled until they beat on his head until he stopped. Then they pulled him outside where he could only lie in the rain and curse and watch.

Of course the Weskers were marvellous craftsmen, and everything had been constructed down to the last detail, following the illustration in the bible. There was the cross, planted firmly on the top of a small hill, the gleaming metal spikes, the hammer. Father Mark was stripped and draped in a carefully pleated loincloth. They led him out of the church.

At the sight of the cross he almost fainted. After that he held his head high and determined to die as he had lived, with faith.

Yet this was hard. It was unbearable even for Garth, who only watched. It is one thing to talk of crucifixion and look at the gentle carved bodies in the dim light of prayer. It is another to see a man naked, ropes cutting into his skin where he hangs from a bar of wood. And to see the needle-tipped spike raised and placed against the soft flesh of his palm, to see the hammer come back with the calm deliberation of an artisan's measured stroke. To hear the thick sound of metal penetrating flesh.

Then to hear the screams.

Few are born to be martyrs; Father Mark was not one of them. With the first blows, the blood ran from his lips where his clenched teeth met. Then his mouth was wide and his head strained back and the guttural horror of his screams sliced through the susurration of the falling rain. It resounded as a silent echo from the masses of watching Weskers, for whatever emotion opened their mouths was now tearing at their bodies with all its force, and row after row of gaping jaws reflected the crucified priest's agony.

Mercifully he fainted as the last nail was driven home. Blood ran from the raw wounds, mixing with the rain to drip faintly pink from his feet as the life ran out of him. At this time, somewhere at this time, sobbing and tearing at his own bonds, numbed from the blows on the head, Garth lost consciousness.

He awoke in his own warehouse and it was dark. Someone was cutting away the woven ropes they had bound him with. The rain still dripped and splashed outside.

'Itin,' he said. It could be no one else.

'Yes,' the alien voice whispered back. 'The others are all talking in the church. Lin died after you struck his head, and Inon is very sick. There are some that say you should be crucified too, and I think that is what will happen. Or perhaps killed by stoning on the head. They have found in the bible where it says . . . '

'I know.' With infinite weariness. 'An eye for an eye. You'll find lots of things like that once you start looking. It's a wonderful book.' His head ached terribly.

'You must go, you can get to your ship without anyone seeing you. There has been enough killing.' Itin as well, spoke with a new-found weariness.

Garth experimented, pulling himself to his feet. He pressed his head to the rough wood of the wall until the nausea stopped. 'He's dead.' He said it as a statement, not a question.

'Yes, some time ago. Or I could not have come away to see you.'

'And buried of course, or they wouldn't be thinking about starting on me next.'

'And buried!' There was almost a ring of emotion in the alien's voice, an echo of the dead priest's. 'He is buried and he will rise on High. It is written and that is the way it will happen. Father Mark will be so happy that it has happened like this.' The voice ended in a sound like a human sob.

Garth painfully worked his way towards the door, leaning against the wall so he wouldn't fall.

'We did the right thing, didn't we?' Itin asked. There was no answer. 'He will rise up, Garth, won't he rise?'

Garth was at the door and enough light came from the brightly lit church to show his torn and bloody hands clutching at the frame. Itin's face swam into sight close to his, and Garth felt the delicate, many fingered hands with the sharp nails catch at his clothes.

'He will rise, won't he, Garth?'

'No,' Garth said, 'he is going to stay buried right where you put him. Nothing is going to happen because he is dead and he is going to stay dead.'

The rain runnelled through Itin's fur and his mouth was opened so wide that he seemed to be screaming into the night. Only with effort could he talk, squeezing out the alien thoughts in an alien language.

'Then we will not be saved? We will not become pure?'

'You were pure,' Garth said, in a voice somewhere between a sob and a laugh. 'That's the horrible ugly dirty part of it. You were pure. Now you are . . . '

'Murderers,' Itin said, and the water ran down from his lowered head and streamed away into the darkness.

The Country of the Kind

Damon Knight

The attendant at the car lot was daydreaming when I pulled up – a big, lazy-looking man in black satin chequered down the front. I was wearing scarlet, myself; it suited my mood. I got out, almost on his toes.

'Park or storage?' he asked automatically, turning around. Then he realized who I was, and ducked his head away.

'Neither,' I told him.

There was a hand torch on a shelf in the repair shed right behind him. I got it and came back. I kneeled down to where I could reach behind the front wheel, and ignited the torch. I turned it on the axle and suspension. They glowed cherry red, then white, and fused together. Then I got up and turned the flame on both tyres until the rubberoid stank and sizzled and melted down to the pavement. The attendant didn't say anything.

I left him there, looking at the mess on his nice clean concrete.

It had been a nice car, too; but I could get another any time. And I felt like walking. I went down the winding road, sleepy in the afternoon sunlight, dappled with shade and smelling of cool leaves. You couldn't see the houses; they were all sunken or hidden by shrubbery, or a little of both. That was the fad I'd heard about; it was what I'd come here to see. Not that anything the dulls did would be worth looking at.

I turned off at random and crossed a rolling lawn, went

through a second hedge of hawthorn in blossom, and came out next to a big sunken games court.

The tennis net was up, and two couples were going at it, just working up a little sweat – young, about half my age, all four of them. Three dark-haired, one blonde. They were evenly matched, and both couples played well together; they were enjoying themselves.

I watched for a minute. But by then the nearest two were beginning to sense I was there, anyhow. I walked down on to the court, just as the blonde was about to serve. She looked at me, frozen across the net, poised on tiptoe. The others stood.

'Off,' I told them. 'Game's over.'

I watched the blonde. She was not especially pretty, as they go, but compactly and gracefully put together. She came down slowly, flatfooted without awkwardness, and tucked the racquet under her arm; then the surprise was over and she was trotting off the court after the other three.

I followed their voices around the curve of the path, between towering masses of lilacs, inhaling the sweetness, until I came to what looked like a little sunning spot. There was a sundial, and a birdbath, and towels lying around on the grass. One couple, the dark-haired pair, was still in sight farther down the path, heads bobbing along. The other couple had disappeared.

I found the handle in the grass without any trouble. The mechanism responded, and an oblong section of turf rose up. It was the stair I had, not the elevator, but that was all right. I ran down the steps and into the first door I saw, and was in the top-floor lounge, an oval room lit with diffused simulated sunlight from above. The furniture was all comfortably bloated, sprawling and ugly; the carpet was deep, and there was a fresh flower scent in the air.

The blonde was over at the near end with her back to me, studying the autochef keyboard. She was half out of her playsuit. She pushed it the rest of the way down and stepped out of it, then turned and saw me.

She was surprised again; she hadn't thought I might follow her down.

I got up close before it occurred to her to move; then it was too late. She knew she couldn't get away from me; she closed her eyes and leaned back against the panelling, turning a little pale. Her lips and her golden brows went up in the middle.

I looked her over and told her a few uncomplimentary things about herself. She trembled, but didn't answer. On impulse, I leaned over and dialled the autochef to hot cheese sauce. I cut the safety out of circuit and put the quantity dial all the way up. I dialled *soup tureen* and then *punch bowl*.

The stuff began to come out in about a minute, steaming hot. I took the tureens and splashed them up and down the wall on either side of her. Then, when the first punch bowl came out, I used the empty bowls as scoops. I clotted the carpet with the stuff; I made streamers of it all along the walls, and dumped puddles into what furniture I could reach. Where it cooled it would harden, and where it hardened it would cling.

I wanted to splash it across her body, but it would've hurt, and we couldn't have that. The punch bowls of hot sauce were still coming out of the autochef, crowding each other around the vent. I punched *cancel*, and then *port wine*.

It came out well chilled in open bottles. I took the first one and had my arm back just about to throw a nice line of the stuff right across her midriff, when a voice said behind me:

'Watch out for cold wine.'

My arm twitched and a little stream of the wine splashed across her thighs. She was ready for it; her eyes had opened at the voice, and she barely jumped.

I whirled around, fighting mad. The man was standing there where he had come out of the stairwell. He was thinner in the face than most, bronzed, wide-chested, with alert blue eyes. If it hadn't been for him, I knew it would have worked – the blonde would have mistaken the cold splash for a hot one.

I could hear the scream in my mind, and I wanted it.

I took a step towards him, and my foot slipped. I went down clumsily, wrenching one knee. I got up shaking and tight all over. I wasn't in control of myself. I screamed, 'You – you – ' I turned and got one of the punch bowls and lifted it in both hands, heedless of how the hot sauce was slopping over onto my wrists, and I had it almost in the air towards him when the sickness took me – that damned buzzing in my head, louder, louder, drowning everything out.

When I came to, they were both gone. I got up off the floor, weak as death, and staggered over to the nearest chair. My clothes were slimed and sticky. I wanted to die. I wanted to drop into that dark furry hole that was yawning for me and never come up; but I made myself stay awake and get out of the chair.

Going down in the elevator, I almost blacked out again. The blonde and the thin man weren't in any of the second-floor bedrooms. I made sure of that, and then I emptied the closets and bureau drawers onto the floor, dragged the whole mess into one of the bathrooms and stuffed the tub with it, then turned on the water.

I tried the third floor: maintenance and storage. It was empty. I turned the furnace on and set the thermostat up as high as it would go. I opened the freezer doors and dialled them to defrost. I propped the stairwell door open and went back up in the elevator.

On the second floor I stopped long enough to open the stairway door there – the water was halfway towards it, creeping across the floor – and then searched the top floor. No one was there. I opened book reels and threw them unwinding across the room; I would have done more, but I could hardly stand. I got up to the surface and collapsed on the lawn; that furry pit swallowed me up, dead and drowned.

While I slept, water poured down the open stairwell and filled the third level. Thawing food packages floated out into the rooms. Water seeped into wall panels and machine housings; circuits shorted and fuses blew. The air conditioning stopped, but the pile kept heating. The water rose.

Spoiled food, floating supplies, grimy water surged up the stairwell. The second and first levels were bigger and would take longer to fill, but they'd fill. Rugs, furnishings, clothing, all the things in the house would be waterlogged and ruined. Probably the weight of so much water would shift the house, rupture water pipes and other fluid intakes. It would take a repair crew more than a day just to clean up the mess. The house itself was done for, not repairable. The blonde and the thin man would never live in it again.

Serve them right.

The dulls could build another house; they built like beavers. There was only one of me in the world.

The earliest memory I have is of some woman, probably the crèchemother, staring at me with an expression of shock and horror. Just that. I've tried to remember what happened directly before or after, but I can't. Before, there's nothing but the dark formless shaft of no-memory that runs back to birth. Afterwards, the big calm.

From my fifth year, it must have been, to my fifteenth, everything I can remember floats in a pleasant dim sea. Nothing was terribly important. I was languid and soft; I drifted. Waking merged into sleep.

In my fifteenth year it was the fashion in loveplay for the young people to pair off for months or longer. 'Loving steady,' we called it. I remember how the older people protested that it was unhealthy; but we were all normal juniors, and nearly as free as adults under law.

All but me.

The first steady girl I had was named Elen. She had blonde hair, almost white, worn long; her lashes were dark and her eyes pale green. Startling eyes: they didn't look as if they were looking at you. They looked blind.

Several times she gave me strange startled glances, something between fright and anger. Once it was because I held her too tightly, and hurt her; other times, it seemed to be for nothing at all.

In our group, a pairing that broke up sooner than four

weeks was a little suspect – there must be something wrong with one partner or both, or the pairing would have lasted longer.

Four weeks and a day after Elen and I made our pairing, she told me she was breaking it.

I'd thought I was ready. But I felt the room spin half around me till the wall came against my palm and stopped.

The room had been in use as a hobby chamber; there was a rack of plasticraft knives under my hand. I took one without thinking, and when I saw it I thought, *I'll frighten her.*

And I saw the startled, half-angry look in her pale eyes as I went towards her; but this is curious: she wasn't looking at the knife. She was looking at my face.

The elders found me later with the blood on me, and put me into a locked room. Then it was my turn to be frightened, because I realized for the first time that it was possible for a human being to do what I had done. And if I could do it to Elen, I thought, surely they could do it to me.

But they couldn't. They set me free: they had to.

And it was then I understood that I was the king of the world.

Something else in me, that had been suppressed and forgotten, rose up with my first blow struck in anger. The sculpture began years afterwards, as an accident; but in that moment I was free, and I was an artist.

One winter, in the AC Archives in Denver, I found a storeroom full of old printed books. I spent months there, reading them, because until then I'd thought I had invented sculpture and drawing. The thing I chiefly wanted to know was, why had it stopped? There was no answer in so many words in any of the books. But reading the histories of those times before the Interregnum, I found one thing that might explain it. Whenever there was a long period of peace and plenty anywhere in the ancient world, art grew poor: decoration, genre painting, imitations of imitations. And as for the great artists, they all belonged to violent periods – Praxiteles, da Vinci, Rembrandt van Rijn, Renoir, Picasso . . .

It had been bred out of the race, evidently. I don't suppose the genetic planners wanted to get rid of it, but they would have shed almost anything to make a homogeneous, rational, sane and healthy world.

So there was only one man to carve the portrait of the Age of Reason. All right; I would have been content, only . . .

The sky was turning clear violet when I woke up, and shadow was spilling out from the hedges. I went down the hill until I saw the ghostly blue of photon tubes glowing in a big oblong, just outside the commerce area. I went that way, by habit.

Other people were lining up at the entrance to show their books and be admitted. I brushed by them, seeing the shocked faces and feeling their bodies flinch away, and went on into the robing chamber.

Straps, aqualungs, masks and flippers were all for the taking. I stripped, dropping the clothes where I stood, and put the underwater equipment on. I strode out to the poolside, monstrous, like a being from another world. I adjusted the lung and the flippers, and slipped into the water.

Underneath it was all crystal blue, with the forms of swimmers sliding through it like pale angels. Schools of small fish scattered as I went down. My heart was beating with a painful joy.

Down, far down, I saw a girl slowly undulating through the motions of a sinuous underwater dance, writhing around and around a ribbed column of imitation coral. She had a suction-tipped fish lance in her hand, but she was not using it; she was only dancing, all by herself, down at the bottom of the water.

I swam after her. She was young and delicately made, and when she saw the deliberately clumsy motions I made in imitation of hers, her eyes glinted with amusement behind her mask. She bowed to me in mockery, and slowly glided off with simple, exaggerated movements, like a child's ballet.

I followed. Around her and around I swam, stiff-legged, first more childlike and awkward than she, then subtly parodying her motions; then improvising on them until I was dancing an intricate, mocking dance around her.

I saw her eyes widen. She matched her rhythm to mine, then, and together, apart, together again we coiled the wake of our dancing. At last, exhausted, we clung together where a bridge of plastic coral arched over us. Her cool body was in the bend of my arm; behind two thicknesses of vitrin – a world away! – her eyes were friendly and kind.

There was a moment when, two strangers yet one flesh, we felt our souls speak to one another across that abyss of matter. It was a truncated embrace – we could not kiss, we could not speak – but her hands lay confidingly on my shoulders, and her eyes looked into mine.

That moment had to end. She gestured towards the surface, and left me. I followed her up. I was feeling drowsy and almost at peace, after my sickness. I thought . . . I don't know what I thought.

We rose together at the side of the pool. She turned to me, removing her mask: and her smile stopped, and melted away. She stared at me with a horrified disgust, wrinkled her nose.

'*Pyah!*' she said, and turned, awkward in her flippers. Watching her, I saw her fall into the arms of a white-haired man, and heard her hysterical voice tumbling over itself.

'But don't you remember?' the man's voice rumbled. 'You should know it by heart.' He turned. 'Hal, is there a copy in the clubhouse?'

A murmur answered him, and in a few moments a young man came out holding a slender brown pamphlet.

I knew that pamphlet. I could even have told you what page the white-haired man opened it to; what sentences the girl was reading as I watched.

I waited. I don't know why.

I heard her voice rising: 'To think that I let him *touch* me!' And the white-haired man reassured her, the words rumbling, too low to hear. I saw her back straighten. She looked across at me . . . only a few yards in that scented, blue-lit air; a world away . . . and folded up the pamphlet into a hard wad, threw it, and turned on her heel.

The pamphlet landed almost at my feet. I touched it with my toe, and it opened to the page I had been thinking of:

. . . sedation until his fifteenth year, when for sexual reasons it became no longer practicable. While the advisers and medical staff hesitated, he killed a girl of the group by violence.

And farther down:

The solution finally adopted was threefold.
1. *A sanction* – the only sanction possible to our humane, permissive society. Excommunication: not to speak to him, touch him willingly, or acknowledge his existence.
2. *A precaution*. Taking advantage of a mild predisposition to epilepsy, a variant of the so-called Kusko analogue technique was employed, to prevent by an epileptic seizure any future act of violence.
3. *A warning*. A careful alteration of his body chemistry was effected to make his exhaled and exuded wastes emit a strongly pungent and offensive odour. In mercy, he himself was rendered unable to detect this smell.
Fortunately, the genetic and environmental accidents which combined to produce this atavism have been fully explained and can never again . . .

The words stopped meaning anything, as they always did at this point. I didn't want to read any further; it was all nonsense, anyway. I was the king of the world.

I got up and went away, out into the night, blind to the dulls who thronged the rooms I passed.

Two squares away was the commerce area. I found a clothing outlet and went in. All the free clothes in the display cases were drab: those were for worthless floaters, not for me. I went past them to the specials, and found a combination I could stand – silver and blue, with a severe black piping down the tunic. A dull would have said it was 'nice'. I punched for it. The automatic looked me over with its dull glassy eye, and croaked, 'Your contribution book, please.'

I could have had a contribution book, for the trouble of stepping out into the street and taking it away from the first passer-by; but I didn't have the patience. I picked up the one-legged table from the refreshment nook, hefted it, and swung it at the cabinet door. The metal shrieked and dented opposite the catch. I swung once more to the same place, and the door sprang open. I pulled out clothing in handfuls till I got a set that would fit me.

I bathed and changed, and then went prowling in the big multi-outlet down the avenue. All those places are arranged pretty much alike, no matter what the local managers do to them. I went straight to the knives, and picked out three in graduated sizes, down to the size of my fingernail. Then I had to take my chance. I tried the furniture department, where I had had good luck once in a while; but this year all they were using was metal. I had to have seasoned wood.

I knew where there was a big cache of cherry wood, in goodsized blocks, in a forgotten warehouse up north at a place called Kootenay. I could have carried some around with me – enough for years – but what for, when the world belonged to me?

It didn't take me long. Down in the workshop section, of all places, I found some antiques – tables and benches, all with wooden tops. While the dulls collected down at the other end of the room, pretending not to notice, I sawed off a good oblong chunk of the smallest bench, and made a base for it out of another.

As long as I was there, it was a good place to work, and I could eat and sleep upstairs, so I stayed.

I knew what I wanted to do. It was going to be a man, sitting with his legs crossed and his forearms resting down along his calves. His head was going to be tilted back, and his eyes closed, as if he were turning his face up to the sun.

In three days it was finished. The trunk and limbs had a shape that was not man and not wood, but something in between: something that hadn't existed before I made it.

Beauty. That was the old word.

I had carved one of the figure's hands hanging loosely, and the other one curled shut. There had to be a time to stop and say it was finished. I took the smallest knife, the one I had been using to scrape the wood smooth, and cut away the handle and ground down what was left of the shaft to a thin spike. Then I drilled a hole into the wood of the figurine's hand, in the hollow between thumb and curled finger. I fitted the knife blade in there; in the small hand it was a sword.

I cemented it in place. Then I took the sharp blade and stabbed my thumb, and smeared the blade.

I hunted most of that day, and finally found the right place – a niche in an outcropping of striated brown rock, in a little triangular half-wild patch that had been left where two roads forked. Nothing was permanent, of course, in a community like this one that might change its houses every five years or so, to follow the fashion; but this spot had been left to itself for a long time. It was the best I could do.

I had the paper ready: it was one of a batch I had printed up a year ago. The paper was treated, and I knew it would stay legible a long time. I hid a little photo capsule in the back of the niche, and ran the control wire to a staple in the base of the figurine. I put the figurine down on top of the paper, and anchored it lightly to the rock with two spots of all-cement. I had done it so often that it came naturally; I knew just how much cement would hold the figurine steady against a casual hand, but yield to one that really wanted to pull it down.

Then I stepped back to look: and the power and the pity of it made my breath come short, and tears start to my eyes.

Reflected light gleamed fitfully on the dark-stained blade that hung from his hand. He was sitting alone in that niche that closed him in like a coffin. His eyes were shut, and his head tilted back, as if he were turning his face up to the sun.

But only rock was over his head. There was no sun for him.

Hunched on the cool bare ground under a pepper tree, I was looking down across the road at the shadowed niche where my figurine sat.

I was all finished here. There was nothing more to keep me, and yet I couldn't leave.

People walked past now and then – not often. The community seemed half deserted, as if most of the people had flocked off to a surf party somewhere, or a contribution meeting, or to watch a new house being dug to replace the one I had wrecked . . . There was a little wind blowing towards me, cool and lonesome in the leaves.

Up the other side of the hollow there was a terrace, and on that terrace, half an hour ago, I had seen a brief flash of colour – a boy's head, with a red cap on it, moving past and out of sight.

That was why I had to stay. I was thinking how that boy might come down from his terrace and into my road, and passing the little wild triangle of land, see my figurine. I was thinking he might not pass by indifferently, but stop: and go closer to look: and pick up the wooden man: and read what was written on the paper underneath.

I believed that sometime it had to happen. I wanted it so hard that I ached.

My carvings were all over the world, wherever I had wandered. There was one in Congo City, carved of ebony, dusty-black; one in Cyprus, of bone; one in New Bombay, of shell; one in Changteh, of jade.

They were like signs printed in red and green, in a colour-blind world. Only the one I was looking for would even pick one of them up, and read the message I knew by heart.

TO YOU WHO CAN SEE, the first sentence said. I OFFER YOU A WORLD . . .

There was a flash of colour up on the terrace. I stiffened. A minute later, here it came again, from a different direction: it was the boy, clambering down the slope, brilliant against the green, with his red, sharp-billed cap like a woodpecker's head.

I held my breath.

He came towards me through the fluttering leaves, ticked off by pencils of sunlight as he passed. He was a brown boy, I could see at this distance, with a serious thin face. His ears stuck out, flickering pink with the sun behind them, and his elbow and knee pads made him look knobbly.

He reached the fork in the road, and chose the path on

my side. I huddled into myself as he came nearer. *Let him see it, let him not see me*, I thought fiercely.

My fingers closed around a stone.

He was nearer, walking jerkily with his hands in his pockets, watching his feet mostly.

When he was almost opposite me, I threw the stone.

It rustled through the leaves below the niche in the rock. The boy's head turned. He stopped, staring; I think he saw the figurine then. I'm sure he saw it.

He took one step.

'Risha!' came floating down from the terrace.

And he looked up. 'Here,' he piped.

I saw the woman's head, tiny at the top of the terrace. She called something I didn't hear; I was standing up, squeezed tight with anger.

Then the wind shifted. It blew from me to the boy. He whirled around, his eyes big, and clapped a hand to his nose.

'Oh, what a stench!'

He turned to shout, 'Coming!' and then he was gone, hurrying back up the road, into the unstable blur of green.

My one chance, ruined. He would have seen the image, I knew, if it hadn't been for the damned woman, and the wind shifting . . . They were all against me, people, wind and all.

And the figurine still sat, blind eyes turned up to the rocky sky.

There was something inside me that told me to take my disappointment and go away from there, and not come back.

I knew I would be sorry. I did it anyway: took the image out of the niche, and the paper with it, and climbed the slope. At the top I heard his clear voice laughing.

There was a thing that might have been an ornamental mound, or the camouflaged top of a buried house. I went around it, tripping over my own feet, and came upon the boy kneeling on the turf. He was playing with a brown and white puppy.

He looked up with the laughter going out of his face. There was no wind, and he could smell me. I knew it was bad. No wind, and the puppy to distract him – everything about it was wrong. But I went to him blindly anyhow, and fell on one knee, and shoved the figurine at his face.

'Look – ' I said.

He went over backwards in his hurry: he couldn't even have seen the image, except as a brown blur coming at him. He scrambled up, with the puppy whining and yapping around his heels, and ran for the mound.

I was up after him, clawing up moist earth and grass as I rose. In the other hand I still had the image clutched, and the paper with it.

A door popped open and swallowed him and popped shut again in my face. With the flat of my hand I beat the vines around it until I hit the doorplate by accident and the door opened. I dived in, shouting, 'Wait,' and was in a spiral passage, lit pearl-grey, winding downwards. Down I went headlong, and came out at the wrong door – an underground conservatory, humid and hot under the yellow lights, with dripping rank leaves in long rows. I went down the aisle raging, overturning the tanks, until I came to a vestibule and an elevator.

Down I went again to the third level and a labyrinth of guest rooms, all echoing, all empty. At last I found a ramp leading upwards, past the conservatory, and at the end of it voices.

The door was clear vitrin, and I paused on the near side of it looking and listening. There was the boy, and a woman old enough to be his mother, just – sister or cousin, more likely – and an elderly woman in a hard chair holding the puppy. The room was comfortable and tasteless, like other rooms.

I saw the shock grow on their faces as I burst in: it was always the same, they knew I would like to kill them, but they never expected that I would come uninvited into a house. It was not done.

There was that boy, so close I could touch him, but the shock of all of them was quivering in the air, smothering, like a blanket that would deaden my voice. I felt I had to shout.

'Everything they tell you is lies!' I said. 'See here – here, this is the truth!' I had the figurine in front of his eyes, but he didn't see.

'Risha, go below,' said the young woman quietly. He turned to obey, quick as a ferret. I got in front of him again. 'Stay,' I said, breathing hard. 'Look – '

'Remember, Risha, don't speak,' said the woman.

I couldn't stand any more. Where the boy went I don't know; I ceased to see him. With the image in one hand and the paper with it, I leaped at the woman. I was almost quick enough; I almost reached her; but the buzzing took me in the middle of a step, louder, louder, like the end of the world.

It was the second time that week. When I came to, I was sick and too faint to move for a long time.

The house was silent. They had gone, of course . . . the house had been defiled, having me in it. They wouldn't live here again, but would build elsewhere.

My eyes blurred. After a while I stood up and looked around at the room. The walls were hung with a grey close-woven cloth that looked as if it would tear, and I thought of ripping it down in strips, breaking furniture, stuffing carpets and bedding into the oubliette . . . But I didn't have the heart for it. I was too tired.

At last I stooped and picked up the figurine, and the paper that was supposed to go under it – crumpled now, with the forlorn look of a message that someone has thrown away unread.

I smoothed it out and read the last part.

YOU CAN SHARE THE WORLD WITH ME. THEY CAN'T STOP YOU. STRIKE NOW – PICK UP A SHARP THING AND STAB, OR A HEAVY THING AND CRUSH. THAT'S ALL. THAT WILL MAKE YOU FREE. ANYONE CAN DO IT.

Anyone. Anyone.

The Machine That Won the War

Isaac Asimov

The celebration had a long way to go and even in the silent depths of Multivac's underground chambers, it hung in the air.

If nothing else, there was the mere fact of isolation and silence – for the first time in a decade, technicians were not scurrying about the vitals of the giant computer, the soft lights did not wink out their erratic patterns, the flow of information in and out had halted.

It would not be halted long, of course, for the needs of peace would be pressing. Yet now, for a day, perhaps for a week, even Multivac might celebrate the great victory, and rest.

Lamar Swift, Executive Director of the Solar Federation, took off the military cap he was wearing and looked down the long and empty main corridor of the enormous computer. He sat down rather wearily in one of the technicians' swing-stools and his uniform, in which he had never been comfortable, took on a heavy and wrinkled appearance.

He said, 'I'll miss it all, in a grisly fashion. It's hard to remember when we weren't at war with Deneb, and it seems against nature now to be at peace and to look at the stars without anxiety.'

The two men with Swift were both younger than he. Neither was as grey, neither looked quite as tired.

John Henderson, thin-lipped and finding it hard to control the relief he felt in the midst of triumph, said, 'They're destroyed! They're destroyed! It's what I keep saying to myself over and over and I still can't believe it. We all talked so much, over so many years, about the menace hanging over Earth and all its worlds, over every human being, and all the time it was true, every word of it. And now we're alive and it's the Denebians who are shattered and destroyed. They'll be no menace now, ever again.'

'Thanks to Multivac,' said Swift, with a quiet glance at the imperturbable Jablonsky, who through all the war had been Chief Interpreter of science's oracle. 'Right, Max?'

Jablonsky shrugged. Automatically, he reached for a cigarette and decided against it. He alone, of all the thousands who had lived in the tunnels within Multivac, had been allowed to smoke, but toward the end he had made definite efforts to avoid making use of the privilege.

He said, 'Well, that's what *they* say.' His broad thumb moved in the direction of his right shoulder, aiming upward.

'Jealous, Max?'

'Because they're shouting for Multivac? Because Multivac is the big hero in this war?' Jablonsky's craggy face took on an air of contempt. 'What's that to me? Let Multivac be the machine that won the war, if it pleases them.'

Henderson looked at the other two out of the corners of his eyes. In this short interlude that the three had instinctively sought out in the one peaceful corner of a metropolis gone mad; in this entr'acte between the dangers of war and the difficulties of peace, when, for one moment, they might all find surcease, he was conscious only of his weight of guilt.

Suddenly, it was as though that weight were too great to be borne longer. It had to be thrown off, along with the war – now!

Henderson said, 'Multivac had nothing to do with victory. It's just a machine.'

'A big one,' said Swift.

'Then just a big machine. No better than the data fed it.' For a moment, he stopped, suddenly unnerved at what he was saying.

Jablonsky looked at him, his thick fingers once again fumbling for a cigarette and once again drawing back. 'You should know. You supplied the data. Or is it just that you're taking the credit?'

'*No*,' said Henderson angrily. 'There is no credit. What do you know of the data Multivac had to use, predigested from a hundred subsidiary computers here on Earth, on the Moon, on Mars, even on Titan? With Titan always delayed and always that feeling that its figures would introduce an unexpected bias.'

'It would drive anyone mad,' said Swift, with gentle sympathy.

Henderson shook his head. 'It wasn't just that. I admit that eight years ago when I replaced Lepont as Chief Programmer, I was nervous. But there was an exhilaration about things in those days. The war was still long range; an adventure without real danger. We hadn't reached the point where manned vessels had had to take over and where interstellar warps could swallow up a planet clean, if aimed correctly. But then, when the real difficulties began – '

Angrily – he could finally permit anger – he said, 'You know nothing about it.'

'Well,' said Swift. 'Tell us. The war is over. We've won.'

'Yes.' Henderson nodded his head. He had to remember that. Earth had won, so all had been for the best. 'Well, the data became meaningless.'

'Meaningless? You mean that literally?' said Jablonsky.

'Literally. What would you expect? The trouble with you two was that you weren't out in the thick of it. Max, you never left Multivac, and you, Mr Director, never left the Mansion except on state visits where you saw exactly what they wanted you to see.'

'I was not as unaware of that,' said Swift, 'as you may have thought.'

'Do you know,' said Henderson, 'to what extent data concerning our production capacity, our resource potential, our trained manpower – everything of importance to the war effort, in fact – had become unreliable and untrustworthy during the last half of the war? Group leaders, both civilian and military, were intent on projecting their own improved image, so to speak, so they obscured the bad and magnified the good. Whatever the machines might do, the men who programmed them and interpreted the results had their own skins to think of and competitors to stab. There was no way of stopping that. I tried, and failed.'

'Of course,' said Swift, in quiet consolation. 'I can see that you would.'

This time Jablonsky decided to light his cigarette. 'Yet I presume you provided Multivac with data in your programming? You said nothing to us about unreliability.'

'How could I tell you? And if I did, how could you afford to believe me?' demanded Henderson. 'Our entire war effort was geared to Multivac. It was the one great weapon on our side, for the Denebians had nothing like it. What else kept up morale in the face of doom but the assurance that Multivac would always predict and circumvent any Denebian move, and would always direct and prevent the circumvention of our moves? Great Space, after our Spy-warp was blasted out of hyperspace we lacked any reliable Denebian data to feed Multivac, and we didn't dare make *that* public.'

'True enough,' said Swift.

'Well, then,' said Henderson, 'if I told you the data were unreliable, what could you have done but replace me and refuse to believe me? I couldn't allow that.'

'What did you do?' said Jablonsky.

'Since the war is over, I'll tell you what I did. I corrected the data.'

'How?' asked Swift.

'Intuition, I presume. I juggled them till they looked right. At first, I hardly dared. I changed a bit here and there to correct what were obvious impossibilities. When the sky didn't collapse about us, I got braver. Toward the end, I scarcely cared. I just wrote out the necessary data as they were needed. I even had Multivac Annex prepare data for me according to a private programming pattern I had devised for the purpose.'

'Random figures?' said Jablonsky.

'Not at all. I introduced a number of necessary biases.'

Jablonsky smiled, quite unexpectedly, his dark eyes

sparkling behind the crinkling of the lower lids. 'Three times a report was brought to me about unauthorized uses of the Annex, and I let it go each time. If it had mattered, I would have followed it up and spotted you, John, and found out what you were doing. But, of course, nothing about Multivac mattered in those days, so you got away with it.'

'What do you mean, nothing mattered?' asked Henderson, suspiciously.

'Nothing did. I suppose if I had told you this at the time, it would have spared you your agony, but then if you had told me what you were doing, it would have spared me mine. What made you think Multivac was in working order, whatever the data you supplied it?'

'Not in working order?' said Swift.

'Not really. Not reliably. After all, where were my technicians in the last years of the war? I'll tell you – they were out feeding computers on a thousand different space devices. They were gone! I had to make do with kids I couldn't trust and veterans who were out of date. Besides, do you think I could trust the solid-state components coming out of Cyogenics in the last years? Cyogenics wasn't any better placed as far as personnel was concerned than I was. To me, it didn't matter whether the data being supplied Multivac were reliable or not. The *results* weren't reliable. That much I knew.'

'What did you do?' asked Henderson.

'I did what you did, John, I introduced the bugger factor. I adjusted matters in accordance with intuition – and that's how the machine won the war.'

Swift leaned back in the chair and stretched his legs out before him. 'Such revelations. It turns out then that the material handed me to guide me in my decision-making capacity was a man-made interpretation of man-made data. Isn't that right?'

'It looks so,' said Jablonsky.

'Then I perceive I was correct in not placing too much reliance upon it,' said Swift.

'You didn't?' Jablonsky, despite what he had just said, managed to look professionally insulted.

'I'm afraid I didn't. Multivac might seem to say: Strike here, not there; Do this, not that; Wait, don't act. But I could never be certain that what Multivac seemed to say, it really did say; or what it really said, it really meant. I could never be certain.'

'But the final report was always plain enough, sir,' said Jablonsky.

'To those who did not have to make the decision, perhaps. Not to me. The horror of the responsibility of such decisions was unbearable and even Multivac was not sufficient to remove the weight . . . But the important point is I was justified in doubting, and there is tremendous relief in that.'

Caught up in the conspiracy of mutual confession, Jablonsky put titles aside. 'What was it you did then, Lamar? After all, you did make decisions. How?'

'Well, it's time to be getting back, perhaps, but – I'll tell you first. Why not? I did make use of a computer, Max, but an older one than Multivac, much older.'

He groped in his pocket and brought out a scattering of small change – old-fashioned coins dating to the first years before the metal shortage had produced a credit system tied to a computer-complex.

Swift smiled rather sheepishly. 'I still need these to make money seem substantial to me. An old man finds it hard to abandon the habits of youth.' He dropped the coins back into his pocket.

He held the last coin between his fingers, staring at it absently. 'Multivac is not the first computer, friends, nor the best-known, nor the one that can most efficiently lift the load of decision from the shoulders of the executive. A machine *did* win the war, John; at least, a very simple computing device did, one that I used every time I had a particularly hard decision to make.'

With a faint smile of reminiscence, he flipped the coin he held. It glinted in the air as it spun and came down in Swift's outstretched palm. His hand closed over it and brought it down on the back of his left hand. His right hand remained in place, hiding the coin.

'Heads or tails, gentlemen?'

Student Body

F. L. Wallace

The first morning that they were fully committed to the planet, the executive officer stepped out of the ship. It was not quite dawn. Executive Hafner squinted in the early light; his eyes opened wider, and he promptly went back insider. Three minutes later, he reappeared with the biologist in tow.

'Last night you said there was nothing dangerous,' said the executive. 'Do you still think it's so?'

Dano Marin stared. 'I do.' What his voice lacked in conviction, it made up in embarrassment. He laughed uncertainly.

'This is no laughing matter. I'll talk to you later.'

The biologist stood by the ship and watched as the executive walked to the row of sleeping colonists.

'Mrs Athyl,' said the executive as he stopped beside the sleeping figure.

She yawned, rubbed her eyes, rolled over, and stood up. The covering that should have been there, however, wasn't. Neither was the garment she had on when she had gone to sleep. She assumed the conventional position of a woman who is astonished to find herself unclad without her knowledge or consent.

'It's all right, Mrs Athyl. I'm not a voyeur myself. Still, I think you should get some clothing on.' Most of the colonists were awake now. Executive Hafner turned to them. 'If you haven't any suitable clothing in the ship, the commissary will issue you some. Explanations will be given later.'

The colonists scattered. There was no compulsive modesty among them, for it couldn't have survived a year and a half in crowded spaceships. Nevertheless, it was a shock to awaken with no clothing on and not know who or what had removed it during the night. It was surprise more than anything else that disconcerted them.

On his way back to the spaceship, Executive Hafner paused. 'Any ideas about it?'

Dano Marin shrugged. 'How could I have? The planet is as new to me as it is to you.'

'Sure. But you're the biologist.'

As the only scientist in a crew of rough-and-ready colonists and builders, Marin was going to be called on to answer a lot of questions that weren't in his field.

'Nocturnal insects, most likely,' he suggested. That was pretty weak, though he knew that in ancient times locusts had stripped fields in a matter of hours. Could they do the same with the clothing of humans and not awaken them? 'I'll look into the matter. As soon as I find anything, I'll let you know.'

'Good.' Hafner nodded and went into the spaceship.

Dano Marin walked to the grove in which the colonists had been sleeping. It had been a mistake to let them bed down there, but at the time the request had been made, there had seemed no reason not to grant it. After eighteen months in crowded ships everyone naturally wanted fresh air and the rustle of leaves overhead.

Marin looked out through the grove. It was empty now; the colonists, both men and women, had disappeared inside the ship, dressing, probably.

The trees were not tall and the leaves were dark bottle-green. Occasional huge white flowers caught sunlight that made them seem larger than they were. It wasn't Earth and therefore the trees couldn't be magnolias. But they reminded Marin of magnolia trees and thereafter he always thought of them as that.

The problem of the missing clothing was ironic. Biological Survey never made a mistake – yet obviously they had. They listed the planet as the most suitable for Man of any so far discovered. Few insects, no dangerous animals, a most equable climate. They had named it Glade because that was the word which fitted best. The whole land mass seemed to be one vast and pleasant meadow.

Evidently there were things about the planet that Biological Survey had missed.

Marin dropped to his knees and began to look for clues. If insects had been responsible, there ought to be a few dead ones, crushed, perhaps, as the colonists rolled over in their sleep. There were no insects, either live or dead.

He stood up in disappointment and walked slowly through the grove. It might be the trees. At night they could exude a vapour which was capable of dissolving the material from which the clothing had been made. Far-fetched, but not impossible. He crumbled a leaf in his hand and rubbed it against his sleeve. A pungent smell, but nothing happened. That didn't disprove the theory, of course.

He looked out through the trees at the blue sun. It was bigger than Sol, but farther away. At Glade, it was about equal to the Sun on Earth.

He almost missed the bright eyes that regarded him from the underbrush. Almost, but didn't – the domain of biology begins at the edge of the atmosphere; it includes the brush and the small creatures that live in it.

He swooped down on it. The creature fled squealing. He ran it down in the grass outside the grove. It collapsed into quaking flesh as he picked it up. He talked to it gently and the terror subsided.

It nibbled contentedly on his jacket as he carried it back to the ship.

Executive Hafner stared unhappily at the cage. It was an undistinguished animal, small and something like an undeveloped rodent. Its fur was sparse and stringy, unglamorous; it would never be an item in the fur export trade.

'Can we exterminate it?' asked Hafner. 'Locally, that is.'

'Hardly. It's ecologically basic.'

The executive looked blank. Dano Marin added the explanation: 'You know how Biological Control works. As soon as a planet has been discovered that looks suitable, they send out a survey ship loaded with equipment. The ship flies low over a good part of the planet and the instruments can distinguish the characteristic neural patterns of anything that has a brain, including insects.

'Anyway, they have a pretty good idea of the kinds of animals on the planet and their relative distribution. Naturally, the survey party takes a few specimens. They have to in order to correlate the pattern with the actual animal, otherwise the neural pattern would be merely a meaningless squiggle on a microfilm.

'The survey shows that this animal is one of only four species of mammals on the planet. It is also the most numerous.'

Hafner grunted. 'So if we kill them off here, others will swarm in from surrounding areas?'

'That's about it. There are probably millions of them on this peninsula. Of course, if you want to put a barrier across the narrow connection to the mainland, you might be able to wipe them out locally.'

The executive scowled. A barrier was possible, but it would involve more work than he cared to expend.

'What do they eat?' he asked truculently.

'A little bit of everything, apparently. Insects, fruits, berries, nuts, succulents and grain.' Dano Marin smiled. 'I guess it could be called an omnivore – now that our clothing is handy, it eats that, too.'

Hafner didn't smile. 'I thought our clothing was supposed to be verminproof.'

Marin shrugged. 'It is, on twenty-seven planets. On the twenty-eighth, we meet up with a little fella that has better digestive fluids, that's all.'

Hafner looked pained. 'Are they likely to bother the crops we plant?'

'Offhand, I would say they aren't. But then I would have said the same about our clothing.'

Hafner made up his mind. 'All right. You worry about the crops. Find some way to keep them out of the fields. Meanwhile, everyone sleeps in the ship until we can build dormitories.'

Individual dwelling units would have been more appropriate in the colony at this stage, thought Marin. But it wasn't for him to decide. The executive was a man who regarded a schedule as something to be exceeded.

'The omnivore – ' began Marin.

Hafner nodded impatiently. 'Work on it,' he said, and walked away.

The biologist sighed. The omnivore really was a queer little creature, but it was by no means the most important thing on Glade. For instance, why were there so few species of land animals on the planet? No reptiles, numerous birds, and only four kinds of mammals.

Every comparable planet teemed with a wild variety of life. Glade, in spite of seemingly ideal conditions, hadn't developed. Why?

He had asked Biological Controls for this assignment because it had seemed an interesting problem. Now, apparently, he was being pressed into service as an exterminator.

He reached in the cage and picked up the omnivore. Mammals on Glade were not unexpected. Parallel development took care of that. Given roughly the same kind of environment, similar animals would usually evolve.

In the Late Carboniferous forest on Earth, there had been creatures like the omnivore, the primitive mammal from which all others had evolved. On Glade, that kind of evolution just hadn't taken place. What had kept nature from exploiting its evolutionary potentialities? There was the real problem, not how to wipe them out.

Marin stuck a needle in the omnivore. It squealed and then relaxed. He drew out the blood and set it back in the cage. He could learn a lot about the animal from trying to kill it.

The quartermaster was shouting, though his normal voice carried quite well.

'How do you know it's mice?' the biologist asked him.

'Look,' said the quartermaster angrily.

Marin looked. The evidence did indicate mice.

Before he could speak, the quartermaster snapped, 'Don't tell me they're only micelike creatures. I know that. The question is: how can I get rid of them?'

'Have you tried poison?'

'Tell me what poison to use and I'll use it.'

It wasn't the easiest question to answer. What was poisonous to an animal he had never seen and knew nothing about? According to Biological Survey, the animal didn't exist.

It was unexpectedly serious. The colony could live off the land, and was expected to. But another group of colonists was due in three years. The colony was supposed to accumulate a surplus of food to feed the increased numbers. If they couldn't store the food they grew any better than the concentrates, that surplus was going to be scanty.

Marin went over the warehouse thoroughly. It was the usual early construction on a colonial world. Not aesthetic, it was sturdy enough. Fused dirt floor, reinforced foot-thick walls, a ceiling slab of the same. The whole was bound together with a molecular cement that made it practically airtight. It had no windows; there were two doors. Certainly it should keep out rodents.

A closer examination revealed an unexpected flaw. The floor was as hard as glass; no animal could gnaw through it, but, like glass, it was also brittle. The crew that had built the warehouse had evidently been in such a hurry to get back to Earth that they hadn't been as careful as they should have been, for here and there the floor was thin. Somewhere under the heavy equipment piled on it, the floor had cracked. There a burrowing animal had means of entry.

Short of building another warehouse, it was too late to do anything about that. Micelike animals were inside and had to be controlled where they were.

The biologist straightened up. 'Catch me a few of them alive and I'll see what I can do.'

In the morning, a dozen live specimens were delivered to the lab. They actually did resemble mice.

Their reactions were puzzling. No two of them were affected by the same poison. A compound that stiffened one in a matter of minutes left the others hale and hearty, and the poison he had developed to control the omnivores was completely ineffective.

The depredations in the warehouse went on. Black mice, white ones, grey and brown, short-tailed and long-eared, or the reverse, they continued to eat the concentrates and spoil what they didn't eat.

Marin conferred with the executive, outlined the problem as he saw it and his ideas on what could be done to combat the nuisance.

'But we can't build another warehouse,' argued Hafner. 'Not until the atomic generator is set up, at any rate. And then we'll have other uses for the power.' The executive rested his head in his hands. 'I like the other solution better. Build one and see how it works.'

'I was thinking of three,' said the biologist.

'One,' Hafner insisted. 'We can't spare the equipment until we know how it works.'

At that he was probably right. They had equipment, as much as three ships could bring. But the more they brought, the more was expected of the colony. The net effect was that equipment was always in short supply.

Marin took the authorization to the engineer. On the way, he privately revised his specifications upward. If he couldn't get as many as he wanted, he might as well get a better one.

In two days, the machine was ready.

It was delivered in a small crate to the warehouse. The crate was opened and the machine leaped out and stood there, poised.

'A cat!' exclaimed the quartermaster, pleased. He stretched out his hand towards the black fuzzy robot.

'If you've touched anything a mouse may have, get your hand away,' warned the biologist. 'It reacts to smell as well as sight and sound.'

Hastily, the quartermaster withdrew his hand. The robot disappeared silently into the maze of stored material.

In one week, though there were still some mice in the warehouse, they were no longer a danger.

The executive called Marin into his office, a small sturdy building located in the centre of the settlement. The colony was growing, assuming an aspect of permanency. Hafner sat in his chair and looked out over that growth with satisfaction.

'A good job on the mouse plague,' he said.

The biologist nodded. 'Not bad, except there shouldn't be any mice here. Biological Survey – '

'Forget it,' said the exec. 'Everybody makes mistakes, even BS.' He leaned back and looked seriously at the biologist. 'I have a job I need done. Just now I'm short of men. If you have no objections . . . '

The exec was always short of men, would be until the planet was overcrowded, and he would try to find someone to do the work his own men should have done. Dano Marin was not directly responsible to Hafner; he was on loan to the expedition from Biological Controls. Still, it was a good idea to cooperate with the executive. He sighed.

'It's not as bad as you think,' said Hafner, interpreting the sound correctly. He smiled. 'We've got the digger together. I want you to run it.'

Since it tied right in with his investigations, Dano Marin looked relieved and showed it.

'Except for food, we have to import most of our supplies,' Hafner explained. 'It's a long haul, and we've got to make use of everything on the planet we can. We need oil. There are going to be a lot of wheels turning, and every one of them will have to have oil. In time we'll set up a synthetic plant, but if we can locate a productive field now, it's to our advantage.'

'You're assuming the geology of Glade is similar to Earth?'

Hafner waggled his hand. 'Why not? It's a nicer twin of Earth.'

Why not? Because you couldn't always tell from the surface, thought Marin. It *seemed* like Earth, but was it? Here was a good chance to find out the history of Glade.

Hafner stood up. 'Any time you're ready, a technician will check you out on the digger. Let me know before you go.'

Actually, the digger wasn't a digger. It didn't move or otherwise displace a gramme of dirt or rock. It was a means of looking down below the surface, to any practical depth. A large crawler, it was big enough for a man to live in without discomfort for a week.

It carried an outsize ultrasonic generator and a device for directing the beam into the planet. That was the sending apparatus. The receiving end began with a large sonic lens which picked up sound beams reflected from any desired depth, converted it into electrical energy and thence into an image which was flashed onto a screen.

At the depth of ten miles, the image was fuzzy, though good enough to distinguish the main features of the strata. At three miles, it was better. It could pick up the sound reflection of a buried coin and convert it into a picture on which the date could be seen.

It was to a geologist as a microscope is to a biologist. Being a biologist, Dano Marin could appreciate the analogy.

He started at the tip of the peninsula and zigzagged across, heading towards the isthmus. Methodically, he covered the territory, sleeping at night in the digger. On the morning of the third day, he discovered oil traces, and by that afternoon he had located the main field.

He should probably have turned back at once, but now that he had found oil, he investigated more deliberately. Starting at the top, he let the image range downwards below the top strata.

It was the reverse of what it should have been. In the top few feet, there were plentiful fossil remains, mostly of the four species of mammals. The squirrel-like creature and the far larger grazing animal were the forest dwellers. Of the plains animals, there were only two, in size fitting neatly between the extremes of the forest dwellers.

After the first few feet, which corresponded to approximately twenty thousand years, he found virtually no fossils. Not until he reached a depth which he could correlate to the Late Carboniferous age on Earth did fossils reappear. Then they were of animals appropriate to the epoch. At that depth and below, the history of Glade was quite similar to Earth's.

Puzzled, he checked again in a dozen widely scattered localities. The results were always the same – fossil history for the first twenty thousand years, then none for roughly a hundred million. Beyond that, it was easy to trace the thread of biological development.

In that period of approximately one hundred million years, something unique had happened to Glade. What was it?

On the fifth day his investigations were interrupted by the sound of the keyed-on radio.

'Marin.'

'Yes?' He flipped on the sending switch.

'How soon can you get back?'

He looked at the photo-map. 'Three hours. Two if I hurry.'

'Make it two. Never mind the oil.'

'I've found oil. But what's the matter?'

'You can see it better than I can describe it. We'll discuss it when you get back.'

Reluctantly, Marin retracted the instruments into the digger. He turned it around and, with not too much regard for the terrain, let it roar. The treads tossed dirt high in the air. Animals fled squealing from in front of him. If the grove was small enough, he went around it, otherwise he went through and left matchsticks behind.

He skidded the crawler ponderously to a halt near the edge of the settlement. The centre of activity was the warehouse. Pickups wheeled in and out, transferring supplies to a cleared area outside. He found Hafner in a corner of the warehouse, talking to the engineer.

Hafner turned around when he came up. 'Your mice have grown, Marin.'

Marin looked down. The robot cat lay on the floor. He knelt and examined it. The steel skeleton hadn't broken; it had been bent, badly. The tough plastic skin had been torn off and, inside, the delicate mechanism had been chewed into an unrecognizable mass.

Around the cat were rats, twenty or thirty of them, huge by any standards. The cat had fought; the dead animals were headless or disembowelled, unbelievably battered. But the robot had been outnumbered.

Biological Survey had said there weren't any rats on Glade. They had also said that about mice. What was the key to their error?

The biologist stood up. 'What are you going to do about it?'

'Build another warehouse, two-foot-thick fused dirt floors, monolithic construction. Transfer all perishables to it.'

Marin nodded. That would do it. It would take time, of course, and power, all they could draw out of the recently set up atomic generator. All other construction would have to be suspended. No wonder Hafner was disturbed.

'Why not build more cats?' Marin suggested.

The executive smiled nastily. 'You weren't here when we opened the doors. The warehouse was swarming with rats. How many robot cats would we need – five, fifteen? I don't know. Anyway the engineer tells me we have enough parts to build three more cats. The one lying there can't be salvaged.'

It didn't take an engineer to see that, thought Marin.

Hafner continued, 'If we need more, we'll have to rob the computer in the spaceship. I refuse to permit that.'

Obviously he would. The spaceship was the only link with Earth until the next expedition brought more colonists. No exec in his right mind would permit the ship to be crippled.

But why had Hafner called him back? Merely to keep him informed of the situation?

Hafner seemed to guess his thoughts. 'At night we'll floodlight the supplies we remove from the warehouse. We'll post a guard armed with decharged rifles until we can move the food into the new warehouse. That'll take about ten days. Meanwhile, our fast crops are ripening. It's my guess the rats will turn to them for food. In order to protect our future food supply, you'll have to activate your animals.'

The biologist started. 'But it's against regulations to loose any animal on a planet until a complete investigation of the possible ill effects is made.'

'That takes ten or twenty years. This is an emergency and I'll be responsible – in writing, if you want.'

The biologist was effectively countermanded. Another rabbit-infested Australia or the planet that the snails took over might be in the making, but there was nothing he could do about it.

'I hardly think they'll be of any use against rats this size,' he protested.

'You've got hormones. Apply them.' The executive turned and began discussing construction with the engineer.

Marin had the dead rats gathered up and placed in the freezer for further study.

After that, he retired to the laboratory and worked out a course of treatment for the domesticated animals that the colonists had brought with them. He gave them the first injections and watched them carefully until they were safely through the initial shock phase of growth. As soon as he saw they were going to survive, he bred them.

Next he turned to the rats. Of note was the wide variation in size. Internally, the same thing was true. They had the usual organs, but the proportions of each varied greatly, more than is normal. Nor were their teeth uniform. Some carried huge fangs set in delicate jaws; others had tiny teeth that didn't match the massive bone structure. As a species, they were the most scrambled the biologist had ever encountered.

He turned the microscope on their tissues and tabulated

the results. There was less difference here between individual specimens, but it was enough to set him pondering. The reproductive cells were especially baffling.

Late in the day, he felt rather than heard the soundless whoosh of the construction machinery. He looked out of the laboratory and saw smoke rolling upwards. As soon as the vegetation was charred, the smoke ceased and heat waves danced into the sky.

They were building on a hill. The little creatures that crept and crawled in the brush attacked in the most vulnerable spot, the food supply. There was no brush, not a blade of grass, on the hill when the colonists finished.

Terriers. In the past, they were the hunting dogs of the agricultural era. What they lacked in size they made up in ferocity towards rodents. They had earned their keep originally in granaries and fields, and, for a brief time, they were doing it again on colonial worlds where conditions were repeated.

The dogs the colonists brought had been terriers. They were still as fast, still with the same anti-rodent disposition, but they were no longer small. It had been a difficult job, yet Marin had done it well, for the dogs had lost none of their skill and speed in growing to the size of a Great Dane.

The rats moved in on the fields of fast crops. Fast crops were made to order for a colonial world. They could be planted, grown, and harvested in a matter of weeks. After four such plantings, the fertility of the soil was destroyed, but that meant nothing in the early years of a colonial planet, for land was plentiful.

The rat tide grew in the fast crops, and the dogs were loosed on the rats. They ranged through the fields, hunting. A rush, a snap of their jaws, the shake of a head, and the rat was tossed aside, its back broken. The dogs went on to the next.

Until they could not see, the dogs prowled and slaughtered. At night they came in bloody, most of it not their own, and exhausted. Marin pumped them full of antibiotics, bandaged their wounds, fed them through their veins, and shot them into sleep. In the morning he awakened them with an injection of stimulant and sent them tingling into battle.

It took the rats two days to learn they could not feed during the day. Not so numerous, they came at night. They climbed on the vines and nibbled the fruit. They gnawed growing grain and ravaged vegetables.

The next day the colonists set up lights. The dogs were with them, discouraging the few rats who were still foolish enough to forage while the sun was overhead.

An hour before dusk, Marin called the dogs in and gave them an enforced rest. He brought them out of it after dark and took them to the fields, staggering. The scent of rats revived them; they were as eager as ever, if not quite so fast.

The rats came from the surrounding meadows, not singly, or in twos and threes, as they had before; this time they came together. Squealing and rustling the grass, they moved towards the fields. It was dark, and though he could not see them, Marin could hear them. He ordered the great lights turned on in the area of the fields.

The rats stopped under the glare, milling around uneasily. The dogs quivered and whined. Marin held them back. The rats resumed their march, and Marin released the dogs.

The dogs charged in to attack, but didn't dare brave the main mass. They picked off the stragglers and forced the rest into a tighter formation. After that the rats were virtually unassailable.

The colonists could have burned the bunched-up rats with the right equipment, but they didn't have it and couldn't get it for years. Even if they'd had it, the use of such equipment would endanger the crops, which they had to save if they could. It was up to the dogs.

The rat formation came to the edge of the fields, and broke. They could face a common enemy and remain united, but in the presence of food, they forgot that unity and scattered – hunger was the great divisor. The dogs leaped joyously in pursuit. They hunted down the starved rodents, one by one, and killed them as they ate.

When daylight came, the rat menace had ended.

The next week the colonists harvested and processed the food for storage and immediately planted another crop.

Marin sat in the lab and tried to analyse the situation. The colony was moving from crisis to crisis, all of them involving food. In itself, each critical situation was minor, but lumped together they could add up to failure. No matter how he looked at it, they just didn't have the equipment they needed to colonize Glade.

The fault seemed to lie with Biological Survey; they hadn't reported the presence of pests that were endangering the food supply. Regardless of what the exec thought about them, Survey knew their business. If they said there were no mice or rats on Glade, then there hadn't been any – *when the survey was made.*

The question was: when did they come and how did they get here?

Marin sat and stared at the wall, turning over hypotheses in his mind, discarding them when they failed to make sense.

His gaze shifted from the wall to the cage of the omnivores, the squirrel-size forest creature. The most numerous animal on Glade, it was a commonplace sight to the colonists.

And yet it was a remarkable animal, more than he had realized. Plain, insignificant in appearance, it might be the most important of any animal Man had encountered on the many worlds he had settled on. The longer he watched, the more Marin became convinced of it.

He sat silent, observing the creature, not daring to move. He sat until it was dark and the omnivore resumed its normal activity.

Normal? The word didn't apply on Glade.

The interlude with the omnivore provided him with one answer. He needed another one; he thought he knew what it was, but he had to have more data, additional observations.

He set up his equipment carefully on the fringes of the settlement. There and in no other place existed the information he wanted.

He spent time in the digger, checking his original investigations. It added up to a complete picture.

When he was certain of his facts, he called on Hafner.

The executive was congenial; it was a reflection of the smoothness with which the objectives of the colony were being achieved.

'Sit down,' he said affably. 'Smoke?'

The biologist sat down and took a cigarette.

'I thought you'd like to know where the mice came from,' he began.

Hafner smiled. 'They don't bother us any more.'

'I've also determined the origin of the rats.'

'They're under control. We're doing nicely.'

On the contrary, thought Marin. He searched for the proper beginning.

'Glade has an Earth-type climate and topography,' he said. 'Has had for the past twenty thousand years. Before that, about a hundred million years ago, it was also like Earth of the comparable period.'

He watched the look of polite interest settle on the executive's face as he stated the obvious. Well, it *was* obvious, up to a point. The conclusions weren't, though.

'Between a hundred million years and twenty thousand years ago, something happened to Glade,' Marin went on. 'I don't know the cause; it belongs to cosmic history and we may never find out. Anyway, whatever the cause – fluctuations in the sun, unstable equilibrium of forces within the planet, or perhaps an encounter with an interstellar dust cloud of variable density – the climate on Glade changed.

'It changed with inconceivable violence and it kept on changing. A hundred million years ago, plus or minus, there was carboniferous forest on Glade. Giant reptiles resembling dinosaurs and tiny mammals roamed through it. The first great change wiped out the dinosaurs, as it did on Earth. It didn't wipe out the still more primitive ancestor of the omnivore, because it could adapt to changing conditions.

'Let me give you an idea how the conditions changed. For a few years a given area would be a desert; after that it would turn into a jungle. Still later a glacier would begin to form. And then the cycle would be repeated, with wild variations. All this might happen – did happen – within a span covered by the lifetime of a single omnivore. This occurred many times. For roughly a hundred million years, it was the norm of existence on Glade. This condition was hardly conducive to the preservation of fossils.'

Hafner saw the significance and was concerned. 'You mean these climatic fluctuations suddenly stopped, twenty thousand years ago? Are they likely to begin again?'

'I don't know,' confessed the biologist. 'We can probably determine it if we're interested.'

The exec nodded grimly. 'We're interested, all right.'

Maybe we are, thought the biologist. He said, 'The point is that survival was difficult. Birds could and did fly to more suitable climates; quite a few of them survived. Only one species of mammals managed to come through.'

'Your facts are not straight,' observed Hafner. 'There are four species, ranging in size from a squirrel to a water buffalo.'

'One species,' Marin repeated doggedly. 'They're the same. If the food supply for the largest animal increases, some of the smaller so-called species grow up. Conversely, if food becomes scarce in any category, the next generation, which apparently can be produced almost instantly, switches to a form which does have an adequate food supply.'

'The mice,' Hafner said slowly.

Marin finished the thought for him. 'The mice weren't here when we got here. They were born of the squirrel-size omnivore.'

Hafner nodded. 'And the rats?'

'Born of the next larger size. After all, we're environment, too – perhaps the harshest the beasts have yet faced.'

Hafner was a practical man, trained to administer a colony. Concepts were not his familiar ground. 'Mutations, then? But I thought – '

The biologist smiled. It was thin and cracked at the edges of his mouth. 'On Earth, it would be mutation. Here it is merely normal evolutionary adaptation.' He shook his head. 'I never told you, but the omnivores, though they could be mistaken for an animal from Earth, have no genes or chromosomes. Obviously they do have heredity, but how it is passed down, I don't know. However it functions, it responds to external conditions far faster than anything we've ever encountered.'

Hafner nodded to himself. 'Then we'll never be free from pests.' He clasped and unclasped his hands. 'Unless, of course, we rid the planet of all animal life.'

'Radioactive dust?' asked the biologist. 'They have survived worse.'

The exec considered alternatives. 'Maybe we should leave the planet and leave it to the animals.'

'Too late,' said the biologist. 'They'll be on Earth, too, and all the planets we've settled on.'

Hafner looked at him. The same pictures formed in his mind that Marin had thought of. Three ships had been sent to colonize Glade. One had remained with the colonists, survival insurance in case anything unforeseen happened. Two had gone back to Earth to carry the report that all was well and that more supplies were needed. They had also carried specimens from the planet.

The cages those creatures were kept in were secure. But a smaller species could get out, must already be free, inhabiting, undetected, the cargo spaces of the ships.

There was nothing they could do to intercept those ships. And once they reached Earth, would the biologists suspect? Not for a long time. First a new kind of rat would appear. A mutation could account for that. Without specific knowledge, there would be nothing to connect it with the specimens picked up from Glade.

'We have to stay,' said the biologist. 'We have to study them and we can do it best here.'

He thought of the vast complex of buildings on Earth. There was too much invested to tear them down and make them verminproof. Billions of people could not be moved off the planet while the work was being done.

They were committed to Glade not as a colony, but as a gigantic laboratory. They had gained one planet and lost the equivalent of ten, perhaps more when the destructive properties of the omnivores were finally assessed.

A rasping animal cough interrupted the biologist's thoughts. Hafner jerked his head and glanced out of the window. Lips tight, he grabbed a rifle off the wall and ran out. Marin followed him.

The exec headed towards the fields where the second fast crop was maturing. On top of a knoll, he stopped and knelt. He flipped the dial to *extreme charge*, aimed, and fired. It was high; he missed the animal in the field. A neat strip of smoking brown appeared in the green vegetation.

He aimed more carefully and fired again. The charge screamed out of the muzzle. It struck the animal on the forepaw. The beast leaped high in the air and fell down, dead and broiled.

They stood over the animal Hafner had killed. Except for the lack of markings, it was a good imitation of a tiger. The exec prodded it with his toe.

'We chase the rats out of the warehouse and they go to the fields,' he muttered. 'We hunt them down in the fields with dogs and they breed tigers.'

'Easier than rats,' said Marin. 'We can shoot tigers.' He bent down over the slain dog near which they had surprised the big cat.

The other dog came whining from the far corner of the field to which he had fled in terror. He was a courageous dog, but he could not face the great carnivore. He whimpered and licked the face of his mate.

The biologist picked up the mangled dog and headed towards the laboratory.

'You can't save her,' said Hafner morosely. 'She's dead.'

'But the pups aren't. We'll need them. The rats won't disappear merely because tigers have showed up.'

The head drooped limply over his arm and blood seeped into his clothing as Hafner followed him up the hill.

'We've been here three months,' the exec said suddenly. 'The dogs have been in the fields only two. And yet the tiger was mature. How do you account for something like that?'

Marin bent under the weight of the dog. Hafner never would understand his bewilderment. As a biologist, all his categories were upset. What did evolution explain? It was a history of organic life on a particular world. Beyond that world, it might not apply.

Even about himself there were many things Man didn't know, dark patches in his knowledge which theory simply had to pass over. About other creatures, his ignorance was sometimes limitless.

Birth was simple; it occurred on countless planets. Meek grazing creatures, fierce carnivores – the most unlikely animals gave birth to their young. It happened all the time. And the young grew up, became mature and mated.

He remembered that evening in the laboratory. It was accidental – what if he had been elsewhere and not witnessed it? They would not know what little they did.

He explained it carefully to Hafner. 'If the survival factor is high and there's a great disparity in size, the young need not ever be young. They may be born as fully functioning adults!'

Although not at the rate it had initially set, the colony progressed. The fast crops were slowed down and a more diversified selection was planted. New buildings were constructed and the supplies that were stored in them were spread out thin, for easy inspection.

The pups survived and within a year shot up to maturity. After proper training, they were released to the fields where they joined the older dogs. The battle against the rats went on; they were held in check, though the damage they caused was considerable.

The original animal, unchanged in form, developed an appetite for electrical insulation. There was no protection except to keep the power on at all times. Even then there were unwelcome interruptions until the short was located and the charred carcass was removed. Vehicles were kept tightly closed or parked only in verminproof buildings. While the plague didn't increase in numbers, it couldn't be eliminated, either.

There was a flurry of tigers, but they were larger animals and were promptly shot down. They prowled at night, so the colonists were assigned to guard the settlement around the clock. Where lights failed to reach, the infra-red 'scope did. As fast as they came, the tigers died. Except for the first one, not a single dog was lost.

The tigers changed, though not in form. Externally, they were all big and powerful killers. But as the slaughter went on, Marin noticed one astonishing fact – the internal organic structure became progressively more immature.

The last one that was brought to him for examination was the equivalent of a newly born cub. That tiny stomach was suited more for the digestion of milk than meat. How it had furnished energy to drive those great muscles was something of a miracle. But drive it had, for a murderous fifteen minutes before the animal was brought down. No lives were lost, though sick bay was kept busy for a while.

That was the last tiger they shot. After that, the attacks ceased.

The seasons passed and nothing new occurred. A space-ship civilization or even that fragment of it represented by the colony was too much for the creature, which Marin by now had come to think of as the 'Omnimal'. It had evolved out of a cataclysmic past, but it could not meet the challenge of the harshest environment.

Or so it seemed.

Three months before the next colonists were due, a new animal was detected. Food was missing from the fields. It was not another tiger: they were carnivorous. Nor rats, for vines were stripped in a manner that no rodent could manage.

The food was not important. The colony had enough in storage. But if the new animal signalled another plague, it was necessary to know how to meet it. The sooner they knew what the animal was, the better defence they could set up against it.

Dogs were useless. The animal roamed the field they were

loose in, and they did not attack nor even seem to know it was there.

The colonists were called upon for guard duty again, but it evaded them. They patrolled for a week and they still did not catch sight of it.

Hafner called them in and rigged up an alarm system in the field most frequented by the animal. It detected that, too, and moved its sphere of operations to a field in which the alarm system had not been installed.

Hafner conferred with the engineer, who devised an alarm that would react to body radiation. It was buried in the original field and the old alarm was moved to another.

Two nights later, just before dawn, the alarm rang.

Marin met Hafner at the edge of the settlement. Both carried rifles. They walked; the noise of any vehicle was likely to frighten the animal. They circled around and approached the field from the rear. The men in the camp had been alerted. If they needed help, it was ready.

They crept silently through the underbrush. It was feeding in the field, not noisily, yet they could hear it. The dogs hadn't barked.

They inched nearer. The blue sun of Glade came up and shone full on their quarry. The gun dropped in Hafner's hand. He clenched his teeth and raised it again.

Marin put out a restraining arm. 'Don't shoot,' he whispered.

'I'm the exec here. I say it's dangerous.'

'Dangerous,' agreed Marin, still in a whisper. 'That's why you can't shoot. It's more dangerous than you know.'

Hafner hesitated and Marin went on. 'The omnimal couldn't compete in the changed environment and so it evolved mice. We stopped the mice and it countered with rats. We turned back the rat and it provided the tiger.

'The tiger was easiest of all for us and so it was apparently stopped for a while. But it didn't really stop. Another animal was being formed, the one you see there. It took the omnimal two years to create it – how, I don't know. A million years were required to evolve it on Earth.'

Hafner hadn't lowered the rifle and he showed no signs of doing so. He looked lovingly into the sights.

'Can't you see?' urged Marin. 'We can't destroy the omnimal. It's on Earth now, and on the other planets, down in the storage areas of our big cities, masquerading as rats. And we've never been able to root out even our own terrestrial rats, so how can we exterminate the omnimal?'

'All the more reason to start now.' Hafner's voice was flat.

Marin struck the rifle down. 'Are their rats better than ours?' he asked wearily. 'Will their pests win or ours be stronger? Or will the two make peace, unite and interbreed, make war on us? It's not impossible; the omnimal could do it if inter-breeding had a high survival factor.

'Don't you still see? There is a progression. After the tiger, it bred this. If this evolution fails, if we shoot it down, what will it create next? This creature I think we can compete with. *It's the one after this that I do not want to face.*'

It heard them. It raised its head and looked around. Slowly it edged away and back towards a nearby grove.

The biologist stood up and called softly. The creature scurried to the trees and stopped just inside the shadows among them.

The two men laid down their rifles. Together they approached the grove, hands spread open to show they carried no weapons.

It came out to meet them. Naked, it had had no time to learn about clothing. Neither did it have weapons. It plucked a large white flower from the tree and extended this mutely as a sign of peace.

'I wonder what it's like,' said Marin. 'It seems adult, but can it be, all the way through? What's inside that body?'

'I wonder what's in his head,' Hafner said worriedly.

It looked very much like a man.

It's a **Good** Life

Jerome Bixby

Aunt Amy was out on the front porch, rocking back and
forth in the highbacked chair and fanning herself, when Bill
Soames rode his bicycle up the road and stopped in front of
the house.

Perspiring under the afternoon 'sun', Bill lifted the box
of groceries out of the big basket over the front wheel of
the bike, and came up the front walk.

Little Anthony was sitting on the lawn, playing with a rat.
He had caught the rat down in the basement – he had made
it think that it smelled cheese, the most rich-smelling and
crumbly-delicious cheese a rat had ever thought it smelled,
and it had come out of its hole, and now Anthony had hold
of it with his mind and was making it do tricks.

When the rat saw Bill Soames coming, it tried to run, but
Anthony thought at it, and it turned a flip-flop on the grass,
and lay trembling, its eyes gleaming in small black terror.

Bill Soames hurried past Anthony and reached the front
steps, mumbling. He always mumbled when he came to the
Fremont house, or passed by it, or even thought of it.
Everybody did. They thought about silly things, things that
didn't mean very much, like two-and-two-is-four-and-
twice-is-eight and so on; they tried to jumble up their
thoughts and keep them skipping back and forth, so Anthony couldn't read their minds. The mumbling helped.
Because if Anthony got anything strong out of your
thoughts, he might take a notion to do something about it
– like curing your wife's sick headaches or your kid's

mumps, or getting your old milk cow back on schedule, or fixing the privy. And while Anthony mightn't actually mean any harm, he couldn't be expected to have much notion of what was the right thing to do in such cases.

That was if he liked you. He might try to help you, in his way. And that could be pretty horrible.

If he didn't like you . . . well, that could be worse.

Bill Soames set the box of groceries on the porch railing, and stopped his mumbling long enough to say, 'Everythin' you wanted, Miss Amy.'

'Oh, fine, William,' Amy Fremont said lightly. 'My, ain't it terrible hot today?'

Bill Soames almost cringed. His eyes pleaded with her. He shook his head violently *no*, and then interrupted his mumbling again, though obviously he didn't want to: 'Oh, don't say that, Miss Amy . . . it's fine, just fine. A real *good* day!'

Amy Fremont got up from the rocking chair, and came across the porch. She was a tall woman, thin, a smiling vacancy in her eyes. About a year ago, Anthony had gotten mad at her, because she'd told him he shouldn't have turned the cat into a cat-rug, and although he had always obeyed her more than anyone else, which was hardly at all, this time he'd snapped at her. With his mind. And that had been the end of Amy Fremont's bright eyes, and the end of Amy Fremont as everyone had known her. And that was when word got around in Peaksville (population: 46) that even the members of Anthony's own family weren't safe. After that, everyone was twice as careful.

Someday Anthony might undo what he'd done to Aunt Amy. Anthony's Mom and Pop hoped he would. When he was older, and maybe sorry. If it was possible, that is. Because Aunt Amy had changed a lot, and besides, now Anthony wouldn't obey anyone.

'Land alive, William,' Aunt Amy said, 'you don't have to mumble like that. Anthony wouldn't hurt you. My goodness, Anthony likes you!' She raised her voice and called to Anthony, who had tired of the rat and was making it eat itself. 'Don't you, dear? Don't you like Mr Soames?'

Anthony looked across the lawn at the grocery man – a bright, wet, purple gaze. He didn't say anything. Bill Soames tried to smile at him. After a second Anthony returned his attention to the rat. It had already devoured its tail, or at least chewed it off – for Anthony had made it bite faster than it could swallow, and little pink and red furry pieces lay around it on the green grass. Now the rat was having trouble reaching its hindquarters.

Mumbling silently, thinking of nothing in particular as hard as he could, Bill Soames went stiff-legged down the walk, mounted his bicycle and pedalled off.

'We'll see you tonight, William,' Aunt Amy called after him.

As Bill Soames pumped the pedals, he was wishing deep down that he could pump twice as fast, to get away from Anthony all the faster, and away from Aunt Amy, who sometimes just forgot how *careful* you had to be. And he shouldn't have thought that. Because Anthony caught it. He caught the desire to get away from the Fremont house as if it was something *bad*, and his purple gaze blinked, and he snapped a small, sulky thought after Bill Soames – just a small one, because he was in a good mood today, and besides, he liked Bill Soames, or at least he didn't dislike him, at least today. Bill Soames wanted to go away – so, petulantly, Anthony helped him.

Pedalling with superhuman speed – or rather, appearing to, because in reality the bicycle was pedalling *him* – Bill Soames vanished down the road in a cloud of dust, his thin, terrified wail drifting back across the summerlike heat.

Anthony looked at the rat. It had devoured half its belly, and had died from pain. He thought it into a grave out deep in the cornfield – his father had once said, smiling, that he might as well do that with the things he killed – and went around the house, casting his odd shadow in the hot, brassy light from above.

In the kitchen, Aunt Amy was unpacking the groceries. She put the Mason-jarred goods on the shelves, and the meat and milk in the icebox, and the beet sugar and coarse flour in big cans under the sink. She put the cardboard box in the corner, by the door, for Mr Soames to pick up next time he came. It was stained and battered and torn and worn fuzzy, but it was one of the few left in Peaksville. In faded red letters it said *Campbell's Soup*. The last cans of soup, or of anything else, had been eaten long ago, except for a small communal hoard which the villagers dipped into for special occasions – but the box lingered on, like a coffin, and when it and the other boxes were gone, the men would have to make some out of wood.

Aunt Amy went out in back, where Anthony's Mom – Aunt Amy's sister – sat in the shade of the house, shelling peas. The peas, every time Mom ran a finger along a pod, went *lollop-lollop-lollop* into the pan on her lap.

'William brought the groceries,' Aunt Amy said. She sat down wearily in the straightbacked chair beside Mom, and began fanning herself again. She wasn't really old; but ever since Anthony had snapped at her with his mind, something had seemed to be wrong with her body as well as her mind, and she was tired all the time.

'Oh, good,' said Mom. *Lollop* went the peas into the pan.

Everybody in Peaksville always said 'Oh, fine,' or 'Good,' or 'Say, that's swell!' when almost anything happened or was mentioned – even unhappy things like accidents or even deaths. They'd always say 'Good,' because if they didn't try to cover up how they really felt, Anthony might overhear with his mind, and then nobody knew what might happen. Like the time Mrs Kent's husband, Sam, had come walking back from the graveyard, because Anthony liked Mrs Kent and had heard her mourning.

Lollop.

'Tonight's television night,' said Aunt Amy. 'I'm glad. I look forward to it so much every week. I wonder what we'll see tonight?'

'Did Bill bring the meat?' asked Mom.

'Yes.' Aunt Amy fanned herself, looking up at the featureless brassy glare of the sky. 'Goodness, it's so hot! I wish Anthony would make it just a little cooler – '

'*Amy!*'

'Oh!' Mom's sharp tone had penetrated, where Bill Soames's agonized expression had failed. Aunt Amy put one thin hand to her mouth in exaggerated alarm. 'Oh . . . I'm sorry, dear.' Her pale blue eyes shuttled around, right and left, to see if Anthony was in sight. Not that it would make any difference if he was or wasn't – he didn't have to be near you to know what you were thinking. Usually, though, unless he had his attention on somebody, he would be occupied with thoughts of his own.

But some things attracted his attention – you could never be sure just what.

'This weather's just *fine*,' Mom said.

Lollop.

'Oh, yes,' Aunt Amy said. 'It's a wonderful day. I wouldn't want it changed for the world!'

Lollop.

Lollop.

'What time is it?' Mom asked.

Aunt Amy was sitting where she could see through the kitchen window to the alarm clock on the shelf above the stove. 'Four thirty,' she said.

Lollop.

'I want tonight to be something special,' Mom said. 'Did Bill bring a good lean roast?'

'Good and lean, dear. They butchered just today, you know, and sent us over the best piece.'

'Dan Hollis will be *so* surprised when he finds out that tonight's television party is a birthday party for him too!'

'Oh, *I* think he will! Are you sure nobody's told him?'

'Everybody swore they wouldn't.'

'That'll be real nice,' Aunt Amy nodded, looking off across the cornfield. 'A birthday party.'

'Well – ' Mom put the pan of peas down beside her, stood up and brushed her apron. 'I'd better get the roast on. Then we can set the table.' She picked up the peas.

Anthony came around the corner of the house. He didn't look at them, but continued on down through the carefully kept garden – *all* the gardens in Peaksville were carefully kept, very carefully kept – and went past the rusting, useless hulk that had been the Fremont family car, and went smoothly over the fence and out into the cornfield.

'Isn't this a lovely day!' said Mom, a little loudly, as they went towards the back door.

Aunt Amy fanned herself. 'A beautiful day, dear. Just *fine!*'

Out in the cornfield, Anthony walked between the tall, rustling rows of green stalks. He liked to smell the corn. The alive corn overhead, and the old dead corn underfoot. Rich Ohio earth, thick with weeds and brown, dry-rotting ears of corn, pressed between his bare toes with every step – he had made it rain last night so everything would smell and feel nice today.

He walked clear to the edge of the cornfield, and over to where a grove of shadowy green trees covered cool, moist, dark ground, and lots of leafy undergrowth, and jumbled moss-covered rocks, and a small spring that made a clear, clean pool. Here Anthony liked to rest and watch the birds and insects and small animals that rustled and scampered and chirped about. He liked to lie on the cool ground and look up through the moving greenness overhead, and watch the insects flit in the hazy soft sunbeams that stood like slanting, glowing bars between ground and treetops. Somehow, he liked the thoughts of the little creatures in this place better than the thoughts outside; and while the thoughts he picked up here weren't very strong or very clear, he could get enough out of them to know what the little creatures liked and wanted, and he spent a lot of time making the grove more like what they wanted it to be. The spring hadn't always been here; but one time he had found thirst in one small furry mind, and had brought subterranean water to the surface in a clear cold flow, and had watched blinking as the creature drank, feeling its pleasure. Later he had made the pool, when he found a small urge to swim.

He had made rocks and trees and bushes and caves, and sunlight here and shadows there, because he had felt in all the tiny minds around him the desire – or the instinctive want – for this kind of resting place, and that kind of mating place, and this kind of place to play, and that kind of home.

And somehow the creatures from all the fields and pastures around the grove had seemed to know that this was a good place, for there were always more of them coming in – every time Anthony came out here there were more creatures than the last time, and more desires and needs to be tended to. Every time there would be some kind of creature he had never seen before, and he would find its mind, and see what it wanted, and then give it to it.

He liked to help them. He liked to feel their simple gratification.

Today, he rested beneath a thick elm, and lifted his purple gaze to a red and black bird that had just come to the grove. It twittered on a branch over his head, and hopped back and forth, and thought its tiny thoughts, and Anthony made a big, soft nest for it, and pretty soon it hopped in.

A long, brown, sleek-furred animal was drinking at the pool. Anthony found its mind next. The animal was thinking about a smaller creature that was scurrying along the ground on the other side of the pool, grubbing for insects. The little creature didn't know that it was in danger. The long, brown animal finished drinking and tensed its legs to leap, and Anthony thought it into a grave in the cornfield.

He didn't like those kinds of thoughts. They reminded him of the thoughts outside the grove. A long time ago some of the people outside had thought that way about *him*, and one night they'd hidden and waited for him to come back from the grove – and he'd just thought them all into the cornfield. Since then, the rest of the people hadn't thought that way – at least, very clearly. Now their thoughts were all mixed up and confusing whenever they thought about him or near him, so he didn't pay much attention.

He liked to help them too, sometimes – but it wasn't simple, or very gratifying either. They never thought happy thoughts when he did – just the jumble. So he spent more time out here.

He watched all the birds and insects and furry creatures for a while, and played with a bird, making it soar and dip and streak madly around tree trunks until, accidentally, when another bird caught his attention for a moment, he ran it into a rock. Petulantly, he thought the rock into a grave in the cornfield; but he couldn't do anything more with the bird. Not because it was dead, though it was; but because it had a broken wing. So he went back to the house. He didn't feel like walking back through the cornfield, so he just *went* to the house, right down into the basement.

It was nice down here. Nice and dark and damp and sort of fragrant, because once Mom had been making preserves in a rack along the far wall, and then she'd stopped coming down ever since Anthony had started spending time here, and the preserves had spoiled and leaked down and spread over the dirt floor, and Anthony liked the smell.

He caught another rat, making it smell cheese, and after he played with it, he thought it into a grave right beside the long animal he'd killed in the grove. Aunt Amy hated rats, and so he killed a lot of them, because he liked Aunt Amy most of all and sometimes did things that Aunt Amy wanted. Her mind was more like the little furry minds out in the grove. She hadn't thought anything bad at all about him for a long time.

After the rat, he played with a big black spider in the corner under the stairs, making it run back and forth until its web shook and shimmered in the light from the cellar window like a reflection in silvery water. Then he drove fruit flies into the web until the spider was frantic trying to wind them all up. The spider liked flies, and its thoughts were stronger than theirs, so he did it. There was something bad in the way it liked flies, but it wasn't clear – and besides, Aunt Amy hated flies too.

He had heard footsteps overhead – Mum moving around in the kitchen. He blinked his purple gaze, and almost decided to make her hold still – but instead he *went* up to the attic, and after looking out the circular window at the front end of the long V-roofed room for a while at the front lawn and the dusty road and Henderson's tip-waving wheatfield beyond, he curled into an unlikely shape and went partly to sleep.

Soon people would be coming for television, he heard Mom think.

He went more to sleep. He liked television night. Aunt Amy had always liked television a lot, so one time he had thought some for her, and a few other people had been there at the time, and Aunt Amy had felt disappointed when they wanted to leave. He'd done something to them for that – and now everybody came to television.

He liked all the attention he got when they did.

Anthony's father came home around 6.30, looking tired and dirty and bloody. He'd been over in Dunn's pasture with the other men, helping pick out the cow to be slaughtered this month and doing the job, and then butchering the meat and salting it away in Soames's icehouse. Not a job he cared for, but every man had his turn. Yesterday, he had helped scythe down old McIntyre's wheat. Tomorrow, they would start threshing. By hand. Everything in Peaksville had to be done by hand.

He kissed his wife on the cheek and sat down at the kitchen table. He smiled and said, 'Where's Anthony?'

'Around someplace,' Mom said.

Aunt Amy was over at the wood-burning stove, stirring the big pot of peas. Mom went back to the oven and opened it and basted the roast.

'Well, it's been a *good* day,' Dad said. By rote. Then he looked at the mixing bowl and breadboard on the table. He sniffed at the dough. 'M'm,' he said. 'I could eat a loaf all by myself, I'm so hungry.'

'No one told Dan Hollis about its being a birthday party, did they?' his wife asked.

'Nope. We kept as quiet as mummies.'

'We've fixed up such a lovely surprise!'

'Um? What?'

'Well . . . you know how much Dan likes music. Well, last week Thelma Dunn found a *record* in her attic!'

'No!'

'Yes! And we had Ethel sort of ask – you know, without

really *asking* – if he had that one. And he said no. Isn't that a wonderful surprise?'

'Well, now, it sure is. A record, imagine! That's a real nice thing to find! What record is it?'

'Perry Como, singing *You Are My Sunshine*.'

'Well, I'll be darned. I always liked that tune.' Some raw carrots were lying on the table. Dad picked up a small one, scrubbed it on his chest, and took a bite. 'How did Thelma happen to find it?'

'Oh, you know – just looking around for new things.'

'M'm.' Dad chewed the carrot. 'Say, who has that picture we found a while back? I kind of liked it – that old clipper sailing along – '

'The Smiths. Next week the Sipichs get it, and they give the Smiths old McIntyre's music-box, and we give the Sipichs – ' and she went down the tentative order of things that would exchange hands among the women at church this Sunday.

He nodded. 'Looks like we can't have the picture for a while, I guess. Look, honey, you might try to get that detective book back from the Reillys. I was so busy the week we had it, I never got to finish all the stories – '

'I'll try,' his wife said doubtfully. 'But I hear the van Husens have a stereoscope they found in the cellar.' Her voice was just a little accusing. 'They had it two whole months before they told anybody about it – '

'Say,' Dad said, looking interested. 'That'd be nice, too. Lots of pictures?'

'I suppose so. I'll see on Sunday. I'd like to have it – but we still owe the van Husens for their canary. I don't know why that bird had to pick *our* house to die . . . it must have been sick when we got it. Now there's just no satisfying Betty van Husen – she even hinted she'd like our *piano* for a while!'

'Well, honey, you try for the stereoscope – or just anything you think we'll like.' At last he swallowed the carrot. It had been a little young and tough. Anthony's whims about the weather made it so that people never knew what crops would come up, or what shape they'd be in if they did. All they could do was plant a lot; and always enough of something came up any one season to live on. Just once there had been a grain surplus; tons of it had been hauled to the edge of Peaksville and dumped off into the nothingness. Otherwise, nobody could have breathed, when it started to spoil.

'You know,' Dad went on. 'It's nice to have the new things around. It's nice to think that there's probably still a lot of stuff nobody's found yet, in cellars and attics and barns and down behind things. They help, somehow. As much as anything can help – '

'Sh-h!' Mom glanced nervously around.

'Oh,' Dad said, smiling hastily. 'It's all right! The new things are *good*! It's *nice* to be able to have something around you've never seen before, and know that something you've given somebody else is making them happy . . . that's a real *good* thing.'

'A good thing,' his wife echoed.

'Pretty soon,' Aunt Amy said, from the stove, 'there won't be any more new things. We'll have found everything there is to find. Goodness, that'll be too bad – '

'*Amy!*'

'Well – ' Her pale eyes were shallow and fixed, a sign of her recurrent vagueness. 'It will be kind of a shame – no new things – '

'Don't *talk* like that,' Mom said, trembling. 'Amy, be *quiet!*'

'It's *good*,' said Dad, in the loud, familiar, wanting-to-be-overheard tone of voice. 'Such talk is *good*. It's okay, honey – don't you see? It's good for Amy to talk any way she wants. It's good for her to feel bad. Everything's good. Everything *has* to be good . . .'

Anthony's mother was pale. And so was Aunt Amy – the peril of the moment had suddenly penetrated the clouds surrounding her mind. Sometimes it was difficult to handle words so that they might not prove disastrous. You just never *knew*. There were so many things it was wise not to say, or even think – but remonstration for saying or thinking them might be just as bad, if Anthony heard and decided to do anything about it. You could just never tell what Anthony was liable to do.

Everything had to be good. Had to be fine just as it was, even if it wasn't. Always. Because any change might be worse. So terribly much worse.

'Oh, my goodness, yes, of course it's good,' Mom said. 'You talk any way you want to, Amy, and it's just fine. Of course, you want to remember that some ways are *better* than others . . .'

Aunt Amy stirred the peas, fright in her pale eyes.

'Oh, yes,' she said. 'But I don't feel like talking right now. It . . . it's *good* that I don't feel like talking.'

Dad said tiredly, smiling, 'I'm going out and wash up.'

They started arriving around eight o'clock. By that time, Mom and Aunt Amy had the big table in the dining-room set, and two more tables off to the side. The candles were burning, and the chairs situated, and Dad had a big fire going in the fireplace.

The first to arrive were the Sipichs, John and Mary. John wore his best suit, and was well-scrubbed and pink-faced after his day in McIntyre's pasture. The suit was neatly pressed, but getting threadbare at elbows and cuffs. Old McIntyre was working on a loom, designing it out of school-books, but so far it was slow going. McIntyre was a capable man with wood and tools, but a loom was a big order when you couldn't get metal parts. McIntyre had been one of the ones who, at first, had wanted to try to get Anthony to make things the villagers needed, like clothes and canned goods and medical supplies and gasoline. Since then, he felt that what had happened to the whole Terrance family and Joe Kinney was his fault, and he worked hard trying to make it up to the rest of them. And since then, no one had tried to get Anthony to do anything.

Mary Sipich was a small, cheerful woman in a simple dress. She immediately set about helping Mom and Aunt Amy put the finishing touches on the dinner.

The next arrivals were the Smiths and the Dunns, who lived right next to each other down the road, only a few yards from the nothingness. They drove up in the Smiths' wagon, drawn by their old horse.

Then the Reillys showed up, from across the darkened wheatfield, and the evening really began. Pat Reilly sat down at the big upright in the front room, and began to play from the popular sheet music on the rack. He played softly, as expressively as he could – and nobody sang. Anthony liked piano playing a whole lot, but not singing; often he would come up from the basement, or down from the attic, or just *come*, and sit on top of the piano, nodding his head as Pat played *Lover* or *Boulevard of Broken Dreams* or *Night and Day*. He seemed to prefer ballads, sweet-sounding songs – but the one time somebody had started to sing, Anthony had looked over from the top of the piano and done something that made everybody afraid of singing from then on. Later, they'd decided that the piano was what Anthony had heard first, before anybody had ever tried to sing, and now anything else added to it didn't sound right and distracted him from his pleasure.

So, every television night, Pat would play the piano, and that was the beginning of the evening. Wherever Anthony was, the music would make him happy, and put him in a good mood, and he would know that they were gathering for television and waiting for him.

By 8.30 everybody had shown up, except for the seventeen children and Mrs Soames who was off watching them in the schoolhouse at the far end of town. The children of Peaksville were never, never allowed near the Fremont house – not since little Fred Smith had tried to play with Anthony on a dare. The younger children weren't even told about Anthony. The others had mostly forgotten about him, or were told that he was a nice, nice goblin, but they must never go near him.

Dan and Ethel Hollis came late, and Dan walked in not suspecting a thing. Pat Reilly had played the piano until his hands ached – he'd worked pretty hard with them today – and now he got up, and everybody gathered around to wish Dan Hollis a happy birthday.

'Well, I'll be darned,' Dan grinned. 'This is swell. I wasn't expecting this at all . . . gosh, this is *swell!*'

They gave him his presents – mostly things they had made by hand, though some were things that people had possessed as their own and now gave him as his. John Sipich gave him a watch charm, hand-carved out of a piece of hickory wood. Dan's watch had broken down a year or so ago, and there was nobody in the village who knew how to fix it, but he still carried it around because it had been his grandfather's and was a fine old heavy thing of gold and silver. He attached the charm to the chain, while everybody laughed and said John had done a nice job of carving. Then Mary Sipich gave him a knitted necktie, which he put on, removing the one he'd worn.

The Reillys gave him a little box they had made, to keep things in. They didn't say what things, but Dan said he'd keep his personal jewellery in it. The Reillys had made it out of a cigar box, carefully peeled off its paper and lined it on the inside with velvet. The outside had been polished, and carefully if not expertly carved by Pat – but his carving got complimented too. Dan Hollis received many other gifts – a pipe, a pair of shoelaces, a tie pin, a knit pair of socks, some fudge, a pair of garters made from old suspenders.

He unwrapped each gift with vast pleasure, and wore as many of them as he could right there, even the garters. He lit up the pipe, and said he'd never had a better smoke; which wasn't quite true, because the pipe wasn't broken in yet. Pete Manners had had it lying around ever since he'd received it as a gift four years ago from an out-of-town relative who hadn't known he'd stopped smoking.

Dan put the tobacco into the bowl very carefully. Tobacco was precious. It was only pure luck that Pat Reilly had decided to try to grow some in his backyard just before what had happened to Peaksville had happened. It didn't grow very well, and then they had to cure it and shred it and all, and it was just precious stuff. Everybody in town used wooden holders old McIntyre had made, to save on butts.

Last of all, Thelma Dunn gave Dan Hollis the record she had found.

Dan's eyes misted even before he opened the package. He knew it was a record.

'Gosh,' he said softly. 'What one is it? I'm almost afraid to look . . . '

'You haven't got it, darling,' Ethel Hollis smiled. 'Don't you remember, I asked about *You Are My Sunshine*?'

'Oh, gosh,' Dan said again. Carefully he removed the wrapping and stood there fondling the record, running his big hands over the worn grooves with their tiny, dulling crosswise scratches. He looked around the room, eyes shining, and they all smiled back, knowing how delighted he was.

'Happy birthday, darling!' Ethel said, throwing her arms around him and kissing him.

He clutched the record in both hands, holding it off to one side as she pressed against him. 'Hey,' he laughed, pulling back his head. 'Be careful . . . I'm holding a priceless object!' He looked around again, over his wife's arms, which were still around his neck. His eyes were hungry. 'Look . . . do you think we could play it? Lord, what I'd give to hear some new music . . . just the first part, the orchestra part, before Como sings?'

Faces sobered. After a minute, John Sipich said, 'I don't think we'd better, Dan. After all, we don't know just where the singer comes in – it'd be taking too much of a chance. Better wait till you get home.'

Dan Hollis reluctantly put the record on the buffet with all his other presents. 'It's *good*,' he said automatically, but disappointedly, 'that I can't play it here.'

'Oh, yes,' said Sipich. 'It's good.' To compensate for Dan's disappointed tone, he repeated, 'It's *good*.'

They ate dinner, the candles lighting their smiling faces, and ate it all right down to the last delicious drop of gravy. They complimented Mom and Aunt Amy on the roast beef, and the peas and carrots, and the tender corn on the cob. The corn hadn't come from the Fremonts' cornfield, naturally

– everybody knew what was out there; and the field was going to weeds.

Then they polished off the dessert – homemade ice cream and cookies. And then they sat back, in the flickering light of the candles, and chatted, waiting for television.

There never was a lot of mumbling on television night – everybody came and had a good dinner at the Fremonts', and that was nice, and afterwards there was television, and nobody really thought much about that – it just had to be put up with. So it was a pleasant enough get-together, aside from your having to watch what you said just as carefully as you always did every place. If a dangerous thought came into your mind, you just started mumbling, even right in the middle of a sentence. When you did that, the others just ignored you until you felt happier again and stopped.

Anthony liked television night. He had done only two or three awful things on television night in the whole past year.

Mom had put a bottle of brandy on the table, and they each had a tiny glass of it. Liquor was even more precious than tobacco. The villagers could make wine, but the grapes weren't right, and certainly the techniques weren't, and it wasn't very good wine. There were only a few bottles of real liquor left in the village – four rye, three Scotch, three brandy, nine real wine and half a bottle of Drambuie belonging to old McIntyre (only for marriages) – and when those were gone, that was it.

Afterward, everybody wished that the brandy hadn't been brought out. Because Dan Hollis drank more of it than he should have, and mixed it with a lot of the homemade wine. Nobody thought anything about it at first, because he didn't show it much outside, and it was his birthday party and a happy party, and Anthony liked these get-togethers and shouldn't see any reason to do anything even if he was listening.

But Dan Hollis got high, and did a fool thing. If they'd seen it coming, they'd have taken him outside and walked him around.

The first thing they knew, Dan stopped laughing right in the middle of the story about how Thelma Dunn had found the Perry Como record and dropped it and it hadn't broken because she'd moved faster than she ever had before in her life and caught it. He was fondling the record again, and looking longingly at the Fremonts' gramophone over in the corner, and suddenly he stopped laughing and his face got slack, and then it got ugly, and he said, 'Oh, *Christ!*'

Immediately the room was still. So still they could hear the whirring movement of the grandfather's clock out in the hall. Pat Reilly had been playing the piano, softly. He stopped, his hands poised over the yellowed keys.

The candles on the dining-room table flickered in a cool breeze that blew through the lace curtains over the bay window.

'Keep playing, Pat,' Anthony's father said softly.

Pat started again. He played *Night and Day*, but his eyes were sidewise on Dan Hollis, and he missed notes.

Dan stood in the middle of the room, holding the record. In his other hand he held a glass of brandy so hard his hand shook.

They were all looking at him.

'*Christ*,' he said again, and he made it sound like a dirty word.

Reverend Younger, who had been talking with Mom and Aunt Amy by the dining-room door, said 'Christ' too – but he was using it in a prayer. His hands were clasped, and his eyes were closed.

John Sipich moved forward. 'Now, Dan . . . it's *good* for you to talk that way. But you don't want to talk too much, you know.'

Dan shook off the hand Sipich put on his arm.

'Can't even play my record,' he said loudly. He looked down at the record, and then around at their faces. 'Oh, my God . . . '

He threw the glassful of brandy against the wall. It splattered and ran down the wallpaper in streaks.

Some of the women gasped.

'Dan,' Sipich said in a whisper. 'Dan, cut it out – '

Pat Reilly was playing *Night and Day* louder, to cover up

the sounds of the talk. It wouldn't do any good, though, if Anthony was listening.

Dan Hollis went over to the piano and stood by Pat's shoulder, swaying a little.

'Pat,' he said. 'Don't play *that*. Play *this*.' And he began to sing. Softly, hoarsely, miserably: 'Happy birthday to me . . . Happy birthday to me . . . '

'*Dan!*' Ethel Hollis screamed. She tried to run across the room to him. Mary Sipich grabbed her arm and held her back. 'Dan,' Ethel screamed again. 'Stop – '

'My God, be quiet!' hissed Mary Sipich, and pushed her towards one of the men, who put his hand over her mouth and held her still.

' – Happy birthday, dear Danny,' Dan sang. 'Happy birthday to me!' He stopped and looked down at Pat Reilly. 'Play it, Pat. Play it, so I can sing right . . . you know I can't carry a tune unless somebody plays it!'

Pat Reilly put his hands on the keys and began *Lover* – in a slow waltz tempo, the way Anthony liked it. Pat's face was white. His hands fumbled.

Dan Hollis stared over at the dining-room door. At Anthony's mother, and at Anthony's father who had gone to join her.

'*You* had him,' he said. Tears gleamed on his cheeks as the candlelight caught them. '*You* had to go and *have* him . . . '

He closed his eyes, and the tears squeezed out. He sang loudly, 'You are my sunshine . . . my only sunshine . . . you make me happy . . . when I am blue . . . '

Anthony *came* into the room.

Pat stopped playing. He froze. Everybody froze. The breeze rippled the curtains. Ethel Hollis couldn't even try to scream – she had fainted.

'Please don't take my sunshine . . . away . . . ' Dan's voice faltered into silence. His eyes widened. He put both hands out in front of him, the empty glass in one, the record in the other. He hiccupped, and said, '*No –*'

'Bad man,' Anthony said, and thought Dan Hollis into something like nothing anyone would have believed possible, and then he thought the thing into a grave deep, deep in the cornfield.

The glass and record thumped on the rug. Neither broke.

Anthony's purple gaze went around the room.

Some of the people began mumbling. They all tried to smile. The sound of mumbling filled the room like a far-off approval. Out of the murmuring came one or two clear voices:

'Oh, it's a very *good* thing,' said John Sipich.

'A good thing,' said Anthony's father, smiling. He'd had more practice in smiling than most of them. 'A wonderful thing.'

'It's swell . . . just swell,' said Pat Reilly, tears leaking from eyes and nose, and he began to play the piano again, softly, his trembling hands feeling for *Night and Day*.

Anthony climbed up on top of the piano, and Pat played for two hours.

Afterwards, they watched television. They all went into the front room, and lit just a few candles, and pulled up chairs around the set. It was a small-screen set, and they couldn't all sit close enough to it to see, but that didn't matter. They didn't even turn the set on. It wouldn't have worked anyway, there being no electricity in Peaksville.

They just sat silently, and watched the twisting, writhing shapes on the screen, and listened to the sounds that came out of the speaker, and none of them had any idea what it was all about. They never did. It was always the same.

'It's real nice,' Aunt Amy said once, her pale eyes on the meaningless flickers and shadows. 'But I liked it a little better when there were cities outside and we could get real – '

'Why, Amy!' said Mom. 'It's good for you to say such a thing. Very good. But how can you mean it? Why, this television is *much* better than anything we ever used to get!'

'Yes,' chimed in John Sipich. 'It's fine. It's the best show we've ever seen!'

He sat on the couch, with two other men, holding Ethel Hollis flat against the cushions, holding her arms and legs and putting their hands over her mouth, so she couldn't start screaming again.

'It's really *good!*' he said again.

Mom looked out of the front window, across the darkened road, across Henderson's darkened wheatfield to the vast, endless, grey nothingness in which the little village of Peaksville floated like a soul – the huge nothingness that was most evident at night, when Anthony's brassy day had gone.

It did no good to wonder where they were . . . no good at all. Peaksville was just someplace. Someplace away from the world. It was wherever it had been since that day three years ago when Anthony had crept from her womb and old Doc Bates – God rest him – had screamed and dropped him and tried to kill him, and Anthony had whined and done the thing. Had taken the village someplace. Or had destroyed the world and left only the village, nobody knew which.

It did no good to wonder about it. Nothing at all did any good – except to live as they must live. Must always, always live, if Anthony would let them.

These thoughts were dangerous, she thought.

She began to mumble. The others started mumbling too. They had all been thinking, evidently.

The men on the couch whispered and whispered to Ethel Hollis, and when they took their hands away, she mumbled too.

While Anthony sat on top of the set and made television, they sat around and mumbled and watched the meaningless, flickering shapes far into the night.

Next day it snowed, and killed off half the crops – but it was a *good* day.

Sister Planet

Poul Anderson

Long afterwards they found a dead man in shabby clothes adrift near San Francisco. The police decided he must have jumped from the Golden Gate Bridge one misty day. That was an oddly clean and lonesome place for some obscure wino to die, but no one was very much interested. Beneath his shirt he carried a Bible with a bookmark indicating a certain passage which had been underlined. Idly curious, a member of the Homicide Squad studied the waterlogged pulp until he deduced the section: Ezekiel vii, 3–4.

1

A squall hit when Shorty McClellan had almost set down. He yanked back the stick; jets snorted and the ferry stood on her tail and reached for heaven. An eyeblink later she was whipping about like a wind-tossed leaf. The viewports showed blackness. Above the wind there was a bongo beat of rain. Then lightning blazed and thunder followed and Nat Hawthorne closed off smitten sense channels.

Welcome back! he thought. Or did he say it aloud? The thunder rolled off, monster wheels if it was not laughter. He felt the vessel steady around him. When the dazzle had cleared from his eyes, he saw clouds and calm. A smoky blueness in the air told him that it was near sunset. What answered to sunset on Venus, he reminded himself. The daylight would linger on for hours, and the night never got truly dark.

'That was a near one,' said Shorty McClellan.

'I thought these craft were designed to ride out storms,' said Hawthorne.

'Sure. But not to double as submarines. We were pretty close to the surface when that one sneaked up on us. We could'a got dunked, and then – ' McClellan shrugged.

'No real danger,' Hawthorne answered. 'We could get out the airlock, I'm sure, with masks, and stay afloat till they picked us up from the station. If Oscar and company didn't rescue us first. You realize there's no trouble from any native life form. They find us every bit as poisonous as we find them.'

'No danger, he says,' groaned McClellan. 'Well, you wouldn't have to account for five million bucks' worth of boat!'

He began whistling tunelessly as he spiralled down for another approach. He was a small, heavy set, quick moving man with a freckled face and sandy hair. For years Hawthorne had only known him casually, as one of the pilots who took cargo between orbiting spaceships and Venus Station: a cocky sort, given to bawdy limericks and improbable narratives about himself and what he called the female race. But on the voyage from Earth, he had ended with shyly passing around stereos of his children and describing plans for opening a little resort on Great Bear Lake when he reached retirement age.

I thank the nonexistent Lord that I am a biologist, thought Hawthorne. *The farcical choice of quitting or accepting a desk job at thirty-five has not yet reached my line of work. I hope I'll still be tracing ecological chains and watching auroras over the Phosphor Sea at eighty.*

As the boat tilted forward, he saw Venus below him. One would never have expected a landless, planet-wide ocean to be so alive. But there were climatic zones, each with its own million restless hues – the colour of light, the quality of living organisms, nowhere the same, so that a sea on Venus was not an arbitrary section of water but an iridescent belt around the world. And then there was the angle of the sun, night-lighting, breezes and gales and typhoons, seasons, solar tides which had no barrier to their 20,000 mile march, and the great biological rhythms which men did not yet understand. No, you could sit for a hundred years in one place, watching, and never see the same thing twice. And all that you saw would be beautiful.

The Phosphor Sea girdled the planet between 55 and 63 degrees north latitude. Now from above, at evening, it had grown indigo, streaked with white; but on the world's very edge it shaded to black in the north and an infinitely clear green in the south. Here and there beneath the surface twined scarlet veins. A floating island, a jungle twisted over giant bladderweeds, upbore flame yellows and a private mistiness. Eastward walked the squall, blue-black and light-ning, the water roaring in its track. The lower western clouds were tinged rose and copper. The permanent sky-layer above ranged from pearl grey in the east to a still blinding white in the west, where the invisible sun burned. A double rainbow arched the horizon.

Hawthorne sighed. It was good to be back.

Air whistled under the ferry's glider wings. Then it touched pontoons to water, bounced, came down again, and taxied for the station. A bow wave broke among those caissons and spouted toward the upper deck and the build-ings which, gyro-stabilized, ignored such disturbances. As usual, the whole station crew had turned out to greet the vessel. Spaceship arrivals were months apart.

'End of the line.' McClellan came to a halt, unbuckled himself, stood up and struggled into his air harness. 'You know,' he remarked, 'I've never felt easy in one of these gizmos.'

'Why not?' Hawthorne, hanging the tank on his own shoulders, looked in surprise at the pilot.

McClellan adjusted his mask. It covered nose and mouth with a tight airseal of celluplastic gasketing. Both men had already slipped ultraviolet-filtering contact lenses over their eyeballs. 'I keep remembering that there isn't an oxygen molecule that's not man-made for twenty-five million miles,' he confessed. The airhose muffled his voice, giving it for

Hawthorne a homelike accent. 'I'd feel safer with a space suit.'

'*De gustibus non disputandum est*,' said Hawthorne, 'which has been translated as, "There is no disputing that Gus is in the east." Me, I was never yet in a space suit that didn't squeak and smell of somebody else's garlic.'

Through the port he saw a long blue back swirl in the water and thresh impatient foam. A grin tugged at his lips. 'Why, I'll bet Oscar knows I'm here,' he said.

'Yeah. Soul mates,' grunted McClellan.

They went out the airlock. Ears popped, adjusting to a slight pressure difference. The masks strained out some water vapor for reasons of comfort, and virtually all the carbon dioxide, for there was enough to kill a man in three gulps. Nitrogen, argon, and trace gases passed on, to be blent with oxygen from the harness tank and breathed. Units existed which electrolysed the Earth-vital element directly from water, but so far they were cumbersome.

A man on Venus did best to keep such an engine handy in his boat or on the dock, for recharging the bottle on his back every few hours. Newcomers from Earth always found that an infernal nuisance, but after a while at Venus Station you fell into a calmer pattern.

A saner one? Hawthorne had often wondered. His latest visit to Earth had about convinced him.

The heat struck like a fist. He had already donned the local costume: loose, flowing garments of synthetic, designed to ward ultraviolet radiation off his skin and not absorb water. Now he paused for a moment, reminded himself that Man was a mammal and able to get along quite well at even higher temperatures, and relaxed. The sea lapped his bare feet where he stood on a pontoon. It felt cool. Suddenly he stopped minding the heat; he forgot it entirely.

Oscar frisked up. Yes, of course it was Oscar. The other cetoids, a dozen or so, were more interested in the ferry, nosing it, rubbing their sleek flanks against the metal, holding their calves up in their foreflippers for a good look.

Oscar paid attention only to Hawthorne. He lifted his

blunt bulky head, nuzzled the biologist's toes, and slapped flukes on water twenty feet away.

Hawthorne squatted. 'Hi, Oscar,' he said. 'Didn't think I'd make it back, did you?' He chucked the beast under the chin. Be damned if the cetoids didn't have true chins. Oscar rolled belly-up and snorted.

'Thought I'd pick up some dame Earthside and forget all about you, huh?' murmured Hawthorne. 'Why, bless your ugly puss, I wouldn't dream of it! Certainly not. I wouldn't waste Earthside time dreaming of abandoning you for a woman. I'd do it! C'mere, creature.'

He scratched the rubbery skin just behind the blowhole. Oscar bumped against the pontoon and wriggled.

'Cut that out, will you?' asked McClellan. 'I don't want a bath just yet.' He threw a hawser. Wim Dykstra caught it, snubbed it around a bollard, and began to haul. The ferry moved slowly to the dock.

'Okay, Oscar, okay, okay,' said Hawthorne. 'I'm home. Let's not get sickening about it.' He was a tall, rather bony man, with dark-blond hair, and a prematurely creased face. 'Yes, I've got a present for you too, same as the rest of the station, but let me get unpacked first. I got you a celluloid duck. Leggo there!'

The cetoid sounded. Hawthorne was about to step off onto the dock ladder when Oscar came back. With great care, the swimmer nudged the man's ankles and then, awkwardly, because this was the regular trading pier, pushed something out of his mouth to lay at Hawthorne's feet. After which Oscar sounded again and Hawthorne muttered total, profane astonishment and felt his eyes sting a little.

He had just been presented with one of the finest firegems on record.

2

After dark, the aurora became visible. The sun was so close, and the Venusian magnetic field so weak, that even in the equator the sky became criss-crossed at times with great banners of light. Here in the Phosphor Sea, the night was royal blue, with rosy curtains and silent white shuddering streamers. And the water itself shone, bioluminescence, each wave laced by cold fires. Where droplets struck the station deck, they glowed for minutes before evaporating, as if gold coals had been strewn at random over its gleaming circumference.

Hawthorne looked out the transparent wall of the ward-room. 'It's good to be back,' he said.

'Get that,' said Shorty McClellan. 'From wine and women competing in droves for the company of a glamorous inter-planetary explorer, it is good to be back. This man is crazy.'

The geophysicist, Wim Dykstra, nodded with seriousness. He was the tall swarthy breed of Dutchman, whose ancestral memories are of Castilian uplands. Perhaps that is why so many of them feel forever homeless.

'I think I understand, Nat,' he said. 'I read between the lines of my mail. Is it that bad on Earth?'

'In some ways.' Hawthorne leaned against the wall, star-ing into Venus' night.

The cetoids were playing about the station. Joyous tor-pedo shapes would hurtle from the water, streaming liquid radiance, arch over and come down in a fountain that burned. And then they threshed the sea and were off around a mile-wide circle, rolling and tumbling. The cannon-crack of bodies and flukes could be heard this far up.

'I was afraid of that. I do not know if I want to take my next furlough when it comes,' said Dykstra.

McClellan looked bewildered. 'What're you fellows talk-ing about?' he asked. 'What's wrong?'

Hawthorne sighed. 'I don't know where to begin,' he said. 'The trouble is, Shorty, you see Earth continually. Get back from a voyage and you're there for weeks or months before taking off again. But we . . . we're gone three, four, five years at a stretch. We notice the changes.'

'Oh, sure.' McClellan shifted his weight uneasily in his chair. 'Sure, I suppose you aren't used to – well, the gangs, or the covées, or the fact that they've begun to ration dwell-ing space in America since the last time you were there. But still, you guys are well paid, and your job has prestige. You rate special privileges. What are *you* complaining about?

'Call it the atmosphere,' said Hawthorne. He sketched a smile. 'If God existed, which thank God He doesn't, I'd say He has forgotten Earth.'

Dykstra flushed. 'God does not forget,' he said. 'Men do.'

'Sorry, Wim,' said Hawthorne. 'But I've seen – not just Earth. Earth is too big to be anything but statistics. I visited my own country, the place where I grew up. And the lake where I went fishing as a kid is an algae farm and my mother has to share one miserable room with a yattering old biddy she can't stand the sight of.

'What's worse, they've cut down Bobolink Grove to put up still another slum mislabelled a housing project, and the gangs are operating in open daylight now. Armed escort has become a major industry. I walk into a bar and not a face is happy. They're just staring stupefied at a telescreen and – ' He pulled up short. 'Never mind. I probably exaggerate.'

'I'll say you do,' said McClellan. 'Why, I can show you places where no man has been since the Indians left – if it's nature you want. You've never been to San Francisco, have you? Well, come with me to a pub I know in North Beach, and I'll show you the time of your life.'

'Sure,' said Hawthorne. 'What I wonder is, how much longer will those fragments survive?'

'Some of them, indefinitely,' said McClellan. 'They're corporate property. These days CP means private estates.'

Wim Dykstra nodded. 'The rich get richer,' he said, 'and the poor get poorer, and the middle class vanishes. Eventually there is the fossilized Empire. I have read history.'

He regarded Hawthorne out of dark, thoughtful eyes. 'Medieval feudalism and monasticism evolved *within* the Roman domain: they were there when it fell apart. I wonder if a parallel development may not already be taking place. The feudalism of the large organizations on Earth; the monasticism of planetary stations like this.'

'Complete with celibacy,' grimaced McClellan. 'Me, I'll take the feudalism!'

Hawthorne sighed again. There was always a price. Sex-suppressive pills, and the memory of fervent lips and clinging arms on Earth, were often poor comfort.

'We're not a very good analogy, Wim,' he argued. 'In the first place, we live entirely off the jewel trade. Because it's profitable, we're allowed to carry on the scientific work which interests us personally: that's part of our wage, in effect. But if the cetoids stopped bringing gems, we'd be hauled home so fast we'd meet ourselves coming back. You know nobody will pay the fabulous cost of interplanetary freight for pure knowledge – only for luxuries.'

Dykstra shrugged. 'What of it? The economics is irrelevant to our monasticism. Have you never drunk Benedictine?'

'Uh . . . yeah, I get it. But also, we're only celibate by necessity. Our big hope is that eventually we can have our own women.'

Dykstra smiled. 'I am not pressing the analogy too close,' he said. 'My point is that we feel ourselves serving a larger purpose, a cultural purpose. Science, in our case, rather than religion, but still a purpose worth all the isolation and other sacrifice. If, in our hearts, we really consider the isolation a sacrifice.'

Hawthorne winced. Sometimes Dykstra was too analytical. Indeed, thought Hawthorne, the station personnel were monks. Wim himself – but he was a passionate man, fortunate enough to be single-minded. Hawthorne, less lucky, had spent fifteen years shaking off a Puritan upbringing, and finally realized that he never would. He had killed his father's unmerciful God, but the ghost would always haunt him.

He could now try to make up for long self-denial by an Earthside leave which was one continuous orgy, but the sense of sin plagued him notwithstanding, disguised as bitterness. I have been iniquitous upon Terra. Ergo, Terra is a sink of evil.

Dykstra continued, with a sudden unwonted tension in his voice: 'The analogy with medieval monasteries holds good in another respect too. They thought they were retreating from the world. Instead, they became the nucleus of its next stage. And we too, unwittingly until now, may have changed history.'

'Uh-uh,' denied McClellan. 'You can't have a history without a next generation, can you? And there's not a woman on all Venus.'

Hawthorne said, quickly, to get away from his own thoughts: 'There was talk in the company offices about that. They'd like to arrange it, if they can, to give all of us more incentive to stay. They think maybe it'll be possible. If trade continues to expand, the station will have to be enlarged, and the new people could just as well be female technicians and scientists.'

'That could lead to trouble,' said McClellan.

'Not if there were enough to go around,' said Hawthorne. 'And nobody signs on here who hasn't long ago given up any hope of enriching their lives with romantic love, or fatherhood.'

'They could have that,' murmured Dykstra. 'Fatherhood, I mean.'

'Kids?' Hawthorne was startled. 'On Venus?'

A look of exultant triumph flickered across Dykstra's face. Hawthorne, reverting to the sensitivity of intimate years, knew that Dykstra had a secret, which he wanted to shout to the universe, but could not yet. Dykstra had discovered something wonderful.

To give him a lead, Hawthorne said: 'I've been so busy swapping gossip, I've had no time for shop talk. What have you learned about this planet since I left?'

'Some promising things,' said Dykstra, evasively. His tone was still not altogether steady.

'Found how the firegems are created?'

'Heavens, no. That would scuttle us, wouldn't it – if they could be synthesized? No . . . you can talk to Chris, if you wish. But I know he has only established that they are a biological product, like pearls. Apparently several strains of bacteroids are involved, which exist only under Venusian deep-sea conditions.'

'Learn more about the life cycle?' asked McClellan. He had a spaceman's somewhat morbid fascination with any organisms that got along without oxygen.

'Yes, Chris and Mamoru and their co-workers have de-

veloped quite a lot of the detailed chemistry,' said Dykstra.
'It is over my head, Nat. But you will want to study it, and
they have been anxious for your help as an ecologist. You
know this business of the plants, if one may call them that,
using solar energy to build up unsaturated compounds,
which the creatures we call animals then oxidize? Oxidation
need not involve oxygen, Shorty.'

'I know that much chemistry,' said McClellan, looking
hurt.

'Well, in a general way the reactions involved did not
seem energetic enough to power animals the size of Oscar.
No enzymes could be identified which – ' He paused, frowning a little. 'Anyhow, Mamoru got to thinking about fer-
mentation, the closest Terrestrial analogy. And it seems that
micro-organisms really *are* involved. The Venusian enzymes
are indistinguishable from . . . shall we call them viruses,
for lack of a better name? Certain forms even seem to
function like genes. How is that for a symbiosis, eh? Puts
the classical examples in the shade.'

Hawthorne whistled.

'I daresay it's a very fascinating new concept,' said
McClellan. 'As for myself, I wish you'd hurry up and give
us our cargo so we can go home. Not that I don't like you
guys, but you're not exactly my type.'

'It will take a few days,' said Dykstra. 'It always does.'

'Well, just so they're Earth days, not Venusian.'

'I may have a most important letter for you to deliver,'
said Dykstra. 'I have not yet gathered the crucial data, but
you must wait for that if nothing else.'

Suddenly he shivered with excitement.

3

The long nights were devoted to study of material gathered
in the daytime. When Hawthorne emerged into sunrise,
where mists smoked along purple waters under a sky like
nacre, the whole station seemed to explode outward around
him. Wim Dykstra had already scooted off with his new
assistant, little Jimmy Cheng-tung of the hopeful grin, and

their two-man sub was over the horizon, picking up data-recording units off the sea bottom. Now boats left the wharf in every direction: Diehl and Matsumoto to gather pseudo-plankton, Vassiliev after some of the beautiful coralite on Erebus Bank, Lafarge continuing his mapping of the currents, Glass heading straight up to investigate the clouds a bit more . . .

The space ferry had been given its first loading during the night. Shorty McClellan walked across a bare deck with Hawthorne and Captain Jevons. 'Expect me back again about local sundown,' he said. 'No use coming before then, with everyone out fossicking.'

'I imagine not.' Jevons, white-haired and dignified, looked wistfully at Lafarge's retreating craft.

Five cetoids frisked in its wake, leaping and spouting and gaily swimming rings around it. Nobody had invited them, but by now few men would have ventured out of station view without such an escort.

More than once, when accidents happened – and they happened often on an entire planet as big and varied as Earth – the cetoids had saved lives. A man could ride on the back of one, if worst came to worst, but more often several would labour to keep a damaged vessel afloat, as if they knew the cost of hauling even a rowboat across space.

'I'd like to go fossicking myself,' said Jevons. He chuckled. 'But someone has to mind the store.'

'Uh, how did the Veenies go for that last lot of stuff?' asked McClellan. 'The plastic jewellery?'

'They didn't,' said Jevons. 'They simply ignored it. Proving, at least, that they have good taste. Do you want the beads back?'

'Lord, no! Chuck 'em in the ocean. Can you recommend any other novelties? Anything you think they might like?'

'Well, said Hawthorne, 'I've speculated about tools such as they could use, designed to be held in the mouth and – '

'We'd better experiment with that right here, before getting samples from Earth,' said Jevons. 'I'm sceptical, myself. What use would a hammer or a knife be to a cetoid?'

'Actually,' said Hawthorne, 'I was thinking about a saw. To cut coralite blocks and make shelters on the sea bottom.'

'Whatever for?' asked McClellan, astonished.

'I don't know,' said Hawthorne. 'There's so little we know. Probably not shelters against undersea weather – though that might not be absolutely fantastic, either. There are cold currents in the depths, I'm sure. What I had in mind, was – I've seen scars on many cetoids, like teeth marks, but left by something gigantic.'

'It's an idea.' Jevons smiled. 'It's good to have you back ideating, Nat. And it's decent of you to volunteer to take your station watch the first thing, right after your return. That wasn't expected of you.'

'Ah, he's got memories to soften the monotony,' said McClellan. 'I saw him in a hostess joint in Chicago. Brother, was he making time!'

The air masks hid most expression, but Hawthorne felt his ears redden. Jevons minded his own business, but he was old-fashioned, and more like a father than the implacable man in black whom Hawthorne dimly remembered. One did not boast of Earthside escapades in Jevons' presence.

'I want to mull over the new biochemical data and sketch out a research programme in the light of it,' said the ecologist hastily. 'And, too, renew my acquaintance with Oscar. I was really touched when he gave me that gem. I felt like a louse, handing it over to the company.'

'At the price it'll command, I'd feel lousy too,' said McClellan.

'No, I don't mean that. I mean – Oh, run along, jetboy!'

Hawthorne and Jevons stood watching the spacecraft taxi off across the water. Its rise was slow at first – much fire and noise, then a gradual acceleration. But by the time it had pierced the clouds, it was a meteor in reverse flight. And still it moved faster, streaking through the planet's thick permanent overcast until it was high in the sky and the clouds to the man inside did not show as grey but as blinding white.

So many miles high, even the air of Venus grew thin and

piercingly cold, and water vapour was frozen out. Thus absorption spectra had not revealed to Earthbound astronomers that this planet was one vast ocean. The first explorers had expected desert and instead they had found water. But still McClellan rode his lightning horse, faster and higher, into a blaze of constellations.

When the rocket noise had faded, Hawthorne came out of his reverie and said: 'At least we've created one beautiful thing with all our ingenuity – just one, space travel. I'm not sure how much destruction and ugliness that makes up for.'

'Don't be so cynical,' said Jevons. 'We've also done Beethoven sonatas, Rembrandt portraits, Shakespearean drama . . . and you, of all people, should be able to rhapsodize on the beauty of science itself.'

'But not of technology,' said Hawthorne. 'Science, pure ordered knowledge, yes. I'll rank that beside anything your Beethoven, and Rembrandts ever made. But this machinery business, gouging a planet so that more people can pullulate – ' It was good to be back with Jevons, he thought. You could dare be serious talking to the captain.

'You've been saddened by your furlough,' said the old man. 'It should be the other way around. You're too young for sadness.'

'New England ancestors.' Hawthorne tried to grin. 'My chromosomes insist that I disapprove of something.'

'I am luckier,' said Jevons. 'Like Pastor Grundtvig, a couple of centuries back, I have made a marvellous discovery. God is *good*.'

'If one can believe in God. You know I can't. The concept just doesn't square with the mess humanity has made of things on Earth.'

'God has to leave us free, Nat. Would you rather be an efficient, will-less puppet?'

'Or He may not care,' said Hawthorne. 'Assuming He does exist, have we any strong empirical grounds for thinking we're His particular favourites? Man may be just another discarded experiment, like the dinosaurs, set aside to gather dust and die. How do you know Oscar's breed don't have souls? And how do you know we do?'

'It's unwise to romanticize the cetoids,' said Jevons. 'They show a degree of intelligence, I'll concede. But – '

'I know. But they don't build spaceships. They haven't got hands, and of course fire is impossible for them. I've heard all that before, Cap. I've argued it a hundred times, here and on Earth. But how can we tell what the cetoids do and don't do on the sea floor? They can stay underwater for days at a time, remember. And even here, I've watched those games of "tag" they play. They are very remarkable games in some respects.

'I swear I can see a pattern, too intricate to make much sense to me, but a distinct pattern notwithstanding. An art form, like our ballet, but using the wind and currents and waves to dance to. And how do you account for their display of taste and discrimination in music, individual taste, so that Oscar goes for those old jazz numbers, and Sambo won't come near them but will pay you carat for carat if you give him some Buxtehude? Why trade at all?'

'Pack rats trade on Earth,' said Jevons.

'Now you're being unfair. The first expedition rafting here thought it was pack rat psychology, too – cetoids snatching oddments off the lower deck and leaving bits of shell, coralite, finally jewels. Sure, I know all that. But by now it's developed into too intricate a price system. The cetoids are shrewd about it – honest, but shrewd. They've got our scale of values figured to an inch: everything from a conchoidal shell to a firegem. Completely to the inch – keep that in mind.

'And why should mere animals go for music tapes, sealed in plastic and run off a thermionic cell? Or for waterproof reproductions of our great art? As for tools? They're often seen helped by schools of specialized fish, rounding up sea creatures, slaughtering and flensing, harvesting pseudo-kelp. They don't need hands, Cap! They use *live* tools!'

'I have been here a good many years,' said Jevons dryly.

Hawthorne flushed. 'Sorry. I gave that lecture so often Earthside, to people who didn't even have the data, that it's become a reflex.'

'I don't mean to downgrade our damp friends,' said the

captain. 'But you know as well as I do that all the years of trying to establish communication with them, symbols, signals – everything has failed.'

'Are you sure?' asked Hawthorne.

'What?'

'How do you know the cetoids have not learned our alphabet off those slates?'

'Well . . . after all – '

'They might have good reasons for not wanting to take a grease pencil in their jaws and scribble messages back to us. A degree of wariness, perhaps. Let's face it, Cap. We're the aliens here, the monsters. Or maybe they simply aren't interested: our vessels are fun to play with, our goods amusing enough to be worth trading for, but we ourselves seem drab. Or, of course – and I think this is the most probable explanation – our minds are too strange. Consider the two planets, how different they are. How alike would you expect the thinking of two wholly different races to be?'

'An interesting speculation,' said Jevons. 'Not new, of course.'

'Well, I'll go set out the latest gadgets for them,' said Hawthorne. He walked a few paces, then stopped and turned around.

'You know,' he said, 'I'm being a fool. Oscar did communicate with us, only last evening. A perfectly unambiguous message, in the form of a firegem.'

4

Hawthorne went past a heavy machine gun, loaded with explosive slugs. He despised the rule that an entire arsenal must always be kept ready. When had Venus ever threatened men with anything but the impersonal consequences of ignorance?

He continued on along the trading pier. Its metal gleamed, nearly awash. Basketlike containers had been lowered overnight, with standard goods. These included recordings and pictures the cetoids already knew, but always seemed to want more of. Did each individual desire some, or did they distribute these things around their world, in the undersea equivalent of museums or libraries?

Then there were the little plastic containers of sodium chloride, aqua ammonia, and other materials, whose taste the cetoids apparently enjoyed. Lacking continents to leach out, the Venusian ocean was less mineralized than Earth's, and these chemicals were exotic. Nevertheless the cetoids had refused plastibulbs of certain compounds, such as the permanganates – and later biochemical research had shown that these were poisonous to Venusian life.

But how had the cetoids known that, without ever crushing a bulb between teeth? They just knew, that was all. Human senses and human science didn't exhaust all the information in the cosmos. The standard list of goods had come to include a few toys, like floating balls, which the cetoids used for some appallingly rough games; and specially devised dressings, to put on injuries . . .

Oh, nobody doubted that Oscar was much more intelligent than a chimpanzee, thought Hawthorne. The problem had always been, was he as highly intelligent as a man?

He pulled up the baskets and took out the equally standardized payments which had been left in them. There were firegems, small and perfect or large and flawed. One was both big and faultless, like a round drop of rainbow. There were particularly beautiful specimens of coralite, which would be made into ornaments on Earth, and several kinds of exquisite shell.

There were specimens of marine life for study, most of them never before seen by Man. How many million species would an entire planet hold? There were a few tools, lost overboard, and only now freed of ooze by shifting currents; a lump of something unidentifiable, light and yellow and greasy to the touch, perhaps a biological product like ambergris, possibly only of slight interest and possibly offering a clue to an entire new field of chemistry. The plunder of a world rattled into Hawthorne's collection boxes.

All novelties had a fixed, rather small value. If the humans took the next such offering, its price would go up, and so on until a stable fee was reached, not too steep for the

Earthmen or too low to be worth the cetoids' trouble. It was amazing how detailed a bargain you could strike without language.

Hawthorne looked down at Oscar. The big fellow had nosed up close to the pier and now lay idly swinging his tail. The blue sheen along his upcurved back was lovely to watch.

'You know,' murmured Hawthorne, 'for years all Earth has been chortling over your giving us such nearly priceless stuff for a few cheaply made geegaws. But I've begun to wonder if it isn't reciprocal. Just how rare are firegems on Venus?'

Oscar spouted a little and rolled a wickedly gleaming eye. A curious expression crossed his face. Doubtless one would be very unscientific to call it a grin. But Hawthorne felt sure that a grin was what Oscar intended.

'Okay,' he said. 'Okay. Now let's see what you think of our gr-r-reat new products, brought to you after years of research for better living. Each and every one of these products, ladies and gentle-cetoids, have been tested in our spotless laboratories, and don't think it was easy to test the patent spot remover in particular. Now – '

The music bubbles of Schoenberg had been rejected. Perhaps other atonalists would be liked, but with spaceship mass ratios what they were, the experiment wasn't going to be done for a long time. On the other hand, a tape of traditional Japanese songs was gone and a two-carat gem had been left, twice the standard price for a novelty: in effect, some cetoid was asking for more of the same.

As usual, every contemporary pictorial artist was refused, but then, Hawthorne agreed they were not to his taste either. Nor did any cetoid want Picasso (middle period), but Mondrian and Matisse had gone well. A doll had been accepted at low valuation, a mere bit of mineral: 'Okay, we (I?) will take just this one sample, but don't bother bringing any more.'

Once again, the waterproof illustrated books had been rejected; the cetoids had never bought books, after the first few. It was an idiosyncrasy, among others, which had led many researchers to doubt their essential basic intelligence and perception.

That doesn't follow, thought Hawthorne. *They haven't got hands, so a printed text isn't natural for them. Because of sheer beauty – or interest, or humour, or whatever they get out of it – some of our best art is worth the trouble of carrying underwater and preserving. But if they're looking for a factual record, they may well have more suitable methods. Such as what? God knows. Maybe they have perfect memories. Maybe, by sheer telepathy or something, they build their messages into the crystal structure of stones on the ocean bed.*

Oscar bustled along the pier, following the man. Hawthorne squatted down and rubbed the cetoid's smooth wet brow. 'Hey, what do you think about me?' he asked aloud. 'Do you wonder if *I* think? All right. All right. My breed came down from the sky and built floating metal settlements and brought all sorts of curious goodies. But ants and termites have pretty intricate behaviour patterns, and you've got similar things on Venus.'

Oscar snorted and nosed Hawthorne's ankles. Out in the water, his people were playing, and foam burned white against purple where they arched skyward and came down again. Still further out, on the hazy edge of vision, a few adults were at work, rounding up a school of 'fish' with the help of three tame (?) species. They seemed to be enjoying the task.

'You have no right to be as smart as you are, Oscar,' said Hawthorne. 'Intelligence is supposed to evolve in response to a rapidly changing environment, and the sea isn't supposed to be changeable enough. Well, maybe the Terrestrial sea isn't. But this is Venus, and what do we know about Venus? Tell me, Oscar, are your dog-type and cattle-type fish just dull-witted animal slaves like the aphids kept by ants, or are they real domestic animals, consciously trained? It's got to be the latter. I'll continue to insist it is, until ants develop a fondness for van Gogh and Beiderbecke.'

Oscar sounded, drenching Hawthorne with carbonated sea water. It foamed spectacularly, and tingled on his skin. A small wind crossed the world, puffing the wetness out of his garments. He sighed. The cetoids were like children, never staying put – another reason why so many psychologists rated them only a cut above Terrestrial apes.

A logically unwarranted conclusion, to say the least. At the quick pace of Venusian life, urgent business might well arise on a second's notice. Or, even if the cetoids were merely being capricious, were they stupid on that account? Man was a heavy-footed beast, who forgot how to play if he was not always being reminded. Here on Venus there might just naturally be more joy in living.

I shouldn't run down my own species the way I do, thought Hawthorne. *'All centuries but this and every country but his own.' We're different from Oscar, that's all. But by the same token, is he any worse than us?*

He turned his mind to the problem of designing a saw which a cetoid could handle. Handle? Manipulate? Not when a mouth was all you had! If the species accepted such tools in trade, it would go a long way towards proving them comparable to man. And if they didn't, it would only show that they had other desires, not necessarily inferior ones.

Quite conceivably, Oscar's race was more intellectual than mankind. Why not? Their bodies and their environment debarred them from such material helps as fire, chipped stone, forged metal, or pictograms. But might this not force their minds into subtler channels? A race of philosophers, unable to talk to Man because it had long ago forgotten baby talk . . .

Sure, it was a far-fetched hypothesis. But the indisputable fact remained, Oscar was far more than a clever animal, even if he was not on a level with Man.

Yet, if Oscar's people had evolved to, say, the equivalent of Pithecanthropus, they had done so because something in Venusian conditions had put a premium on intelligence. The same factor should continue to operate. In another half-million years or so, almost certainly, the cetoids would have as much brain and soul as Man today. (And Man himself might be extinct, or degraded.) Maybe more soul – more sense of beauty and mercy and laughter – if you extrapolated their present behaviour.

In short, Oscar was (a) already equal to Man, or (b) already beyond Man, or (c) on the way up, and his descendants would in time achieve (a) and then (b). Welcome, my brother!

The pier quivered. Hawthorne glanced down again. Oscar had returned. He was nosing the metal impatiently and making gestures with his foreflipper. Hawthorne went over and looked at him. Oscar curved up his tail and whacked his own back, all the time beckoning.

'Hey, wait!' Hawthorne got the idea. He hoped. 'Wait, do you want me to come for a ride?' he asked.

The cetoid blinked both eyes. Was the blink the counterpart of a nod? And if so, had Oscar actually understood the English words?

Hawthorne hurried off to the oxygen electrolyser. Skindiving equipment was stored in the locker beside it. He wriggled into the flexible, heat-retaining Long John. Holding his breath, he unclipped his mask from the tank and air mixer he wore, and put on a couple of oxynitro flasks instead, thus converting it to an aqualung.

For a moment he hesitated. Should he inform Jevons, or at least take the collection boxes inside? No, to hell with it! This wasn't Earth, where you couldn't leave an empty beer bottle unwatched without having it stolen. Oscar might lose patience. The Venusians – damn it, he *would* call them that, and the devil take scientific caution! – had rescued distressed humans, but never before had offered a ride without utilitarian purpose. Hawthorne's pulse beat loudly.

He ran back. Oscar lay level with the pier. Hawthorne straddled him, grasping a small cervical fin and leaning back against the muscular dorsal. The long body glided from the station. Water rippled sensuously around Hawthorne's bare feet. Where his face was not masked, the wind was fresh upon it. Oscar's flukes churned up foam like a snowstorm.

Low overhead there scudded rainclouds, and lightning veined the west. A small polypoid went by, its keelfin submerged, its iridescent membrane-sail driving it on a broad reach. A nearby cetoid slapped the water with his tail in a greeting.

The motion was so smooth that Hawthorne was finally startled to glance behind and see the station five miles off. Then Oscar submerged.

Hawthorne had done a lot of skin-diving, as well as more extensive work in submarines or armour. He was not surprised by the violet clarity of the first yards, nor the rich darkening as he went on down. The glowfish which passed him like rainbow comets were familiar. But he had never before felt the living play of muscles between his thighs; suddenly he knew why a few wealthy men on Earth still kept horses.

When he was in cool, silent, absolute blackness, he felt Oscar begin to travel. Almost, he was torn off by the stream; he lost himself in the sheer exhilaration of hanging on. With other senses than vision he was aware how they twisted through caves and canyons in buried mountains. An hour had passed when light glowed before him, a spark. It took another half hour to reach its source.

He had often seen luminous coralite banks. But never this one. It lay not far from the station as Venusian distances went, but even a twenty-mile radius sweeps out a big territory and men had not chanced by here. And the usual reef was a good bit like its Terrestrial counterpart, a ragged jumble of spires, bluffs and grottos, eerie but unorganized beauty.

Here, the coralite was shaped. A city of merfolk opened up before Hawthorne.

Afterwards he did not remember just how it looked. The patterns were so strange that his mind was not trained to register them. He knew there were delicate fluted columns, arched chambers with arabesque walls, a piling of clean masses at one spot and a Gothic humoresque elsewhere. He saw towers enspiralled like a narwhal's tusk, arches and buttresses of fragile filigree, an overall unity of pattern at once as light as spindrift and as strong as the world-circling tide, immense, complex and serene.

A hundred species of coralite, each with its own distinctive glow, were blended to make the place, so that there was a subtle play of colour, hot reds and icy blues and living greens and yellows, against ocean black. And from some source, he never knew what, came a thin crystal sound, a continuous contrapuntal symphony which he did not understand but which recalled to him frost flowers on the windows of his childhood home.

Oscar let him swim about freely and look. He saw a few other cetoids, also drifting along, often accompanied by young. But plainly, they didn't live here. Was this a memorial, an art gallery, or – Hawthorne didn't know. The place was huge, it reached farther downward than he could see, farther than he could go before pressure killed him, at least half a mile straight down to the sea bottom. Yet this miraculous place had never been fashioned for any 'practical' reason. Or had it? Perhaps the Venusians recognized what Earth had forgotten, though the ancient Greeks had known it – that the contemplation of beauty is essential to thinking life.

The underwater blending of so much that was constructively beautiful could not be a freak of nature. But neither had it been carved out of some pre-existing mountain. No matter how closely he looked, and the flameless fire was adequate to see by, Hawthorne found no trace of chisel or mould. He could only decide that in some unknown way, Oscar's people had grown this thing.

He lost himself. It was Oscar who finally nudged him – a reminder that he had better go back before he ran out of air. When they reached the pier and Hawthorne had stepped off, Oscar nuzzled the man's foot, very briefly, like a kiss, and then he sounded in a tremendous splash.

5

Towards the close of the forty-three-hour daylight period, the boats came straggling in. For most it had been a routine shift, a few dozen discoveries, books and instruments filled with data to be wrestled with and perhaps understood. The men landed wearily, unloaded their craft, stashed their findings and went off for food and rest. Later would come the bull sessions.

Wim Dykstra and Jimmy Cheng-tung had returned earlier than most, with armfuls of recording meters. Hawthorne knew in a general way what they were doing. By seismographs, sonic probes, core studies, mineral analyses, measurements of temperature and radioactivity and a hundred other facets, they tried to understand the planet's inner structure. It was part of an old enigma. Venus had 80 per cent of Earth's mass, and the chemical composition was nearly identical.

The two planets should have been sisters. Instead, the Venusian magnetic field was so weak that iron compasses were useless; the surface was so nearly smooth that no land rose above the water; volcanic and seismic activity were not only less, but showed unaccountably different patterns; lava flows and shock waves here had their own laws; the rocks were of odd types and distributions. And there was a galaxy of other technicalities which Hawthorne did not pretend to follow.

Jevons had remarked that in the past weeks Dykstra had been getting more and more excited about something. The Dutchman was the cautious type of scientist, who said never a word about his results until they were nailed down past argument. He had been spending Earthdays on end in calculations. When someone finally insisted on a turn at the computer, Dykstra often continued figuring with a pencil. One gathered he was well on the way to solving the geological problem of Venus.

'Or aphroditological?' Jevons had murmured. 'But I know Wim. There's more behind this than curiosity, or a chance at glory. Wim has something very big afoot, and very close to his heart. I hope it won't take him too long!'

Today Dykstra had rushed downstairs and sworn nobody would get at the computer until he was through. Cheng-tung hung around for a while, brought him sandwiches, and finally wandered up on deck with the rest of the station to watch Shorty McClellan come in again.

Hawthorne sought him out. 'Hey, Jimmy,' he said. 'You don't have to keep up that mysterious act. You're among friends.'

The Chinese grinned. 'I have not the right to speak,' he said. 'I am only the apprentice. When I have my own doctorate, then you will hear me chatter till you wish I'd learn some Oriental inscrutability.'

'Yes, but hell, it's obvious what you're doing in general outline,' said Hawthorne. 'I understand Wim has been calculating in advance what sort of data he ought to get if his theory is sound. Now he's reducing those speculative assumptions for comparison. So okay, what *is* his theory?'

'There is nothing secret about its essence,' said Cheng-tung. 'It is only a confirmation of a hypothesis made more than a hundred years ago, before anyone had even left Earth. The idea is that Venus has a core unlike our planet's, and that this accounts for the gross differences we've observed.

'Dr Dykstra has been elaborating it, and data so far have confirmed his beliefs. Today we brought in what may be the crucial measurements – chiefly seismic echoes from depth bombs exploded in undersea wells.'

'M-m-m, yeah, I do know something about it.' Hawthorne stared across the ocean. No cetoids were in sight. Had they gone down to their beautiful city? And if so, why? *It's a good thing the questions aren't answered,* he thought. *If there were no more riddles on Venus, I don't know what I'd do with my life.*

'The core here is supposed to be considerably smaller and less dense than Earth's, isn't it?' he went on. His curiosity was actually no more than mild, but he wanted to make conversation while they waited for the spacecraft.

The young Chinese had arrived on the same ship which had taken Hawthorne home to furlough. Now they would be together for a long time, and it was well to show quick friendliness. He seemed a likable little fellow anyhow.

'True,' nodded Cheng-tung. 'Though "supposed" is the wrong word. The general assertion was proven quite satisfactorily quite some time ago. Since then Dr Dykstra has been studying the details.'

'I seem to have read somewhere that Venus ought by rights not to have a core at all,' said Hawthorne. 'Not enough mass to make enough pressure, or something of the sort. The planet ought to have a continuous rocky character right to the centre, like Mars.'

'Your memory is not quite correct,' said Cheng-tung. His sarcasm was gentle and inoffensive. 'But then, the situation is a trifle complex. You see, if you use quantum laws to calculate the curve of pressure at a planet's centre, versus the planet's mass, you do not get a simple figure.

'Up to about eight-tenths of an Earth-mass it rises smoothly, but there is a change at what is called the Y-point. The curve doubles back, as if mass were decreasing with added pressure, and only after it has thus jogged back a certain amount – equivalent to about two per cent of Earth's mass – does the curve resume a steady rise.'

'What happens at this Y-point?' asked Hawthorne rather absently.

'The force becomes great enough to start collapsing the central matter. First crystals, which had already assumed their densest possible form, break down completely. Then, as more mass is added to the planet, the atoms themselves collapse. Not their nuclei, of course. That requires mass on the order of a star's.

'But the electron shells are squeezed into the smallest possible compass. Only when this stage of quantum degeneracy has been reached – when the atoms will not yield any further, and there is a true core, with a specific gravity of better than ten – only thereafter will increased mass again mean a steady rise in internal pressure.'

'Uh . . . yes. I do remember Wim speaking of it, quite some time ago. But he never did like to talk shop, either, except to fellow specialists. Otherwise he'd rather debate history. I take it, then, that Venus has a core which is not collapsed as much as it might be?'

'Yes. At its present internal temperature, Venus is just past the Y-point. If more mass should somehow be added to this planet, its radius would actually decrease. This, not very incidentally, accounts rather well for the observed peculiarities. You can see how the accretion of material in the beginning, when the planets were formed, reached a point where Venus began to shrink – and then, as it happened, stopped, not going on to produce maximum core density and thereafter a steadily increasing size like Earth.

'This means a smooth planet, with no upthrust masses to reach above the hydrosphere and form continents. With no exposed rocks, there was nothing to take nearly all the CO_2 from the air. So life evolved for a different atmosphere. The relatively large mantle, as well as the low-density core, lead to a non-Terrestrial seismology, vulcanology, and mineralogy. The Venusian core is less conductive than Earth's – conductivity tends to increase with degeneracy – so the currents circulating in it are much smaller. Hence, the weak planetary magnetism.'

'Very interesting,' said Hawthorne. 'But why the big secret? I mean, it's a good job of work, but all you've shown is that Venusian atoms obey quantum laws. That's hardly a surprise to spring on the universe.'

Cheng-tung's small body shivered a bare trifle. 'It has been more difficult than one might suspect,' he said. 'But yes, it is true. Our data now reveal unequivocally that Venus has just the type of core which it could have under present conditions.'

Since Cheng-tung had during the night hours asked Hawthorne to correct any mistakes in his excellent English, the American said, 'You mean, the type of core it should have.'

'I mean precisely what I said, and it is not a tautology.' The grin was dazzling. Cheng-tung hugged himself and did a few dance steps. 'But it is Dr Dykstra's brainchild. Let him midwife it.' Abruptly he changed the conversation.

Hawthorne felt puzzled, but dismissed the emotion. And presently McClellan's ferry blazed out of the clouds and came to rest. It was a rather splendid sight, but Hawthorne found himself watching it with only half an eye. Mostly he was still down under the ocean, in the living temple of the Venusians.

Several hours past nightfall, Hawthorne laid the sheaf of reports down on his desk. Chris Diehl and Mamoru Matsumoto had done a superb task. Even in this earliest pioneering stage, their concept of enzymatic symbiosis offered possibilities beyond imagination. Here there was work for a century of science to come. And out of that work would be gotten a deeper insight into living processes, including those of Earth, than men had yet hoped for.

And who could tell what practical benefits? The prospect was heartcatching. Hawthorne had already realized a little of what he himself could do, and yes, in a hazy fashion he could even begin to see, if not understand, how the Venusians had created that lovely thing beneath the water . . . . But a person can only concentrate so long at a time. Hawthorne left his cubbyhole office and wandered down a passageway towards the wardroom.

The station murmured around him. He saw a number of its fifty men at work. Some did their turn at routine chores, maintenance of apparatus, sorting and baling of trade goods, and the rest. Others puttered happily with test tubes, microscopes, spectroscopes, and less understandable equipment. Or they perched on lab benches, brewing coffee over a Bunsen burner while they argued, or sat feet on desk, pipe in mouth, hands behind head and laboured. Those who noticed Hawthorne hailed him as he passed. The station itself muttered familiarly, engines, ventilators, a faint quiver from the surrounding forever unrestful waters.

It was good to be home again.

Hawthorne went up a companionway, down another corridor, and into the wardroom. Jevons sat in a corner with his beloved Montaigne. McClellan and Cheng-tung were shooting dice. Otherwise the long room was deserted. Its transparent wall opened on seas which tonight were almost black, roiled and laced with gold luminosity.

The sky seemed made from infinite layerings of blue and grey, a low haze diffusing the aurora, and a rainstorm was approaching from the west with its blackness and lightning. The only sign of life was a forty-foot sea snake, quickly writhing from one horizon to another, its crested jaws dripping phosphorescence.

McClellan looked up. 'Hi, Nat,' he said. 'Want to sit in?'

'Right after Earth leave?' said Hawthorne. 'What would

I use for money?' He went over to the samovar and tapped himself a cup.

'Eighter from Decatur,' chanted Jimmy Cheng-tung. 'Come on, boys, let's see that good old Maxwell distribution.'

Hawthorne sat down at the table. He was still wondering how to break his news about Oscar and the holy place. He should have reported it immediately to Jevons, but for hours after returning he had been dazed, and then the inadequacy of words had reared a barrier. He was too conditioned against showing emotion to want to speak about it at all.

He had, though, prepared some logical conclusions. The Venusians were at least as intelligent as the builders of the Taj Mahal; they had finally decided the biped strangers were fit to be shown something and would presumably have a whole planet's riches and mysteries to show on later occasions. Hawthorne scalded his tongue on red bitterness.

'Cap,' he said.

'Yes?' Jevons lowered his dog-eared volume, patient as always at the interruption.

'Something happened today,' said Hawthorne.

Jevons looked at him keenly. Cheng-tung finished a throw but did not move further, nor did McClellan. Outside there could be heard the heavy tread of waves and a rising wind.

'Go ahead,' invited Jevons finally.

'I was on the trading pier and while I was standing there – '

Wim Dykstra entered. His shoes rang on the metal floor. Hawthorne's voice stumbled into silence. The Dutchman dropped fifty clipped-together sheets of paper on the table. It seemed they should have clashed, like a sword thrown in challenge, but only the wind spoke.

Dykstra's eyes blazed. 'I have it,' he said.

'By God!' exploded Cheng-tung.

'What on Earth?' said Jevons' mild voice.

'You mean off Earth,' said McClellan. But tightness grew in him as he regarded Dykstra.

The geophysicist looked at them all for several seconds. He laughed curtly. 'I was trying to think of a suitable

dramatic phrase,' he said. 'None came to mind. So much
for historic moments.'

McClellan picked up the papers, shuddered, and dropped
them again. 'Look, maths is okay, but let's keep it within
reason,' he said. 'What do those squiggles mean?'

Dykstra took out a cigarette and made a ceremony of
lighting it. When smoke was in his lungs, he said shakily:
'I have spent the past weeks working out the details of an
old and little-known hypothesis, first made by Ramsey in
nineteen fifty-one, and applying it to Venusian conditions.
The data obtained here have just revealed themselves as
final proof of my beliefs.'

'There isn't a man on this planet who doesn't hope for a
Nobel Prize,' said Jevons.

His trick of soothing dryness didn't work this time.
Dykstra pointed the glowing cigarette like a weapon and
answered: 'I do not care about that. I am interested in the
largest and most significant engineering project of history.'

They waited. Hawthorne began for no good reason to
feel cold.

'The colonization of Venus,' said Dykstra.

6

Dykstra's words fell into silence as if into a well. And then,
like the splash, Shorty McClellan said, 'Huh? Isn't the Min-
danao Deep closer to home?'

But Hawthorne spilled hot tea over his own fingers.

Dykstra began to pace, up and down, smoking in short
nervous drags. His words rattled out: 'The basic reason for
the steady decay of Terrestrial civilization is what one may
call crampedness. Every day we have more people and fewer
resources. There are no longer any exotic foreigners to
challenge and stimulate any frontier . . . no, we can only sit
and brew an eventual, inevitable atomic civil war.

'If we had some place to go, what a difference! Oh, one
could not relieve much population pressure by emigration
to another planet – though an increased demand for such
transportation would surely lead to better, more economical

spaceships. But the fact that men could go, somehow, perhaps to hardship but surely to freedom and opportunity, that fact would make a difference even to the stay-at-homes. At worst, if civilization on Earth must die, its best elements would be on Venus, carrying forward what was good, forgetting what was evil. A second chance for humankind – do you see?'

'It's a pleasant theory, at least,' said Jevons slowly, 'but as for Venus. No, I don't believe a permanent colony forced to live on elaborated rafts and to wear masks every minute outdoors could be successful.'

'Of course not,' said Dykstra. 'That is why I spoke of an engineering project. The transformation of Venus to another Earth.'

'Now wait a minute!' cried Hawthorne, springing up.

No one noticed him. For them, in that moment, only the dark man who spoke like a prophet had reality. Hawthorne clenched his fists together and sat down, muscle by muscle, forcing himself.

Dykstra said through a veil of smoke: 'Do you know the structure of this planet? Its mass puts it just beyond the Y-point – '

Even then, McClellan had to say, 'No, I don't know. Tell me, w'y point?'

But that was automatic, and ignored. Dykstra was watching Jevons, who nodded.

The geophysicist went on, rapidly, 'Now in the region where the mass-pressure curve jogs back, it is not a single-valued function. A planet with the mass of Venus has three possible central pressures. There is the one it does actually have, corresponding to a small core of comparatively low density and a large rocky mantle. But there is also a higher-pressure situation, where the planet has a large degenerate core, hence a greater overall density and smaller radius. And, on the other side of the Y-point, there is the situation of lower central pressure. This means that the planet has no true core but, like Mars, is merely built in layers of rock and magma.

'Now such an ambiguous condition is unstable. It is

possible for the small core which exists to change phase. This would not be true on Earth, which has too much mass, or on Mars, which does not have enough. But Venus is very near the critical point. If the lower mantle collapsed, to make a larger core and smaller total radius, the released energy would appear as vibrations and ultimately as heat.'

He paused an instant, as if to give weight to his words. 'If, on the other hand, the at-present collapsed atoms of the small core were to revert to a higher energy level, there would be blast waves travelling to the surface, disruption on a truly astronomical scale – and, when things had quietened down, Venus would be larger and less dense than at present, *without any core at all*.'

McClellan said, 'Wait a bit, pal! Do you mean this damn golf ball is liable to explode under us at any minute?'

'Oh, no,' said Dykstra more calmly. 'Venus does have a mass somewhat above the critical for existing temperatures. Its core is in a metastable rather than unstable condition, and there would be no reason to worry for billions of years. Also, if temperature did increase enough to cause an expansion, it would not be quite as violent as Ramsey believed, because the Venusian mass *is* greater than his Y-point value. The explosion would not actually throw much material into space. But it would, of course, raise continents.'

'Hey!' That was from Jevons. He jumped up. (Hawthorne sat slumped into nightmare. Outside, the wind lifted, and the storm moved closer across the sea.) 'You mean . . . increased planetary radius, magnifying surface irregularities – '

'And the upthrust of lighter rocks,' added Dykstra, nodding. 'It is all here in my calculations. I can even predict the approximate area of dry land resulting – about equal to that on Earth. The newly exposed rocks will consume carbon dioxide in huge amounts, to form carbonates. At the same time, specially developed strains of Terrestrial photosynthetic life – very like those now used to maintain the air on spaceships – can be sown.

'They will thrive, liberating oxygen in quantity, until a

balance is struck. I can show that this balance can be made identical with the balance which now exists in Earth's atmosphere. The oxygen will form an ozone layer, thus blocking the now dangerous level of ultraviolet radiation. Eventually, another Earth. Warmer, of course – a milder climate, nowhere too hot for man – cloudy still, because of the closer sun – but nevertheless, New Earth!'

Hawthorne shook himself, trying to find a strength which seemed drained from him. He thought dully that one good practical objection would end it all, and then he could wake up.

'Hold on, there,' he said in a stranger's voice. 'It's a clever idea, but these processes you speak of – I mean, all right, perhaps continents could be raised in hours or days, but changing the atmosphere, that would take millions of years. Too long to do humans any good.'

'Ah, no,' said Dykstra. 'This also I have investigated. There are such things as catalysts. Also, the growth of micro-organisms under favourable conditions, without any natural enemies, presents no difficulties. Using only known techniques, I calculate that Venus could be made so a man can safely walk naked on its surface in fifty years.

'In fact, if we wanted to invest more effort, money, and research, it could be done faster. To be sure, then must come the grinding of stone into soil, the fertilizing and planting, the slow painful establishment of an ecology. But that, again, needs only to be started. The first settlers on Venus could make oases for themselves, miles wide, and thereafter expand these at their leisure. By using specialized plants, agriculture can even be practised in the original desert.

'Oceanic life would expand much more rapidly, of course, without any human attentions. Hence the Venusians could soon carry on fishing and pelagiculture. I have good estimates to show that the development of the planet could even exceed the population growth. The firstcomers would have hope – their grandchildren will have wealth!'

Hawthorne sat back. 'There are already Venusians,' he mumbled.

Nobody heard him. 'Say,' objected McClellan, 'how do you propose to blow up this balloon in the first place?'

'Is it not obvious?' said Dykstra. 'Increased core temperature can supply the energy to push a few tons of matter into a higher quantum state. This would lower the pressure enough to trigger the rest. A single large hydrogen bomb at the very centre of the planet would do it. Since this is unfortunately not attainable, we must tap several thousand deep wells in the ocean floor, and touch off a major nuclear explosion in all simultaneously.

'That would be no trick at all. Very little fallout would result, and what did get into the atmosphere would be gone again in a few years. The bombs are available. In fact, they exist already in far larger amounts than would be needed for this project. Would this not be a better use for them than using them as a stockpile to destroy human life?'

'Who would pay the bill?' asked Cheng-tung unexpectedly.

'Whatever government has the foresight – if all the governments on Earth cannot get together on it. I am not greatly concerned about that. Regimes and policies go, nations die, cultures are forgotten. But I want to be sure that *Man* will survive. The cost would not be great – comparable, at most, to one military satellite, and the rewards are enormous even on the crassest immediate terms. Consider what a wealth of uranium and other materials, now in short supply on Earth, would become accessible.'

Dykstra turned to the transparent wall. The storm had reached them. Under the station caissons, the sea raged and struck and shattered in radiant foam. The deep, strong force of those blows travelled up through steel and concrete like the play of muscles in a giant's shoulders. Rain began to smash in great sheets on the deck. A continuous lightning flickered across Dykstra's lean countenance, and thunder toned.

'A world,' he whispered.

Hawthorne stood up again. He leaned forward, his fingertips resting on the table. They were cold. His voice still came to him like someone else's. 'No,' he said. 'Absolutely not.'

'Eh?' Dykstra turned almost reluctantly from watching the storm. 'What is wrong, Nat?'

'You'd sterilize a living planet,' said Hawthorne.

'Well . . . true,' admitted Dykstra. 'Yes. Humanely, though. The first shock wave would destroy all organisms before they even had time to feel it.'

'But that's murder!' cried Hawthorne.

'Come, now,' said Dykstra. 'Let us not get sentimental. I admit it will be a pity to destroy life so interesting, but when children starve and one nation after another is driven to despotism – ' He shrugged and smiled.

Jevons, still seated, stroked a thin hand across his book, as if he wanted to recall a friend five hundred years dead. There was trouble on his face. 'This is too sudden to digest, Wim,' he said. 'You must give us time.'

'Oh, there will be time enough, years of it,' said Dykstra. He laughed. 'First my report must go to Earth, and be published, and debated, and publicized, and wrangled about, and then they will send elaborate expeditions to do my work all over again, and they will haggle and – Have no fears, it will be at least a decade before anything is actually done. And thereafter we of the station, with our experience, will be quite vital to the project.'

'Shucks,' said McClellan, speaking lightly to conceal the way he felt, 'I wanted to take a picnic lunch and watch the planet go up next Fourth of July.'

'I don't know.' Jevons stared into emptiness. 'There's a question of . . . prudence? Call it what you will, but Venus can teach us so much as it is. A thousand years is not too long to study everything here. We may gain a few more continents at the price of understanding what life is all about, or the means for immortality – if that's a goal to be desired – or perhaps a philosophy. I don't know.'

'Well, it is debatable,' conceded Dykstra. 'But let all mankind debate it, then.'

Jimmy Cheng-tung smiled at Hawthorne. 'I believe the captain is right,' he said. 'And I can see your standpoint, as a scientist. It is not fair to take your lifework away from you. I shall certainly argue in favour of waiting at least a hundred years.'

'That may be too long,' warned Dykstra. 'Without some safety valve, technological civilization on Earth may not last another century.'

'*You don't understand.*'

Hawthorne shouted it at them, as he looked into their eyes. Dykstra's gaze in particular caught the light in such a way that it seemed blank, Dykstra was a skull with two white circles for eyes. Hawthorne had the feeling that he was talking to deaf men. Or men already dead.

'You don't understand,' he repeated. 'It isn't my job, or science, or any such thing I'm worried about. It's the brutal fact of murder. The murder of an entire intelligent race. How would you like it if beings came from Jupiter and proposed to give Earth a hydrogen atmosphere? My God, what kind of monsters are we, that we can even think seriously about such a thing?'

'Oh, no!' muttered McClellan. 'Here we go again. Lecture Twenty-eight-B. I listened to it all the way from Earth.'

'Please,' said Cheng-tung. 'The issue is important.'

'The cetoids do pose an embarrassing problem,' conceded Jevons. 'Though I don't believe any scientist has ever objected to vivisection – even the use of close cousins like the apes – for human benefit.'

'The cetoids aren't apes!' protested Hawthorne, his lips whitening. 'They're more human than you are!'

'Wait a minute,' said Dykstra. He moved from his vision of lightning, towards Hawthorne. His face had lost its glory. It was concerned. 'I realize you have opinions about this, Nat. But after all, you have no more evidence – '

'I do!' gasped Hawthorne. 'I've got it at last. I've been wondering all day how to tell you, but now I must.'

What Oscar had shown him came out in words, between peals of thunder.

At the end, even the gale seemed to pause, and for a while only rain, and the *brroom-brroom* of waves far below, continued to speak. McClellan stared at his hands, which twisted a die between the fingers. Cheng-tung rubbed his chin and smiled with scant mirth. Jevons, however, became serenely resolute. Dykstra was harder to read, his face flickered from one expression to the next. Finally he got very busy lighting a new cigarette.

When the silence had become too much, Hawthorne said, 'Well?' in a cracked tone.

'This does indeed put another complexion on the matter,' said Cheng-tung.

'It isn't proof,' snapped Dykstra. 'Look at what bees and bower birds do on Earth.'

'Hey,' said McClellan. 'Be careful, Wim, or you'll prove that we're just glorified ants ourselves.'

'Exactly,' said Hawthorne. 'I'll take you out in a submarine tomorrow and show you, if Oscar himself won't guide us. Add this discovery to all the other hints we've had, and damn it, you can no longer deny that the cetoids are intelligent. They don't think precisely as we do, but they think at least as well.'

'And could doubtless teach us a great deal,' said Cheng-tung. 'Consider how much your people and mine learned from each other: and they were of the same species.'

Jevons nodded. 'I wish you had told me this earlier, Nat,' he said. 'Of course there would have been no argument.'

'Oh, well,' said McClellan, 'guess I'll have to go back to blowing up squibs on the Fourth.'

The rain, wind-flung, hissed against the wall. Lightning still flickered, blue-white, but the thunder wagon was rolling off. The sea ran with wild frosty fires.

Hawthorne looked at Dykstra. The Dutchman was tense as a wire. Hawthorne felt his own briefly relaxing sinews grow taut again.

'Well, Wim?' he said.

'Certainly, certainly!' said Dykstra. He had grown pale. The cigarette fell unnoticed from his lips. 'I am still not absolutely convinced, but that may be only my own disappointment. The chance of genocide is too great to take.'

'Good boy,' smiled Jevons.

Dykstra smote a fist into his palm. 'But my report,' he said. 'What shall I do with my report?'

So much pain was in his voice that Hawthorne felt shock, even though the ecologist had known this question must arise.

McClellan said, startled: 'Well, it's still a nice piece of research, isn't it?'

Then Cheng-tung voiced the horror they all felt.

'I am afraid we must suppress the report, Dr Dykstra,' he said. 'Regrettably, our species cannot be trusted with the information.'

Jevons bit his lip. 'I hate to believe that,' he said. 'We wouldn't deliberately and cold-bloodedly exterminate a billion or more sentient beings for our own . . . convenience.'

'We have done similar things often enough in the past,' said Dykstra woodenly.

I've read enough history myself, Wim, to give a very partial roll call, thought Hawthorne. And he began to tick off on his fingers. *Troy. Jericho. Carthage. Jerusalem. The Albigensians. Buchenwald.*

That's enough for now, he thought, feeling a wish to vomit.

'But surely – ' began Jevons. 'By now, at least – '

'It is barely possible that humane considerations may stay Earth's hand for a decade or two,' said Dykstra. 'The rate at which brutality is increasing gives me little hope even of that, but let us assume so. However, a century? A millennium? How long can we live in our growing poverty with such a temptation? I do not think forever.'

'If it came to a choice between taking over Venus and watching our civilization go under,' said McClellan, 'frankly, I myself would say too bad for Venus. I've got a wife and kids.'

'Be glad, then, that the choice will not be so clearcut in your lifetime,' said Cheng-tung.

Jevons nodded. He had suddenly become an old man, whose work neared an end. 'You have to destroy that report, Wim,' he said. 'Totally. None of us here can ever speak a word about it.'

And now Hawthorne wanted to weep, but could not. There was a barrier in him, like fingers closing on his throat.

Dykstra drew a long breath. 'Fortunately,' he said, 'I have been close-mouthed. No hint escaped me. I only trust the company will not sack me for having been lazy and produced nothing all these months.'

'I'll see to it that they don't, Wim,' said Jevons. His tone was immensely gentle beneath the rain.

Dykstra's hands shook a little, but he tore the first sheet off his report and crumpled it in an ashtray and set fire to it.

Hawthorne flung out of the room.

7

The air was cool outside, at least by contrast with daytime. The squall had passed and only a mild rain fell, sluicing over his bare skin. In the absence of the sun he could go about with no more than shorts and mask. That was a strangely light sensation, like being a boy again in a summer forest which men had since cut down. Rain washed on the decks and into the water, two distinct kinds of noise, marvellously clear.

The waves themselves still ran strong, swish and boom and a dark swirling. Through the air shone a very faint auroral trace, barely enough to tinge the sky with a haze of rose. But mostly, when Nat Hawthorne had left lighted windows behind him, the luminance came from the ocean, where combers glowed green along their backs and utter white when they foamed. Here and there a knife of blackness cut the water, as some quick animal surged.

Hawthorne went down past the machine gun to the trading pier. Heavy seas broke over it, reaching to his knees and spattering him with phosphor glow. He clung to the rail and peered into rain, hoping Oscar would come.

'The worst of it is,' he said aloud, 'they all mean so well.'

A winged being passed overhead, only a shadow and whisper.

'The proverb is wrong,' babbled Hawthorne. He gripped

the rail, though he knew a certain hope that a wave would sweep him loose . . . and afterwards the Venusians would retrieve his bones and take no payment.

'Who shall watch the watchmen? Simple. The watchmen themselves who are of no use anyway, if they aren't honourable. But what about the thing watched? It's on the enemy's side. Wim and Cap and Jimmy and Shorty – and I. We can keep a secret. But nature can't. How long before someone else repeats this work? We hope to expand the station. There'll be more than one geophysicist here, and – and – Oscar! Oscar, where the hell are you, Oscar?'

The ocean gave him reply, but in no language he knew.

He shivered, teeth clapping in his jaws. There was no reason to hang around here. It was perfectly obvious what had to be done. The sight of Oscar's ugly, friendly face wouldn't necessarily make the job easier. It might even make it harder. Impossible, perhaps.

Oscar might make me sane, thought Hawthorne. Ghosts of Sinaic thunder walked in his skull. *I can't have that. Not yet. Lord God of Hosts, why must I be this fanatical? Why not register my protest when the issue arises, like any normal decent crusader, organize pressure groups, struggle by all the legal proper means? Or, if the secret lasts out my lifetime, why should I care what may happen afterwards? I won't be aware of it.*

No. That isn't enough. I require certainty, not that justice will done, for that is impossible, but that injustice will not be done. For I am possessed.

No man, he thought in the wet blowing night, no man could foresee everything. But he could make estimates, and act on them. His brain was as clear as glass, and about as alive, when he contemplated purely empirical data.

If Venus Station stopped paying off, Venus would not be visited again. Not for a very long time, during which many things could happen . . . a Venusian race better able to defend itself, or even a human race that had learned self-control. Perhaps men would never return. Technological civilization might well crumble and not be rebuilt. Maybe that was best, each planet working out its own lonely destiny. But all this was speculation. There were immediate facts at hand.

Item: If Venus Station was maintained, not to speak of its possible expansion, Dykstra's discovery was sure to be repeated. If one man had found the secret, once in a few years of curiosity, another man or two or three would hardly need more than a decade to grope their way to the same knowledge.

Item: Venus Station was at present economically dependent on the cooperation of the cetoids.

Item: If Venus Station suffered ruin due to the reported hostile action of the cetoids, the company was unlikely to try rebuilding it.

Item: Even if the company did make such an attempt, it would soon be abandoned again if the cetoids really did shun it.

Item: Venus would then be left alone.

Item: If you believed in God and sin and so forth, which Hawthorne did not, you could argue that the real benefactor would be humankind, saved from the grisliest burden of deeds since a certain momentous day on Golgotha.

The worst of this for me, Hawthorne came to realize, *is that I don't care very much about humankind. It's Oscar I want to save. And how much hate for one race can hide under love for another?*

He felt dimly that there might be some way to flee nightmare. But the only path down which a man, flipperless and breathing oxygen, could escape, was back through the station.

He hurried along a quiet, brightly lit corridor to a stairwell sloping towards the bowels of the station and down. No one else was about. He might have been the last life in a universe turned ashen.

But when he entered the stockroom, it was a blow that another human figure stood there. Ghosts, ghosts . . . what right had the ghost of a man not yet dead to walk at this moment?

The man turned about. It was Chris Diehl, the biochemist. 'Why, hi, Nat,' he said. 'What are you doing at this hour?'

Hawthorne wet his lips. The Earthlike air seemed to wither him. 'I need a tool,' he said. 'A drill, yes – a small electric drill.'

'Help yourself,' said Diehl.

Hawthorne lifted a drill off the rack. His hands began to shake so much that he dropped it. Diehl stared at him.

'What's wrong, Nat?' he asked softly. 'You look like secondhand custard.'

'I'm all right,' whispered Hawthorne. 'Quite all right.'

Hawthorne picked up the drill and went out.

The locked arsenal was low in the station hull. Hawthorne could feel Venus' ocean surge below the deckplates. That gave him the strength to drill the lock open and enter, to break the cases of explosive and lay a fuse. But he never remembered having set a time cap on the fuse. He only knew he had done so.

His next recollection was of standing in a boathouse, loading oceanographic depth bombs into one of the little submarines. Again, no one stirred. No one was there to question him. What had the brothers of Venus Station to fear?

Hawthorne slipped into the submarine and guided it out the sea gate. Minutes later he felt the shock of an explosion. It was not large, but it made so much noise in him that he was stunned and did not see Venus Station go to the bottom. Only afterwards did he observe that the place was gone. The waters swirled wildfire above it, a few scraps of wreckage bobbing in sheeting spindrift.

He took a compass bearing and submerged. Before long, the coralite city glowed before him. For a long moment he looked at its spires and grottos and lovelinesses, until fear warned him that he might make himself incapable of doing what was necessary. So he dropped his bombs, hastily, and felt his vessel shudder with their force, and saw the temple become a ruin.

And next he remembered surfacing. He went out on deck and his skin tasted rain. The cetoids were gathering. He could not see them, except in glimpses, a fluke or a back, phosphor streaming off into great waves, with once a face glimpsed just under the low rail, almost like a human baby's in that uncertain light.

He crouched by the machine gun, screaming, but they couldn't understand and anyway the wind made a rag of his voice. 'I have to do this! I have no choice, don't you see? How else can I explain to you what my people are like when their greed dominates them? How else can I make you avoid them, which you've got to do if you want to live? Can you realize that? Can you? But no, you can't, you mustn't. You have to learn hate from us, since you've never learned it from each other – '.

And he fired into the bewildered mass of them.

The machine gun raved for a long time, even after no more living Venusians were around. Hawthorne didn't stop shouting until he ran out of ammunition. Then he regained consciousness. His mind felt quiet and very clear, as if a fever had possessed him and departed. He remembered summer mornings when he was a boy, and early sunlight slanting in his bedroom window and across his eyes. He re-entered the turret and radioed the spaceship with total rationality.

'Yes, Captain, it was the cetoids, beyond any possibility of doubt. I don't know how they did it. Maybe they disarmed some of our probe bombs, brought them back and exploded them. But anyhow the station has been destroyed. I got away in a submarine. I glimpsed two other men in an open boat, but before I could reach them the cetoids had attacked. They stove in the boat, and killed the men as I watched . . . God, no, I can't imagine why! Never mind why! Let's just get away from here!'

He heard the promise of rescue by ferry, set an automatic location signal, and lay down on the bunk. It was over now, he thought in a huge grateful weariness. No human would ever learn the truth. Given time, he himself might forget it.

The space vessel descended at dawn, when the sky was turning to mother-of-pearl. Hawthorne came out on deck. Some dozen Venusian corpses rolled alongside the hull. He didn't want to see them, but there they were, and suddenly he recognized Oscar.

Oscar gaped blindly into the sky. Small pincered crustaceans were eating him. His blood was green.

Oh, God, thought Hawthorne, *please exist. Please make a hell for me.*